America's Greatest Satirist
KURT VONNEGUT
is . . .

"UNIQUE . . . one of the writers who map our landscapes for us, who give names to the places we know best."

—DORIS LESSING
The New York Times Book Review

"OUR FINEST BLACK-HUMORIST. . . . We laugh in self-defense."

—*The Atlantic Monthly*

"AN UNIMITATIVE AND INIMITABLE SOCIAL SATIRIST."

—*Harper's Magazine*

"A CAUSE FOR CELEBRATION."

—*Chicago Sun-Times*

"A LAUGHING PROPHET OF DOOM."

—*The New York Times*

Dell Books by Kurt Vonnegut

A LAUREL BOOK
Published by
Dell Publishing
a division of
Bantam Doubleday Dell Publishing Group, Inc.
1540 Broadway
New York, New York 10036

ISBN: 0-440-13148-0

Cover design: Carin Goldberg
Cover illustration: Gene Greif

Reprinted by arrangement with Delacorte Press/Seymour Lawrence

Printed in the United States of America

Published simultaneously in Canada

November 1991

49   48   47   46   45   44   43   42

0PM

OR

By

KURT VONNEGUT

➧ with drawings by the author

LAUREL

In Memory of Phoebe Hurty,
who comforted me in Indianapolis—
during the Great Depression.

When he hath tried me,
I shall come forth as gold.

—JOB

Breakfast of Champions ▶

Preface

The expression "Breakfast of Champions" is a registered trademark of General Mills, Inc., for use on a breakfast cereal product. The use of the identical expression as the title for this book is not intended to indicate an association with or sponsorship by General Mills, nor is it intended to disparage their fine products.

◆ The person to whom this book is dedicated, Phoebe Hurty, is no longer among the living, as they say. She was an Indianapolis widow when I met her late in the Great Depression. I was sixteen or so. She was about forty.

She was rich, but she had gone to work every weekday of her adult life, so she went on doing that. She wrote a sane and funny advice-to-the-lovelorn column for the

Indianapolis *Times*, a good paper which is now defunct. Defunct.

She wrote ads for the William H. Block Company, a department store which still flourishes in a building my father designed. She wrote this ad for an end-of-the-summer sale on straw hats: "For prices like this, you can run them through your horse and put them on your roses."

◗ Phoebe Hurty hired me to write copy for ads about teen-age clothes. I had to wear the clothes I praised. That was part of the job. And I became friends with her two sons, who were my age. I was over at their house all the time.

She would talk bawdily to me and her sons, and to our girlfriends when we brought them around. She was funny. She was liberating. She taught us to be impolite in conversation not only about sexual matters, but about American history and famous heroes, about the distribution of wealth, about school, about everything.

I now make my living by being impolite. I am clumsy at it. I keep trying to imitate the impoliteness which was so graceful in Phoebe Hurty. I think now that grace was easier for her than it is for me because of the mood of the Great Depression. She believed what so many Americans believed then: that the nation would be happy and just and rational when prosperity came.

I never hear that word anymore: *Prosperity*. It used to be a synonym for *Paradise*. And Phoebe Hurty was able to believe that the impoliteness she recommended would give shape to an American paradise.

Now her sort of impoliteness is fashionable. But nobody believes anymore in a new American paradise. I sure miss Phoebe Hurty.

▶ As for the suspicion I express in this book, that human beings are robots, are machines: It should be noted that people, mostly men, suffering from the last stages of syphilis, from *locomotor ataxia*, were common spectacles in downtown Indianapolis and in circus crowds when I was a boy.

Those people were infested with carnivorous little corkscrews which could be seen only with a microscope. The victims' vertebrae were welded together after the corkscrews got through with the meat between. The syphilitics seemed tremendously dignified—erect, eyes straight ahead.

I saw one stand on a curb at the corner of Meridian and Washington Streets one time, underneath an overhanging clock which my father designed. The intersection was known locally as *"The Crossroads of America."*

This syphilitic man was thinking hard there, at the Crossroads of America, about how to get his legs to step off the curb and carry him across Washington Street. He shuddered gently, as though he had a small motor which was idling inside. Here was his problem: his brains, where the instructions to his legs originated, were being eaten alive by corkscrews. The wires which had to carry the instructions weren't insulated anymore, or were eaten clear through. Switches along the way were welded open or shut.

This man looked like an old, old man, although he might have been only thirty years old. He thought and thought. And then he kicked two times like a chorus girl.

He certainly looked like a machine to me when I was a boy.

▶ I tend to think of human beings as huge, rubbery test tubes, too, with chemical reactions seething inside. When I was a boy, I saw a lot of people with goiters. So did Dwayne Hoover, the Pontiac dealer who is the hero of this book. Those unhappy Earthlings had such swollen thyroid glands that they seemed to have zucchini squash growing from their throats.

All they had to do in order to have ordinary lives, it turned out, was to consume less than one-millionth of an ounce of iodine every day.

My own mother wrecked her brains with chemicals, which were supposed to make her sleep.

When I get depressed, I take a little pill, and I cheer up again.

And so on.

So it is a big temptation to me, when I create a character for a novel, to say that he is what he is because of faulty wiring, or because of microscopic amounts of chemicals which he ate or failed to eat on that particular day.

▶ What do I myself think of this particular book? I feel lousy about it, but I always feel lousy about my books. My friend Knox Burger said one time that a certain cumbersome novel ". . . read as though it had been written by Philboyd Studge." That's who I think I am when I write what I am seemingly programmed to write.

▶ This book is my fiftieth birthday present to myself. I feel as though I am crossing the spine of a roof—having ascended one slope.

I am programmed at fifty to perform childishly—to insult "The Star-Spangled Banner," to scrawl pictures of a Nazi flag and an asshole and a lot of other things with a felt-tipped pen. To give an idea of the maturity of my illustrations for this book, here is my picture of an asshole:

♦ I think I am trying to clear my head of all the junk in there—the assholes, the flags, the underpants. Yes—there is a picture in this book of underpants. I'm throwing out characters from my other books, too. I'm not going to put on any more puppet shows.

I think I am trying to make my head as empty as it was when I was born onto this damaged planet fifty years ago.

I suspect that this is something most white Americans, and nonwhite Americans who imitate white Americans, should do. The things other people have put into *my* head, at any rate, do not fit together nicely, are often useless and ugly, are out of proportion with one another, are out of proportion with life as it really is outside my head.

I have no culture, no humane harmony in my brains. I can't live without a culture anymore.

Kurt Vonnegut

◗ So this book is a sidewalk strewn with junk, trash which I throw over my shoulders as I travel in time back to November eleventh, nineteen hundred and twenty-two.

I will come to a time in my backwards trip when November eleventh, accidentally my birthday, was a sacred day called *Armistice Day*. When I was a boy, and when Dwayne Hoover was a boy, all the people of all the nations which had fought in the First World War were silent during the eleventh minute of the eleventh hour of Armistice Day, which was the eleventh day of the eleventh month.

It was during that minute in nineteen hundred and eighteen, that millions upon millions of human beings stopped butchering one another. I have talked to old men who were on battlefields during that minute. They have told me in one way or another that the sudden silence was the Voice of God. So we still have among us some men who can remember when God spoke clearly to mankind.

◗ Armistice Day has become Veterans' Day. Armistice Day was sacred. Veterans' Day is not.

So I will throw Veterans' Day over my shoulder. Armistice Day I will keep. I don't want to throw away any sacred things.

What else is sacred? Oh, *Romeo and Juliet*, for instance.

And all music is.

—PHILBOYD STUDGE

6

Chapter 1

This is a tale of a meeting of two lonesome, skinny, fairly old white men on a planet which was dying fast.

One of them was a science-fiction writer named Kilgore Trout. He was a nobody at the time, and he supposed his life was over. He was mistaken. As a consequence of the meeting, he became one of the most beloved and respected human beings in history.

The man he met was an automobile dealer, a *Pontiac* dealer named Dwayne Hoover. Dwayne Hoover was on the brink of going insane.

▶ Listen:

Trout and Hoover were citizens of the United States of America, a country which was called *America* for short.

7

Kurt Vonnegut

This was their national anthem, which was pure balder-
dash, like so much they were expected to take seriously:

> O, say can you see by the dawn's early light
> What so proudly we hailed at the twilight's
>   last gleaming,
> Whose broad stripes and bright stars,
>   thru the perilous fight
> O'er the ramparts we watched were so
>   gallantly streaming?
> And the rockets' red glare, the bombs
>   bursting in air,
> Gave proof through the night that our
>   flag was still there.
> O, say does that star-spangled banner
>   yet wave
> O'er the land of the free and the home
>   of the brave?

There were one quadrillion nations in the Universe, but
the nation Dwayne Hoover and Kilgore Trout belonged to
was the only one with a national anthem which was gibberish sprinkled with question marks.

Here is what their flag looked like:

It was the law of their nation, a law no other nation on the planet had about its flag, which said this: *"The flag shall not be dipped to any person or thing."*

Flag-dipping was a form of friendly and respectful salute, which consisted of bringing the flag on a stick closer to the ground, then raising it up again.

▶ The motto of Dwayne Hoover's and Kilgore Trout's nation was this, which meant in a language nobody spoke anymore, *Out of Many, One: "E pluribus unum."*

The undippable flag was a beauty, and the anthem and the vacant motto might not have mattered much, if it weren't for this: a lot of citizens were so ignored and cheated and insulted that they thought they might be in the wrong country, or even on the wrong planet, that some terrible mistake had been made. It might have comforted them some if their anthem and their motto had mentioned fairness or brotherhood or hope or happiness, had somehow welcomed them to the society and its real estate.

If they studied their paper money for clues as to what their country was all about, they found, among a lot of other baroque trash, a picture of a truncated pyramid with a radiant eye on top of it, like this:

Not even the President of the United States knew what that was all about. It was as though the country were saying to its citizens, *"In nonsense is strength."*

▶ A lot of the nonsense was the innocent result of playfulness on the part of the founding fathers of the nation of Dwayne Hoover and Kilgore Trout. The founders were aristocrats, and they wished to show off their useless education, which consisted of the study of hocus-pocus from ancient times. They were bum poets as well.

But some of the nonsense was evil, since it concealed great crimes. For example, teachers of children in the United States of America wrote this date on blackboards again and again, and asked the children to memorize it with pride and joy:

1492

The teachers told the children that this was when their continent was discovered by human beings. Actually, millions of human beings were already living full and imaginative lives on the continent in 1492. That was simply the year in which sea pirates began to cheat and rob and kill them.

Here was another piece of evil nonsense which children were taught: that the sea pirates eventually created a government which became a beacon of freedom to human beings everywhere else. There were pictures and statues of this supposed imaginary beacon for children to see. It was sort of an ice-cream cone on fire. It looked like this:

Actually, the sea pirates who had the most to do with the creation of the new government owned human slaves. They used human beings for machinery, and, even after slavery was eliminated, because it was so embarrassing, they and their descendants continued to think of ordinary human beings as machines.

◆ The sea pirates were white. The people who were already on the continent when the pirates arrived were copper-colored. When slavery was introduced onto the continent, the slaves were black.

Color was everything.

◗ Here is how the pirates were able to take whatever they wanted from anybody else: they had the best boats in the world, and they were meaner than anybody else, and they had gunpowder, which was a mixture of potassium nitrate, charcoal, and sulphur. They touched this seemingly listless powder with fire, and it turned violently into gas. This gas blew projectiles out of metal tubes at terrific velocities. The projectiles cut through meat and bone very easily; so the pirates could wreck the wiring or the bellows or the plumbing of a stubborn human being, even when he was far, far away.

The chief weapon of the sea pirates, however, was their capacity to astonish. Nobody else could believe, until it was much too late, how heartless and greedy they were.

◗ When Dwayne Hoover and Kilgore Trout met each other, their country was by far the richest and most powerful country on the planet. It had most of the food and minerals and machinery, and it disciplined other countries by threatening to shoot big rockets at them or to drop things on them from airplanes.

Most other countries didn't have doodley-squat. Many of them weren't even inhabitable anymore. They had too many people and not enough space. They had sold everything that was any good, and there wasn't anything to eat anymore, and still the people went on fucking all the time.

Fucking was how babies were made.

◗ A lot of the people on the wrecked planet were *Communists*. They had a theory that what was left of the planet should be shared more or less equally among all the people, who hadn't asked to come to a wrecked planet in the first place. Meanwhile, more babies were arriving all the time—kicking and screaming, yelling for milk.

In some places people would actually try to eat mud or suck on gravel while babies were being born just a few feet away.

And so on.

◆ Dwayne Hoover's and Kilgore Trout's country, where there was still plenty of everything, was opposed to Communism. It didn't think that Earthlings who had a lot should share it with others unless they really wanted to, and most of them didn't want to.

So they didn't have to.

◆ Everybody in America was supposed to grab whatever he could and hold onto it. Some Americans were very good at grabbing and holding, were fabulously well-to-do. Others couldn't get their hands on doodley-squat.

Dwayne Hoover was fabulously well-to-do when he met Kilgore Trout. A man whispered those exact words to a friend one morning as Dwayne walked by: "Fabulously well-to-do."

And here's how much of the planet Kilgore Trout owned in those days: doodley-squat.

And Kilgore Trout and Dwayne Hoover met in Midland City, which was Dwayne's home town, during an Arts Festival there in autumn of 1972.

As has already been said: Dwayne was a Pontiac dealer who was going insane.

Dwayne's incipient insanity was mainly a matter of

chemicals, of course. Dwayne Hoover's body was manufacturing certain chemicals which unbalanced his mind. But Dwayne, like all novice lunatics, needed some bad ideas, too, so that his craziness could have shape and direction.

Bad chemicals and bad ideas were the Yin and Yang of madness. Yin and Yang were Chinese symbols of harmony. They looked like this:

The bad ideas were delivered to Dwayne by Kilgore Trout. Trout considered himself not only harmless but invisible. The world had paid so little attention to him that he supposed he was dead.

He *hoped* he was dead.

But he learned from his encounter with Dwayne that he was alive enough to give a fellow human being ideas which would turn him into a monster.

Here was the core of the bad ideas which Trout gave to Dwayne: Everybody on Earth was a robot, with one exception—Dwayne Hoover.

Of all the creatures in the Universe, only Dwayne was thinking and feeling and worrying and planning and so on. Nobody else knew what pain was. Nobody else had any choices to make. Everybody else was a fully automatic machine, whose purpose was to stimulate Dwayne. Dwayne was a new type of creature being tested by the Creator of the Universe.

Only Dwayne Hoover had free will.

◗ Trout did not expect to be believed. He put the bad ideas into a science-fiction novel, and that was where Dwayne found them. The book wasn't addressed to Dwayne alone. Trout had never heard of Dwayne when he wrote it. It was addressed to anybody who happened to open it up. It said to simply anybody, in effect, "Hey— guess what: You're the only creature with free will. How does that make you feel?" And so on.

It was a *tour de force*. It was a *jeu d'esprit*.

But it was mind poison to Dwayne.

◗ It shook up Trout to realize that even *he* could bring evil into the world—in the form of bad ideas. And, after Dwayne was carted off to a lunatic asylum in a canvas camisole, Trout became a fanatic on the importance of ideas as causes and cures for diseases.

But nobody would listen to him. He was a dirty old man in the wilderness, crying out among the trees and underbrush, "Ideas or the lack of them can cause disease!"

◗ Kilgore Trout became a pioneer in the field of mental health. He advanced his theories disguised as science-fiction. He died in 1981, almost twenty years after he made Dwayne Hoover so sick.

He was by then recognized as a great artist and scientist. The American Academy of Arts and Sciences caused a monument to be erected over his ashes. Carved in its face was a quotation from his last novel, his two-hundred-and-ninth novel, which was unfinished when he died. The monument looked like this:

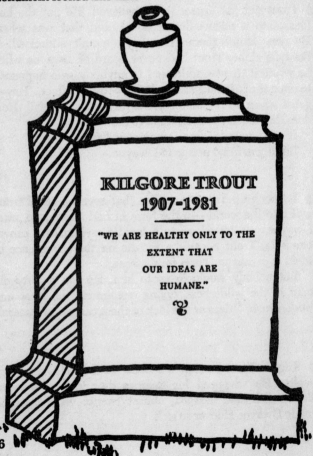

KILGORE TROUT
1907-1981

"WE ARE HEALTHY ONLY TO THE
EXTENT THAT
OUR IDEAS ARE
HUMANE."

Chapter 2

Dwayne was a widower. He lived alone at night in a dream house in Fairchild Heights, which was the most desirable residential area in the city. Every house there cost at least one hundred thousand dollars to build. Every house was on at least four acres of land.

Dwayne's only companion at night was a Labrador retriever named *Sparky*. Sparky could not wag his tail—because of an automobile accident many years ago, so he had no way of telling other dogs how friendly he was. He had to fight all the time. His ears were in tatters. He was lumpy with scars.

 Dwayne had a black servant named Lottie Davis. She cleaned his house every day. Then she cooked his supper for him and served it. Then she went home. She was descended from slaves.

Lottie Davis and Dwayne didn't talk much, even though they liked each other a lot. Dwayne reserved most of his conversation for the dog. He would get down on the floor and roll around with Sparky, and he would say things like, "You and me, Spark," and "How's my old buddy?" and so on.

And that routine went on unrevised, even after Dwayne started to go crazy, so Lottie had nothing unusual to notice.

◊ Kilgore Trout owned a parakeet named *Bill*. Like Dwayne Hoover, Trout was all alone at night, except for his pet. Trout, too, talked to his pet.

But while Dwayne babbled to his Labrador retriever about love, Trout sneered and muttered to his parakeet about the end of the world.

"Any time now," he would say. "And high time, too."

It was Trout's theory that the atmosphere would become unbreathable soon.

Trout supposed that when the atmosphere became poisonous, Bill would keel over a few minutes before Trout did. He would kid Bill about that. "How's the old respiration, Bill?" he'd say, or, "Seems like you've got a touch of the old emphysema, Bill," or, "We never discussed what kind of a funeral you want, Bill. You never even told me what your religion is." And so on.

He told Bill that humanity deserved to die horribly, since it had behaved so cruelly and wastefully on a planet so sweet. "We're all Heliogabalus, Bill," he would say. This was the name of a Roman emperor who had a sculptor make a hollow, life-size iron bull with a door on it. The door could be locked from the outside. The bull's mouth was open. That was the only other opening to the outside.

Heliogabalus would have a human being put into the bull through the door, and the door would be locked. Any sounds the human being made in there would come out of the mouth of the bull. Heliogabalus would have guests in for a nice party, with plenty of food and wine and beautiful women and pretty boys—and Heliogabalus would have a servant light kindling. The kindling was under dry firewood—which was under the bull.

◗ Trout did another thing which some people might have considered eccentric: he called mirrors *leaks*. It amused him to pretend that mirrors were holes between two universes.

If he saw a child near a mirror, he might wag his finger at a child warningly, and say with great solemnity, "Don't get too near that leak. You wouldn't want to wind up in the other universe, would you?"

Sometimes somebody would say in his presence, "Excuse me, I have to take a leak." This was a way of saying that the speaker intended to drain liquid wastes from his body through a valve in his lower abdomen.

And Trout would reply waggishly, "Where I come from, that means you're about to steal a mirror."

And so on.

By the time of Trout's death, of course, everybody called mirrors *leaks*. That was how respectable even his jokes had become.

◗ In 1972, Trout lived in a basement apartment in Cohoes, New York. He made his living as an installer of aluminum combination storm windows and screens. He had nothing to do with the sales end of the business—because he had no *charm*. Charm was a scheme for making strangers like and trust a person immediately, no matter what the charmer had in mind.

◗ Dwayne Hoover had oodles of charm.

◗ I can have oodles of charm when I want to.

◗ A lot of people have oodles of charm.

◗ Trout's employer and co-workers had no idea that he was a writer. No reputable publisher had ever heard of him, for that matter, even though he had written one hundred and seventeen novels and two thousand short stories by the time he met Dwayne.

He made carbon copies of nothing he wrote. He mailed off manuscripts without enclosing stamped, self-addressed envelopes for their safe return. Sometimes he didn't even include a return address. He got names and addresses of publishers from magazines devoted to the writing business, which he read avidly in the periodical rooms of public libraries. He thus got in touch with a firm called World Classics Library, which published hard-core pornography in Los Angeles, California. They used his stories, which usually didn't even have women in them, to give bulk to books and magazines of salacious pictures.

They never told him where or when he might expect to find himself in print. Here is what they paid him: doodley-squat.

◆ They didn't even send him complimentary copies of the books and magazines in which he appeared, so he had to search them out in pornography stores. And the titles he gave to his stories were often changed. "Pan Galactic Straw-boss," for instance, became "Mouth Crazy."

Most distracting to Trout, however, were the illustrations his publishers selected, which had nothing to do with his tales. He wrote a novel, for instance, about an Earthling named Delmore Skag, a bachelor in a neighborhood where everybody else had enormous families. And Skag was a scientist, and he found a way to reproduce himself in chicken soup. He would shave living cells from the palm of his right hand, mix them with the soup, and expose the soup to cosmic rays. The cells turned into babies which looked exactly like Delmore Skag.

Pretty soon, Delmore was having several babies a day, and inviting his neighbors to share his pride and happiness. He had mass baptisms of as many as a hundred babies at a time. He became famous as a family man.

And so on.

◆ Skag hoped to force his country into making laws against excessively large families, but the legislatures and the courts declined to meet the problem head-on. They passed stern laws instead against the possession by unmarried persons of chicken soup.

And so on.

The illustrations for this book were murky photographs of several white women giving blow jobs to the same black man, who, for some reason, wore a Mexican sombrero.

At the time he met Dwayne Hoover, Trout's most widely-distributed book was *Plague on Wheels*. The publisher didn't change the title, but he obliterated most of it and all of Trout's name with a lurid banner which made this promise:

WIDE-OPEN BEAVERS INSIDE!

A wide-open beaver was a photograph of a woman not wearing underpants, and with her legs far apart, so that the mouth of her vagina could be seen. The expression was first used by news photographers, who often got to see up women's skirts at accidents and sporting events and from underneath fire escapes and so on. They needed a code word to yell to other newsmen and friendly policemen and firemen and so on, to let them know what could be seen, in case they wanted to see it. The word was this: "Beaver!"

A beaver was actually a large rodent. It loved water, so it built dams. It looked like this:

The sort of beaver which excited news photographers so much looked like this:

This was where babies came from.

♦ When Dwayne was a boy, when Kilgore Trout was a boy, when I was a boy, and even when we became middle-aged men and older, it was the duty of the police and the courts to keep representations of such ordinary apertures from being examined and discussed by persons not engaged in the practice of medicine. It was somehow decided that wide-open beavers, which were ten thousand times as common as real beavers, should be the most massively defended secret under law.

So there was a madness about wide-open beavers. There was also a madness about a soft, weak metal, an element, which had somehow been declared the most desirable of all elements, which was gold.

♦ And the madness about wide-open beavers was extended to underpants when Dwayne and Trout and I were boys. Girls concealed their underpants at all costs, and boys tried to see their underpants at all costs.

Female underpants looked like this:

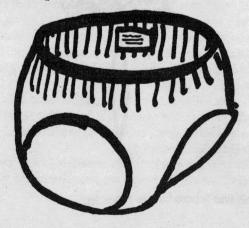

One of the first things Dwayne learned in school as a little boy, in fact, was a poem he was supposed to scream in case he saw a girl's underpants by accident in the playground. Other students taught it to him. This was it:

> *I see England,*
> *I see France;*
> *I see a little girl's*
> *Underpants!*

When Kilgore Trout accepted the Nobel Prize for Medicine in 1979, he declared: "Some people say there is no such thing as progress. The fact that human beings are now the only animals left on Earth, I confess, seems a confusing sort of victory. Those of you familiar with the nature of my earlier published works will understand why I mourned especially when the last beaver died.

"There were two monsters sharing this planet with us when I was a boy, however, and I celebrate their extinction today. They were determined to kill us, or at least to make our lives meaningless. They came close to success. They were cruel adversaries, which my little friends the beavers were not. Lions? No. Tigers? No. Lions and tigers snoozed most of the time. The monsters I will name never snoozed. They inhabited our heads. They were the arbitrary lusts for gold, and, God help us, for a glimpse of a little girl's underpants.

"I thank those lusts for being so ridiculous, for they taught us that it was possible for a human being to believe anything, and to behave passionately in keeping with that belief—*any* belief.

"So now we can build an unselfish society by devoting to unselfishness the frenzy we once devoted to gold and to underpants."

He paused, and then he recited with wry mournfulness the beginning of a poem he had learned to scream in Bermuda, when he was a little boy. The poem was all the more poignant, since it mentioned two nations which no longer existed as such. "I see England," he said, "I see France—"

◗ Actually, women's underpants had been drastically devalued by the time of the historic meeting between Dwayne Hoover and Trout. The price of gold was still on the rise.

Photographs of women's underpants weren't worth the paper they were printed on, and even high quality color motion pictures of wide-open beavers were going begging in the marketplace.

There had been a time when a copy of Trout's most popular book to date, *Plague on Wheels*, had brought as much as twelve dollars, because of the illustrations. It was now being offered for a dollar, and people who paid even that much did so not because of the pictures. They paid for the words.

◗ The words in the book, incidentally, were about life on a dying planet named *Lingo-Three*, whose inhabitants resembled American automobiles. They had wheels. They were powered by internal combustion engines. They ate fossil fuels. They weren't manufactured, though. They reproduced. They laid eggs containing baby automobiles, and the babies matured in pools of oil drained from adult crankcases.

Lingo-Three was visited by space travelers, who learned that the creatures were becoming extinct for this reason: they had destroyed their planet's resources, including its atmosphere.

The space travelers weren't able to offer much in the way of material assistance. The automobile creatures hoped to borrow some oxygen, and to have the visitors carry at least one of their eggs to another planet, where it might hatch, where an automobile civilization could begin again. But the smallest egg they had was a forty-eight pounder, and the space travelers themselves were only an inch high, and their space ship wasn't even as big as an Earthling shoebox. They were from Zeltoldimar.

The spokesman for the Zeltoldimarians was Kago. Kago said that all he could do was to tell others in the Universe about how wonderful the automobile creatures had been. Here is what he said to all those rusting junkers who were out of gas: "You will be gone, but not forgotten."

The illustration for the story at this point showed two Chinese girls, seemingly identical twins, seated on a couch with their legs wide open.

▶ So Kago and his brave little Zeltoldimarian crew, which was all homosexual, roamed the Universe, keeping the memory of the automobile creatures alive. They came at last to the planet Earth. In all innocence, Kago told the Earthlings about the automobiles. Kago did not know that human beings could be as easily felled by a single idea as by cholera or the bubonic plague. There was no immunity to cuckoo ideas on Earth.

◗ And here, according to Trout, was the reason human beings could not reject ideas because they were bad: "Ideas on Earth were badges of friendship or enmity. Their content did not matter. Friends agreed with friends, in order to express friendliness. Enemies disagreed with enemies, in order to express enmity.

"The ideas Earthlings held didn't matter for hundreds of thousands of years, since they couldn't do much about them anyway. Ideas might as well be badges as anything.

"They even had a saying about the futility of ideas: 'If wishes were horses, beggars would ride.'

"And then Earthlings discovered tools. Suddenly agreeing with friends could be a form of suicide or worse. But agreements went on, not for the sake of common sense or decency or self-preservation, but for friendliness.

"Earthlings went on being friendly, when they should have been thinking instead. And even when they built computers to do some thinking for them, they designed them not so much for wisdom as for friendliness. So they were doomed. Homicidal beggars could ride."

Chapter 3

Within a century of little Kago's arrival on Earth, according to Trout's novel, every form of life on that once peaceful and moist and nourishing blue-green ball was dying or dead. Everywhere were the shells of the great beetles which men had made and worshipped. They were automobiles. They had killed everything.

Little Kago himself died long before the planet did. He was attempting to lecture on the evils of the automobile in a bar in Detroit. But he was so tiny that nobody paid any attention to him. He lay down to rest for a moment, and a drunk automobile worker mistook him for a kitchen match. He killed Kago by trying to strike him repeatedly on the underside of the bar.

▶ Trout received only one fan letter before 1972. It was

from an eccentric millionaire, who hired a private detective agency to discover who and where he was. Trout was so invisible that the search cost eighteen thousand dollars.

The fan letter reached him in his basement in Cohoes. It was hand-written, and Trout concluded that the writer might be fourteen years old or so. The letter said that *Plague on Wheels* was the greatest novel in the English language, and that Trout should be President of the United States.

Trout read the letter out loud to his parakeet. "Things are looking up, Bill," he said. "Always knew they would. Get a load of this." And then he read the letter. There was no indication in the letter that the writer, whose name was Eliot Rosewater, was a grownup, was fabulously well-to-do.

◗ Kilgore Trout, incidentally, could never be President of the United States without a Constitutional amendment. He hadn't been born inside the country. His birthplace was Bermuda. His father, Leo Trout, while remaining an American citizen, worked there for many years for the Royal Ornithological Society—guarding the only nesting place in the world for Bermuda Erns. These great green sea eagles eventually became extinct, despite anything anyone could do.

◗ As a child, Trout had seen those Erns die, one by one. His father had assigned him the melancholy task of measuring wingspreads of the corpses. These were the largest creatures ever to fly under their own power on the planet.

And the last corpse had the greatest wingspread of all, which was nineteen feet, two and three-quarters inches.

After all the Erns were dead, it was discovered what had killed them. It was a fungus, which attacked their eyes and brains. Men had brought the fungus to their rookery in the innocent form of athlete's foot.

Here is what the flag of Kilgore Trout's native island looked like:

♦ So Kilgore Trout had a depressing childhood, despite all of the sunshine and fresh air. The pessimism that overwhelmed him in later life, which destroyed his three marriages, which drove his only son, Leo, from home at the age of fourteen, very likely had its roots in the bittersweet mulch of rotting Erns.

♦ The fan letter came much too late. It wasn't good news.

It was perceived as an invasion of privacy by Kilgore Trout. The letter from Rosewater promised that he would make Trout famous. This is what Trout had to say about that, with only his parakeet listening: "Keep the hell out of my body bag."

A body bag was a large plastic envelope for a freshly killed American soldier. It was a new invention.

◆ I do not know who invented the body bag. I do know who invented Kilgore Trout. I did.

I made him snaggle-toothed. I gave him hair, but I turned it white. I wouldn't let him comb it or go to a barber. I made him grow it long and tangled.

I gave him the same legs the Creator of the Universe gave to my father when my father was a pitiful old man. They were pale white broomsticks. They were hairless. They were embossed fantastically with varicose veins.

And, two months after Trout received his first fan letter, I had him find in his mailbox an invitation to be a speaker at an arts festival in the American Middle West.

◆ The letter was from the Festival's chairman, Fred T. Barry. He was respectful, almost reverent about Kilgore Trout. He beseeched him to be one of several distinguished out-of-town participants in the Festival, which would last for five days. It would celebrate the opening of the Mildred Barry Memorial Center for the Arts in Midland City.

The letter did not say so, but Mildred Barry was the late mother of the Chairman, the wealthiest man in Midland City. Fred T. Barry had paid for the new Center of the Arts, which was a translucent sphere on stilts. It had no windows. When illuminated inside at night, it resembled a rising harvest moon.

Fred T. Barry, incidentally, was exactly the same age as Trout. They had the same birthday. But they certainly didn't look anything alike. Fred T. Barry didn't even look like a white man anymore, even though he was of pure English stock. As he grew older and older and happier and happier, and all his hair fell out everywhere, he came to look like an ecstatic old Chinaman.

He looked so much like a Chinaman that he had taken to dressing like a Chinaman. Real Chinamen often mistook him for a real Chinaman.

◗ Fred T. Barry confessed in his letter that he had not read the works of Kilgore Trout, but that he would joyfully do so before the Festival began. "You come highly recommended by Eliot Rosewater," he said, "who assures me that you are perhaps the greatest living American novelist. There can be no higher praise than that."

Clipped to the letter was a check for one thousand dollars. Fred T. Barry explained that this was for travel expenses and an honorarium.

It was a lot of money. Trout was suddenly fabulously well-to-do.

◗ Here is how Trout happened to be invited: Fred T. Barry wanted to have a fabulously valuable oil painting as a focal point for the Midland City Festival of the Arts. As rich as he was, he couldn't afford to buy one, so he looked for one to borrow.

The first person he went to was Eliot Rosewater, who owned an El Greco worth three million dollars or more. Rosewater said the Festival could have the picture on one condition: that it hire as a speaker the greatest living writer in the English language, who was Kilgore Trout.

Trout laughed at the flattering invitation, but he felt fear after that. Once again, a stranger was tampering with the privacy of his body bag. He put this question to his parakeet haggardly, and he rolled his eyes: "Why all this sudden interest in Kilgore Trout?"

He read the letter again. "They not only want Kilgore Trout," he said, "they want him in a *tuxedo*, Bill. Some mistake has been made."

He shrugged. "Maybe they invited me because they know I have a tuxedo," he said. He really did own a tuxedo. It was in a steamer trunk which he had lugged from place to place for more than forty years. It contained toys from childhood, the bones of a Bermuda Ern, and many other curiosities—including the tuxedo he had worn to a senior dance just prior to his graduation from Thomas Jefferson High School in Dayton, Ohio, in 1924. Trout was born in Bermuda, and attended grammar school there. But then his family moved to Dayton.

His high school was named after a slave owner who was also one of the world's greatest theoreticians on the subject of human liberty.

◆ Trout got his tuxedo out of the trunk and he put it on. It was a lot like a tuxedo I'd seen my father put on when he was an old, old man. It had a greenish patina of mold. Some of the growths it supported resembled patches of fine rabbit fur. "This will do nicely for the evenings," said Trout. "But tell me, Bill—what does one wear in Midland City in October before the sun goes down?" He hauled up his pants legs so that his grotesquely ornamental shins were exposed. "Bermuda shorts and bobby socks, eh, Bill? After all—I *am* from Bermuda."

He dabbed at his tuxedo with a damp rag, and the fungi came away easily. "Hate to do this, Bill," he said of the fungi he was murdering. "Fungi have as much right to life as I do. They know what they want, Bill. Damned if *I* do anymore."

Then he thought about what Bill himself might want. It was easy to guess. "Bill," he said, "I like you so much, and I am such a big shot in the Universe, that I will make your three biggest wishes come true." He opened the door of the cage, something Bill couldn't have done in a thousand years.

Bill flew over to a windowsill. He put his little shoulder against the glass. There was just one layer of glass between Bill and the great out-of-doors. Although Trout was in the storm window business, he had no storm windows on his own abode.

"Your second wish is about to come true," said Trout, and he again did something which Bill could never have done. He opened the window. But the opening of the window was such an alarming business to the parakeet that he flew back to his cage and hopped inside.

Trout closed the door of the cage and latched it. "That's the most intelligent use of three wishes I ever heard of," he told the bird. "You made sure you'd still have something worth wishing for—to get out of the cage."

◗ Trout made the connection between his lone fan letter and the invitation, but he couldn't believe that Eliot Rosewater was a grownup. Rosewater's handwriting looked like this:

You ought to be President of the United States!

"Bill," said Trout tentatively, "some teen-ager named Rosewater got me this job. His parents must be friends of the Chairman of the Arts Festival, and they don't know anything about books out that way. So when he said I was good, they believed him."

Trout shook his head. "I'm not going, Bill. I don't want out of my cage. I'm too smart for that. Even if I did want out, though, I wouldn't go to Midland City to make a laughing stock of myself—and my only fan."

◗ He left it at that. But he reread the invitation from time to time, got to know it by heart. And then one of the subtler messages on the paper got through to him. It was in the letterhead, which displayed two masks intended to represent comedy and tragedy:

One mask looked like this:

The other one looked like this:

"They don't want anything but smilers out there," Trout said to his parakeet. "Unhappy failures need not apply." But his mind wouldn't leave it alone at that. He got an idea which he found very tangy: "But maybe an unhappy failure is exactly what they *need* to see."

He became energetic after that. "Bill, Bill—" he said, "listen, I'm leaving the cage, but I'm coming back. I'm going out there to show them what nobody has ever seen at an arts festival before: a representative of all the thousands of artists who devoted their entire lives to a search for truth and beauty—and didn't find doodley-squat!"

37

▶ Trout accepted the invitation after all. Two days before the Festival was to begin, he delivered Bill into the care of his landlady upstairs, and he hitchhiked to New York City—with five hundred dollars pinned to the inside of his underpants. The rest of the money he had put in a bank.

He went to New York first—because he hoped to find some of his books in pornography stores there. He had no copies at home. He despised them, but now he wanted to read out loud from them in Midland City—as a demonstration of a tragedy which was ludicrous as well.

He planned to tell the people out there what he hoped to have in the way of a tombstone.

This was it:

SOMEBODY

[Sometime to Sometime]

He Tried

Chapter 4

Dwayne was meanwhile getting crazier all the time. He saw eleven moons in the sky over the new Mildred Barry Memorial Center for the Arts one night. The next morning, he saw a huge duck directing traffic at the intersection of Arsenal Avenue and Old County Road. He didn't tell anybody what he saw. He maintained secrecy.

And the bad chemicals in his head were fed up with secrecy. They were no longer content with making him feel and see queer things. They wanted him to *do* queer things, also, and make a lot of noise.

They wanted Dwayne Hoover to be *proud* of his disease.

 People said later that they were furious with themselves for not noticing the danger signals in Dwayne's behavior, for ignoring his obvious cries for help. After Dwayne ran amok, the local paper ran a deeply sympathetic editorial about it, begging people to watch each other for danger signals. Here was its title:

A CRY FOR HELP

But Dwayne wasn't all that weird before he met Kilgore Trout. His behavior in public kept him well within the limits of acceptable acts and beliefs and conversations in Midland City. The person closest to him, Francine Pefko, his white secretary and mistress, said that Dwayne seemed to be getting happier and happier all the time during the month before Dwayne went public as a maniac.

"I kept thinking," she told a newspaper reporter from her hospital bed, "'He is finally getting over his wife's suicide.'"

⬧ Francine worked at Dwayne's principal place of business, which was *Dwayne Hoover's Exit Eleven Pontiac Village,* just off the Interstate, next door to the new Holiday Inn.

Here is what made Francine think he was becoming happier: Dwayne began to sing songs which had been popular in his youth, such as "The Old Lamp Lighter," and "Tippy-Tippy-Tin," and "Hold Tight," and "Blue Moon," and so on. Dwayne had never sung before. Now he did it loudly as he sat at his desk, when he took a customer for a ride in a demonstrator, when he watched a mechanic service a car. One day he sang loudly as he crossed the lobby of the new Holiday Inn, smiling and gesturing at people as though he had been hired to sing for their pleasure. But nobody thought that was necessarily a hint of derangement, either—especially since Dwayne owned a piece of the Inn.

A black bus boy and a black waiter discussed this singing. "Listen at him sing," said the bus boy.

"If I owned what he owns, I'd sing, too," the waiter replied.

◆ The only person who said out loud that Dwayne was going crazy was Dwayne's white sales manager at the Pontiac agency, who was Harry LeSabre. A full week before Dwayne went off his rocker, Harry said to Francine Pefko, "Something has come over Dwayne. He used to be so charming. I don't find him so charming anymore."

Harry knew Dwayne better than did any other man. He had been with Dwayne for twenty years. He came to work for him when the agency was right on the edge of the Nigger part of town. A Nigger was a human being who was black.

"I know him the way a combat soldier knows his buddy," said Harry. "We used to put our lives on the line every day, when the agency was down on Jefferson Street. We got held up on the average of fourteen times a year. And I tell you that the Dwayne of today is a Dwayne I never saw before."

◆ It was true about the holdups. That was how Dwayne bought a Pontiac agency so cheaply. White people were the only people with money enough to buy new automobiles, except for a few black criminals, who always wanted Cadillacs. And white people were scared to go anywhere on Jefferson Street anymore.

◆ Here is where Dwayne got the money to buy the agency: He borrowed it from the Midland County National Bank. For collateral, he put up stock he owned in a company which was then called *The Midland City Ordnance Company*. It later became *Barrytron, Limited*. When Dwayne first got the stock, in the depths of the Great Depression, the company was called *The Robo-Magic Corporation of America*.

The name of the company kept changing through the years because the nature of its business changed so much. But its management hung on to the company's original motto—for old time's sake. The motto was this:

GOODBYE, BLUE MONDAY.

◆ Listen:

Harry LeSabre said to Francine, "When a man has been in combat with another man, he gets so he can sense the slightest change in his buddy's personality, and Dwayne has changed. You ask Vernon Garr."

Vernon Garr was a white mechanic who was the only other employee who had been with Dwayne before Dwayne moved the agency out to the Interstate. As it happened, Vernon was having trouble at home. His wife, Mary, was a schizophrenic, so Vernon hadn't noticed whether Dwayne had changed or not. Vernon's wife believed that Vernon was trying to turn her brains into plutonium.

♦ Harry LeSabre was entitled to talk about combat. He had been in actual combat in a war. Dwayne hadn't been in combat. He was a civilian employee of the United States Army Air Corps during the Second World War, though. One time he got to paint a message on a five-hundred-pound bomb which was going to be dropped on Hamburg, Germany. This was it:

♦ "Harry," said Francine, "everybody is entitled to a few bad days. Dwayne has fewer than anybody I know, so when he does have one like today, some people are hurt and surprised. They shouldn't be. He's human like anybody else."

"But why should he single out *me*?" Harry wanted to know. He was right: Dwayne *had* singled him out for astonishing insults and abuse that day. Everybody else still found Dwayne nothing but charming.

Later on, of course, Dwayne would assault all sorts of people, even three strangers from Erie, Pennsylvania, who had never been to Midland City before. But Harry was an isolated victim now.

◗ "Why *me?*" said Harry. This was a common question in Midland City. People were always asking that as they were loaded into ambulances after accidents of various kinds, or arrested for disorderly conduct, or burglarized, or socked in the nose and so on: "*Why me?*"

"Probably because he felt that you were man enough and friend enough to put up with him on one of his few bad days," said Francine.

"How would you like it if he insulted your clothes?" said Harry. This is what Dwayne had done to him: insulted his clothes.

"I would remember that he was the best employer in town," said Francine. This was true. Dwayne paid high wages. He had profit-sharing and Christmas bonuses at the end of every year. He was the first automobile dealer in his part of the State to offer his employees Blue Cross-Blue Shield, which was health insurance. He had a retirement plan which was superior to every retirement plan in the city with the exception of the one at Barrytron. His office door was always open to any employee who had troubles to discuss, whether they had to do with the automobile business or not.

For instance, on the day he insulted Harry's clothing, he also spent two hours with Vernon Garr, discussing the hallucinations Vernon's wife was having. "She sees things that aren't there," said Vernon.

"She needs rest, Vern," said Dwayne.

"Maybe I'm going crazy, too," said Vernon. "Christ, I go home and I talk for hours to my fucking dog."

"That makes two of us," said Dwayne.

44

❧ Here is the scene between Harry and Dwayne which upset Harry so much:

Harry went into Dwayne's office right after Vernon left. He expected no trouble, because he had never had any serious trouble with Dwayne.

"How's my old combat buddy today?" he said to Dwayne.

"As good as can be expected," said Dwayne. "Anything special bothering you?"

"No," said Harry.

"Vern's wife thinks Vern is trying to turn her brains into plutonium," said Dwayne.

"What's plutonium?" said Harry, and so on. They rambled along, and Harry made up a problem for himself just to keep the conversation lively. He said he was sad sometimes that he had no children. "But I'm glad in a way, too," he went on. "I mean, why should I contribute to overpopulation?"

Dwayne didn't say anything.

"Maybe we should have adopted one," said Harry, "but it's too late now. And the old lady and me—we have a good time just horsing around with ourselves. What do we need a kid for?"

It was after the mention of adoption that Dwayne blew up. He himself had been adopted—by a couple who had moved to Midland City from West Virginia in order to make big money as factory workers in the First World War. Dwayne's real mother was a spinster school teacher who wrote sentimental poetry and claimed to be descended from Richard the Lion-Hearted, who was a king. His real father was an itinerant typesetter, who seduced his mother by setting her poems in type. He didn't sneak them into a newspaper or anything. It was enough for her that they were set in type.

She was a defective child-bearing machine. She destroyed herself automatically while giving birth to Dwayne. The printer disappeared. He was a disappearing machine.

◆ It may be that the subject of adoption caused an unfortunate chemical reaction in Dwayne's head. At any rate, Dwayne suddenly snarled this at Harry: "Harry, why don't you get a bunch of cotton waste from Vern Garr, soak it in *Blue Sunoco*, and burn up your fucking wardrobe? You make me feel like I'm at *Watson Brothers*." *Watson Brothers* was the name of the funeral parlor for white people who were at least moderately well-to-do. *Blue Sunoco* was a brand of gasoline.

Harry was startled, and then pain set in. Dwayne had never said anything about his clothes in all the years he'd known him. The clothes were conservative and neat, in Harry's opinion. His shirts were white. His ties were black or navy blue. His suits were gray or dark blue. His shoes and socks were black.

"Listen, Harry," said Dwayne, and his expression was mean, "Hawaiian Week is coming up, and I'm absolutely serious: burn your clothes and get new ones, or apply for work at Watson Brothers. Have yourself embalmed while you're at it."

◆ Harry couldn't do anything but let his mouth hang open. The Hawaiian Week Dwayne had mentioned was a sales promotion scheme which involved making the agency look as much like the Hawaiian Islands as possible. People who bought new or used cars, or had repairs done in excess of five hundred dollars during the week would be entered automatically in a lottery. Three lucky people would each win a free, all-expenses-paid trip to Las Vegas and San Francisco and then Hawaii for a party of two.

"I don't mind that you have the name of a Buick, Harry, when you're supposed to be selling Pontiacs—" Dwayne went on. He was referring to the fact that the Buick division of General Motors put out a model called the *Le Sabre*. "You can't help that." Dwayne now patted the top of his desk softly. This was somehow more menacing than if he had pounded the desk with his fist. "But there *are* a hell of a lot of things you *can* change, Harry. There's a long weekend coming up. I expect to see some big changes in you when I come to work on Tuesday morning."

The weekend was extra-long because the coming Monday was a national holiday, *Veterans' Day*. It was in honor of people who had served their country in uniform.

◆ "When we started selling Pontiacs, Harry," said Dwayne, "the car was sensible transportation for school teachers and grandmothers and maiden aunts." This was true. "Perhaps you haven't noticed, Harry, but the Pontiac has now become a glamorous, youthful adventure for people who want a *kick* out of life! And you dress and act like this was a mortuary! Look at yourself in a mirror, Harry, and ask yourself, 'Who could ever associate a man like this with a Pontiac?'"

Harry LeSabre was too choked up to point out to

Dwayne that, no matter what he looked like, he was generally acknowledged to be one of the most effective sales managers for Pontiac not only in the State, but in the entire Middle West. Pontiac was the best-selling automobile in the Midland City area, despite the fact that it was not a low-price car. It was a medium-price car.

◗ Dwayne Hoover told poor Harry LeSabre that the Hawaiian Festival, only a long weekend away, was Harry's golden opportunity to loosen up, to have some fun, to encourage other people to have some fun, too.

"Harry," said Dwayne. "I have some news for you: modern science has given us a whole lot of wonderful new colors, with strange, exciting names like *red!*, *orange!*, *green!*, and *pink!*, Harry. We're not stuck any more with just black, gray and white! Isn't that good news, Harry? And the State Legislature has just announced that it is no longer a crime to smile during working hours, Harry, and I have the personal promise of the Governor that never again will anybody be sent to the Sexual Offenders' Wing of the Adult Correctional Institution for telling a joke!"

◗ Harry LeSabre might have weathered all this with only minor damage, if only Harry hadn't been a secret transvestite. On weekends he liked to dress up in women's clothing, and not drab clothing, either. Harry and his wife would pull down the window blinds, and Harry would turn into a bird of paradise.

Nobody but Harry's wife knew his secret.

When Dwayne razzed him about the clothes he wore to

work, and then mentioned the Sexual Offenders' Wing of the Adult Correctional Institution at Shepherdstown, Harry had to suspect that his secret was out. And it wasn't merely a comical secret, either. Harry could be arrested for what he did on weekends. He could be fined up to three thousand dollars and sentenced to as much as five years at hard labor in the Sexual Offenders' Wing of the Adult Correctional Institution at Shepherdstown.

So poor Harry spent a wretched Veterans' Day weekend after that. But Dwayne spent a worse one.

Here is what the last night of that weekend was like for Dwayne: his bad chemicals rolled him out of bed. They made him dress as though there were some sort of emergency with which he had to deal. This was in the wee hours. Veterans' Day had ended at the stroke of twelve.

Dwayne's bad chemicals made him take a loaded thirty-eight caliber revolver from under his pillow and stick it in his mouth. This was a tool whose only purpose was to make holes in human beings. It looked like this:

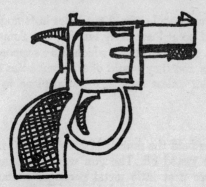

In Dwayne's part of the planet, anybody who wanted one could get one down at his local hardware store. Policemen all had them. So did the criminals. So did the people caught in between.

Criminals would point guns at people and say, "Give me all your money," and the people usually would. And policemen would point their guns at criminals and say, "Stop" or whatever the situation called for, and the criminals usually would. Sometimes they wouldn't. Sometimes a wife would get so mad at her husband that she would put a hole in him with a gun. Sometimes a husband would get so mad at his wife that he would put a hole in her. And so on.

In the same week Dwayne Hoover ran amok, a fourteen-year-old Midland City boy put holes in his mother and father because he didn't want to show them the bad report card he had brought home. His lawyer planned to enter a plea of temporary insanity, which meant that at the time of the shooting the boy was unable to distinguish the difference between right and wrong.

◗ Sometimes people would put holes in famous people so they could be at least fairly famous, too. Sometimes people would get on airplanes which were supposed to fly to someplace, and they would offer to put holes in the pilot and co-pilot unless they flew the airplane to someplace else.

◗ Dwayne held the muzzle of his gun in his mouth for a while. He tasted oil. The gun was loaded and cocked. There were neat little metal packages containing charcoal, potassium nitrate and sulphur only inches from his brains. He had only to trip a lever, and the powder would turn to gas. The gas would blow a chunk of lead down a tube and through Dwayne's brains.

But Dwayne elected to shoot up one of his tiled bathrooms instead. He put chunks of lead through his toilet and a washbasin and a bathtub enclosure. There was a picture of a flamingo sandblasted on the glass of the bathtub enclosure. It looked like this:

Dwayne shot the flamingo.

He snarled at his recollection of it afterwards. Here is what he snarled: "Dumb fucking bird."

◆ Nobody heard the shots. All the houses in the neighborhood were too well insulated for sound ever to get in or out. A sound wanting in or out of Dwayne's dreamhouse, for instance, had to go through an inch and a half of plasterboard, a polystyrene vapor barrier, a sheet of aluminum foil, a three-inch airspace, another sheet of aluminum foil, a three-inch blanket of glass wool, another sheet of aluminum foil, one inch of insulating board made of pressed sawdust, tarpaper, one inch of wood sheathing, more tarpaper, and then aluminum siding which was hollow. The space in the siding was filled with a miracle insulating material developed for use on rockets to the Moon.

◆ Dwayne turned on the floodlights around his house, and he played basketball on the blacktop apron outside his five-car garage.

Dwayne's dog Sparky hid in the basement when Dwayne shot up the bathroom. But he came out now. Sparky watched Dwayne play basketball.

"You and me, Sparky," said Dwayne. And so on. He sure loved that dog.

Nobody saw him playing basketball. He was screened from his neighbors by trees and shrubs and a high cedar fence.

▶ He put the basketball away, and he climbed into a black Plymouth *Fury* he had taken in trade the day before. The Plymouth was a Chrysler product, and Dwayne himself sold General Motors products. He had decided to drive the Plymouth for a day or two in order to keep abreast of the competition.

As he backed out of his driveway, he thought it important to explain to his neighbors why he was in a Plymouth *Fury*, so he yelled out the window: "Keeping abreast of the competition!" He blew his horn.

▶ Dwayne zoomed down Old County Road and onto the Interstate, which he had all to himself. He swerved into Exit Ten at a high rate of speed, slammed into a guardrail, spun around and around. He came out onto Union Avenue going backwards, jumped a curb, and came to a stop in a vacant lot. Dwayne owned the lot.

Nobody saw or heard anything. Nobody lived in the area. A policeman was supposed to cruise by about once every hour or so, but he was cooping in an alley behind a Western Electric warehouse about two miles away. *Cooping* was police slang for sleeping on the job.

▶ Dwayne stayed in his vacant lot for a while. He played the radio. All the Midland City stations were asleep for the night, but Dwayne picked up a country music station in West Virginia, which offered him ten different kinds of flowering shrubs and five fruit trees for six dollars, C.O.D.

"Sounds good to me," said Dwayne. He meant it. Almost all the messages which were sent and received in his

53

country, even the telepathic ones, had to do with buying or selling some damn thing. They were like lullabies to Dwayne.

Chapter 5

While Dwayne Hoover listened to West Virginia, Kilgore Trout tried to fall asleep in a movie theater in New York City. It was much cheaper than a night in a hotel. Trout had never done it before, but he knew sleeping in movie houses was the sort of thing really dirty old men did. He wished to arrive in Midland City as the dirtiest of all old men. He was supposed to take part in a symposium out there entitled "The Future of the American Novel in the Age of McLuhan." He wished to say at that symposium, "I don't know who McLuhan is, but I know what it's like to spend the night with a lot of other dirty old men in a movie theater in New York City. Could we talk about that?"

He wished to say, too, "Does this McLuhan, whoever

he is, have anything to say about the relationship between wide-open beavers and the sales of books?"

▶ Trout had come down from Cohoes late·that afternoon. He had since visited many pornography shops and a shirt store. He had bought two of his own books, *Plague on Wheels* and *Now It Can Be Told*, a magazine containing a short story of his, and a tuxedo shirt. The name of the magazine was *Black Garterbelt*. The tuxedo shirt had a cascade of ruffles down its bosom. On the shirt salesman's advice, Trout had also bought a packaged ensemble consisting of a cumberbund, a boutonnière, and a bow tie. They were all the color of tangerines.

These goodies were all in his lap, along with a crackling brown paper parcel containing his tuxedo, six new pairs of jockey shorts, six new pairs of socks, his razor and a new toothbrush. Trout hadn't owned a toothbrush for years.

▶ The jackets of *Plague on Wheels* and *Now It Can Be Told* both promised plenty of wide-open beavers inside. The picture on the cover of *Now It Can Be Told*, which was the book which would turn Dwayne Hoover into a homicidal maniac, showed a college professor being undressed by a group of naked sorority girls. A library tower could be seen through a window in the sorority house. It was daytime outside, and there was a clock in the tower. The clock looked like this:

The professor was stripped down to his candy-striped underwear shorts and his socks and garters and his mortarboard, which was a hat which looked like this:

There was absolutely nothing about a professor or a sorority or a university anywhere in the body of the book.

The book was in the form of a long letter from the Creator of the Universe to the only creature in the Universe who had free will.

◆ As for the story in *Black Garterbelt* magazine: Trout had no idea that it had been accepted for publication. It had been accepted years ago, apparently, for the date on the magazine was April, 1962. Trout found it by chance in a bin of tame old magazines near the front of the store. They were underpants magazines.

When he bought the magazine, the cashier supposed Trout was drunk or feeble-minded. All he was getting, the cashier thought, was pictures of women in their underpants. Their legs were apart, all right, but they had on underpants, so they were certainly no competition for the wide-open beavers on sale in the back of the store.

"I hope you enjoy it," said the cashier to Trout. He meant that he hoped Trout would find some pictures he could masturbate to, since that was the only point of all the books and magazines.

"It's for an arts festival," said Trout.

◆ As for the story itself, it was entitled "The Dancing Fool." Like so many Trout stories, it was about a tragic failure to communicate.

Here was the plot: A flying saucer creature named Zog arrived on Earth to explain how wars could be prevented and how cancer could be cured. He brought the information from Margo, a planet where the natives conversed by means of farts and tap dancing.

Zog landed at night in Connecticut. He had no sooner

touched down than he saw a house on fire. He rushed into the house, farting and tap dancing, warning the people about the terrible danger they were in. The head of the house brained Zog with a golfclub.

◗ The movie theater where Trout sat with all his parcels in his lap showed nothing but dirty movies. The music was soothing. Phantasms of a young man and a young woman sucked harmlessly on one another's soft apertures on the silver screen.

And Trout made up a new novel while he sat there. It was about an Earthling astronaut who arrived on a planet where all the animal and plant life had been killed by pollution, except for humanoids. The humanoids ate food made from petroleum and coal.

They gave a feast for the astronaut, whose name was Don. The food was terrible. The big topic of conversation was censorship. The cities were blighted with motion picture theaters which showed nothing but dirty movies. The humanoids wished they could put them out of business somehow, but without interfering with free speech.

They asked Don if dirty movies were a problem on Earth, too, and Don said, "Yes." They asked him if the movies were *really* dirty, and Don replied, "As dirty as movies could get."

This was a challenge to the humanoids, who were sure their dirty movies could beat anything on Earth. So everybody piled into air-cushion vehicles, and they floated to a dirty movie house downtown.

It was intermission time when they got there, so Don had some time to think about what could possibly be dirtier than what he had already seen on Earth. He became sexually excited even before the house lights went down. The women in his party were all twittery and squirmy.

So the theater went dark and the curtains opened. At first there wasn't any picture. There were slurps and moans from loudspeakers. Then the picture itself appeared. It was a high quality film of a male humanoid eating what looked like a pear. The camera zoomed in on his lips and tongue and teeth, which glistened with saliva. He took his time about eating the pear. When the last of it had disappeared into his slurpy mouth, the camera focussed on his Adam's apple. His Adam's apple bobbed obscenely. He belched contentedly, and then these words appeared on the screen, but in the language of the planet:

THE END

◗ It was all faked, of course. There weren't any pears anymore. And the eating of a pear wasn't the main event of the evening anyway. It was a short subject, which gave the members of the audience time to settle down.

Then the main feature began. It was about a male and a female and their two children, and their dog and their cat. They ate steadily for an hour and a half—soup, meat, biscuits, butter, vegetables, mashed potatoes and gravy, fruit, candy, cake, pie. The camera rarely strayed more than a foot from their glistening lips and their bobbing Adam's apples. And then the father put the cat and dog on the table, so they could take part in the orgy, too.

After a while, the actors couldn't eat any more. They were so stuffed that they were goggle-eyed. They could hardly move. They said they didn't think they could eat again for a week, and so on. They cleared the table slowly. They went waddling out into the kitchen, and they dumped about thirty pounds of leftovers into a garbage can.

The audience went wild.

▶ When Don and his friends left the theater, they were accosted by humanoid whores, who offered them eggs and oranges and milk and butter and peanuts and so on. The whores couldn't actually deliver these goodies, of course.

The humanoids told Don that if he went home with a whore, she would cook him a meal of petroleum and coal products at fancy prices.

And then, while he ate them, she would talk dirty about how fresh and full of natural juices the food was, even though the food was fake.

Chapter 6

Dwayne Hoover sat in the used Plymouth *Fury* in his own vacant lot for an hour, listening to West Virginia. He was told about health insurance for pennies a day, about how to get better performance from his car. He was told what to do about constipation. He was offered a Bible which had everything that God or Jesus had actually said out loud printed in red capital letters. He was offered a plant which would attract and eat disease-carrying insects in his home.

All this was stored away in Dwayne's memory, in case he should need it later on. He had all kinds of stuff in there.

◗ While Dwayne sat there so alone, the oldest inhabitant of Midland City was dying in the County Hospital, at the foot of Fairchild Boulevard, which was nine miles away. She was Mary Young. She was one hundred and eight years old. She was black. Mary Young's parents had been human slaves in Kentucky.

There was a tiny connection between Mary Young and Dwayne Hoover. She did the laundry for Dwayne's family for a few months, back when Dwayne was a little boy. She told Bible stories and stories about slavery to little Dwayne. She told him about a public hanging of a white man she had seen in Cincinnati, when she was a little girl.

◆ A black intern at the County Hospital now watched Mary Young die of pneumonia.

The intern did not know her. He had been in Midland City for only a week. He wasn't even a fellow-American, although he had taken his medical degree at Harvard. He was an Indaro. He was a Nigerian. His name was Cyprian Ukwende. He felt no kinship with Mary or with any American blacks. He felt kinship only with Indaros.

As she died, Mary was as alone on the planet as were Dwayne Hoover or Kilgore Trout. She had never reproduced. There were no friends or relatives to watch her die. So she spoke her very last words on the planet to Cyprian Ukwende. She did not have enough breath left to make her vocal chords buzz. She could only move her lips noiselessly.

Here is all she had to say about death: "Oh my, oh my."

◆ Like all Earthlings at the point of death, Mary Young

sent faint reminders of herself to those who had known her. She released a small cloud of telepathic butterflies, and one of these brushed the cheek of Dwayne Hoover, nine miles away.

Dwayne heard a tired voice from somewhere behind his head, even though no one was back there. It said this to Dwayne: "Oh my, oh my."

◖ Dwayne's bad chemicals now made him put his car in gear. He drove out of the vacant lot, proceeded sedately down Union Avenue, which paralleled the Interstate.

He went past his principal place of business, which was *Dwayne Hoover's Exit Eleven Pontiac Village*, and he turned into the parking lot of the new Holiday Inn next door. Dwayne owned a third of the Inn—in partnership with Midland City's leading orthodontist, Dr. Alfred Maritimo, and Bill Miller, who was Chairman of the Parole Board at the Adult Correctional Institution at Shepherdstown, among other things.

Dwayne went up the Inn's back steps to the roof without meeting anybody. There was a full moon. There were *two* full moons. The new Mildred Barry Memorial Center for the Arts was a translucent sphere on stilts, and it was illuminated from the inside now—and it looked like a moon.

◖ Dwayne gazed over the sleeping city. He had been born there. He had spent the first three years of his life in an orphanage only two miles from where he stood. He had been adopted and educated there.

He owned not only the Pontiac agency and a piece of

the new Holiday Inn. He owned three Burger Chefs, too, and five coin-operated car washes, and pieces of the Sugar Creek Drive-In Theatre, Radio Station WMCY, the Three Maples Par-Three Golf Course, and seventeen hundred shares of common stock in Barrytron, Limited, a local electronics firm. He owned dozens of vacant lots. He was on the Board of Directors of the Midland County National Bank.

But now Midland City looked unfamiliar and frightening to Dwayne. "Where am I?" he said.

He even forgot that his wife Celia had committed suicide, for instance, by eating Drāno—a mixture of sodium hydroxide and aluminum flakes, which was meant to clear drains. Celia became a small volcano, since she was composed of the same sorts of substances which commonly clogged drains.

Dwayne even forgot that his only child, a son, had grown up to be a notorious homosexual. His name was George, but everybody called him "Bunny." He played piano in the cocktail lounge of the new Holiday Inn.

"Where am I?" said Dwayne.

Chapter 7

Kilgore Trout took a leak in the men's room of the New York City movie house. There was a sign on the wall next to the roller towel. It advertised a massage parlor called *The Sultan's Harem*. Massage parlors were something new and exciting in New York. Men could go in there and photograph naked women, or they could paint the women's naked bodies with water-soluble paints. Men could be rubbed all over by a woman until their penises squirted jism into Turkish towels.

"It's a full life and a merry one," said Kilgore Trout.

There was a message written in pencil on the tiles by the roller towel. This was it:

*What is
the purpose
of life?*

Trout plundered his pockets for a pen or pencil. He had an answer to the question. But he had nothing to write with, not even a burnt match. So he left the question unanswered, but here is what he would have written, if he had found anything to write with:

> *To be
> the eyes
> and ears
> and conscience
> of the Creator of the Universe,
> you fool.*

◆ When Trout headed back for his seat in the theater, he played at being the eyes and ears and conscience of the Creator of the Universe. He sent messages by telepathy to the Creator, wherever He was. He reported that the men's room had been clean as a whistle. "The carpeting under my feet," he signaled from the lobby, "is springy and new. I think it must be some miracle fiber. It's blue. You know what I mean by *blue?*" And so on.

When he got to the auditorium itself, the house lights were on. Nobody was there but the manager, who was also the ticket-taker and the bouncer and the janitor. He was sweeping filth from between the seats. He was a middle-aged white man. "No more fun tonight, grandfather," he said to Trout. "Time to go home."

Trout didn't protest. Neither did he leave immediately. He examined a green enameled steel box in the back of the auditorium. It contained the projector and the sound system and the films. There was a wire that led from the box to a plug in the wall. There was a hole in the front of the box. That was how the pictures got out. On the side of the box was a simple switch. It looked like this:

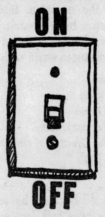

◗ It intrigued Trout to know that he had only to flick the switch, and the people would start fucking and sucking again.

"Good night, Grandfather," said the manager pointedly.

Trout took his leave of the machine reluctantly. He said this about it to the manager: "It fills such a *need*, this machine, and it's so easy to operate."

‣ As Trout departed, he sent this telepathic message to the Creator of the Universe, serving as His eyes and ears and conscience: "Am headed for Forty-second Street now. How much do you already know about Forty-second Street?"

Chapter 8

Trout wandered out onto the sidewalk of Forty-second Street. It was a dangerous place to be. The whole city was dangerous—because of chemicals and the uneven distribution of wealth and so on. A lot of people were like Dwayne: they created chemicals in their own bodies which were bad for their heads. But there were thousands upon thousands of other people in the city who bought bad chemicals and ate them or sniffed them—or injected them into their veins with devices which looked like this:

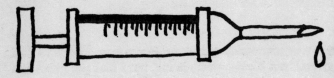

Sometimes they even stuffed bad chemicals up their assholes. Their assholes looked like this:

◆ People took such awful chances with chemicals and their bodies because they wanted the quality of their lives to improve. They lived in ugly places where there were only ugly things to do. They didn't own doodley-squat, so they couldn't improve their surroundings. So they did their best to make their insides beautiful instead.

The results had been catastrophic so far—suicide, theft, murder, and insanity and so on. But new chemicals were coming onto the market all the time. Twenty feet away from Trout there on Forty-second Street, a fourteen-year-old white boy lay unconscious in the doorway of a pornography store. He had swallowed a half pint of a new type of paint remover which had gone on sale for the first time only the day before. He had also swallowed two pills which were intended to prevent contagious abortion in cattle, which was called *Bang's disease.*

◆ Trout was petrified there on Forty-second Street. I had given him a life not worth living, but I had also given him an iron will to live. This was a common combination on the planet Earth.

The theater manager came out and locked the door behind him.

And two young black prostitutes materialized from nowhere. They asked Trout and the manager if they would like to have some fun. They were cheerful and unafraid—because of a tube of Norwegian hemorrhoid remedy which they had eaten about half an hour before. The manufacturer had never intended the stuff to be eaten. People were supposed to squirt it up their assholes.

These were country girls. They had grown up in the rural south of the nation, where their ancestors had been used as agricultural machinery. The white farmers down there weren't using machines made out of meat anymore, though, because machines made out of metal were cheaper and more reliable, and required simpler homes.

So the black machines had to get out of there, or starve to death. They came to cities because everyplace else had signs like this on the fences and trees:

▶ Kilgore Trout once wrote a story called "This Means You." It was set in the Hawaiian Islands, the place where the lucky winners of Dwayne Hoover's contest in Midland City were supposed to go. Every bit of land on the islands was owned by only about forty people, and, in the story, Trout had those people decide to exercise their property rights to the full. They put up *no trespassing* signs on everything.

This created terrible problems for the million other people on the islands. The law of gravity required that they stick somewhere on the surface. Either that, or they could go out into the water and bob offshore.

But then the Federal Government came through with an emergency program. It gave a big balloon full of helium to every man, woman and child who didn't own property.

▶ There was a cable with a harness on it dangling from each balloon. With the help of the balloons, Hawaiians could go on inhabiting the islands without always sticking to things other people owned.

▶ The prostitutes worked for a pimp now. He was splendid and cruel. He was a god to them. He took their free will away from them, which was perfectly all right. They didn't want it anyway. It was as though they had surrendered themselves to Jesus, for instance, so they could live unselfishly and trustingly—except that they had surrendered to a pimp instead.

Their childhoods were over. They were dying now. Earth was a tinhorn planet as far as they were concerned.

When Trout and the theater manager, two tinhorns,

said they didn't want any tinhorn fun, the dying children sauntered off, their feet sticking to the planet, coming unstuck, then sticking again. They disappeared around a corner. Trout, the eyes and ears of the Creator of the Universe, sneezed.

🖙 "God bless you," said the manager. This was a fully automatic response many Americans had to hearing a person sneeze.

"Thank you," said Trout. Thus a temporary friendship was formed.

Trout said he hoped to get safely to a cheap hotel. The manager said he hoped to get to the subway station on Times Square. So they walked together, encouraged by the echoes of their footsteps from the building façades.

The manager told Trout a little about what the planet looked like to him. It was a place where he had a wife and two kids, he said. They didn't know he ran a theater which showed blue movies. They thought he was doing consulting work as an engineer so late at night. He said that the planet didn't have much use for engineers his age anymore. It had adored them once.

"Hard times," said Trout.

The manager told of being in on the development of a miraculous insulating material, which had been used on rocket ships to the Moon. This was, in fact, the same material which gave the aluminum siding of Dwayne Hoover's dream house in Midland City its miraculous insulating qualities.

The manager reminded Trout of what the first man to set foot on the Moon had said: "One small step for man, one great leap for mankind."

"Thrilling words," said Trout. He looked over his shoulder, perceived that they were being followed by a white Oldsmobile *Toronado* with a black vinyl roof. This four hundred horsepower, front-wheel drive vehicle was burbling along at about three miles an hour, ten feet behind them and close to the curb.

That was the last thing Trout remembered—seeing the Oldsmobile back there.

◆ The next thing he knew, he was on his hands and knees on a handball court underneath the Queensboro Bridge at Fifty-ninth Street, with the East River nearby. His trousers and underpants were around his ankles. His money was gone. His parcels were scattered around him—the tuxedo, the new shirt, the books. Blood seeped from one ear.

The police caught him in the act of pulling up his trousers. They dazzled him with a spotlight as he leaned against the backboard of the handball court and fumbled foolishly with his belt and the buttons on his fly. The police supposed that they had caught him committing some public nuisance, had caught him working with an old man's limited palette of excrement and alcohol.

He wasn't quite penniless. There was a ten-dollar bill in the watch pocket of his pants.

◆ It was determined at a hospital that Trout was not seriously hurt. He was taken to a police station, where he was questioned. All he could say was that he had been kidnapped by pure evil in a white Oldsmobile. The police wanted to know how many people were in the car, their ages, their sexes, the colors of their skins, their manners of speech.

"For all I know, they may not even have been Earthlings," said Trout: "For all I know, that car may have been occupied by an intelligent gas from Pluto."

◗ Trout said this so innocently, but his comment turned out to be the first germ in an epidemic of mind-poisoning. Here is how the disease was spread: a reporter wrote a story for the *New York Post* the next day, and he led off with the quotation from Trout.

The story appeared under this headline:

PLUTO BANDITS
KIDNAP PAIR

Trout's name was given as Kilmer Trotter, incidentally, address unknown. His age was given as eighty-two.

Other papers copied the story, rewrote it some. They all hung onto the joke about Pluto, spoke knowingly of *The Pluto Gang*. And reporters asked police for any new information on *The Pluto Gang*, so police went looking for information on *The Pluto Gang*.

◗ So New Yorkers, who had so many nameless terrors, were easily taught to fear something seemingly specific—*The Pluto Gang*. They bought new locks for their doors and gratings for their windows, to keep out *The Pluto Gang*. They stopped going to theaters at night, for fear of *The Pluto Gang*.

Foreign newspapers spread the terror, ran articles on how persons thinking of visiting New York might keep to a certain few streets in Manhattan and stand a fair chance of avoiding *The Pluto Gang.*

⬧ In one of New York City's many ghettos for dark-skinned people, a group of Puerto Rican boys gathered together in the basement of an abandoned building. They were small, but they were numerous and volatile. They wished to become frightening, in order to defend themselves and their friends and families, something the police wouldn't do. They also wanted to drive the drug peddlers out of the neighborhood, and to get enough publicity, which was very important, to catch the attention of the Government, so that the Government would do a better job of picking up the garbage and so on.

One of them, José Mendoza, was a fairly good painter. So he painted the emblem of their new gang on the backs of the members' jackets. This was it:

Chapter 9

While Kilgore Trout was inadvertently poisoning the collective mind of New York City, Dwayne Hoover, the demented Pontiac dealer, was coming down from the roof of his own Holiday Inn in the Middle West.

Dwayne went into the carpeted lobby of the place not long before sunrise, to ask for a room. As queer as the hour was, there was a man ahead of him, and a black one at that. This was Cyprian Ukwende, the Indaro, the physician from Nigeria, who was staying at the Inn until he could find a suitable apartment.

Dwayne awaited his turn humbly. He had forgotten that he was a co-owner of the Inn. As for staying at a place where black men stayed, Dwayne was philosophical. He experienced a sort of bittersweet happiness as he told himself, "Times change. Times change."

▶ The night clerk was new. He did not know Dwayne. He had Dwayne fill out a registration in full. Dwayne, for his part, apologized for not knowing what the number of his license plate was. He felt guilty about that, even though he knew he had done nothing he should feel guilty about.

He was elated when the clerk let him have a room key. He had passed the test. And he adored his room. It was so new and cool and clean. It was so *neutral!* It was the brother of thousands upon thousands of rooms in Holiday Inns all over the world.

Dwayne Hoover might be confused as to what his life was all about, or what he should do with it next. But this much he has done correctly: He had delivered himself to an irreproachable container for a human being.

It awaited anybody. It awaited Dwayne.

Around the toilet seat was a band of paper like this, which he would have to remove before he used the toilet:

This loop of paper guaranteed Dwayne that he need have no fear that corkscrew-shaped little animals would crawl up his asshole and eat up his wiring. That was one less worry for Dwayne.

79

◗ There was a sign hanging on the inside doorknob, which Dwayne now hung on the outside doorknob. It looked like this:

Dwayne pulled open his floor-to-ceiling draperies for a moment. He saw the sign which announced the presence of the Inn to weary travelers on the Interstate. Here is what it looked like:

He closed his draperies. He adjusted the heating and ventilating system. He slept like a lamb.

A lamb was a young animal which was legendary for sleeping well on the planet Earth. It looked like this:

Chapter 10

Kilgore Trout was released by the Police Department of the City of New York like a weightless thing—at two hours before dawn on the day after Veterans' Day. He crossed the island of Manhattan from east to west in the company of Kleenex tissues and newspapers and soot.

He got a ride in a truck. It was hauling seventy-eight thousand pounds of Spanish olives. It picked him up at the mouth of the Lincoln Tunnel, which was named in honor of a man who had had the courage and imagination to make human slavery against the law in the United States of America. This was a recent innovation.

The slaves were simply turned loose without any property. They were easily recognizable. They were black. They were suddenly free to go exploring.

◗ The driver, who was white, told Trout that he would have to lie on the floor of the cab until they reached open country, since it was against the law for him to pick up hitchhikers.

◗ It was still dark when he told Trout he could sit up. They were crossing the poisoned marshes and meadows of New Jersey. The truck was a General Motors Astro-95 Diesel tractor, hooked up to a trailer forty feet long. It was so enormous that it made Trout feel that his head was about the size of a piece of bee-bee shot.

The driver said he used to be a hunter and a fisherman, long ago. It broke his heart when he imagined what the marshes and meadows had been like only a hundred years before. "And when you think of the shit that most of these factories make—wash day products, catfood, pop—"

◗ He had a point. The planet was being destroyed by manufacturing processes, and what was being manufactured was lousy, by and large.

Then Trout made a good point, too. "Well," he said, "I used to be a conservationist. I used to weep and wail about people shooting bald eagles with automatic shotguns from helicopters and all that, but I gave it up. There's a river in Cleveland which is so polluted that it catches fire about once a year. That used to make me sick, but I laugh about it now. When some tanker accidently dumps its load in the ocean, and kills millions of birds and billions of fish, I say, 'More power to Standard Oil,' or whoever it was that dumped it." Trout raised his arms in celebration. "'Up your ass with Mobil gas,'" he said.

The driver was upset by this. "You're kidding," he said.

"I realized," said Trout, "that God wasn't any conservationist, so for anybody else to be one was sacrilegious and a waste of time. You ever see one of His volcanoes or tornadoes or tidal waves? Anybody ever tell you about the Ice Ages he arranges for every half-million years? How about Dutch Elm disease? There's a nice conservation measure for you. That's God, not man. Just about the time we got our rivers cleaned up, he'd probably have the whole galaxy go up like a celluloid collar. That's what the Star of Bethlehem was, you know."

"What *was* the Star of Bethlehem?" said the driver.

"A whole galaxy going up like a celluloid collar," said Trout.

◗ The driver was impressed. "Come to think about it," he said, "I don't think there's anything about conservation anywhere in the Bible."

"Unless you want to count the story about the Flood," said Trout.

◗ They rode in silence for a while, and then the driver made another good point. He said he knew that his truck was turning the atmosphere into poison gas, and that the planet was being turned into pavement so his truck could go anywhere. "So I'm committing suicide," he said.

"Don't worry about it," said Trout.

"My brother is even worse," the driver went on. "He works in a factory that makes chemicals for killing plants and trees in Viet Nam." Viet Nam was a country where America was trying to make people stop being communists by dropping things on them from airplanes. The chemicals he mentioned were intended to kill all the foliage, so it would be harder for communists to hide from airplanes.

"Don't worry about it," said Trout.

"In the long run, *he's* committing suicide," said the driver. "Seems like the only kind of job an American can get these days is committing suicide in some way."

"Good point," said Trout.

◗ "I can't tell if you're serious or not," said the driver.

"I won't know myself until I find out whether *life* is serious or not," said Trout. "It's *dangerous*, I know, and it can hurt a lot. That doesn't necessarily mean it's *serious*, too."

◗ After Trout became famous, of course, one of the biggest mysteries about him was whether he was kidding or not. He told one persistent questioner that he always crossed his fingers when he was kidding.

"And please note," he went on, "that when I gave you that priceless piece of information, my fingers were crossed."

And so on.

He was a pain in the neck in a lot of ways. The truck driver got sick of him after an hour or two. Trout used the silence to make up an anticonservation story he called "Gilgongo!"

"Gilgongo!" was about a planet which was unpleasant because there was too much creation going on.

The story began with a big party in honor of a man

who had wiped out an entire species of darling little panda bears. He had devoted his life to this. Special plates were made for the party, and the guests got to take them home as souvenirs. There was a picture of a little bear on each one, and the date of the party. Underneath the picture was the word:

GILGONGO!

In the language of the planet, that meant "Extinct!"

◆ People were glad that the bears were *gilgongo*, because there were too many species on the planet already, and new ones were coming into being almost every hour. There was no way anybody could prepare for the bewildering diversity of creatures and plants he was likely to encounter.

The people were doing their best to cut down on the number of species, so that life could be more predictable. But Nature was too creative for them. All life on the planet was suffocated at last by a living blanket one hundred feet thick. The blanket was composed of passenger pigeons and eagles and Bermuda Erns and whooping cranes.

◆ "At least it's olives," the driver said.

"What?" said Trout.

"Lots worse things we could be hauling than olives."

"Right," said Trout. He had forgotten that the main thing they were doing was moving seventy-eight thousand pounds of olives to Tulsa, Oklahoma.

◗ The driver talked about politics some.

Trout couldn't tell one politician from another one. They were all formlessly enthusiastic chimpanzees to him. He wrote a story one time about an optimistic chimpanzee who became President of the United States. He called it "Hail to the Chief."

The chimpanzee wore a little blue blazer with brass buttons, and with the seal of the President of the United States sewed to the breast pocket. It looked like this:

Everywhere he went, bands would play "Hail to the Chief." The chimpanzee loved it. He would bounce up and down.

🔥 They stopped at a diner. Here is what the sign in front of the diner said:

So they ate.

Trout spotted an idiot who was eating, too. The idiot was a white male adult—in the care of a white female nurse. The idiot couldn't talk much, and he had a lot of trouble feeding himself. The nurse put a bib around his neck.

But he certainly had a wonderful appetite. Trout watched him shovel waffles and pork sausage into his mouth, watched him guzzle orange juice and milk. Trout marveled at what a big animal the idiot was. The idiot's happiness was fascinating, too, as he stoked himself with calories which would get him through yet another day.

Trout said this to himself: "Stoking up for another day."

🔥 "Excuse me," said the truck driver to Trout, "I've got to take a leak."

"Back where I come from," said Trout, "that means you're going to steal a mirror. We call mirrors *leaks*."

"I never heard that before," said the driver. He repeated the word: "Leaks." He pointed to a mirror on a cigarette machine. "You call that a *leak*?"

"Doesn't it look like a leak to you?" said Trout.

"No," said the driver. "Where did you say you were from?"

"I was born in Bermuda," said Trout.

About a week later, the driver would tell his wife that mirrors were called *leaks* in Bermuda, and she would tell her friends.

▶ When Trout followed the driver back to the truck, he took his first good look at their form of transportation from a distance, saw it whole. There was a message written on the side of it in bright orange letters which were eight feet high. This was it:

Trout wondered what a child who was just learning to read would make of a message like that. The child would suppose that the message was terrifically important, since somebody had gone to the trouble of writing it in letters so big.

And then, pretending to be a child by the roadside, he read the message on the side of another truck. This was it:

Chapter 11

Dwayne Hoover slept until ten at the new Holiday Inn. He was much refreshed. He had a Number Five Breakfast in the popular restaurant of the Inn, which was the *Tally-Ho Room*. The drapes were drawn at night. They were wide open now. They let the sunshine in.

At the next table, also alone, was Cyprian Ukwende, the Indaro, the Nigerian. He was reading the classified ads in the Midland City *Bugle-Observer*. He needed a cheap place to live. The Midland County General Hospital was footing his bills at the Inn while he looked around, and they were getting restless about that.

He needed a woman, too, or a bunch of women who would fuck him hundreds of times a week, because he was so full of lust and jism all the time. And he ached to be with his Indaro relatives. Back home, he had six hundred relatives he knew by name.

Ukwende's face was impassive as he ordered the Number Three Breakfast with whole-wheat toast. Behind his mask was a young man in the terminal stages of nostalgia and lover's nuts.

◗ Dwayne Hoover, six feet away, gazed out at the busy, sunny Interstate Highway. He knew where he was. There was a familiar moat between the parking lot of the Inn and the Interstate, a concrete trough which the engineers had built to contain Sugar Creek. Next came a familiar resilient steel barrier which prevented cars and trucks from tumbling into Sugar Creek. Next came the three familiar west-bound lanes, and then the familiar grassy median divider. After that came the three familiar east-bound lanes, and then another familiar steel barrier. After that came the familiar Will Fairchild Memorial Airport—and then the familiar farmlands beyond.

◗ It was certainly flat out there—flat city, flat township, flat county, flat state. When Dwayne was a little boy, he had supposed that almost everybody lived in places that were treeless and flat. He imagined that oceans and mountains and forests were mainly sequestered in state and national parks. In the third grade, little Dwayne scrawled an essay which argued in favor of creating a national park at a bend in Sugar Creek, the only significant surface water within eight miles of Midland City.

Dwayne said the name of that familiar surface water to himself now, silently: "Sugar Creek."

◆ Sugar Creek was only two inches deep and fifty yards wide at the bend, where little Dwayne thought the park should be. Now they had put the Mildred Barry Memorial Center for the Arts there instead. It was beautiful.

Dwayne fiddled with his lapel for a moment, felt a badge pinned there. He unpinned it, having no recollection of what it said. It was a boost for the Arts Festival, which would begin that evening. All over town people were wearing badges like Dwayne's. Here is what the badges said:

◆ Sugar Creek flooded now and then. Dwayne remembered about that. In a land so flat, flooding was a queerly pretty thing for water to do. Sugar Creek brimmed over silently, formed a vast mirror in which children might safely play.

The mirror showed the citizens the shape of the valley they lived in, demonstrated that they were hill people who inhabited slopes rising one inch for every mile that separated them from Sugar Creek.

Dwayne silently said the name of the water again: "Sugar Creek."

◆ Dwayne finished his breakfast, and he dared to suppose that he was no longer mentally diseased, that he had been cured by a simple change of residence, by a good night's sleep.

His bad chemicals let him cross the lobby and then the cocktail lounge, which wasn't open yet, without experiencing anything strange. But when he stepped out of the side door of the cocktail lounge, and onto the asphalt prairie which surrounded both his Inn and his Pontiac agency, he discovered that someone had turned the asphalt into a sort of trampoline.

It sank beneath Dwayne's weight. It dropped Dwayne to well below street level, then slowly brought him only part way up again. He was in a shallow, rubbery dimple. Dwayne took another step in the direction of his automobile agency. He sank down again, came up again, and stood in a brand new dimple.

He gawked around for witnesses. There was only one. Cyprian Ukwende stood on the rim of the dimple, not sinking in. This was all Ukwende had to say, even though Dwayne's situation was extraordinary:

"Nice day."

◆ Dwayne progressed from dimple to dimple.

He blooped across the used car lot now.

He stopped in a dimple, looked up at another young black man. This one was polishing a maroon 1970 Buick *Skylark* convertible with a rag. The man wasn't dressed for that sort of work. He wore a cheap blue suit and a white shirt and a black necktie. Also: he wasn't merely polishing the car—he was *burnishing* it.

The young man did some more burnishing. Then he smiled at Dwayne blindingly, then he burnished the car again.

Here was the explanation: this young black man had just been paroled from the Adult Correctional Institution at Shepherdstown. He needed work right away, or he would starve to death. So he was showing Dwayne how hard a worker he was.

He had been in orphanages and youth shelters and prisons of one sort or another in the Midland City area since he was nine years old. He was now twenty-six.

⏺ He was free at last!

⏺ Dwayne thought the young man was an hallucination.

⏺ The young man went back to burnishing the automobile. His life was not worth living. He had a feeble will to survive. He thought the planet was terrible, that he never should have been sent there. Some mistake had been made. He had no friends or relatives. He was put in cages all the time.

He had a name for a better world, and he often saw it in dreams. Its name was a secret. He would have been ridiculed, if he had said its name out loud. It was such a *childish* name.

The young black jailbird could see the name any time he wanted to, written in lights on the inside of his skull. This is what it looked like:

◗ He had a photograph of Dwayne in his wallet. He used to have photographs of Dwayne on the walls of his cell at Shepherdstown. They were easy to get, because Dwayne's smiling face, with his motto underneath, was a part of every ad he ran in the *Bugle-Observer*. The picture was changed every six months. The motto hadn't varied in twenty-five years.

Here was the motto:

ASK ANYBODY—
YOU CAN TRUST
DWAYNE.

◗ The young ex-convict smiled yet again at Dwayne. His teeth were in perfect repair. The dental program at Shepherdstown was excellent. So was the food.

"Good morning, sir," said the young man to Dwayne. He was dismayingly innocent. There was so much he had to learn. He didn't know anything about women, for instance. Francine Pefko was the first woman he had spoken to in eleven years.

"Good morning," said Dwayne. He said it softly, so his voice wouldn't carry very far, in case he was conversing with an hallucination.

"Sir—I have read your ads in the newspapers with great interest, and I have found pleasure in your radio advertising, too," the parolee said. During the last year in prison, he had been obsessed by one idea: that he would work for Dwayne someday, and live happily ever after. It would be like Fairyland.

Dwayne made no reply to this, so the young man went on: "I am a very hard worker, sir, as you can see. I hear nothing but good things about you. I think the good Lord meant for me to work for you."

"Oh?" said Dwayne.

"Our names are so close," said the young man, "it's the good Lord telling us *both* what to do."

Dwayne Hoover didn't ask him what his name was, but the young man told him anyway, radiantly: "My name, sir, is Wayne Hoobler."

All around Midland City, Hoobler was a common Nigger name.

◗ Dwayne Hoover broke Wayne Hoobler's heart by shaking his head vaguely, then walking away.

◗ Dwayne entered his showroom. The ground wasn't blooping underneath him anymore, but now he saw something else for which there could be no explanation: A palm tree was growing out of the showroom floor. Dwayne's bad chemicals made him forget all about Hawaiian Week. Actually, Dwayne had designed the palm tree himself. It was a sawed-off telephone pole—swaddled in burlap. It had real coconuts nailed to the top of it. Sheets of green plastic had been cut to resemble leaves.

The tree so bewildered Dwayne that he almost swooned. Then he looked around and saw pineapples and ukuleles scattered everywhere.

And then he saw the most unbelievable thing of all: His sales manager, Harry LeSabre, came toward him leeringly, wearing a lettuce-green leotard, straw sandals, a grass skirt, and a pink T-shirt which looked like this:

♦ Harry and his wife had spent all weekend arguing about whether or not Dwayne suspected that Harry was a transvestite. They concluded that Dwayne had no reason to suspect it. Harry never talked about women's clothes to Dwayne. He had never entered a transvestite beauty contest or done what a lot of transvestites in Midland City did, which was join a big transvestite club over in Cincinnati. He never went into the city's transvestite bar, which was *Ye Old Rathskeller*, in the basement of the Fairchild Hotel. He had never exchanged Polaroid pictures with any other transvestites, had never subscribed to a transvestite magazine.

Harry and his wife concluded that Dwayne had meant nothing more than what he said, that Harry had better put on some wild clothes for Hawaiian Week, or Dwayne would can him.

So here was the new Harry now, rosy with fear and excitement. He felt uninhibited and beautiful and lovable and suddenly free.

He greeted Dwayne with the Hawaiian word which meant both *hello* and *goodbye*. "Aloha," he said.

Chapter 12

Kilgore Trout was far away, but he was steadily closing the distance between himself and Dwayne. He was still in the truck named *Pyramid*. It was crossing a bridge named in honor of the poet Walt Whitman. The bridge was veiled in smoke. The truck was about to become a part of Philadelphia now. A sign at the foot of the bridge said this:

YOU ARE NOW ENTERING
THE CITY OF
BROTHERLY LOVE

◗ As a younger man, Trout would have sneered at the sign about brotherhood—posted on the rim of a bomb crater, as anyone could see. But his head no longer sheltered ideas of how things could be and should be on the planet, as opposed to how they really were. There was only one way for the Earth to be, he thought: the way it was.

Everything was necessary. He saw an old white woman fishing through a garbage can. That was necessary. He saw a bathtub toy, a little rubber duck, lying on its side on the grating over a storm sewer. It *had* to be there.

And so on.

◗ The driver mentioned that the day before had been Veterans' Day.

"Um," said Trout.

"You a veteran?" said the driver.

"No," said Trout. "Are you?"

"No," said the driver.

Neither one of them was a veteran.

◗ The driver got onto the subject of friends. He said it was hard for him to maintain friendships that meant anything because he was on the road most of the time. He joked about the time when he used to talk about his "best friends." He guessed people stopped talking about best friends after they got out of junior high school.

He suggested that Trout, since Trout was in the combination aluminum storm window and screen business, had opportunities to build many lasting friendships in the course of his work. "I mean," he said, "you get men working together day after day, putting up those windows, they get to know each other pretty well."

"I work alone," said Trout.

The driver was disappointed. "I assumed it would take two men to do the job."

"Just one," said Trout. "A weak little kid could do it without any help."

The driver wanted Trout to have a rich social life so that he could enjoy it vicariously. "All the same," he insisted, "you've got buddies you see after work. You have a few beers. You play some cards. You have some laughs."

Trout shrugged.

"You walk down the same streets every day," the driver told him. "You know a lot of people, and they know you, because it's the same streets for you, day after day. You say, 'Hello,' and they say 'Hello,' back. You call them by name. They call you by name. If you're in a real jam, they'll help you, because you're one of 'em. You *belong*. They see you every day."

Trout didn't want to argue about it.

◗ Trout had forgotten the driver's name.

Trout had a mental defect which I, too, used to suffer from. He couldn't remember what different people in his life looked like—unless their bodies or faces were strikingly unusual.

When he lived on Cape Cod, for instance, the only person he could greet warmly and by name was Alfy Bearse, who was a one-armed albino. "Hot enough for you, Alfy?" he would say. "Where you been keeping yourself, Alfy?" he'd say. "You're a sight for sore eyes, Alfy," he'd say.

And so on.

Now that Trout lived in Cohoes, the only person he called by name was a red-headed Cockney midget, Durling Heath. He worked in a shoe repair shop. Heath had an executive-type nameplate on his workbench, in case anybody wished to address him by name. The nameplate looked like this:

Trout would drop into the shop from time to time, and say such things as, "Who's gonna win the World Series this year, Durling?" and "You have any idea what all the sirens were blowing about last night, Durling?" and, "You're looking good today, Durling—where'd you get that shirt?" And so on.

Trout wondered now if his friendship with Heath was over. The last time Trout had been in the shoe repair place, saying this and that to Durling, the midget had unexpectedly screamed at him.

This is what he had screamed in his Cockney accent: "Stop bloody *hounding* me!"

◆ The Governor of New York, Nelson Rockefeller, shook Trout's hand in a Cohoes grocery story one time. Trout had no idea who he was. As a science-fiction writer, he should have been flabbergasted to come so close to such a man. Rockefeller wasn't merely Governor. Because of the peculiar laws in that part of the planet, Rockefeller was allowed to own vast areas of Earth's surface, and the petroleum and other valuable minerals underneath the surface, as well. He owned or controlled more of the planet than many nations. This had been his destiny since infancy. He had been *born* into that cockamamie proprietorship.

"How's it going, fella?" Governor Rockefeller asked him.

"About the same," said Kilgore Trout.

◆ After insisting that Trout had a rich social life, the driver pretended, again for his own gratification, that Trout had begged to know what the sex life of a transcontinental truck driver was like. Trout had begged no such thing.

"You want to know how truck drivers make out with women, right?" the driver said. "You have this idea that every driver you see is fucking up a storm from coast to coast, right?"

Trout shrugged.

The truck driver became embittered by Trout, scolded him for being so salaciously misinformed. "Let me tell you, Kilgore—" he hesitated. "That's your name, right?"

"Yes," said Trout. He had forgotten the driver's name a hundred times. Every time Trout looked away from him, Trout forgot not only his name but his face, too.

"Kilgore, God damn it—" the driver said, "if I was to have my rig break down in Cohoes, for instance, and I was to have to stay there for two days while it was worked on, how easy you think it would be for me to get laid while I was there—a stranger, looking the way I do?"

"It would depend on how *determined* you were," said Trout.

The driver sighed. "Yeah, God—" he said, and he despaired for himself, "that's probably the story of my life: not enough determination."

◗ They talked about aluminum siding as a technique for making old houses look new again. From a distance, these sheets, which never needed painting, looked like freshly painted wood.

The driver wanted to talk about *Perma-Stone*, too, which was a competitive scheme. It involved plastering the sides of old houses with colored cement, so that, from a distance, they looked as though they were made of stone.

"If you're in aluminum storm windows," the driver said to Trout, "you must be in aluminum siding, too." All over the country, the two businesses went hand-in-hand.

"My company sells it," said Trout, "and I've seen a lot of it. I've never actually worked on an installation."

The driver was thinking seriously of buying aluminum siding for his home in Little Rock, and he begged Trout to give him an honest answer to this question: "From what you've seen and heard—the people who get aluminum siding, are they *happy* with what they get?"

"Around Cohoes," said Trout. "I think those were about the only really happy people I ever saw."

◆ "I know what you mean," said the driver. "One time I saw a whole family standing outside their house. They couldn't believe how nice their house looked after the aluminum siding went on. My question to you, and you can give me an honest answer, on account of we'll never have to do business, you and me: Kilgore, how long will that happiness last?"

"About fifteen years," said Trout. "Our salesmen say you can easily afford to have the job redone with all the money you've saved on paint and heat."

"*Perma-Stone* looks a lot richer, and I suppose it lasts a lot longer, too," said the driver. "On the other hand, it costs a lot more."

"You get what you pay for," said Kilgore Trout.

◆ The truck driver told Trout about a gas hot-water heater he had bought thirty years ago, and it hadn't given him a speck of trouble in all that time.

"I'll be damned," said Kilgore Trout.

◆ Trout asked about the truck, and the driver said it was the greatest truck in the world. The tractor alone cost twenty-eight thousand dollars. It was powered by a three hundred and twenty-four horsepower Cummins Diesel engine, which was turbo-charged, so it would function well at high altitudes. It had hydraulic steering, air brakes, a thirteen-speed transmission, and was owned by his brother-in-law.

His brother-in-law, he said, owned twenty-eight trucks, and was President of the Pyramid Trucking Company.

"Why did he name his company *Pyramid*?" asked

Trout. "I mean——this thing can go a hundred miles an hour, if it has to. It's fast and useful and unornamental. It's as up-to-date as a rocket ship. I never saw anything that was less like a pyramid than this truck."

A pyramid was a sort of huge stone tomb which Egyptians had built thousands and thousands of years before. The Egyptians didn't build them anymore. The tombs looked like this, and tourists would come from far away to gaze at them:

"Why would anybody in the business of highspeed transportation name his business and his trucks after buildings which haven't moved an eighth of an inch since Christ was born?"

The driver's answer was prompt. It was peevish, too, as though he thought Trout was stupid to have to ask a question like that. "He liked the *sound* of it," he said. "Don't you like the *sound* of it?"

Trout nodded in order to keep things friendly. "Yes," he said, "it's a very nice sound."

◆ Trout sat back and thought about the conversation. He shaped it into a story, which he never got around to writing until he was an old, old man. It was about a planet where the language kept turning into pure music, because the creatures there were so enchanted by sounds. Words became musical notes. Sentences became melodies. They were useless as conveyors of information, because nobody knew or cared what the meanings of words were anymore.

So leaders in government and commerce, in order to function, had to invent new and much uglier vocabularies and sentence structures all the time, which would resist being transmuted to music.

◆ "You married, Kilgore?" the driver asked.

"Three times," said Trout. It was true. Not only that, but each of his wives had been extraordinarily patient and loving and beautiful. Each had been shriveled by his pessimism.

"Any kids?"

"One," said Trout. Somewhere in the past, tumbling among all the wives and stories lost in the mails was a son named Leo. "He's a man now," said Trout.

Leo left home forever at the age of fourteen. He lied bout his age, and he joined the Marines. He sent a note his father from boot camp. It said this: "I pity you. ou've crawled up your own asshole and died."

That was the last Trout heard from Leo, directly or directly, until he was visited by two agents from the ederal Bureau of Investigation. Leo had deserted from s division in Viet Nam, they said. He had committed gh treason. He had joined the Viet Cong.

Here was the F.B.I. evaluation of Leo's situation on the anet at that time: "Your boy's in bad trouble," they id.

Chapter 13

When Dwayne Hoover saw Harry LeSabre, his sale[s]
manager, in leaf-green leotards and a grass skirt and al[l]
that, he could not believe it. So he made himself not se[e]
it. He went into his office, which was also cluttered wit[h]
ukuleles and pineapples.

Francine Pefko, his secretary, looked normal, excep[t]
that she had a rope of flowers around her neck and [a]
flower behind one ear. She smiled. This was a war widow
with lips like sofa pillows and bright red hair. She adore[d]
Dwayne. She adored Hawaiian Week, too.

"Aloha," she said.

◗ Harry LeSabre, meanwhile, had been destroyed by
Dwayne.

When Harry presented himself to Dwayne so ridicu[lous]

lously, every molecule in his body awaited Dwayne's reaction. Each molecule ceased its business for a moment, put some distance between itself and its neighbors. Each molecule waited to learn whether its galaxy, which was called *Harry LeSabre*, would or would not be dissolved.

When Dwayne treated Harry as though he were invisible, Harry thought he had revealed himself as a revolting transvestite, and that he was fired on that account.

Harry closed his eyes. He never wanted to open them again. His heart sent this message to his molecules: "For reasons obvious to us all, this galaxy is *dissolved!*"

Dwayne didn't know anything about that. He leaned on Francine Pefko's desk. He came close to telling her how sick he was. He warned her: "This is a very tough day, for some reason. So no jokes, no surprises. Keep everything simple. Keep anybody the least bit nutty out of here. No telephone calls."

Francine told Dwayne that the twins were waiting for him in the inner office. "Something bad is happening to the cave, I think," she told him.

Dwayne was grateful for a message that simple and clear. The twins were his younger stepbrothers, Lyle and Kyle Hoover. The cave was Sacred Miracle Cave, a tourist trap just south of Shepherdstown, which Dwayne owned in partnership with Lyle and Kyle. It was the sole source of income for Lyle and Kyle, who lived in identical yellow ranch houses on either side of the gift shop which sheltered the entrance to the cave.

All over the State, nailed to trees and fence posts, were arrow-shaped signs, which pointed in the direction of the cave and said how far away it was—for example:

♦ Before Dwayne entered his inner office, he read one of many comical signs which Francine had put up on the wall in order to amuse people, to remind them of what they so easily forgot: that people didn't have to be serious all the time.

Here was the text of the sign Dwayne read:

YOU DON'T HAVE TO BE CRAZY
TO WORK HERE, BUT IT SURE HELPS!

There was a picture of a crazy person to go with the text. This was it:

Francine wore a button on her bosom which showed a creature in a healthier, more enviable frame of mind. This was the button:

Lyle and Kyle sat side-by-side on the black leather couch in Dwayne Hoover's inner office. They looked so much alike that Dwayne had not been able to tell them apart until 1954, when Lyle got in a fight over a woman at the Roller Derby. After that, Lyle was the one with the broken nose. As babies in crib, Dwayne remembered now, they used to suck each other's thumbs.

Here is how Dwayne happened to have stepbrothers, incidentally, even though he had been adopted by people who couldn't have children of their own. Their adopting him triggered something to their bodies which made it possible for them to have children after all. This was a common phenomenon. A lot of couples seemed to be programmed that way.

Dwayne was so glad to see them now—these two little men in overalls and work shoes, each wearing a pork-pie hat. They were familiar, they were *real*. Dwayne closed his door on the chaos outside. "All right—" he said, "what's happened at the cave?"

Ever since Lyle had had his nose broken, the twins agreed that Lyle should do the talking for the two. Kyle hadn't said a thousand words since 1954.

"Them bubbles is halfway up to the *Cathedral* now," said Lyle. "The way they're coming, they'll be up to *Moby Dick* in a week or two."

Dwayne understood him perfectly. The underground stream which passed through the bowels of Sacred Miracle Cave was polluted by some sort of industrial waste which formed bubbles as tough as ping-pong balls. These bubbles were shouldering one another up a passage which led to a big boulder which had been painted white to resemble *Moby Dick, the Great White Whale*. The bubbles would soon engulf *Moby Dick* and invade the *Cathedral of Whispers*, which was the main attraction at the cave. Thousands of people had been married in the *Cathedral of Whispers*—including Dwayne and Lyle and Kyle. Harry LeSabre, too.

▶ Lyle told Dwayne about an experiment he and Kyle had performed the night before. They had gone into the cave with their identical Browning Automatic Shotguns and they had opened fire on the advancing wall of bubbles.

"They let loose a stink you wouldn't believe," said Lyle. He said it smelled like athlete's foot. "It drove me and Kyle right out of there. We run the ventilating system for an hour, and then we went back in. The paint was blistered on *Moby Dick*. He ain't even got eyes anymore."

Moby Dick used to have long-lashed blue eyes as big as dinner plates.

◆ "The organ turned black, and the ceiling turned a kind of dirty yellow," said Lyle. "You can't hardly see the *Sacred Miracle* no more."

The organ was the *Pipe Organ of the Gods,* a thicket of stalactites and stalagmites which had grown together in one corner of the *Cathedral.* There was a loudspeaker in back of it, through which music for weddings and funerals was played. It was illuminated by electric lights, which changed colors all the time.

The Sacred Miracle was a cross on the ceiling of the *Cathedral.* It was formed by the intersection of two cracks. "It never *was* real easy to see," said Lyle, speaking of the cross. "I ain't even sure it's there anymore." He asked Dwayne's permission to order a load of cement. He wanted to plug up the passage between the stream and the Cathedral.

"Just forget about *Moby Dick* and *Jesse James* and the slaves and all that," said Lyle, "and save the *Cathedral.*"

Jesse James was a skeleton which Dwayne's stepfather had bought from the estate of a doctor back during the Great Depression. The bones of its right hand mingled with the rusted parts of a .45 caliber revolver. Tourists were told that it had been found that way, that it probably belonged to some railroad robber who had been trapped in the cave by a rockslide.

As for the slaves: these were plaster statues of black men in a chamber fifty feet down the corridor from *Jesse James.* The statues were removing one another's chains with hammers and hacksaws. Tourists were told that real slaves had at one time used the cave after escaping to freedom across the Ohio River.

❧ The story about the slaves was as fake as the one about Jesse James. The cave wasn't discovered until 1937, when a small earthquake opened it up a crack. Dwayne Hoover himself discovered the crack, and then he and his stepfather opened it with crowbars and dynamite. Before that, not even small animals had been in there.

The only connection the cave had with slavery was this: the farm on which it was discovered was started by an ex-slave, Josephus Hoobler. He was freed by his master, and he came north and started the farm. Then he went back and bought his mother and a woman who became his wife.

Their descendants continued to run the farm until the Great Depression, when the Midland County Merchants Bank foreclosed on the mortgage. And then Dwayne's stepfather was hit by an automobile driven by a white man who had bought the farm. In an out-of-court settlement for his injuries, Dwayne's stepfather was given what he called contemptuously ". . . a God damn Nigger farm."

Dwayne remembered the first trip the family took to see it. His father ripped a Nigger sign off the Nigger mailbox, and he threw it into a ditch. Here is what it said:

Chapter 14

⬇

The truck carrying Kilgore Trout was in West Virginia now. The surface of the State had been demolished by men and machinery and explosives in order to make it yield up its coal. The coal was mostly gone now. It had been turned into heat.

The surface of West Virginia, with its coal and trees and topsoil gone, was rearranging what was left of itself in conformity with the laws of gravity. It was collapsing into all the holes which had been dug into it. Its mountains, which had once found it easy to stand by themselves, were sliding into valleys now.

The demolition of West Virginia had taken place with the approval of the executive, legislative, and judicial branches of the State Government, which drew their power from the people.

Here and there an inhabited dwelling still stood.

◆ Trout saw a broken guardrail ahead. He gazed into a gully below it, saw a 1968 Cadillac *El Dorado* capsized in a brook. It had Alabama license plates. There were also several old home appliances in the brook—stoves, a washing machine, a couple of refrigerators.

An angel-faced white child, with flaxen hair, stood by the brook. She waved up at Trout. She clasped an eighteen-ounce bottle of *Pepsi-Cola* to her breast.

◆ Trout asked himself out loud what the people did for amusement, and the driver told him a queer story about a night he spent in West Virginia, in the cab of his truck, near a windowless building which droned monotonously.

"I'd see folks go in, and I'd see folks come out," he said, "but I couldn't figure out what kind of a machine it was that made the drone. The building was a cheap old frame thing set up on cement blocks, and it was out in the middle of nowhere. Cars came and went, and the folks sure seemed to like whatever was doing the droning," he said.

So he had a look inside. "It was full of folks on roller-skates," he said. "They went around and around. Nobody smiled. They just went around and around."

◆ He told Trout about people he'd heard of in the area who grabbed live copperheads and rattlesnakes during church services, to show how much they believed that Jesus would protect them.

"Takes all kinds of people to make up a world," said Trout.

Trout marveled at how recently white men had arrived in West Virginia, and how quickly they had demolished it—for heat.

Now the heat was all gone, too—into outer space, Trout supposed. It had boiled water, and the steam had made steel windmills whiz around and around. The windmills had made rotors in generators whiz around and around. America was jazzed with electricity for a while. Coal had also powered old-fashioned steamboats and choo-choo trains.

Choo-choo trains and steamboats and factories had whistles which were blown by steam when Dwayne Hoover and Kilgore Trout and I were boys—when our fathers were boys, when our grandfathers were boys. The whistles looked like this:

Steam from water boiled by burning coal was sent raging through the whistles, which made harshly beautiful laments, as though they were the voice boxes of mating or dying dinosaurs—cries such as *wooooooooo-uh, wooooo-uh,* and *torrrrrrrrrrrrrrrrrrrrrrrrrrrrrrrrnnnnnnnnnnnnn,* and so on.

◗ A dinosaur was a reptile as big as a choo-choo train. It looked like this:

It had two brains, one for its front end and one for its rear end. It was extinct. Both brains combined were smaller than a pea. A pea was a legume which looked like this:

Coal was a highly compressed mixture of rotten trees and flowers and bushes and grasses and so on, and dinosaur excrement.

◗ Kilgore Trout thought about the cries of steam whistles he had known, and about the destruction of West Virginia, which made their songs possible. He supposed that the heart-rending cries had fled into outer space, along with the heat. He was mistaken.

Like most science-fiction writers, Trout knew almost nothing about science, was bored stiff by technical details. But no cry from a whistle had got very far from Earth for this reason: sound could only travel in an atmosphere, and the atmosphere of Earth relative to the planet wasn't even as thick as the skin of an apple. Beyond that lay an all-but-perfect vacuum.

An apple was a popular fruit which looked like this:

◗ The driver was a big eater. He pulled into a Mac-Donald's Hamburger establishment. There were many different chains of hamburger establishments in the country. *MacDonald's* was one. *Burger Chef* was another. Dwayne Hoover, as has already been said, owned franchises for several *Burger Chefs*.

◗ A hamburger was made out of an animal which looked like this:

The animal was killed and ground up into little bits, then shaped into patties and fried, and put between two pieces of bread. The finished product looked like this:

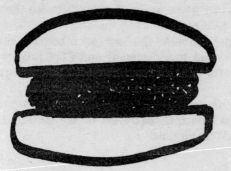

And Trout, who had so little money left, ordered a cup of coffee. He asked an old, old man on a stool next to him at the table if he had worked in the coal mines.

The old man said this: "From the time I was ten till I was sixty-two."

"You glad to be out of 'em?" said Trout.

"Oh, God," said the man, "you never get out of 'em—even when you sleep. I *dream* mines."

Trout asked him what it had felt like to work for an industry whose business was to destroy the countryside, and the old man said he was usually too tired to care.

"Don't matter if you care," the old miner said, "if you don't own what you care about." He pointed out that the mineral rights to the entire county in which they sat were owned by the Rosewater Coal and Iron Company, which had acquired these rights soon after the end of the Civil War. "The law says," he went on, "when a man owns something under the ground and he wants to get at it, you got to let him tear up anything between the surface and what he owns."

Trout did not make the connection between the Rosewater Coal and Iron Company and Eliot Rosewater, his only fan. He still thought Eliot Rosewater was a teenager.

The truth was that Rosewater's ancestors had been among the principal destroyers of the surface and the people of West Virginia.

◆ "It don't seem right, though," the old miner said to Trout, "that a man can own what's underneath another man's farm or woods or house. And any time the man wants to get what's underneath all that, he's got a right to wreck what's on top to get at it. The rights of the people on top of the ground don't amount to nothing compared to the rights of the man who owns what's underneath."

He remembered out loud when he and other miners used to try to force the Rosewater Coal and Iron Company to treat them like human beings. They would fight small wars with the company's private police and the State Police and the National Guard.

"I never saw a Rosewater," he said, "but Rosewater always won. I walked on Rosewater. I dug holes for Rosewater in Rosewater. I lived in Rosewater houses. I ate Rosewater food. I'd fight Rosewater, whatever Rosewater is, and Rosewater would beat me and leave me for dead. You ask people around here and they'll tell you: this whole world is Rosewater as far as *they're* concerned."

▶ The driver knew Trout was bound for Midland City. He didn't know Trout was a writer on his way to an arts festival. Trout understood that honest working people had no use for the arts.

"Why would anybody in his right mind go to Midland City?" the driver wanted to know. They were riding along again.

"My sister is sick," said Trout.

"Midland City is the asshole of the Universe," said the driver.

"I've often wondered where the asshole was," said Trout.

"If it isn't in Midland City," said the driver, "it's in Libertyville, Georgia. You ever see Libertyville?"

"No," said Trout.

"I was arrested for speeding down there. They had a speed trap, where you all of a sudden had to go from fifty down to fifteen miles an hour. It made me mad. I had some words with the policeman, and he put me in jail.

"The main industry there was pulping up old newspapers and magazines and books, and making new paper out of 'em," said the driver. "Trucks and trains were bringing in hundreds of tons of unwanted printed material every day."

"Um," said Trout.

"And the unloading process was sloppy, so there were pieces of books and magazines and so on blowing all over town. If you wanted to start a library, you could just go over to the freight yard, and carry away all the books you wanted."

"Um," said Trout. Up ahead was a white man hitchhiking with his pregnant wife and nine children.

"Looks like Gary Cooper, don't he?" said the truck driver of the hitchhiking man.

"Yes, he does," said Trout. Gary Cooper was a movie star.

♦ "Anyway," said the driver, "they had so many books in Libertyville, they used books for toilet paper in the jail. They got me on a Friday, late in the afternoon, so I couldn't have a hearing in court until Monday. So I sat there in the calaboose for two days, with nothing to do but read my toilet paper. I can still remember one of the stories I read."

"Um," said Trout.

"That was the *last* story I ever read," said the driver. "My God—that must be all of fifteen years ago. The story was about another planet. It was a crazy story. They had museums full of paintings all over the place, and the government used a kind of roulette wheel to decide what to put in the museums, and what to throw out."

Kilgore Trout was suddenly woozy with *déjà vu*. The truck driver was reminding him of the premise of a book he hadn't thought about for years. The driver's toilet paper in Libertyville, Georgia, had been *The Barring-gaffner of Bagnialto*, or *This Year's Masterpiece*, by Kilgore Trout.

♦ The name of the planet where Trout's book took place was *Bagnialto*, and a "Barring-gaffner" there was a government official who spun a wheel of chance once a year. Citizens submitted works of art to the government, and these were given numbers, and then they were assigned cash values according to the Barring-gaffner's spins of the wheel.

The viewpoint of character of the tale was not the Barring-gaffner, but a humble cobbler named Gooz. Gooz lived alone, and he painted a picture of his cat. It was the only picture he had ever painted. He took it to the Barring-gaffner, who numbered it and put it in a warehouse crammed with works of art.

The painting by Gooz had an unprecedented gush of luck on the wheel. It became worth eighteen thousand *lambos*, the equivalent of one billion dollars on Earth. The Barring-gaffner awarded Gooz a check for that amount, most of which was taken back at once by the tax collector. The picture was given a place of honor in the National Gallery, and people lined up for miles for a chance to see a painting worth a billion dollars.

There was also a huge bonfire of all the paintings and statues and books and so on which the wheel had said were worthless. And then it was discovered that the wheel was rigged, and the Barring-gaffner committed suicide.

◗ It was an amazing coincidence that the truck driver had read a book by Kilgore Trout. Trout had never met a reader before, and his response now was interesting: He did not admit that he was the father of the book.

◗ The driver pointed out that all the mailboxes in the area had the same last name painted on them.

"There's another one," he said, indicating a mailbox which looked like this:

The truck was passing through the area where Dwayne Hoover's stepparents had come from. They had trekked from West Virginia to Midland City during the First World War, to make big money at the Keedsler Automobile Company, which was manufacturing airplanes and trucks. When they got to Midland City, they had their name changed legally from *Hoobler* to *Hoover*, because there were so many black people in Midland City named Hoobler.

As Dwayne Hoover's stepfather explained to him one time, "It was embarrassing. Everybody up here naturally assumed Hoobler was a *Nigger* name."

Chapter 15

Dwayne Hoover got through lunch all right that day. He remembered now about Hawaiian Week. The ukuleles and so on were no longer mysterious. The pavement between his automobile agency and the new Holiday Inn was no longer a trampoline.

He drove to lunch alone in an air-conditioned demonstrator, a blue Pontiac *Le Mans* with a cream interior, with his radio on. He heard several of his own radio commercials, which drove home the point: "You can always trust Dwayne."

Though his mental health had improved remarkably since breakfast, a new symptom of illness made itself known. It was incipient echolalia. Dwayne found himself wanting to repeat out loud whatever had just been said.

So when the radio told him, "You can always trust Dwayne," he echoed the last word. "Dwayne," he said.

When the radio said there had been a tornado in Texas, Dwayne said this out loud: "Texas."

Then he heard that husbands of women who had been raped during the war between India and Pakistan wouldn't have anything to do with their wives anymore. The women, in the eyes of their husbands, had become *unclean,* said the radio.

"Unclean," said Dwayne.

◆ As for Wayne Hoobler, the black ex-convict whose only dream was to work for Dwayne Hoover: he had learned to play hide-and-seek with Dwayne's employees. He did not wish to be ordered off the property for hanging around the used cars. So, when an employee came near, Wayne would wander off to the garbage and trash area behind the Holiday Inn, and gravely study the remains of club sandwiches and empty packs of Salem cigarettes and so on in the cans back there, as though he were a health inspector or some such thing.

When the employee went away, Wayne would drift back to the used cars, keeping the boiled eggs of his eyes peeled for the real Dwayne Hoover.

The real Dwayne Hoover, of course, had in effect denied that he was Dwayne. So, when the real Dwayne came out at lunch time, Wayne, who had nobody to talk to but himself, said this to himself: "That ain't Mr. Hoover. Sure *look* like Mr. Hoover, though. Maybe Mr. Hoover sick today." And so on.

◆ Dwayne had a hamburger and French fries and a Coke at his newest Burger Chef, which was out on Crestview

Avenue, across the street from where the new John. F.
Kennedy High School was going up. John F. Kennedy
had never been in Midland City, but he was a President
of the United States who was shot to death. Presidents of
the country were often shot to death. The assassins were
confused by some of the same bad chemicals which troubled Dwayne.

Dwayne certainly wasn't alone, as far as having bad
chemicals inside of him was concerned. He had plenty of
company throughout all history. In his own lifetime, for
instance, the people in a country called Germany were so
full of bad chemicals for a while that they actually built
factories whose only purpose was to kill people by the
millions. The people were delivered by railroad trains.

When the Germans were full of bad chemicals, their
flag looked like this:

Here is what their flag looked like after they got well again:

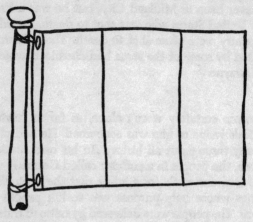

After they got well again, they manufactured a cheap and durable automobile which became popular all over the world, especially among young people. It looked like this:

People called it "the beetle." A real beetle looked like this:

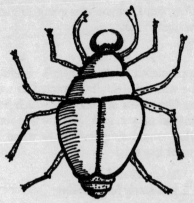

The mechanical beetle was made by Germans. The real beetle was made by the Creator of the Universe.

Dwayne's waitress at the Burger Chef was a seventeen-year-old white girl named Patty Keene. Her hair was yellow. Her eyes were blue. She was very old for a mammal. Most mammals were senile or dead by the time they were seventeen. But Patty was a sort of mammal which developed very slowly, so the body she rode around in was only now mature.

She was a brand-new adult, who was working in order to pay off the tremendous doctors' and hospital bills her father had run up in the process of dying of cancer of the colon and then cancer of the everything.

This was in a country where everybody was expected to pay his own bills for everything, and one of the most

expensive things a person could do was get sick. Patty
Keene's father's sickness cost ten times as much as all the
trips to Hawaii which Dwayne was going to give away at
the end of Hawaiian Week.

◗ Dwayne appreciated Patty Keene's brand-newness,
even though he was not sexually attracted to women that
young. She was like a new automobile, which hadn't even
had its radio turned on yet, and Dwayne was reminded of
a ditty his father would sing sometimes when his father
was drunk. It went like this:

> *Roses are red,*
> *And ready for plucking.*
> *You're sixteen,*
> *And ready for high school.*

◗ Patty Keene was stupid on purpose, which was the case
with most women in Midland City. The women all had
big minds because they were big animals, but they did
not use them much for this reason: unusual ideas could
make enemies, and the women, if they were going to
achieve any sort of comfort and safety, needed all the
friends they could get.

So, in the interests of survival, they trained themselves
to be agreeing machines instead of thinking machines. All
their minds had to do was to discover what other people
were thinking, and then they thought that, too.

◗ Patty knew who Dwayne was. Dwayne didn't know
who Patty was. Patty's heart beat faster when she waited

on him—because Dwayne could solve so many of her problems with the money and power he had. He could give her a fine house and new automobiles and nice clothes and a life of leisure, and he could pay all the medical bills—as easily as she had given him his hamburger and his French fries and his Coke.

Dwayne could do for her what the Fairy Godmother did for Cinderella, if he wanted to, and Patty had never been so close to such a magical person before. She was in the presence of the supernatural. And she knew enough about Midland City and herself to understand that she might never be this close to the supernatural ever again.

Patty Keene actually imagined Dwayne's waving a magic wand at her troubles and dreams. It looked like this:

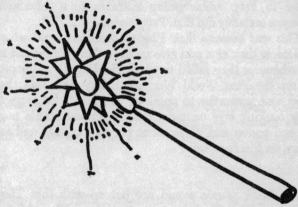

She spoke up bravely, to learn if supernatural assistance was possible in her case. She was willing to do without it, expected to do without it—to work hard all her life, to get not much in return, and to associate with other men and women who were poor and powerless, and in debt. She said this to Dwayne:

"Excuse me for calling you by name, Mr. Hoover, but I can't help knowing who you are, with your picture in all your ads and everything. Besides—everybody else who works here told me who you were. When you came in, they just buzzed and buzzed."

"Buzzed," said Dwayne. This was his echolalia again.

◆ "I guess that isn't the right word," she said. She was used to apologizing for her use of language. She had been encouraged to do a lot of that in school. Most white people in Midland City were insecure when they spoke, so they kept their sentences short and their words simple, in order to keep embarrassing mistakes to a minimum. Dwayne certainly did that. Patty certainly did that.

This was because their English teachers would wince and cover their ears and give them flunking grades and so on whenever they failed to speak like English aristocrats before the First World War. Also: they were told that they were unworthy to speak or write their language if they couldn't love or understand incomprehensible novels and poems and plays about people long ago and far away, such as *Ivanhoe*.

◆ The black people would not put up with this. They went on talking English every *which* way. They refused to read books they couldn't understand—on the grounds they couldn't understand them. They would ask such impudent questions as, "Whuffo I want to read no *Tale of Two Cities*? Whuffo?"

Patty Keene flunked English during the semester when he had to read and appreciate *Ivanhoe*, which was about men in iron suits and the women who loved them. And he was put in a remedial reading class, where they made her read *The Good Earth*, which was about Chinamen.

It was during this same semester that she lost her virginity. She was raped by a white gas-conversion unit installer named Don Breedlove in the parking lot outside the Bannister Memorial Fieldhouse at the County Fairgrounds after the Regional High School Basketball Playoffs. She never reported it to the police. She never reported it to anybody, since her father was dying at the time.

There was enough trouble already.

The Bannister Memorial Fieldhouse was named in honor of George Hickman Bannister, a seventeen-year-old boy who was killed while playing high school football in 1924. George Hickman Bannister had the largest tombstone in Calvary Cemetery, a sixty-two-foot obelisk with a marble football on top.

The marble football looked like this:

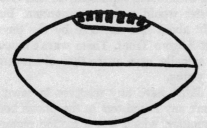

Football was a war game. Two opposing teams fought over the ball while wearing armor made out of leather and cloth and plastic.

George Hickman Bannister was killed while trying to get a hold of the ball on Thanksgiving Day. Thanksgiving Day was a holiday when everybody in the country was expected to express gratitude to the Creator of the Universe, mainly for food.

▶ George Hickman Bannister's obelisk was paid for by public subscription, with the Chamber of Commerce matching every two dollars raised with a dollar of its own. It was for many years the tallest structure in Midland City. A city ordinance was passed which made it illegal to erect anything taller than that, and it was called *The George Hickman Bannister Law.*

The ordinance was junked later on to allow radio towers to go up.

▶ The two largest monuments in town, until the new Mildred Barry Memorial Arts Center went up in Sugar Creek, were constructed supposedly so that George Hickman Bannister would never be forgotten. But nobody ever thought about him anymore by the time Dwayne Hoover met Kilgore Trout. There wasn't much to think about him, actually; even at the time of his death, except that he was young.

And he didn't have any relatives in town anymore. There weren't any Bannisters in the phone book, except for *The Bannister,* which was a motion picture theater. Actually, there wouldn't even be a *Bannister Theater* in here after the new phonebooks came out. The Bannister had been turned into a cut-rate furniture store.

George Hickman Bannister's father and mother and sister, Lucy, moved away from town before either the tombstone or the fieldhouse was completed, and they couldn't be located for the dedication ceremonies.

It was a very restless country, with people tearing around all the time. Every so often, somebody would stop to put up a monument.

There were monuments all over the country. But it was certainly unusual for somebody from the common people to have not one but *two* monuments in his honor, as was the case with George Hickman Bannister.

Technically, though, only the tombstone had been erected specifically for him. The fieldhouse would have gone up anyway. The money was appropriated for the fieldhouse two years before George Hickman Bannister was cut down in his prime. It didn't cost anything extra to name it after him.

Calvary Cemetery, where George Hickman Bannister was at rest, was named in honor of a hill in Jerusalem, thousands of miles away. Many people believed that the son of the Creator of the Universe had been killed on that hill thousands of years ago.

Dwayne Hoover didn't know whether to believe that or not. Neither did Patty Keene.

And they certainly weren't worrying about it now.

They had other fish to fry. Dwayne was wondering how long his attack of echolalia was likely to last, and Patty Keene had to find out if her brand-newness and prettiness and outgoing personality were worth a lot to a sweet, sort of sexy, middle-aged old Pontiac dealer like Dwayne.

"Anyway," she said, "it certainly is an honor to have you visit us, and those aren't the right words, either, but I hope you know what I mean."

"Mean," said Dwayne.

"Is the food all right?" she said.

"All right," said Dwayne.

"It's what everybody else gets," she said. "We didn't do anything special for you."

"You," said Dwayne.

◗ It didn't matter much what Dwayne said. It hadn't mattered much for years. It didn't matter much what most people in Midland City said out loud, except when they were talking about money or structures or travel or machinery—or other measurable things. Every person had a clearly defined part to play—as a black person, a female high school drop-out, a Pontiac dealer, a gynecologist, a gas-conversion burner installer. If a person stopped living up to expectations, because of bad chemicals or one thing or another, everybody went on imagining that the person was living up to expectations anyway.

That was the main reason the people in Midland City were so slow to detect insanity in their associates. Their imaginations insisted that nobody changed much from day to day. Their imaginations were flywheels on the ramshackle machinery of the awful truth.

When Dwayne left Patty Keene and his Burger Chef, when he got into his demonstrator and drove away, Patty Keene was persuaded that she could make him happy with her young body, with her bravery and cheerfulness. She wanted to cry about the lines in his face, and the fact that his wife had eaten Drāno, and that his dog had to fight all the time because it couldn't wag its tail, about the fact that his son was a homosexual. She knew all those things about Dwayne. Everybody knew those things about Dwayne.

She gazed at the tower of radio station WMCY, which Dwayne Hoover owned. It was the tallest structure in Midland City. It was eight times as tall as the tombstone of George Hickman Bannister. It had a red light on top of it—to keep airplanes away.

She thought about all the new and used cars Dwayne owned.

Earth scientists had just discovered something fascinating about the continent Patty Keene was standing on, accidentally. It was riding on a slab about forty miles thick, and the slab was drifting around on molten glurp. And all the other continents had slabs of their own. When one slab crashed into another one, mountains were made.

The mountains of West Virginia, for instance, were heaved up when a huge chunk of Africa crashed into North America. And the coal in the state was formed from forests which were buried by the crash.

Patty Keene hadn't heard the big news yet. Neither had Dwayne. Neither had Kilgore Trout. I only found out about it day before yesterday. I was reading a magazine, and I also had the television on. A group of scientists was on television, saying that the theory of floating, crashing, grinding slabs was more than a theory. They could prove it was true now, and that Japan and San Francisco, for instance, were in hideous danger, because that was where some of the most violent crashing and grinding was going on.

They said, too, that ice ages would continue to occur. Mile-thick glaciers would, geologically speaking, continue to go down and up like window blinds.

◗ Dwayne Hoover, incidentally, had an unusually large penis, and didn't even know it. The few women he had had anything to do with weren't sufficiently experienced to know whether he was average or not. The world average was five and seven-eighths inches long, and one and one-half inches in diameter when engorged with blood. Dwayne's was seven inches long and two and one-eighth inches in diameter when engorged with blood.

Dwayne's son Bunny had a penis that was exactly average.

Kilgore Trout had a penis seven inches long, but only one and one-quarter inches in diameter.

This was an inch:

Harry LeSabre, Dwayne's sales manager, had a penis five inches long and two and one-eighth inches in diameter.

Cyprian Ukwende, the black physician from Nigeria, had a penis six and seven-eighths inches long and one and three-quarters inches in diameter.

Don Breedlove, the gas-conversion unit installer who raped Patty Keene, had a penis five and seven-eighths inches long and one and seven-eighths inches in diameter.

↟ Patty Keene had thirty-four-inch hips, a twenty-six-inch waist, and a thirty-four-inch bosom.

Dwayne's late wife had thirty-six-inch hips, a twenty-eight-inch waist, and a thirty-eight-inch bosom when he married her. She had thirty-nine-inch hips, a thirty-one-inch waist, and a thirty-eight-inch bosom when she ate Drāno.

His mistress and secretary, Francine Pefko, had thirty-seven-inch hips, a thirty-inch waist, and a thirty-nine-inch bosom.

His stepmother at the time of her death had thirty-four-inch hips, a twenty-four-inch waist, and a thirty-three-inch bosom.

↟ So Dwayne went from the Burger Chef to the construction site of the new high school. He was in no hurry to get back to his automobile agency, particularly since he had developed echolalia. Francine was perfectly capable of running the place herself, without any advice from Dwayne. He had trained her well.

So he kicked a little dirt down into the cellar hole. He

spat down into it. He stepped into mud. It sucked off his right shoe. He dug the shoe out with his hands, and he wiped it. Then he leaned against an old apple tree while he put the shoe back on. This had all been farmland when Dwayne was a boy. There had been an apple orchard here.

◆ Dwayne forgot all about Patty Keene, but she certainly hadn't forgotten him. She would get up enough nerve that night to call him on the telephone, but Dwayne wouldn't be home to answer. He would be in a padded cell in the County Hospital by then.

And Dwayne wandered over to admire a tremendous earth-moving machine which had cleared the site and dug the cellar hole. The machine was idle now, caked with mud. Dwayne asked a white workman how many horsepower drove the machine. All the workmen were white.

The workman said this: "I don't know how many horsepower, but I know what we call it."

"What do you call it?" said Dwayne, relieved to find his echolalia was subsiding.

"We call it *The Hundred-Nigger Machine*," said the workman. This had reference to a time when black men had done most of the heavy digging in Midland City.

◆ The largest human penis in the United States was fourteen inches long and two and a half inches in diameter.

The largest human penis in the world was sixteen and seven-eighths inches long and two and one-quarter inches in diameter.

The blue whale, a sea mammal, had a penis ninety-six inches long and fourteen inches in diameter.

◆ One time Dwayne Hoover got an advertisement through the mail for a penis-extender, made out of rubber. He could slip it over the end of his real penis, according to the ad, and thrill his wife or sweetheart with extra inches. They also wanted to sell him a lifelike rubber vagina for when he was lonesome.

◆ Dwayne went back to work at about two in the afternoon, and he avoided everybody—because of his echolalia. He went into his inner office, and he ransacked his desk drawers for something to read or think about. He came across the brochure which offered him the penis-extender and the rubber vagina for lonesomeness. He had received it two months before. He still hadn't thrown it away.

The brochure also offered him motion pictures such as the ones Kilgore Trout had seen in New York. There were still photographs taken from the movies, and these caused the sex excitation center in Dwayne's brain to send nerve impulses down to an erection center in his spine.

The erection center caused the dorsal vein in his penis to tighten up, so blood could get in all right, but it couldn't get out again. It also relaxed the tiny arteries in his penis, so they filled up the spongy tissue of which Dwayne's penis was mainly composed, so that the penis got hard and stiff—like a plugged-up garden hose.

So Dwayne called Francine Pefko on the telephone, even though she was only eleven feet away. "Francine—?" he said.

"Yes?" she said.

Dwayne fought down his echolalia. "I am going to ask you to do something I have never asked you to do before. Promise me you'll say yes."

"I promise," she said.

"I want you to walk out of here with me this very moment," he said, "and come with me to the Quality Motor Court at Shepherdstown."

▶ Francine Pefko was willing to go to the Quality Motor Court with Dwayne. It was her duty to go, she thought—especially since Dwayne seemed so depressed and jangled. But she couldn't simply walk away from her desk for the afternoon, since her desk was the nerve center of Dwayne Hoover's Exit Eleven Pontiac Village.

"You ought to have some crazy young teen-ager, who can rush off whenever you want her to," Francine told Dwayne.

"I don't want a crazy teen-ager," said Dwayne. "I want *you.*"

"Then you're going to have to be patient," said Francine. She went back to the Service Department, to beg Gloria Browning, the white cashier back there, to man her desk for a little while.

Gloria didn't want to do it. She had had a hysterectomy only a month before, at the age of twenty-five—after a botched abortion at the Ramada Inn down in Green County, on Route 53, across from the entrance to Pioneer Village State Park.

There was a mildly amazing coincidence here: the father of the destroyed fetus was Don Breedlove, the white gas-conversion unit installer who had raped Patty

Keene in the parking lot of the Bannister Memorial Field-house.

This was a man with a wife and three kids.

● Francine had a sign on the wall over her desk, which had been given to her as a joke at the automobile agency's Christmas party at the new Holiday Inn the year before.

It spelled out the truth of her situation. This was it:

Gloria said she didn't want to man the nerve center. "I don't want to man anything," she said.

● But Gloria took over Francine's desk anyway. "I don't have nerve enough to commit suicide," she said, "so I might as well do anything anybody says—in the service of mankind."

149

◗ Dwayne and Francine headed for Shepherdstown in separate cars, so as not to call attention to their love affair. Dwayne was in a demonstrator again. Francine was in her own red GTO. GTO stood for *Gran Turismo Omologato.* She had a sticker on her bumper which said this:

VISIT SACRED
MIRACLE CAVE

It was certainly loyal of her to put that sticker on her car. She was always doing loyal things like that, always rooting for her man, always rooting for Dwayne.

And Dwayne tried to reciprocate in little ways. For instance, he had been reading articles and books on sexual intercourse recently. There was a sexual revolution going on in the country, and women were demanding that men pay more attention to women's pleasure during sexual intercourse, and not just think of themselves. The key to their pleasure, they said, and scientists backed them up, was the clitoris, a tiny meat cylinder which was right above the hole in women where men were supposed to stick their much larger cylinders.

Men were supposed to pay more attention to the clitoris, and Dwayne had been paying a lot more attention to Francine's, to the point where she said he was paying too much attention to it. This did not surprise him. The things he had read about the clitoris had said that this was a danger—that a man could pay too much attention to it.

So, driving out to the Quality Motor Court that day, Dwayne was hoping that he would pay exactly the right amount of attention to Francine's clitoris.

▶ Kilgore Trout once wrote a short novel about the importance of the clitoris in love-making. This was in response to a suggestion by his second wife, Darlene, that he could make a fortune with a dirty book. She told him that the hero should understand women so well that he could seduce anyone he wanted. So Trout wrote *The Son of Jimmy Valentine.*

Jimmy Valentine was a famous made-up person in another writer's books, just as Kilgore Trout was a famous made-up person in my books. Jimmy Valentine in the other writer's books sandpapered his fingertips, so they were extrasensitive. He was a safe-cracker. His sense of feel was so delicate that he could open any safe in the world by feeling the tumblers fall.

Kilgore Trout invented a son for Jimmy Valentine, named Ralston Valentine. Ralston Valentine also sandpapered his fingertips. But he wasn't a safe-cracker. Ralston was so good at touching women the way they wanted to be touched, that tens of thousands of them became his willing slaves. They abandoned their husbands or lovers for him, in Trout's story, and Ralston Valentine became President of the United States, thanks to the votes of women.

◗ Dwayne and Francine made love in the Quality Motor Court. Then they stayed in bed for a while. It was a water bed. Francine had a beautiful body. So did Dwayne. "We never made love in the afternoon before," said Francine.

"I felt so *tense*," said Dwayne.

"I know," said Francine. "Are you better now?"

"Yes." He was lying on his back. His ankles were crossed. His hands were folded behind his head. His great wang lay across his thigh like a salami. It slumbered now.

"I love you so much," said Francine. She corrected herself. "I know I promised not to say that, but that's a promise I can't help breaking all the time." The thing was: Dwayne had made a pact with her that neither one of them was ever to mention love. Since Dwayne's wife had eaten Drāno, Dwayne never wanted to hear about love ever again. The subject was too painful.

Dwayne snuffled. It was customary for him to communicate by means of snuffles after sexual intercourse. The snuffles all had meanings which were bland: "That's all right . . . forget it . . . who could blame you?" And so on.

"On Judgment Day," said Francine, "when they ask me what bad things I did down here, I'm going to have to tell them, 'Well—there was a promise I made to a man I loved, and I broke it all the time. I promised him never to say I loved him.' "

This generous, voluptuous woman, who had only ninety-six dollars and eleven cents a week in take-home pay, had lost her husband, Robert Pefko, in a war in Viet Nam. He was a career officer in the Army. He had a penis six and one-half inches long and one and seven-eighths inches in diameter.

He was a graduate of West Point, a military academy which turned young men into homicidal maniacs for use in war.

Francine followed Robert from West Point to Parachute School at Fort Bragg, and then to South Korea, where Robert managed a Post Exchange, which was a department store for soldiers, and then to the University of Pennsylvania, where Robert took a Master's Degree in Anthropology, at Army expense, and then back to West Point, where Robert was an Assistant Professor of Social Sciences for three years.

After that, Francine followed Robert to Midland City, where Robert oversaw the manufacture of a new sort of booby trap. A booby trap was an easily hidden explosive device, which blew up when it was accidentally twiddled in some way. One of the virtues of the new type of booby trap was that it could not be smelled by dogs. Various armies at that time were training dogs to sniff out booby traps.

When Robert and Francine were in Midland City, there weren't any other military people around, so they made their first civilian friends. And Francine took a job with Dwayne Hoover, in order to augment her husband's salary and fill her days.

But then Robert was sent to Viet Nam.

Shortly after that, Dwayne's wife ate Drāno and Robert was shipped home in a plastic body bag.

◆ "I pity men," said Francine, there in the Quality Motor Court. She was sincere. "I wouldn't want to be a man— they take such chances, they work so hard." They were on the second floor of the motel. Their sliding glass doors gave them a view of an iron railing and a concrete terrace outside—and then Route 103, and then the wall and the rooftops of the Adult Correctional Institution beyond that.

"I don't wonder you're tired and nervous," Francine went on. "If I was a man, I'd be tired and nervous, too. I guess God made women so men could relax and be treated like little babies from time to time." She was more than satisfied with this arrangement.

Dwayne snuffled. The air was rich with the smell of raspberries, which was the perfume in the disinfectant and roach-killer the motel used.

Francine mused about the prison, where the guards were all white and most of the prisoners were black. "Is it true," she said, "that nobody ever escaped from there?"

"It's true," said Dwayne.

◆ "When was the last time they used the electric chair?" said Francine. She was asking about a device in the basement of the prison, which looked like this:

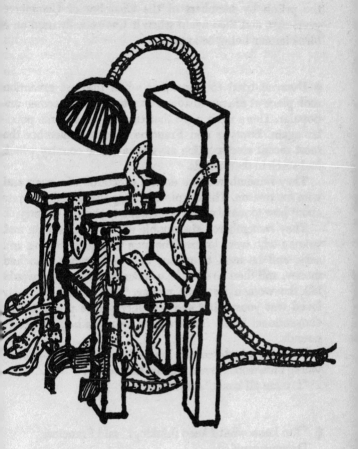

The purpose of it was to kill people by jazzing them with more electricity than their bodies could stand. Dwayne Hoover had seen it twice—once during a tour of

the prison by members of the Chamber of Commerce
years ago, and then again when it was actually used on a
black human being he knew.

◆ Dwayne tried to remember when the last execution
took place at Shepherdstown. Executions had become un-
popular. There were signs that they might become popular again. Dwayne and Francine tried to remember the
most recent electrocution anywhere in the country which
had stuck in their minds.

They remembered the double execution of a man and
wife for treason. The couple had supposedly given secrets
about how to make a hydrogen bomb to another country.

They remembered the double execution of a man and
woman who were lovers. The man was good-looking and
sexy, and he used to seduce ugly old women who had
money, and then he and the woman he really loved would
kill the women for their money. The woman he really
loved was young, but she certainly wasn't pretty in the
conventional sense. She weighed two hundred and forty
pounds.

Francine wondered out loud why a thin, good-looking
young man would love a woman that heavy.

"It takes all kinds," said Dwayne.

◆ "You know what I keep thinking?" said Francine.
Dwayne snuffled.

"This would be a very good location for a Colonel Sanders Kentucky Fried Chicken franchise."

Dwayne's relaxed body contracted as though each
muscle in it had been stung by a drop of lemon juice.

Here was the problem: Dwayne wanted Francine to love him for his body and soul, not for what his money could buy. He thought Francine was hinting that he should buy her a Colonel Sanders Kentucky Fried Chicken franchise, which was a scheme for selling fried chicken.

A chicken was a flightless bird which looked like this:

The idea was to kill it and pull out all its feathers, and cut off its head and feet and scoop out its internal organs —and then chop it into pieces and fry the pieces, and put the pieces in a waxed paper bucket with a lid on it, so it looked like this:

▶ Francine, who had been so proud of her capacity to make Dwayne relax, was now ashamed to have made him tighten up again. He was as rigid as an ironing board. "Oh my God—" she said, "what's the matter now?"

"If you're going to ask me for presents," said Dwayne, "just do me a favor—and don't hint around right after e've made love. Let's keep love-making and presents parate. O.K.?"

"I don't even know what you think I asked for," said rancine.

Dwayne mimicked her cruelly in a falsetto voice: "'I on't even know what you think I asked you for,'" he aid. He looked about as pleasant and relaxed as a coiled attlesnake now. It was his bad chemicals, of course, hich were compelling him to look like that. A real ratesnake looked like this:

The Creator of the Universe had put a rattle on its tail. he Creator had also given it front teeth which were ypodermic syringes filled with deadly poison.

⬥ Sometimes I wonder about the Creator of the Univers

⬥ Another animal invented by the Creator of the Un
verse was a Mexican beetle which could make a blan
cartridge gun out of its rear end. It could detonate i
own farts and knock over other bugs with shock waves.

Word of Honor—I read about it in an article on strang
animals in *Diners' Club Magazine*.

⬥ So Francine got off the bed in order not to share it wit
the seeming rattlesnake. She was aghast. All she could sa
over and over again was, "You're my *man*. You're m
man." This meant that she was willing to agree abou
anything with Dwayne, to do anything for him, no matte
how difficult or disgusting, to think up nice things to d
for him that he didn't even notice, to die for him, if nece
sary, and so on.

She honestly tried to live that way. She couldn't imag
ine anything better to do. So she fell apart when Dway
persisted in his nastiness. He told her that every woma
was a whore, and every whore had her price, and Fra
cine's price was what a Colonel Sanders Kentucky Frie
Chicken franchise would cost, which would be well ov
one hundred thousand dollars by the time adequate park
ing and exterior lighting and all that was taken into co
sideration, and so on.

Francine replied in blubbering gibberish that she ha
never wanted the franchise for herself, that she ha
wanted it for Dwayne, that everything she wanted wa
for Dwayne. Some of the words came through. "I though
of all the people who come out here to visit their relativ

in prison, and I realized how most of them were black, and I thought how much black people liked fried chicken," she said.

"So you want me to open a Nigger joint?" said Dwayne. And so on. So Francine now had the distinction of being the second close associate of Dwayne's who discovered how vile he could be.

"Harry LeSabre was right," said Francine. She was backed up against the cement block wall of the motel room now, with her fingers spread over her mouth. Harry LeSabre, of course, was Dwayne's transvestite sales manager. "He said you'd changed," said Francine. She made a cage of fingers around her mouth. "Oh, God, Dwayne—" she said, "you've changed, you've changed."

"Maybe it was time!" said Dwayne. "I never felt better in my life!" And so on.

▶ Harry LeSabre was at that moment crying, too. He was at home—in bed. He had a purple velvet sheet over his head. He was well-to-do. He had invested in the stock market very intelligently and luckily over the years. He had bought one hundred shares of Xerox, for instance, for eight dollars a share. With the passage of time, his shares had become one hundred times as valuable, simply lying in the total darkness and silence of a safe-deposit box.

There was a lot of money magic like that going on. It was almost as though some blue fairy were flitting about that part of the dying planet, waving her magic wand over certain deeds and bonds and stock certificates.

▶ Harry's wife, Grace, was stretched out on a chaise longue at some distance from the bed. She was smoking a small cigar in a long holder made from the legbone of a stork. A stork was a large European bird, about half the size of a Bermuda Ern. Children who wanted to know where babies came from were sometimes told that they were brought by storks. People who told their children such a thing felt that their children were too young to think intelligently about wide-open beavers and all that.

And there were actually pictures of storks delivering babies on birth announcements and in cartoons and so on, for children to see. A typical one might look like this:

Dwayne Hoover and Harry LeSabre saw pictures like that when they were very little boys. They believed them, too.

◗ Grace LeSabre expressed her contempt for the good opinion of Dwayne Hoover, which her husband felt he had lost. "Fuck Dwayne Hoover," she said. "Fuck Midland City. Let's sell the God damn Xerox stock and buy a condominium on Maui." Maui was one of the Hawaiian Islands. It was widely believed to be a paradise.

"Listen," said Grace, "we're the only white people in Midland City with any kind of sex life, as nearly as I can tell. You're not a freak. Dwayne Hoover's the freak! How many orgasms do you think he has a month?"

"I don't know," said Harry from his humid tent.

Dwayne's monthly orgasm rate on the average over the past ten years, which included the last years of his marriage, was two and one-quarter. Grace's guess was close. "One point five," she said. Her own monthly average over the same period was eighty-seven. Her husband's average was thirty-six. He had been slowing up in recent years, which was one of many reasons he had for feeling panicky.

Grace now spoke loudly and scornfully about Dwayne's marriage. "He was so scared of sex," she said, "he married a woman who had never heard of the subject, who was guaranteed to destroy herself, if she ever *did* hear about it." And so on. "Which she finally did," she said.

◗ "Can the reindeer hear you?" said Harry.

"Fuck the reindeer," said Grace. Then she added, "No
the reindeer cannot hear." *Reindeer* was their code word
for the black maid, who was far away in the kitchen a
the time. It was their code word for black people in gen
eral. It allowed them to speak of the black problem in the
city, which was a big one, without giving offense to any
black person who might overhear.

"The reindeer's asleep—or reading the *Black Panthe
Digest*," she said.

🔹 The reindeer problem was essentially this: Nobody
white had much use for black people anymore—excep
for the gangsters who sold the black people used cars an
dope and furniture. Still, the reindeer went on reproduc
ing. There were these useless, big black animals every
where, and a lot of them had very bad dispositions. They
were given small amounts of money every month, so they
wouldn't have to steal. There was talk of giving them
very cheap dope, too—to keep them listless and cheerful
and uninterested in reproduction.

The Midland City Police Department, and the Midland
County Sheriff's Department, were composed mainly o
white men. They had racks and racks of sub-machine
guns and twelve-gauge automatic shotguns for an open
season on reindeer, which was bound to come.

"Listen—I'm serious," said Grace to Harry. "This is the
asshole of the Universe. Let's split to a condominium on
Maui and *live* for a change."

So they did.

🔹 Dwayne's bad chemicals meanwhile changed his man

ner toward Francine from nastiness to pitiful dependency. He apologized to her for ever thinking that she wanted a Colonel Sanders Kentucky Fried Chicken franchise. He gave her full credit for unflagging unselfishness. He begged her to just hold him for a while, which she did.

"I'm so confused," he said.

"We all are," she said. She cradled his head against her breasts.

"I've got to talk to somebody," said Dwayne.

"You can talk to Mommy, if you want," said Francine. She meant that *she* was *Mommy*.

"Tell me what life is all about," Dwayne begged her fragrant bosom.

"Only God knows that," said Francine.

▶ Dwayne was silent for a while. And then he told her haltingly about a trip he had made to the headquarters of the Pontiac Division of General Motors at Pontiac, Michigan, only three months after his wife ate Drāno.

"We were given a tour of all the research facilities," he said. The thing that impressed him most, he said, was a series of laboratories and out-of-doors test areas where various parts of automobiles and even entire automobiles were destroyed. Pontiac scientists set upholstery on fire, threw gravel at windshields, snapped crankshafts and driveshafts, staged head-on collisions, tore gearshift levers out by the roots, ran engines at high speeds with almost no lubrication, opened and closed glove compartment doors a hundred times a minute for days, cooled dashboard clocks to within a few degrees of absolute zero, and so on.

"Everything you're not supposed to do to a car, they did to a car," Dwayne said to Francine. "And I'll never forget the sign on the front door of the building where all that torture went on." Here was the sign Dwayne described to Francine:

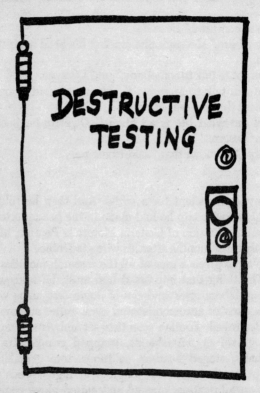

"I saw that sign," said Dwayne, "and I couldn't help wondering if that was what God put me on Earth for—to find out how much a man could take without breaking."

♦ "I've lost my way," said Dwayne. "I need somebody to take me by the hand and lead me out of the woods."

"You're tired," she said. "Why wouldn't you be tired? You work *so* hard. I feel sorry for men, they work so hard. You want to sleep for a while?"

"I can't sleep," said Dwayne, "until I get some answers."

"You want to go to a doctor?" said Francine.

"I don't want to hear the kinds of things doctors say," said Dwayne. "I want to talk to somebody brand new. Francine," he said, and he dug his fingers into her soft arm, "I want to hear new things from new people. I've heard everything anybody in Midland City ever said, ever *will* say. It's got to be somebody new."

"Like who?" said Francine.

"I don't know," said Dwayne. "Somebody from Mars, maybe."

"We could go to some other city," said Francine.

"They're all like here. They're all the same," said Dwayne.

Francine had an idea. "What about all these painters and writers and composers coming to town?" she said. "You never talked to anybody like that before. Maybe you should talk to one of them. They don't think like other people."

"I've tried everything else," said Dwayne. He brightened. He nodded. "You're right! The Festival could give me a brand new viewpoint on life!" he said.

"That's what it's for," said Francine. "*Use* it!"

"I *will*," said Dwayne. This was a bad mistake.

♦ Kilgore Trout, hitchhiking westward, ever westward,

had meanwhile become a passenger in a Ford *Galaxie*.
The man at the controls of the *Galaxie* was a traveling
salesman for a device which engulfed the rear ends of
trucks at loading docks. It was a telescoping tunnel of
rubberized canvas, and it looked like this in action:

The idea of the gadget was to allow people in a building to load or unload trucks without losing cold air in
the summertime or hot air in the wintertime to the out-of-
doors.

The man in control of the *Galaxie* also sold large spools
for wire and cable and rope. He also sold fire extin-
guishers. He was a manufacturer's representative, he explained. He was his own boss, in that he represented
products whose manufacturers couldn't afford salesmen
of their own.

"I make my own hours, and I pick the products I sell.
The products don't sell me," he said. His name was Andy.

Lieber. He was thirty-two. He was white. He was a good deal overweight like so many people in the country. He was obviously a happy man. He drove like a maniac. The *Galaxie* was going ninety-two miles an hour now. "I'm one of the few remaining free men in America," he said.

He had a penis one inch in diameter and seven and a half inches long. During the past year, he had averaged twenty-two orgasms per month. This was far above the national average. His income and the value of his life insurance policies at maturity were also far above average.

Trout wrote a novel one time which he called *How You Doin'?* and it was about national averages for this and that. An advertising agency on another planet had a successful campaign for the local equivalent of Earthling peanut butter. The eye-catching part of each ad was the statement of some sort of average—the average number of children, the average size of the male sex organ on that particular planet—which was two inches long, with an inside diameter of three inches and an outside diameter of four and a quarter inches—and so on. The ads invited the readers to discover whether they were superior or inferior to the majority, in this respect or that one—whatever the respect was for that particular ad.

The ad went on to say that superior and inferior people alike ate such and such brand of peanut butter. Except that it wasn't really peanut butter on that planet. It was *Shazzbutter*.

And so on.

Chapter 16

And the peanut butter-eaters on Earth were preparing to conquer the shazzbutter-eaters on the planet in the book by Kilgore Trout. By this time, the Earthlings hadn't just demolished West Virginia and Southeast Asia. They had demolished everything. So they were ready to go pioneering again.

They studied the shazzbutter-eaters by means of electronic snooping, and determined that they were too numerous and proud and resourceful ever to allow themselves to be pioneered.

So the Earthlings infiltrated the ad agency which had the shazzbutter account, and they buggered the statistics in the ads. They made the average for everything so high that everybody on the planet felt inferior to the majority in every respect.

And then the Earthling armored space ships came in and discovered the planet. Only token resistance was offered here and there, because the natives felt so below average. And then the pioneering began.

◗ Trout asked the happy manufacturer's representative what it felt like to drive a *Galaxie*, which was the name of the car. The driver didn't hear him, and Trout let it go. It was a dumb play on words, so that Trout was asking simultaneously what it was like to drive the car and what it was like to steer something like the Milky Way, which was one hundred thousand light-years in diameter and ten thousand light-years thick. It revolved once every two hundred million years. It contained about one hundred billion stars.

And then Trout saw that a simple fire extinguisher in the *Galaxie* had this brand name:

As far as Trout knew, this word meant *higher* in a dead language. It was also a thing a fictitious mountain climber in a famous poem kept yelling as he disappeared into a blizzard up above. And it was also the trade name for wood shavings which were used to protect fragile objects inside packages.

"Why would anybody name a fire extinguisher *Excelsior*?" Trout asked the driver.

The driver shrugged. "Somebody must have liked the *sound* of it," he said.

▶ Trout looked out at the countryside, which was smeared by high velocity. He saw this sign:

So he was getting really close to Dwayne Hoover. And, as though the Creator of the Universe or some other supernatural power were preparing him for the meeting, Trout felt the urge to thumb through his own book, *Now*

Can Be Told. This was the book which would soon turn
wayne into a homicidal maniac.

The premise of the book was this: Life was an experi-
ent by the Creator of the Universe, Who wanted to test
new sort of creature He was thinking of introducing
to the Universe. It was a creature with the ability to
ake up its own mind. All the other creatures were fully-
:ogrammed robots.

The book was in the form of a long letter from The
reator of the Universe to the experimental creature. The
reator congratulated the creature and apologized for all
e discomfort he had endured. The Creator invited him
 a banquet in his honor in the Empire Room of the
aldorf Astoria Hotel in New York City, where a black
bot named Sammy Davis, Jr., would sing and dance.

And the experimental creature wasn't killed after the
anquet. He was transferred to a virgin planet instead.
iving cells were sliced from the palms of his hands,
hile he was unconscious. The operation didn't hurt at
l.

And then the cells were stirred into a soupy sea on the
rgin planet. They would evolve into ever more compli-
ited life forms as the eons went by. Whatever shapes
ey assumed, they would have free will.

Trout didn't give the experimental creature a proper
ume. He simply called him *The Man.*

On the virgin planet, The Man was Adam and the sea
as Eve.

◆ The Man often sauntered by the sea. Sometimes h
waded in his Eve. Sometimes he swam in her, but she wa
too soupy for an invigorating swim. She made her Ada
feel sleepy and sticky afterwards, so he would dive int
an icy stream that had just jumped off a mountain.

He screamed when he dived into the icy wate
screamed again when he came up for air. He bloodied h
shins and laughed about it when he scrambled up roc
to get out of the water.

He panted and laughed some more, and he thought
something amazing to yell. The Creator never knew wh
he was going to yell, since The Creator had no contr
over him. The Man himself got to decide what he wa
going to do next—and why. After a dip one day, for in
stance, The Man yelled this: "Cheese!"

Another time he yelled, "Wouldn't you really rath
drive a Buick?"

◆ The only other big animal on the virgin planet was a
angel who visited The Man occasionally. He was a mes
senger and an investigator for the Creator of the Un
verse. He took the form of an eight hundred pound ma
cinnamon bear. He was a robot, too, and so was Th
Creator, according to Kilgore Trout.

The bear was attempting to get a line on why The Ma
did what he did. He would ask, for instance, "Why d
you yell, 'Cheese'?"

And The Man would tell him mockingly, "Because
felt like it, you stupid machine."

▶ Here is what The Man's tombstone on the virgin planet looked like at the end of the book by Kilgore Trout:

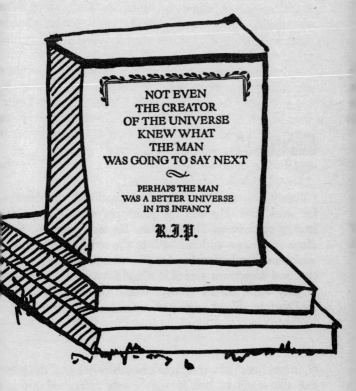

NOT EVEN
THE CREATOR
OF THE UNIVERSE
KNEW WHAT
THE MAN
WAS GOING TO SAY NEXT

PERHAPS THE MAN
WAS A BETTER UNIVERSE
IN ITS INFANCY

R.I.P.

Chapter 17

▼

Bunny Hoover, Dwayne's homosexual son, was dressing for work now. He was the piano player in the cocktail lounge of the new Holiday Inn. He was poor. He lived alone in a room without bath in the old Fairchild Hotel, which used to be fashionable. It was a flophouse now—in the most dangerous part of Midland City.

Very soon, Bunny Hoover would be seriously injured by Dwayne, would soon share an ambulance with Kilgore Trout.

● Bunny was pale, the same unhealthy color of the blind fish that used to live in the bowels of Sacred Miracle Cave. Those fish were extinct. They had all turned belly-up years ago, had been flushed from the cave and into the

Ohio River—to turn belly-up, to go *bang* in the noonday sun.

Bunny avoided the sunshine, too. And the water from the taps of Midland City was becoming more poisonous every day. He ate very little. He prepared his own food in his room. The preparation was simple, since vegetables and fruits were all he ate, and he munched them raw.

He not only did without dead meat—he did without living meat, too, without friends or lovers or pets. He had once been highly popular. When he was at Prairie Military Academy, for instance, the student body was unanimous in electing him Cadet Colonel, the highest rank possible, in his senior year.

When Bunny played the piano bar at the Holiday Inn, he had many, many secrets. One of them was this: he wasn't really there. He was able to absent himself from the cocktail lounge, and from the planet itself, for that matter, by means of Transcendental Meditation. He learned this technique from Maharishi Mahesh Yogi, who once stopped off in Midland City during a world-wide lecture tour.

Maharishi Mahesh Yogi, in exchange for a new handkerchief, a piece of fruit, a bunch of flowers, and thirty-five dollars, taught Bunny to close his eyes, and to say this euphonious nonsense word to himself over and over again: "Aye-eeeeem, aye-eeeeem, aye-eeeeem." Bunny sat on the edge of his bed in the hotel room now, and he did it. "Aye-eeeeem, aye-eeeeem," he said to himself—internally. The rhythm of the chant matched one syllable with each two beats in his heart. He closed his eyes. He

became a skin diver in the depths of his mind. The depth
were seldom used.

His heart slowed. His respiration nearly stopped. A sin
gle word floated by in the depths. It had somehow e
caped from the busier parts of his mind. It wasn't con
nected to anything. It floated by lazily, a translucen
scarf-like fish. The word was untroubling. Here was th
word: "Blue." Here is what it looked like to Bunn
Hoover:

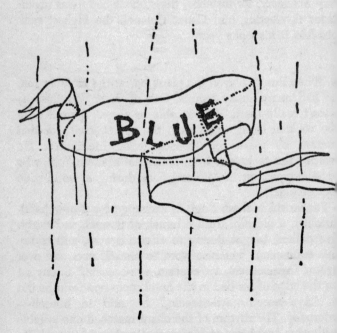

And then another lovely scarf swam by. It looked like his:

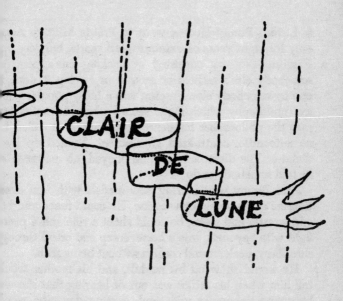

Fifteen minutes later, Bunny's awareness bobbed to the urface of its own accord. Bunny was refreshed. He got p from the bed, and he brushed his hair with the mili-ary brushes his mother had given him when he was lected Cadet Colonel so long ago.

Bunny was sent away to military school, an institution levoted to homicide and absolutely humorless obedience, vhen he was only ten years old. Here is why: He told

Dwayne that he wished he were a woman instead of
man, because what men did was so often cruel and ugl

◗ Listen: Bunny Hoover went to Prairie Military Aca
emy for eight years of uninterrupted sports, buggery an
Fascism. Buggery consisted of sticking one's penis i
somebody else's asshole or mouth, or having it done t
one by somebody else. Fascism was a fairly popular pol
ical philosophy which made sacred whatever nation an
race the philosopher happened to belong to. It called fo
an autocratic, centralized government, headed up by
dictator. The dictator had to be obeyed, no matter wha
he told somebody to do.

And Bunny would bring new medals with him ever
time he came home for vacation. He could fence and bo
and wrestle and swim, he could shoot a rifle and a pisto
fight with bayonets, ride a horse, creep and crawl throug
shrubbery, peek around corners without being seen.

He would show off his medals, and his mother woul
tell him when his father was out of hearing that she wa
becoming unhappier with each passing day. She woul
hint that Dwayne was a monster. It wasn't true. It was a
in her head.

She would begin to tell Bunny what was so vile abou
Dwayne, but she always stopped short. "You're too youn
to hear about such things," she'd say, even when Bunn
was sixteen years old. "There's nothing you or anybod
could do about them anyway." She would pretend to loc
her lips with a key, and then whisper to Bunny, "The
are secrets I will carry to my grave."

Her biggest secret, of course, was one that Bunn
didn't detect until she knocked herself off with Drāne

Celia Hoover was crazy as a bedbug.
My mother was, too.

◆ Listen: Bunny's mother and my mother were different
sorts of human beings, but they were both beautiful in
exotic ways, and they both boiled over with chaotic talk
about love and peace and wars and evil and desperation,
of better days coming by and by, of worse days coming
by and by. And both our mothers committed suicide.
Bunny's mother ate Drāno. My mother ate sleeping pills,
which wasn't nearly as horrible.

◆ And Bunny's mother and my mother had one really
bizarre symptom in common: neither one could stand to
have her picture taken. They were usually fine in the
daytime. They usually concealed their frenzies until late
at night. But, if somebody aimed a camera at either one
of them during the daytime, the mother who was aimed
at would crash down on her knees and protect her head
with her arms, as though somebody was about to club her
to death. It was a scary and pitiful thing to see.

◆ At least Bunny's mother taught him how to control a
piano, which was a music machine. At least Bunny
Hoover's mother taught him a trade. A good piano con-
troller could get a job making music in cocktail lounges
almost anywhere in the world, and Bunny was a good
one. His military training was useless, despite all the
medals he won. The armed forces knew he was a homosexual, that he was certain to fall in love with other fight-

ing men, and the armed forces didn't want to put up with such love affairs.

◗ So Bunny Hoover now got ready to practice his trade. He slipped a black velvet dinner jacket over a black turtleneck sweater now. Bunny looked out his only window at the alleyway. The better rooms afforded views of Fairchild Park, where there had been fifty-six murders in the past two years. Bunny's room was on the second floor, so his window framed a piece of the blank brick side of what used to be the Keedsler Opera House.

There was an historical marker on the front of the former opera house. Not many people could understand it, but this is what it said:

JENNY LIND
"THE SWEDISH NIGHTINGALE"
SANG HERE
AVGVST 11
ANNO DOMINI MDCCCLXXXI

The Opera House used to be the home of the Midland City Symphony Orchestra, which was an amateur group of music enthusiasts. But they became homeless in 1927, when the Opera House became a motion picture house, *The Bannister.* The orchestra remained homeless, too, until the Mildred Barry Memorial Center for the Arts went up.

And *The Bannister* was the city's leading movie house for many years, until it was engulfed by the high crime district, which was moving north all the time. So it wasn't a theater anymore, even though there were still busts of Shakespeare and Mozart and so on gazing down from niches in the walls inside.

The stage was still in there, too, but it was crowded with dinette sets now. The Empire Furniture Company had taken over the premises now. It was gangster-controlled.

◆ The nickname for Bunny's neighborhood was *Skid Row.* Every American town of any size had a neighborhood with the same nickname: Skid Row. It was a place where people who didn't have any friends or relatives or property or usefulness or ambition were supposed to go.

People like that would be treated with disgust in other neighborhoods, and policemen would keep them moving. They were as easy to move, usually, as toy balloons.

And they would drift hither and yon, like balloons filled with some gas slightly heavier than air, until they came to rest in Skid Row, against the foundations of the old Fairchild Hotel.

They could snooze and mumble to each other all day long. They could beg. They could get drunk. The basic

scheme was this one: they were to stay there and n
bother anybody anywhere else—until they were mu
dered for thrills, or until they were frozen to death by th
wintertime.

▶ Kilgore Trout wrote a story one time about a tow
which decided to tell derelicts where they were and wha
was about to happen to them by putting up actual stree
signs like this:

Bunny now smiled at himself in the mirror, in the *leak*
He called himself to attention for a moment, becam
again the insufferably brainless, humorless, heartless so
dier he had learned to be in military school. He mu
mured the motto of the school, a motto he used to have t

hout about a hundred times a day—at dawn, at meals, at
he start of every class, at games, at bayonet practice, at
unset, at bedtime:

"Can do," he said. "Can do."

Chapter 18

The *Galaxie* in which Kilgore Trout was a passenger
was on the Interstate now, close to Midland City. It was
creeping. It was trapped in rush hour traffic from Barrytron and Western Electric and Prairie Mutual. Trout
looked up from his reading, saw a billboard which said
this:

So Sacred Miracle Cave had become a part of the past.

As an old, old man, Trout would be asked by Dr. Thor
embrig, the Secretary-General of the United Nations, if
e feared the future. He would give this reply:
"Mr. Secretary-General, it is the *past* which scares the
ejesus out of me."

Dwayne Hoover was only four miles away. He was sit-
ng alone on a zebra-skin banquette in the cocktail
unge of the new Holiday Inn. It was dark in there, and
uiet, too. The glare and uproar of rush hour traffic on
he Interstate was blocked out by thick drapes of crimson
elvet. On each table was a hurricane lamp with a candle
side, although the air was still.
On each table was a bowl of dry-roasted peanuts, too,
nd a sign which allowed the staff to refuse service to
nyone who was inharmonious with the mood of the
unge. Here is what it said:

THIS TABLE
RESERVED

◗ Bunny Hoover was controlling the piano. He had no looked up when his father came in. Neither had his fathe glanced in his direction. They had not exchanged greet ings for many years.

Bunny went on playing his white man's blues. The were slow and tinkling, with capricious silences here an there. Bunny's blues had some of the qualities of a musi box, a tired music box. They tinkled, stopped, then relu tantly, torpidly, they managed a few tinkles more.

Bunny's mother used to collect tinkling music boxes among other things.

◗ Listen: Francine Pefko was at Dwayne's automobil agency next door. She was catching up on all the wor she should have done that afternoon. Dwayne would bea her up very soon.

And the only other person on the property with her a she typed and filed was Wayne Hoobler, the black pa role, who still lurked among the used cars. Dwayn would try to beat him up, too, but Wayne was a genius a dodging blows.

Francine was pure machinery at the moment, a ma chine made of meat—a typing machine, a filing machine

Wayne Hoobler, on the other hand, had nothin machine-like to do. He ached to be a useful machine. Th used cars were all locked up tight for the night. Now an then aluminum propellors on a wire overhead would b turned by a lazy breeze, and Wayne would respond t them as best he could. "Go," he would say to them. "Spi 'roun'."

He established a sort of relationship with the traffic on he Interstate, too, appreciating its changing moods. Everybody goin' home," he said during the rush hour um. "Everybody home now," he said later on, when the affic thinned out. Now the sun was going down.

"Sun goin' down," said Wayne Hoobler. He had no lues as to where to go next. He supposed without mind-ng much that he might die of exposure that night. He ad never seen death by exposure, had never been threat-ned by it, since he had so seldom been out-of-doors. He new of death by exposure because the papery voice of he little radio in his cell told of people's dying of expo-ure from time to time.

He missed that papery voice. He missed the clash of teel doors. He missed the bread and the stew and the itchers of milk and coffee. He missed fucking other men 1 the mouth and the asshole, and being fucked in the 1outh and the asshole, and jerking off—and fucking cows 1 the prison dairy, all events in a normal sex life on the lanet, as far as he knew.

Here would be a good tombstone for Wayne Hoobler vhen he died:

Kurt Vonnegut

▶ The dairy at the prison provided milk and cream an
butter and cheese and ice cream not only for the priso
and the County Hospital. It sold its products to the out
side world, too. Its trademark didn't mention prison. Thi
was it:

▶ Wayne couldn't read very well. The words *Hawaii* an
Hawaiian, for instance, appeared in combination wit
more familiar words and symbols in signs painted on th

windows of the showroom and on the windshields of some used cars. Wayne tried to decode the mysterious words phonetically, without any satisfaction. "Wahee-io," he would say, and "Hoo-he-woo-hi," and so on.

Wayne Hoobler smiled now, not because he was happy but because, with so little to do, he thought he might as well show off his teeth. They were excellent teeth. The Adult Correctional Institution at Shepherdstown was proud of its dentistry program.

It was such a famous dental program, in fact, that it had been written up in medical journals and in the *Reader's Digest*, which was the dying planet's most popular magazine. The theory behind the program was that many ex-convicts could not or would not get jobs because of their appearances, and good looks began with good teeth.

The program was so famous, in fact, that police even in neighboring states, when they picked up a poor man with expensively maintained teeth, fillings and bridgework and all that, were likely to ask him, "All right, boy—how many years you spend in Shepherdstown?"

Wayne Hoobler heard some of the orders which a waitress called to the bartender in the cocktail lounge. Wayne heard her call, "Gilbey's and quinine, with a twist." He had no idea what that was—or a Manhattan or a brandy Alexander or a sloe gin fizz. "Give me a Johnny Walker Rob Roy," she called, "and a Southern Comfort on the rocks, and a Bloody Mary with Wolfschmidt's."

Wayne's only experiences with alcohol had had to do

with drinking cleaning fluids and eating shoe polish and s
on. He had no fondness for alcohol.

◗ "Give me a Black and White and water," he heard th
waitress say, and Wayne should have pricked up his ea
at that. That particular drink wasn't for any ordinary pe
son. That drink was for the person who had created a
Wayne's misery to date, who could kill him or make hi
a millionaire or send him back to prison or do whateve
he damn pleased with Wayne. That drink was for me.

◗ I had come to the Arts Festival incognito. I was ther
to watch a confrontation between two human beings
had created: Dwayne Hoover and Kilgore Trout. I wa
not eager to be recognized. The waitress lit the hurrican
lamp on my table. I pinched out the flame with m
fingers. I had bought a pair of sunglasses at a Holiday In
outside of Ashtabula, Ohio, where I spent the night before
I wore them in the darkness now. They looked like this

The lenses were silvered, were mirrors to anyone look
ing my way. Anyone wanting to know what my eye
were like was confronted with his or her own twin reflec

ns. Where other people in the cocktail lounge had eyes,
ad two holes into another universe. I had *leaks*.

There was a book of matches on my table, next to my
ll Mall cigarettes.
Here is the message on the book of matches, which I
ad an hour and a half later, while Dwayne was beating
e daylights out of Francine Pefko:
"It's easy to make $100 a week in your spare time by
owing comfortable, latest style Mason shoes to your
ends. EVERYBODY goes for Mason Shoes with their
any special comfort features! We'll send FREE money-
aking kit so you can run your business from home. We'll
en tell you how you can earn shoes FREE OF COST as
bonus for taking profitable orders!"
And so on.

"This is a very bad book you're writing," I said to my-
lf behind my *leaks*.
"I know," I said.
"You're afraid you'll kill yourself the way your mother
d," I said.
"I know," I said.

There in the cocktail lounge, peering out through my
aks at a world of my own invention, I mouthed this
ord: *schizophrenia*.
The sound and appearance of the word had fascinated
e for many years. It sounded and looked to me like a
man being sneezing in a blizzard of soapflakes.

I did not and do not know for certain that I have th[e] disease. This much I knew and know: I was making m[y] self hideously uncomfortable by not narrowing my [at] tention to details of life which were immediately imp[or] tant, and by refusing to believe what my neighb[ors] believed.

◗ I am better now.
Word of honor: I am better now.

◗ I was really sick for a while, though. I sat there [in] a cocktail lounge of my own invention, and I star[ed] through my *leaks* at a white cocktail waitress of my ow[n] invention. I named her Bonnie MacMahon. I had h[er] bring Dwayne Hoover his customary drink, which was [a] House of Lords martini with a twist of lemon peel. S[he] was a longtime acquaintance of Dwayne's. Her husba[nd] was a guard in the Sexual Offenders' Wing of the Ad[ult] Correctional Institution. Bonnie had to work as a waitr[ess] because her husband lost all their money by investing [it] in a car wash in Shepherdstown.

Dwayne had advised them not to do it. Here is h[ow] Dwayne knew her and her husband Ralph: They h[ad] bought nine Pontiacs from him over the past sixte[en] years.

"We're a Pontiac family," they'd say.

Bonnie made a joke now as she served him his marti[ni.] She made the same joke every time she served anybody [a] martini. "Breakfast of Champions," she said.

The expression "Breakfast of Champions" is a registered trademark of General Mills, Inc., for use on a breakfast cereal product. The use of the identical expression as the title for this book as well as throughout the book is not intended to indicate an association with or sponsorship by General Mills, nor is it intended to disparage their fine products.

Dwayne was hoping that some of the distinguished visitors to the Arts Festival, who were all staying at the inn, would come into the cocktail lounge. He wanted to talk to them, if he could, to discover whether they had truths about life which he had never heard before. Here is what he hoped new truths might do for him: enable him to laugh at his troubles, to go on living, and to keep out of the North Wing of the Midland County General Hospital, which was for lunatics.

While he waited for an artist to appear, he consoled himself with the only artistic creation of any depth and mystery which was stored in his head. It was a poem he had been forced to learn by heart during his sophomore year in Sugar Creek High School, the elite white high school at the time. Sugar Creek High was a Nigger high school now. Here was the poem:

> *The Moving Finger writes; and, having writ,*
> *Moves on: nor all your Piety nor Wit*
> *Shall lure it back to cancel half a Line*
> *Nor all your Tears wash out a Word of it.*

Some poem!

◆ And Dwayne was so open to new suggestions about the meaning of life that he was easily hypnotized. So, when he looked down into his martini, he was put into a trance by dancing myriads of winking eyes on the surface of his drink. The eyes were beads of lemon oil.

Dwayne missed it when two distinguished visitors to the Arts Festival came in and sat down on barstools next to Bunny's piano. They were white. They were Beatrice Keedsler, the Gothic novelist, and Rabo Karabekian, the minimal painter.

Bunny's piano, a Steinway baby grand, was armored with pumpkin-colored Formica and ringed with stools. People could eat and drink from the piano. On the previous Thanksgiving, a family of eleven had had Thanksgiving dinner served on the piano. Bunny played.

◆ This *has* to be the asshole of the Universe," said Rabo Karabekian, the minimal painter.

Beatrice Keedsler, the Gothic novelist, had grown up in Midland City. "I was petrified about coming home after all these years," she said to Karabekian.

"Americans are always afraid of coming home," said Karabekian, "with good reason, may I say."

"They *used* to have good reason," said Beatrice, "but not anymore. The past has been rendered harmless. I would tell any wandering American now, 'Of course you can go home again, and as often as you please. It's just a motel.'"

◆ Traffic on the westbound barrel of the Interstate had come to a halt a mile east of the new Holiday Inn—

cause of a fatal accident on Exit 10A. Drivers and assengers got out of their cars—to stretch their legs and nd out, if they could, what the trouble was up ahead.

Kilgore Trout was among those who got out. He arned from others that the new Holiday Inn was within asy walking distance. So he gathered up his parcels from e front seat of the *Galaxie*. He thanked the driver, hose name he had forgotten, and he began to trudge.

He also began to assemble in his mind a system of eliefs which would be appropriate to his narrow mission Midland City, which was to show provincials, who ere bent on exalting creativity, a would-be creator who ad failed and failed. He paused in his trudge to examine imself in the rearview mirror, the rearview *leak*, of a uck locked up in traffic. The tractor was pulling two ailers instead of one. Here was the message the owners f the rig saw fit to shriek at human beings wherever it ent:

Trout's image in the *leak* was as shocking as he had oped it would be. He had not washed up after his drubing by *The Pluto Gang*, so there was caked blood on one arlobe, and more under his left nostril. There was dog uit on a shoulder of his coat. He had collapsed into og shit on the handball court under the Queensboro ridge after the robbery.

By an unbelievable coincidence, that shit came fro
the wretched greyhound belonging to a girl I knew.

♦ The girl with the greyhound was an assistant lightin
director for a musical comedy about American histor
and she kept her poor greyhound, who was name
Lancer, in a one-room apartment fourteen feet wide an
twenty-six feet long, and six flights of stairs above stree
level. His entire life was devoted to unloading his excre
ment at the proper time and place. There were two prope
places to put it: in the gutter outside the door seventy
two steps below, with the traffic whizzing by, or in
roasting pan his mistress kept in front of the Westing
house refrigerator.

Lancer had a very small brain, but he must have su
pected from time to time, just as Wayne Hoobler di
that some kind of terrible mistake had been made.

♦ Trout trudged onward, a stranger in a strange land. Hi
pilgrimage was rewarded with new wisdom, which woul
never have been his had he remained in his basement i
Cohoes. He learned the answer to a question many huma
beings were asking themselves so frantically: "What
blocking traffic on the westbound barrel of the Midlan
City stretch of the Interstate?"

The scales fell from the eyes of Kilgore Trout. He sa
the explanation: a *Queen of the Prairies* milk truck wa
lying on its side, blocking the flow. It had been hit har
by a ferocious 1971 Chevrolet *Caprice* two-door. Th
Chevy had jumped the median divider strip. The Chevy
passenger hadn't used his seat belt. He had shot righ

through the shatterproof windshield. He was lying dead now in the concrete trough containing Sugar Creek. The Chevy's driver was also dead. He had been skewered by the post of his steering wheel.

The Chevy's passenger was bleeding blood as he lay dead in Sugar Creek. The milk truck was bleeding milk. Milk and blood were about to be added to the composition of the stinking ping-pong balls which were being manufactured in the bowels of Sacred Miracle Cave.

Chapter 19

I was on a par with the Creator of the Universe there in the dark in the cocktail lounge. I shrunk the Universe to a ball exactly one light-year in diameter. I had it explode. I had it disperse itself again.

Ask me a question, any question. How old is the Universe? It is one half-second old, but that half-second has lasted one quintillion years so far. Who created it? Nobody created it. It has always been here.

What is time? It is a serpent which eats its tail, like this:

This is the snake which uncoiled itself long enough to er Eve the apple, which looked like this:

What was the apple which Eve and Adam ate? It was e Creator of the Universe.

And so on.

Symbols can be so beautiful, sometimes.

Listen:

The waitress brought me another drink. She wanted to ght my hurricane lamp again. I wouldn't let her. "Can u see anything in the dark, with your sunglasses on?" e asked me.

"The big show is inside my head," I said.

"Oh," she said.

"I can tell fortunes," I said. "You want your fortune ld?"

"Not right now," she said. She went back to the bar, d she and the bartender had some sort of conversation

about me, I think. The bartender took several anxio
looks in my direction. All he could see were the *leaks* ov
my eyes. I did not worry about his asking me to leave t
establishment. I had created him, after all. I gave him
name: Harold Newcomb Wilbur. I awarded him the S
ver Star, the Bronze Star, the Soldier's Medal, the Go
Conduct Medal, and a Purple Heart with two Oak-Le
Clusters, which made him the second most decorat
veteran in Midland City. I put all his medals under l
handkerchiefs in a dresser drawer.

He won all those medals in the Second World W
which was staged by robots so that Dwayne Hoov
could give a free-willed reaction to such a holocaust. T
war was such an extravaganza that there was scarcely
robot anywhere who didn't have a part to play. Haro
Newcomb Wilbur got his medals for killing Japane:
who were yellow robots. They were fueled by rice.

And he went on staring at me, even though I wanted
stop him now. Here was the thing about my control ov
the characters I created: I could only guide their mov
ments approximately, since they were such big anima
There was inertia to overcome. It wasn't as though I w
connected to them by steel wires. It was more as though
was connected to them by stale rubberbands.

So I made the green telephone in back of the bar rir
Harold Newcomb Wilbur answered it, but he kept l
eyes on me. I had to think fast about who was on t
other end of the telephone. I put the first most decorat
veteran in Midland City on the other end. He had
penis eight hundred miles long and two hundred ar
ten miles in diameter, but practically all of it was in t
fourth dimension. He got his medals in the war in Vi
Nam. He had also fought yellow robots who ran on ri

"Cocktail lounge," said Harold Newcomb Wilbur.

"Hal—?"

"Yes?"

"This is Ned Lingamon."

"I'm busy."

"Don't hang up. The cops got me down at City Jail.
.ey only let me have one call, so I called you."

"Why me?"

"You're the only friend I got left."

"What they got you in for?"

"They say I killed my baby."

And so on.

This man, who was white, had all the medals Harold
ewcomb Wilbur had, plus the highest decoration for
roism which an American soldier could receive, which
oked like this:

He had now also committed the lowest crime which a American could commit, which was to kill his own chil Her name was Cynthia Anne, and she certainly didn't liv very long before she was made dead again. She got kille for crying and crying. She wouldn't shut up.

First she drove her seventeen-year-old mother awa with all her demands, and then her father killed her.

And so on.

◗ As for the fortune I might have told for the waitres this was it: "You will be swindled by termite extermina tors and not even know it. You will buy steel-belted radi tires for the front wheels of your car. Your cat will b killed by a motorcyclist named Headley Thomas, and yo will get another cat. Arthur, your brother in Atlanta, wi find eleven dollars in a taxicab."

◗ I might have told Bunny Hoover's fortune, too: "You father will become extremely ill, and you will respond s grotesquely that there will be talk of putting you in th booby hatch, too. You will stage scenes in the hospita waiting room, telling doctors and nurses that you are t blame for your father's disease. You will blame yourse for trying for so many years to kill him with hatred. Yo will redirect your hatred. You will hate your mom."

And so on.

And I had Wayne Hoobler, the black ex-convict, stan bleakly among the garbage cans outside the back door o the Inn, and examine the currency which had been give to him at the prison gate that morning. He had nothin else to do.

He studied the pyramid with the blazing eye on top. He wished he had more information about the pyramid and the eye. There was so much to learn!

Wayne didn't even know the Earth revolved around the Sun. He thought the Sun revolved around the Earth, because it certainly looked that way.

A truck sizzled by on the Interstate, seemed to cry out in pain to Wayne, because he read the message on the side of it phonetically. The message told Wayne that the truck was in agony, as it hauled things from here to there. This was the message, and Wayne said it out loud:

Here was what was going to happen to Wayne in about four days—because I wanted it to happen to him: He would be picked up and questioned by policemen, because he was behaving suspiciously outside the back gate of Barrytron, Ltd., which was involved in super-secret weapons work. They thought at first that he might be pretending to be stupid and ignorant, that he might, in fact, be a cunning spy for the Communists.

A check of his fingerprints and his wonderful dental work proved that he was who he said he was. But there was still something else he had to explain: What was he doing with a membership card in the Playboy Club of America, made out in the name of Paulo di Capistrano. He had found it in a garbage can in back of the new Holiday Inn.

And so on.

 And it was time now for me to have Rabo Karabekian, the minimalist painter, and Beatrice Keedsler, the novelist, say and do some more stuff for the sake of this book. I did not want to spook them by staring at them as I worked their controls, so I pretended to be absorbed in drawing pictures on my tabletop with a damp fingertip.

I drew the Earthling symbol for *nothingness*, which was this:

I drew the Earthling symbol for *everything*, which was this:

Dwayne Hoover and Wayne Hoobler knew the first one, but not the second one. And now I drew a symbol in vanishing mist which was bitterly familiar to Dwayne but not to Wayne. This was it:

DRĀNO

And now I drew a symbol whose meaning Dwayne had known for a few years in school, a meaning which had once eluded him. The symbol would have looked like the end of a table in a prison dining hall to Wayne. It represented the ratio of the circumference of a circle to its diameter. This ratio could also be expressed as a number, and even as Dwayne and Wayne and Karabekian and Beatrice Keedsler and all the rest of us went about our business, Earthling scientists were monotonously radioing that number into outer space. The idea was to show other inhabited planets, in case they were listening, how intelligent we were. We had tortured circles until they coughed up this symbol of their secret lives:

And I made an invisible duplicate on my Formica tabletop of a painting by Rabo Karabekian, entitled *The Temptation of Saint Anthony*. My duplicate was a miniature of the real thing, and mine was not in color, but I had captured the picture's form and the spirit, too. This is what I drew.

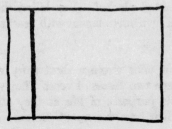

The original was twenty feet wide and sixteen feet high. The field was *Hawaiian Avocado*, a green wall paint manufactured by the O'Hare Paint and Varnish Company in Hellertown, Pennsylvania. The vertical stripe was day-glo orange reflecting tape. This was the most expensive piece of art, not counting buildings and tombstones, and not counting the statue of Abraham Lincoln in front of the old Nigger high school.

It was a scandal what the painting cost. It was the first purchase for the permanent collection of the Mildred Barry Memorial Center for the Arts. Fred T. Barry, the Chairman of the Board of Barrytron, Ltd., had coughed up fifty thousand dollars of his own for the picture.

Midland City was outraged. So was I.

So was Beatrice Keedsler, but she kept her dismay to herself as she sat at the piano bar with Karabekian. Karabekian, who wore a sweatshirt imprinted with the likeness of Beethoven, knew he was surrounded by people who hated him for getting so much money for so little work. He was amused.

Like everybody else in the cocktail lounge, he was softening his brain with alcohol. This was a substance produced by a tiny creature called yeast. Yeast organisms ate sugar and excreted alcohol. They killed themselves by destroying their own environment with yeast shit.

Kilgore Trout once wrote a short story which was a dialogue between two pieces of yeast. They were discussing the possible purposes of life as they ate sugar and suffocated in their own excrement. Because of their lim

ed intelligence, they never came close to guessing that
ney were making champagne.

So I had Beatrice Keedsler say to Rabo Karabekian
here at the piano bar, "This is a dreadful confession, but
don't even know who Saint Anthony was. Who was he,
nd why should anybody have wanted to tempt him?"

"I don't know, and I would hate to find out," said Kara-
ekian.

"You have no use for truth?" said Beatrice.

"You know what truth is?" said Karabekian. "It's some
razy thing my neighbor believes. If I want to make
riends with him, I ask him what he believes. He tells me,
nd I say, 'Yeah, yeah—ain't it the truth?' "

I had no respect whatsoever for the creative works of
ither the painter or the novelist. I thought Karabekian
with his meaningless pictures had entered into a con-
piracy with millionaires to make poor people feel stupid.
thought Beatrice Keedsler had joined hands with other
ld-fashioned storytellers to make people believe that life
ad leading characters, minor characters, significant de-
ils, insignificant details, that it had lessons to be
earned, tests to be passed, and a beginning, a middle,
nd an end.

As I approached my fiftieth birthday, I had become
nore and more enraged and mystified by the idiot deci-
ions made by my countrymen. And then I had come
uddenly to pity them, for I understood how innocent and
atural it was for them to behave so abominably, and
with such abominable results: They were doing their best

to live like people invented in story books. This was th
reason Americans shot each other so often: It was
convenient literary device for ending short stories an
books.

Why were so many Americans treated by their govern
ment as though their lives were as disposable as pape
facial tissues? Because that was the way authors cus
tomarily treated bit-part players in their made-up tales.

And so on.

Once I understood what was making America such
dangerous, unhappy nation of people who had nothing t
do with real life, I resolved to shun storytelling. I woul
write about life. Every person would be exactly as impor
tant as any other. All facts would also be given equa
weightiness. Nothing would be left out. Let others brin
order to chaos. I would bring chaos to order, instead
which I think I have done.

If all writers would do that, then perhaps citizens no
in the literary trades will understand that there is n
order in the world around us, that we must adapt our
selves to the requirements of chaos instead.

It is hard to adapt to chaos, but it can be done. I ar
living proof of that: It can be done.

◗ Adapting to chaos there in the cocktail lounge, I now
had Bonnie MacMahon, who was exactly as important a
anybody else in the Universe, bring more yeast excremen
to Beatrice Keedsler and Karabekian. Karabekian's drin
was a Beefeater's dry martini with a twist of lemon pee
so Bonnie said to him, "Breakfast of Champions."

"That's what you said when you brought me my firs
martini," said Karabekian.

"I say it every time I give anybody a martini," said onnie.

"Doesn't that get tiresome?" said Karabekian. "Or aybe that's why people found cities in Godforsaken laces like this—so they can make the same jokes over d over again, until the Bright Angel of Death stops eir mouths with ashes."

"I just try to cheer people up," said Bonnie. "If that's a rime, I never heard about it till now. I'll stop saying it om now on. I beg your pardon. I did not mean to give ffense."

Bonnie detested Karabekian, but she was as sweet as ie to him. She had a policy of never showing her anger bout anything there in the cocktail lounge. The largest art of her income by far came from tips, and the way to t big tips was to smile, smile, smile, no matter what. onnie had only two goals in life now. She meant to re- up all the money her husband had lost in the car wash Shepherdstown, and she ached to have steel-belted dial tires for the front wheels of her automobile.

Her husband, meanwhile, was at home watching pro-ssional golfers on television, and getting smashed on east excrement.

Saint Anthony, incidentally, was an Egyptian who unded the very first monastery, which was a place here men could live simple lives and pray often to the reator of the Universe, without the distractions of ambi-on and sex and yeast excrement. Saint Anthony himself ld everything he had when he was young, and he went t into the wilderness and lived alone for twenty years. He was often tempted during all those years of perfect

solitude by visions of good times he might have had wi
food and men and women and children and the marke
place and so on.

His biographer was another Egyptian, Saint Athan
sius, whose theories on the Trinity, the Incarnation, an
the divinity of the Holy Spirit, set down three hundre
years after the murder of Christ, were considered val
by Catholics even in Dwayne Hoover's time.

The Catholic high school in Midland City, in fact, w
named in honor of Saint Athanasius. It was named
honor of Saint Christopher at first, but then the Pop
who was head of Catholic churches everywhere, a
nounced that there probably never had been a Sai
Christopher, so people shouldn't honor him anymore.

◗ A black male dishwasher stepped out of the kitchen
the Inn now for a Pall Mall cigarette and some fresh a
He wore a large button on his sweat-soaked white T-shi
which said this:

There were bowls of such buttons around the Inn, for anybody to help himself to, and the dishwasher had taken one in a spirit of levity. He had no use for works of art, except for cheap and simple ones which weren't meant to live very long. His name was Eldon Robbins, and he had penis nine inches long and two inches in diameter.

Eldon Robbins, too, had spent time in the Adult Correctional Institution, so it was easy for him to recognize Wayne Hoobler, out among the garbage cans, as a new parolee. "Welcome to the real world, Brother," he said gently and with wry lovingness to Wayne. "When was the last time you ate? This mornin'?"

Wayne shyly acknowledged that this was true. So Eldon took him through a kitchen to a long table where the kitchen staff ate. There was a television set back there, and it was on, and it showed Wayne the beheading of Queen Mary of Scotland. Everybody was all dressed up, and Queen Mary put her head on the block of her own accord.

Eldon arranged for Wayne to get a free steak and mashed potatoes and gravy and anything else he wanted, all prepared by other black men in the kitchen. There was a bowl of Arts Festival buttons on the table, and Eldon made Wayne put one on before he ate. "Wear this at all times," he told Wayne gravely, "and no harm can come to you."

Eldon revealed to Wayne a peephole, which kitchen workers had drilled through the wall and into the cocktail lounge. "When you get tarred of watchin' television," he said, "you can watch the animals in the zoo."

Eldon himself had a look through the peephole, told

Wayne that there was a man seated at the piano bar who
had been paid fifty thousand dollars for sticking a piece
of yellow tape to a green piece of canvas. He insisted that
Wayne take a *good* look at Karabekian. Wayne obeyed.

And Wayne wanted to remove his eye from the peep
hole after a few seconds, because he didn't have nearly
enough background information for any sort of understanding of what was going on in the cocktail lounge. The
candles puzzled him, for instance. He supposed that the
electricity in there had failed, and that somebody had
gone to change a fuse. Also, he did not know what to
make of Bonnie MacMahon's costume, which consisted of
white cowboy boots and black net stockings with crimson
garters plainly showing across several inches of bare
thigh, and a tight sequin sort of bathing suit with a puff
of pink cotton pinned to its rear.

Bonnie's back was to Wayne, so he could not see that
she wore octagonal, rimless trifocals, and was a horse-
faced woman forty-two years old. He could not see
either, that she was smiling, smiling, smiling, no matter
how insulting Karabekian became. He could read Karabekian's lips, however. He was good at reading lips, as
was anyone who had spent any time in Shepherdstown.
The rule of silence was enforced in the corridors and at
meals in Shepherdstown.

◗ Karabekian was saying this to Bonnie, indicating Beatrice Keedsler with a wave of his hand: "This distinguished lady is a famous storyteller, and also a native of
this railroad junction. Perhaps you could tell her some
recent true stories about her birthplace."

"I don't know any," said Bonnie.

"Oh come now," said Karabekian. "Every human being in this room must be worth a great novel." He pointed at Dwayne Hoover. "What is the life story of that man?"

Bonnie limited herself to telling about Dwayne's dog, Sparky, who couldn't wag his tail. "So he has to fight all the time," she said.

"Wonderful," said Karabekian. He turned to Beatrice. "I'm sure you can use that somewhere."

"As a matter of fact, I can," said Beatrice. "That's an enchanting detail."

"The more details the better," said Karabekian. "Thank God for novelists. Thank God there are people willing to write everything down. Otherwise, so much would be forgotten!" He begged Bonnie for more true stories.

Bonnie was deceived by his enthusiasm and energized by the idea that Beatrice Keedsler honestly needed true stories for her books. "Well—" she said, "would you consider Shepherdstown part of Midland City, more or less?"

"Of course," said Karabekian, who had never heard of Shepherdstown. "What would Midland City be without Shepherdstown? And what would Shepherdstown be without Midland City?"

"Well—" said Bonnie, and she thought she had what was maybe a really good story to tell, "my husband is a guard at the Shepherdstown Adult Correctional Institution, and he used to have to keep people who were going to be electrocuted company—back when they used to electrocute people all the time. He'd play cards with them, or read parts of the Bible out loud to them, or whatever they wanted to do, and he had to keep a white man named Leroy Joyce company."

Bonnie's costume gave off a faint, fishy, queer glow as she spoke. This was because her garments were heavily

impregnated with fluorescent chemicals. So was the bar
tender's jacket. So were the African masks on the walls.
The chemicals would shine like electric signs when
ultraviolet lights in the ceiling were energized. The lights
weren't on just now. The bartender turned them on at
random times, at his own whim, in order to give the cus
tomers a delightful and mystifying surprise.

The power for the lights and for everything electrical
in Midland City, incidentally, was generated by coal from
strip mines in West Virginia, through which Kilgore
Trout had passed not many hours before.

♦ "Leroy Joyce was so dumb," Bonnie went on, "he
couldn't play cards. He couldn't understand the Bible. He
could hardly talk. He ate his last supper, and then he sat
still. He was going to be electrocuted for rape. So my
husband sat out in the corridor outside the cell, and he
read to himself. He heard Leroy moving around in his
cell, but he didn't worry about it. And then Leroy rattled
his tin cup on the bars. My husband thought Leroy
wanted some more coffee. So he got up and went over and
took the cup. Leroy was smiling as though everything
was all right now. He wouldn't have to go to the electric
chair after all. He'd cut off his whatchamacallit and put it
in the cup."

♦ This book is made up, of course, but the story I had
Bonnie tell actually happened in real life—in the death
house of a penitentiary in Arkansas.

As for Dwayne Hoover's dog Sparky, who couldn't wag
his tail: Sparky is modeled after a dog my brother owns.

ho has to fight all the time, because he can't wag his
il. There really *is* such a dog.

Rabo Karabekian asked Bonnie MacMahon to tell him
mething about the teen-age girl on the cover of the
rogram for the Festival of the Arts. This was the only
iternationally famous human being in Midland City. She
as Mary Alice Miller, the Women's Two Hundred
Ieter Breast Stroke Champion of the World. She was
ily fifteen, said Bonnie.

Mary Alice was also the Queen of the Festival of the
rts. The cover of the program showed her in a white
athing suit, with her Olympic Gold Medal hanging
round her neck. The medal looked like this:

Mary Alice was smiling at a picture of Saint Sebastian,
the Spanish painter El Greco. It had been loaned to
.e Festival by Eliot Rosewater, the patron of Kilgore
rout. Saint Sebastian was a Roman soldier who had
ved seventeen hundred years before me and Mary Alice

Miller and Wayne and Dwayne and all the rest of us. I
had secretly become a Christian when Christianity w.
against the law.

And somebody squealed on him. The Emperor Dioc
tian had him shot by archers. The picture Mary Ali
smiled at with such uncritical bliss showed a huma
being who was so full of arrows that he looked like
porcupine.

Something almost nobody knew about Saint Sebastia
incidentally, since painters liked to put so many arrov
into him, was that he survived the incident. He actuall
got well.

He walked around Rome praising Christianity and bac
mouthing the Emperor, so he was sentenced to death
second time. He was beaten to death by rods.

And so on.

And Bonnie MacMahon told Beatrice and Karabekia
that Mary Alice's father, who was a member of the Paro
Board out at Shepherdstown, had taught Mary Alice
swim when she was eight months old, and that he ha
made her swim at least four hours a day, every day, sin
she was three.

Rabo Karabekian thought this over, and then he sa
loudly, so a lot of people could hear him, "What kind of
man would turn his daughter into an outboard motor?"

⬥ And now comes the spiritual climax of this book, for
is at this point that I, the author, am suddenly tran
formed by what I have done so far. This is why I ha
gone to Midland City: to be born again. And Chaos a
nounced that it was about to give birth to a new me I
putting these words in the mouth of Rabo Karabekia

What kind of a man would turn his daughter into an outboard motor?"

Such a small remark was able to have such thundering consequences because the spiritual matrix of the cocktail lounge was in what I choose to call a *pre-earthquake condition.* Terrific forces were at work on our souls, but they could do no work, because they balanced one another so nicely.

But then a grain of sand crumbled. One force had a sudden advantage over another, and spiritual continents began to shrug and heave.

One force, surely, was the lust for money which invested so many people in the cocktail lounge. They knew what Rabo Karabekian had been paid for his painting, and they wanted fifty thousand dollars, too. They could have a lot of fun with fifty thousand dollars, or so they believed. But they had to earn money the hard way, just a few dollars at a time, instead. It wasn't right.

Another force was the fear in these same people that their lives might be ridiculous, that their entire city might be ridiculous. Now the worst had happened: Mary Alice Miller, the one thing about their city which they had supposed was ridicule-proof had just been lazily ridiculed by a man from out-of-town.

And my own pre-earthquake condition must be taken into consideration, too, since I was the one who was being reborn. Nobody else in the cocktail lounge was reborn, as far as I know. The rest got their minds changed, some of them, about the value of modern art.

As for myself: I had come to the conclusion that there was nothing sacred about myself or about any human being, that we were all machines, doomed to collide and collide and collide. For want of anything better to do, we became fans of collisions. Sometimes I wrote well about collisions, which meant I was a writing machine in good repair. Sometimes I wrote badly, which meant I was writing machine in bad repair. I no more harbored sacredness than did a Pontiac, a mousetrap, or a South Bend Lathe.

I did not expect Rabo Karabekian to rescue me. I had created him, and he was in my opinion a vain and weak and trashy man, no artist at all. But it is Rabo Karabekian who made me the serene Earthling which I am this day.

Listen:

"What kind of a man would turn his daughter into an outboard motor?" he said to Bonnie MacMahon.

Bonnie MacMahon blew up. This was the first time she had blown up since she had come to work in the cocktail lounge. Her voice became as unpleasant as the noise of bandsaw's cutting galvanized tin. It was *loud*, too. "Oh yeah?" she said. "Oh yeah?"

Everybody froze. Bunny Hoover stopped playing the piano Nobody wanted to miss a word.

"You don't think much of Mary Alice Miller?" she said. "Well, we don't think much of your painting. I've seen better pictures done by a five-year-old."

Karabekian slid off his barstool so he could face all those enemies standing up. He certainly surprised me. expected him to retreat in a hail of olives, maraschino cherries and lemon rinds. But he was majestic up there. "Listen—" he said so calmly, "I have read the editorial against my painting in your wonderful newspaper. I have read every word of the hate mail you have been thoughtful enough to send to New York."

This embarrassed people some.

"The painting did not exist until I made it," Karabekian ent on. "Now that it does exist, nothing would make me ppier than to have it reproduced again and again, and stly improved upon, by all the five-year-olds in town. I ould love for your children to find pleasantly and play- lly what it took me many angry years to find.

"I now give you my word of honor," he went on, "that e picture your city owns shows everything about e which truly matters, with nothing left out. It is a cture of the awareness of every animal. It is the imma- rial core of every animal—the 'I am' to which all mes- ges are sent. It is all that is alive in any of us—in a ouse, in a deer, in a cocktail waitress. It is unwavering d pure, no matter what preposterous adventure may fall us. A sacred picture of Saint Anthony alone is one rtical, unwavering band of light. If a cockroach were ar him, or a cocktail waitress, the picture would show vo such bands of light. Our awareness is all that is alive d maybe sacred in any of us. Everything else about us dead machinery.

"I have just heard from this cocktail waitress here, this rtical band of light, a story about her husband and an iot who was about to be executed at Shepherdstown. ery well—let a five-year-old paint a sacred interpreta- on of that encounter. Let that five-year-old strip away e idiocy, the bars, the waiting electric chair, the uni- rm of the guard, the gun of the guard, the bones and at of the guard. What is that perfect picture which any e-year-old can paint? Two unwavering bands of light."

Ecstasy bloomed on the barbaric face of Rabo Kara- kian. "Citizens of Midland City, I salute you," he said. You have given a home to a masterpiece!"

Kurt Vonnegut

▶ Dwayne Hoover, incidentally, wasn't taking any of th
in. He was still hypnotized, turned inward. He was thin
ing about moving fingers writing and moving on, and s
forth. He had bats in his bell tower. He was off his rocke
He wasn't playing with a full deck of cards.

Chapter 20

⬇

While my life was being renewed by the words of Rabo Karabekian, Kilgore Trout found himself standing on the shoulder of the Interstate, gazing across Sugar Creek in its concrete trough at the new Holiday Inn. There were no bridges across the creek. He would have to wade.

So he sat down on a guardrail, removed his shoes and socks, rolled his pantlegs to his knees. His bared shins were rococo with varicose veins and scars. So were the shins of my father when he was an old, old man.

Kilgore Trout had my father's shins. They were a present from me. I gave him my father's feet, too, which were long and narrow and sensitive. They were azure. They were artistic feet.

Trout lowered his artistic feet into the concrete trough

containing Sugar Creek. They were coated at once with clear plastic substance from the surface of the creek When, in some surprise, Trout lifted one coated foot from the water, the plastic substance dried in air instantly sheathed his foot in a thin, skin-tight bootie resembling mother-of-pearl. He repeated the process with his other foot.

The substance was coming from the Barrytron plant The company was manufacturing a new anti-personnel bomb for the Air Force. The bomb scattered plastic pellets instead of steel pellets, because the plastic pellets were cheaper. They were also impossible to locate in the bodies of wounded enemies by means of x-ray machines.

Barrytron had no idea it was dumping this waste into Sugar Creek. They had hired the Maritimo Brothers Construction Company, which was gangster-controlled, to build a system which would get rid of the waste. They knew the company was gangster-controlled. Everybody knew that. But the Maritimo Brothers were usually the best builders in town. They had built Dwayne Hoover's house, for instance, which was a solid house.

But every so often they would do something amazingly criminal. The Barrytron disposal system was a case in point. It was expensive, and it appeared to be complicated and busy. Actually, though, it was old junk hooked up every which way, concealing a straight run of stolen sewer pipe running directly from Barrytron to Sugar Creek.

Barrytron would be absolutely sick when it learned what a polluter it had become. Throughout its history, it had attempted to be a perfect model of corporate good citizenship, no matter what it cost.

Trout now crossed Sugar Creek on my father's legs and et, and those appendages became more nacreous with very wading stride. He carried his parcels and his shoes nd socks on his head, although the water scarcely ached his kneecaps.

He knew how ridiculous he looked. He expected to be eceived abominably, dreamed of embarrassing the Festi-al to death. He had come all this distance for an orgy of asochism. He wanted to be treated like a cockroach.

His situation, insofar as he was a machine, was com-lex, tragic, and laughable. But the sacred part of him, is awareness, remained an unwavering band of light.

And this book is being written by a meat machine in ooperation with a machine made of metal and plastic. he plastic, incidentally, is a close relative of the gunk in ugar Creek. And at the core of the writing meat machine something sacred, which is an unwavering band of ght.

At the core of each person who reads this book is a and of unwavering light.

My doorbell has just rung in my New York apartment. nd I know what I will find when I open my front door: n unwavering band of light.

God bless Rabo Karabekian!

Listen: Kilgore Trout climbed out of the trough and nto the asphalt desert which was the parking lot. It was is plan to enter the lobby of the Inn on wet bare feet, to ave footprints on the carpet—like this:

It was Trout's fantasy that somebody would be ou[t]
raged by the footprints. This would give him the oppo[r]
tunity to reply grandly, "What is it that offends you so? [I]
am simply using man's first printing press. You are rea[d]
ing a bold and universal headline which says, 'I am her[e,]
I am here, I am here.'"

⏵ But Trout was no walking printing press. His feet le[ft]
no marks on the carpet, because they were sheathed

astic and the plastic was dry. Here was the structure of
e plastic molecule:

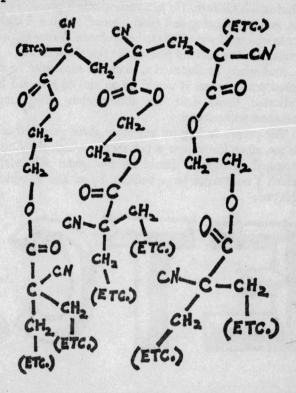

The molecule went on and on and on, repeating itself
rever to form a sheet both tough and poreless.

This molecule was the monster Dwayne's twin step-
others, Lyle and Kyle, had attacked with their auto-
atic shotguns. This was the same stuff which was fuck-
g up Sacred Miracle Cave.

♦ The man who told me how to diagram a segment of molecule of plastic was Professor Walter H. Stockmayer Dartmouth College. He is a distinguished physical chem ist, and an amusing and useful friend of mine. I did n make him up. I would like to be Professor Walter H. Stoc mayer. He is a brilliant pianist. He skis like a dream.

And when he sketched a plausible molecule, he ind cated points where it would go on and on just as I hav indicated them—with an abbreviation which mea sameness without end.

The proper ending for any story about people it seer to me, since life is now a polymer in which the Earth wrapped so tightly, should be that same abbreviatio which I now write large because I feel like it, which this one:

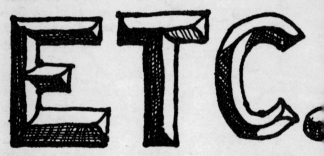

♦ And it is in order to acknowledge the continuity of t polymer that I begin so many sentences with "And" a "So," and end so many paragraphs with "... and so on."

And so on.

"It's all like an ocean!" cried Dostoevski. I say it's like cellophane.

So Trout entered the lobby as an inkless printing press, but he was still the most grotesque human being who had ever come in there.

All around him were what other people called *mirrors*, which he called *leaks*. The entire wall which separated the lobby from the cocktail lounge was a *leak* ten feet high and thirty-feet long. There was another *leak* on the cigarette machine and yet another on the candy machine. And when Trout looked through them to see what was going on in the other universe, he saw a red-eyed, filthy old creature who was barefoot, who had his pants rolled up to his knees.

As it happened, the only other person in the lobby at the time was the beautiful young desk clerk, Milo Maritimo. Milo's clothing and skin and eyes were all the colors that olives can be. He was a graduate of the Cornell Hotel School. He was the homosexual grandson of Guillermo "Little Willie" Maritimo, a bodyguard of the notorious Chicago gangster, Al Capone.

Trout presented himself to this harmless man, stood before his desk with his bare feet far apart and his arms outspread. "The Abominable Snowman has arrived," he said to Milo. "If I'm not as clean as most abominable snowmen are, it is because I was kidnapped as a child from the slopes of Mount Everest, and taken as a slave to a bordello in Rio de Janeiro, where I have been cleaning the unspeakably filthy toilets for the past fifty years. A visitor to our whipping room there screamed in a transport of agony and ecstasy that there was to be an arts festival in Midland City. I escaped down a rope of sheets taken from a reeking hamper. I have come to Midland City to have myself acknowledged, before I die, as the great artist I believe myself to be."

Milo Maritimo greeted Trout with luminous adoration. "Mr. Trout," he said in rapture, "I'd know you anywhere. Welcome to Midland City. We *need* you so!"

"How do you know who I am?" said Kilgore Trout. Nobody had ever known who he was before.

"You *had* to be you," said Milo.

Trout was deflated—*neutralized*. He dropped his arms, became child-like now. "Nobody ever knew who I was before," he said.

"I know," said Milo. "We have discovered you, and we hope you will discover us. No longer will Midland City be known merely as the home of Mary Alice Miller, the Women's Two Hundred Meter Breast Stroke Champion of the World. It will also be the city which first acknowledged the greatness of Kilgore Trout."

Trout simply walked away from the desk and sat down on a brocaded Spanish-style settee. The entire lobby, except for the vending machines, was done in Spanish style.

Milo now used a line from a television show which had been popular a few years back. The show wasn't on the air anymore, but most people still remembered the line. Much of the conversation in the country consisted of lines from television shows, both present and past. The show Milo's line was from consisted of taking some old person, usually fairly famous, into what looked like an ordinary room, only it was actually a stage, with an audience out front and television cameras hidden all around. There were also people who had known the person in the older days hidden around. They would come out and tell anecdotes about the person later on.

Milo now said what the master of ceremonies would

have said to Trout, if Trout had been on the show and the curtain was going up: "Kilgore Trout! This is your life!"

♦ Only there wasn't any audience or curtain or any of that. And the truth was that Milo Maritimo was the only person in Midland City who knew anything about Kilgore Trout. It was wishful thinking on his part that the upper crust of Midland City was about to be as ga-ga as he was about the works of Kilgore Trout.

"We are so ready for a Renaissance, Mr. Trout! You will be our Leonardo!"

"How could you *possibly* have heard of me?" said Trout dazedly.

"In getting ready for the Midland City Renaissance," said Milo, "I made it my business to read everything I could by and about every artist who was on his way here."

"There isn't anything by me or about me anywhere," protested Trout.

Milo came from behind his desk. He brought with him what appeared to be a lopsided old softball, swaddled in many different sorts of tape. "When I couldn't find out anything about you," he said, "I wrote to Eliot Rosewater, the man who said we had to bring you here. He has a private collection of forty-one of your novels and sixty-three of your short stories, Mr. Trout. He let me read them all." He held out the seeming baseball, which was actually a book from Rosewater's collection. Rosewater used his science-fiction library hard. "This is the only book I haven't finished, and I'll finish it before the sun comes up tomorrow," said Milo.

◗ The novel in question, incidentally, was *The Sma
Bunny*. The leading character was a rabbit who lived li
all the other wild rabbits, but who was as intelligent :
Albert Einstein or William Shakespeare. It was a fema
rabbit. She was the only female leading character in ar
novel or story by Kilgore Trout.

She led a normal female rabbit's life, despite her ba
looning intellect. She concluded that her mind was us
less, that it was a sort of tumor, that it had no usefulne
within the rabbit scheme of things.

So she went hippity-hop, hippity-hop toward the cit
to have the tumor removed. But a hunter named Dudle
Farrow shot and killed her before she got there. Farro
skinned her and took out her guts, but then he and h
wife Grace decided that they had better not eat her b
cause of her unusually large head. They thought what sl
had thought when she was alive—that she must be di
eased.

And so on.

◗ Kilgore Trout had to change into his only other ga
ments, his high school tuxedo and his new evening shi
and all, right away. The lower parts of his rolled-up tro
sers had become impregnated with the plastic substan
from the creek, so he couldn't roll them down again. The
were as stiff as flanges on sewer pipes.

So Milo Maritimo showed him to his suite, which w
two ordinary Holiday Inn rooms with a door betwee
them open. Trout and every distinguished visitor had
suite, with two color television sets, two tile baths, fo
double beds equipped with *Magic Fingers*. Magic Finge
were electric vibrators attached to the mattress springs

bed. If a guest put a quarter into a little box on his dside table, the Magic Fingers would jiggle his bed.

There were enough flowers in Trout's room for a atholic gangster's funeral. They were from Fred T. rry, the Chairman of the Arts Festival, and from the idland City Association of Women's Clubs, and from e Chamber of Commerce, and on and on.

Trout read a few of the cards on the flowers, and he mmented, "The town certainly seems to be getting be- nd the arts in a great big way."

Milo closed his olive eyes tight, wincing with a tangy ony. "It's *time*. Oh God, Mr. Trout, we were starving for long, without even knowing what we were hungering r," he said. This young man was not only a descendant master criminals, he was a close relative of felons erating in Midland City at the present time. The part- rs in the Maritimo Brothers Construction Company, for stance, were his uncles. Gino Maritimo, Milo's first usin once removed, was the dope king of the city.

"Oh, Mr. Trout," nice Milo went on, there in Trout's ite, "teach us to sing and dance and laugh and cry. e've tried to survive so long on money and sex and envy d real estate and football and basketball and automo- es and television and alcohol—on sawdust and broken ass!"

"Open your eyes!" said Trout bitterly. "Do I look like a ncer, a singer, a man of joy?" He was wearing his tux- o now. It was a size too large for him. He had lost ch weight since high school. His pockets were crammed th mothballs. They bulged like saddlebags.

"Open your eyes!" said Trout. "Would a man nourished

by beauty look like this? You have nothing but desolati●
and desperation here, you say? I bring you more of t●
same!"

"My eyes *are* open," said Milo warmly, "and I see e●
actly what I *expect* to see. I see a man who is terrib●
wounded—because he has dared to pass through the fir●
of truth to the other side, which we have never seen. A●
then he has come back again—to tell us about the oth●
side."

◗ And I sat there in the new Holiday Inn, and made ●
disappear, then appear again, then disappear, then a●
pear again. Actually, there was nothing but a big op●
field there. A farmer had put it into rye.

It was high time, I thought, for Trout to meet Dway●
Hoover, for Dwayne to run amok.

I knew how this book would end. Dwayne would hu●
a lot of people. He would bite off one joint of the rig●
index finger of Kilgore Trout.

And then Trout, with his wound dressed, would wa●
out into the unfamiliar city. He would meet his Creat●
who would explain everything.

Chapter 21

ilgore Trout entered the cocktail lounge. His feet were
y hot. They were encased not only in shoes and socks,
in clear plastic, too. They could not sweat, they could
breathe.

abo Karabekian and Beatrice Keedsler did not see
come in. They were surrounded by new affectionate
nds at the piano bar. Karabekian's speech had been
ndidly received. Everybody agreed now that Midland
had one of the greatest paintings in the world.

All you had to do was explain," said Bonnie Mac-
on. "I understand now."

I didn't think there was anything *to* explain," said
lo Maritimo, the builder, wonderingly. "But there
, by God."

be Cohen, the jeweler, said to Karabekian, "If artists

would explain more, people would like art more. You
alize that?"

And so on.

Trout was feeling spooky. He thought maybe a lot
people were going to greet him as effusively as M
Maritimo had done, and he had had no experience w
celebrations like that. But nobody got in his way. His
friend Anonymity was by his side again, and the two
them chose a table near Dwayne Hoover and me. All
could see of me was the reflection of candle flames in
mirrored glasses, in my *leaks*.

Dwayne Hoover was still mentally absent from acti
ties in the cocktail lounge. He sat like a lump of n
putty, staring at something long ago and far away.

Dwayne moved his lips as Trout sat down. He v
saying this soundlessly, and it had nothing to do w
Trout or me: "Goodbye, Blue Monday."

♦ Trout had a fat manila envelope with him. Milo M
timo had given it to him. It contained a program for
Festival of the Arts, a letter of welcome to Trout fr
Fred T. Barry, the Chairman of the Festival, a timeta
of events during the coming week—and some ot
things.

Trout also carried a copy of his novel *Now It Can*
Told. This was the wide-open beaver book wh
Dwayne Hoover would soon take so seriously.

So there the three of us were. Dwayne and Trout an
could have been included in an equilateral triangle ab
twelve feet on a side.

As three unwavering bands of light, we were sim
and separate and beautiful. As machines, we were fla

s of ancient plumbing and wiring, of rusty hinges and ble springs. And our interrelationships were Byzantine. After all, I had created both Dwayne and Trout, and w Trout was about to drive Dwayne into full-blown anity, and Dwayne would soon bite off the tip of out's finger.

Wayne Hoobler was watching us through a peephole in kitchen. There was a tap on his shoulder. The man o had fed him now told him to leave.

So he wandered outdoors, and he found himself among ayne's used cars again. He resumed his conversation h the traffic on the Interstate.

The bartender in the cocktail lounge now flicked on the raviolet lights in the ceiling. Bonnie MacMahon's uni-m, since it was impregnated with fluorescent materials, up like an electric sign.

So did the bartender's jacket and the African masks on walls.

So did Dwayne Hoover's shirt, and the shirts of several er men. The reason was this: Those shirts had been ndered in washday products which contained fluores-t materials. The idea was to make clothes look ghter in sunlight by making them actually fluorescent. When the same clothes were viewed in a dark room der ultraviolet light, however, they became ridicu-sly bright.

Bunny Hoover's teeth also lit up, since he used a tooth-te containing fluorescent materials, which was sup-sed to make his smile look brighter in daylight. He

grinned now, and he appeared to have a mouthful of lit
Christmas tree lights.

But the brightest new light in the room by far was t
bosom of Kilgore Trout's new evening shirt. Its brilliar
twinkled and had depth. It might have been the top o
slumping, open sack of radioactive diamonds.

But then Trout hunched forward involuntarily, buc
ling the starched shirt bosom, forming it into a parabo
dish. This made a searchlight of the shirt. Its beam w
aimed at Dwayne Hoover.

The sudden light roused Dwayne from his trance. I
thought perhaps he had died. At any rate, somethi
painless and supernatural was going on. Dwayne smi
trustingly at the holy light. He was ready for anything.

◗ Trout had no explanation for the fantastic transform
tion of certain garments around the room. Like mc
science-fiction writers, he knew almost nothing abo
science. He had no more use for solid information th
did Rabo Karabekian. So now he could only be flabb
gasted.

My own shirt, being an old one which had be
washed many times in a Chinese laundry which us
ordinary soap, did not fluoresce.

Dwayne Hoover now lost himself in the bosom
Trout's shirt, just as he had earlier lost himself in twi
kling beads of lemon oil. He remembered now a thing I
stepfather had told him when he was only ten years o
which was this: Why there were no Niggers in She
herdstown.

This was not a completely irrelevant recollectio
Dwayne had, after all, been talking to Bonnie Ma

hon, whose husband had lost so much money in a car
sh in Shepherdstown. And the main reason the car
sh had failed was that successful car washes needed
eap and plentiful labor, which meant black labor—and
re were no Niggers in Shepherdstown.

"Years ago," Dwayne's stepfather told Dwayne when
ayne was ten, "Niggers was coming up north by the
lions—to Chicago, to Midland City, to Indianapolis,
Detroit. The World War was going on. There was such
abor shortage that even Niggers who couldn't read or
ite could get good factory jobs. Niggers had money like
y never had before.

"Over at Shepherdstown, though," he went on, "the
ite people got smart quick. They didn't want Niggers
their town, so they put up signs on the main roads at
city limits and in the railroad yard." Dwayne's step-
her described the signs, which looked like this:

NIGGER! THIS IS
SHEPHERDSTOWN
GOD HELP YOU IF
THE SUN EVER
SETS ON YOU
HERE!

"One night—" Dwayne's stepfather said, "a Nig
family got off a boxcar in Shepherdstown. Maybe t
didn't see the sign. Maybe they couldn't read it. May
they couldn't believe it." Dwayne's stepfather was out
work when he told the story so gleefully. The Great I
pression had just begun. He and Dwayne were on
weekly expedition in the family car, hauling garbage a
trash out into the country, where they dumped it all
Sugar Creek.

"Anyway, they moved into an empty shack that nig
Dwayne's stepfather went on. "They got a fire going
the stove and all. So a mob went down there at midnig
They took out the man, and they sawed him in two on
top strand of a barbed-wire fence." Dwayne remember
clearly that a rainbow of oil from the trash was spread
prettily over the surface of Sugar Creek when he he
that.

"Since that night, which was a long time ago now,"
stepfather said, "there ain't been a Nigger even spend
night in Shepherdstown."

◆ Trout was itchingly aware that Dwayne was staring
his bosom so loonily. Dwayne's eyes swam, and Tr
supposed they were swimming in alcohol. He could
know that Dwayne was seeing an oil slick on Sugar Cr
which had made rainbows forty long years ago.

Trout was aware of me, too, what little he could see
me. I made him even more uneasy than Dwayne did. 7
thing was: Trout was the only character I ever crea
who had enough imagination to suspect that he might
the creation of another human being. He had spoken
this possibility several times to his parakeet. He had sa

instance, "Honest to God, Bill, the way things are
g, all I can think of is that I'm a character in a book
somebody who wants to write about somebody who
rs all the time."

ow Trout was beginning to catch on that he was sit-
very close to the person who had created him. He
embarrassed. It was hard for him to know how to
ond, particularly since his responses were going to be
thing I said they were.

went easy on him, didn't wave, didn't stare. I kept my
ses on. I wrote again on my tabletop, scrawled the
bols for the interrelationship between matter and
rgy as it was understood in my day:

$$E = Mc^2$$

was a flawed equation, as far as I was concerned.
re should have been an "A" in there somewhere for
reness—without which the "E" and the "M" and the
which was a mathematical constant, could not exist.

ll of us were stuck to the surface of a ball, inci-
tally. The planet was ball-shaped. Nobody knew why
didn't fall off, even though everybody pretended to
l of understand it.

he really smart people understood that one of the best
s to get rich was to own a part of the surface people
to stick to.

▶ Trout dreaded eye contact with either Dwayne or
so he went through the contents of the manila envel
which had been waiting for him in his suite.

The first thing he examined was a letter from Free
Barry, the Chairman of the Festival of the Arts, the de
of the Mildred Barry Memorial Center for the Arts,
the founder and Chairman of the Board of Director
Barrytron, Ltd.

Clipped to the letter was one share of common st
in Barrytron, made out in the name of Kilgore Tr
Here was the letter:

"Dear Mr. Trout:" it said, "It is a pleasure and an ho
to have such a distinguished and creative person give
precious time to Midland City's first Festival of the A
It is our wish that you feel like a member of our fan
while you are here. To give you and other distinguis
visitors a deeper sense of participation in the life of
community, I am making a gift to each of you of
share in the company which I founded, the company
which I am now Chairman of the Board. It is not only
company now, but yours as well.

"Our company began as The Robo-Magic Corporat
of America in 1934. It had three employees in the be
ning, and its mission was to design and manufacture
first fully automatic washing machine for use in
home. You will find the motto of that washing mach
on the corporate emblem at the top of the stock cer
cate."

The emblem consisted of a Greek goddess on an or
chaise longue. She held a flagstaff from which a long p
nant streamed. Here is what the pennant said:

The motto of the old Robo-Magic washing machine verly confused two separate ideas people had about nday. One idea was that women traditionally did their ndry on Monday. Monday was simply washday, and an especially depressing day on that account.

People who had horrible jobs during the week used to l Monday "Blue Monday" sometimes, though, because ey hated to return to work after a day of rest. When ed T. Barry made up the Robo-Magic motto as a young n, he pretended that Monday was called "Blue Mon-/" because doing the laundry disgusted and exhausted men.

The Robo-Magic was going to cheer them up.

It wasn't true, incidentally, that most women did their ndry on Monday at the time the Robo-Magic was in-ated. They did it any time they felt like it. One of vayne Hoover's clearest recollections from the Great pression, for instance, was when his stepmother de-ed to do the laundry on Christmas Eve. She was bitter

about the low estate to which the family had fallen, a
she suddenly clumped down into the basement, do
among the black beetles and the millipedes, and did
laundry.

"Time to do the Nigger work," she said.

▶ Fred T. Barry began advertising the Robo-Magic
1933, long before there was a reliable machine to s
And he was one of the few persons in Midland City w
could afford billboard advertising during the Great I
pression, so the Robo-Magic sales message did not h
to jostle and shriek for attention. It was practically
only symbol in town.

One of Fred's ads was on a billboard outside the m.
gate of the defunct Keedsler Automobile Compa
which the Robo-Magic Corporation had taken over.
showed a high society woman in a fur coat and pea
She was leaving her mansion for a pleasant afternoon
idleness, and a balloon was coming out of her mou
These were the words in the balloon:

OFF TO THE BRIDGE
CLUB WHILE MY
ROBO-MAGIC
DOES THE WASH!
GOODBYE, BLUE
MONDAY!

Another ad, which was painted on a billboard by the
lroad depot, showed two white deliverymen who were
nging a Robo-Magic into a house. A black maid was
tching them. Her eyes were popping out in a comical
iy. There was a balloon coming out of her mouth, too,
d she was saying this:

FEETS, GET MOVIN'! DEY'S GOT THEIRSELVES A ROBO-MAGIC! DEY AIN'T GONNA BE NEEDIN' US 'ROUN' HERE NO MO'!

Fred T. Barry wrote these ads himself, and he pre-
:ted at the time that Robo-Magic appliances of various
ts would eventually do what he called "all the Nigger
rk of the world," which was lifting and cleaning and
king and washing and ironing and tending children
d dealing with filth.

Dwayne Hoover's stepmother wasn't the only white
man who was a terrible sport about doing work like
at. My own mother was that way, too, and so was my
ter, may she rest in peace. They both flatly refused to
Nigger work.

The white men wouldn't do it either, of course. They
led it *women's work,* and the women called it *Nigger
rk.*

Kurt Vonnegut

♦ I am going to make a wild guess now: I think that the end of the Civil War in my country frustrated the white people in the North, who won it, in a way which has never been acknowledged before. Their descendants inherited that frustration, I think, without ever knowing what it was.

The victors in that war were cheated out of the most desirable spoils of that war, which were human slaves.

♦ The Robo-Magic dream was interrupted by World War Two. The old Keedsler Automobile Works became an armory instead of an appliance factory. All that survived of the Robo-Magic itself was its brain, which had told the rest of the machine when to let the water in, when to let the water out, when to slosh, when to rinse, when to spin dry, and so on.

That brain became the nerve center of the so-called "BLINC System" during the Second World War. It was installed on heavy bombers, and it did the actual dropping of bombs after a bombardier pressed his bright red "bombs away" button. The button activated the BLINC System, which then released the bombs in such a way as to achieve a desired pattern of explosions on the plains below. "BLINC" was an abbreviation of "Blast Interval Normalization Computer."

Chapter 22

And I sat there in the cocktail lounge of the new Holiday Inn, watching Dwayne Hoover stare into the bosom
of the shirt of Kilgore Trout. I was wearing a bracelet
which looked like this:

WO1 stood for Warrant Officer First Class, which was
the rank of Jon Sparks.
The bracelet had cost me two dollars and a half. It was

a way of expressing my pity for the hundreds of Americans who had been taken prisoner during the war in Viet
Nam. Such bracelets were becoming popular. Each one
bore the name of an actual prisoner of war, his rank, and
the date of his capture.

Wearers of the bracelets weren't supposed to take them
off until the prisoners came home or were reported dead or
missing.

I wondered how I might fit my bracelet into my story,
and hit on the good idea of dropping it somewhere for
Wayne Hoobler to find.

Wayne would assume that it belonged to a woman who
loved somebody named WOl Jon Sparks, and that the
woman and WOl had become engaged or married or
something important on March 19th, 1971.

Wayne would mouth the unusual first name tentatively. "Woo-ee?" he would say. "Woe-ee? Woe-eye?
Woy?"

♦ There in the cocktail lounge, I gave Dwayne Hoover
credit for having taken a course in speed-reading at night
at the Young Men's Christian Association. This would enable him to read Kilgore Trout's novel in minutes instead
of hours.

♦ There in the cocktail lounge, I took a white pill which
a doctor said I could take in moderation, two a day, in
order not to feel blue.

♦ There in the cocktail lounge, the pill and the alcohol

ve me a terrific sense of urgency about explaining all
 things I hadn't explained yet, and then hurtling on
h my tale.

Let's see: I have already explained Dwayne's uncharac-
istic ability to read so fast. Kilgore Trout probably
ldn't have made his trip from New York City in the
e I allotted, but it's too late to bugger around with
t. Let it stand, let it stand!

Let's see, let's see. Oh, yes—I have to explain a jacket
ut will see at the hospital. It will look like this from
 back:

Here is the explanation: There used to be only one
ger high school in Midland City, and it was an all-
ger high school still. It was named after Crispus
ucks, a black man who was shot by British troops in
ston in 1770. There was an oil painting of this event in

the main corridor of the school. Several white peo
were stopping bullets, too. Crispus Attucks himself ha
hole in his forehead which looked like the front door o
birdhouse.

But the black people didn't call the school *Crispus
tucks High School* anymore. They called it *Innocent
stander High.*

And when another Nigger high school was built af
the Second World War, it was named after George Wa
ington Carver, a black man who was born into slave
but who became a famous chemist anyway. He disc
ered many remarkable new uses for peanuts.

But the black people wouldn't call that school by
proper name, either. On the day it opened, there w
already young black people wearing jackets which loo
like this from the back:

I have to explain, too, see, why so many black people in dland City were able to imitate birds from various ts of what used to be the British Empire. The thing s, see, that Fred T. Barry and his mother and father re almost the only people in Midland City who could ord to hire Niggers to do the Nigger work during the at Depression. They took over the old Keedsler Man- n, where Beatrice Keedsler, the novelist, had been born. ey had as many as twenty servants working there, all at e time.

Fred's father got so much money during the prosperity the twenties as a bootlegger and as a swindler in stocks l bonds. He kept all his money in cash, which turned to be a bright thing to do, since so many banks failed ring the Great Depression. Also: Fred's father was an nt for Chicago gangsters who wanted to buy legiti- te businesses for their children and grandchildren. rough Fred's father, those gangsters bought almost ry desirable property in Midland City for anything m a tenth to a hundredth of what it was really worth.

And before Fred's mother and father came to the ited States after the First World War, they were music l entertainers in England. Fred's father played the sical saw. His mother imitated birds from various ts of what was still the British Empire.

She went on imitating them for her own amusement, ll into the Great Depression. "The Bulbul of Malaysia," e would say, for instance, and then she would imitate t bird.

"The Morepark Owl of New Zealand," she would say, l then she would imitate that bird.

And all the black people who worked for her thought r act was the funniest thing they had ever seen, though

they never laughed out loud when she did it. And,
order to double up their friends and relatives with laug
ter, they, too, learned how to imitate the birds.

The craze spread. Black people who had never bee
near the Keedsler mansion could imitate the Lyre Bi
and the Willy Wagtail of Australia, the Golden Oriole
India, the Nightingale and the Chaffinch and the Wre
and the Chiffchaff of England itself.

They could even imitate the happy screech of the e
tinct companion of Kilgore Trout's island childhoo
which was the Bermuda Ern.

When Kilgore Trout hit town, the black people coul
still imitate those birds, and say word for word wh
Fred's mother had said before each imitation. If one
them imitated a Nightingale, for instance, he or sl
would say this first: "What adds peculiar beauty to tl
call of the Nightingale, much beloved by poets, is the fa
that it will *only* sing by moonlight."

And so on.

♦ There in the cocktail lounge, Dwayne Hoover's ba
chemicals suddenly decided that it was time for Dwayı
to demand from Kilgore Trout the secrets of life.

"Give me the message," cried Dwayne. He tottered u
from his own banquette, crashed down again next
Trout, throwing off heat like a steam radiator. "The me
sage, please."

And here Dwayne did something extraordinarily ur
natural. He did it because I wanted him to. It was som
thing I had ached to have a character do for years ar
years. Dwayne did to Trout what the Duchess did
Alice in Lewis Carroll's *Alice's Adventures in Wonde*

nd. He rested his chin on poor Trout's shoulder, dug in ith his chin.

"The message?" he said, digging in his chin, digging in chin.

Trout made no reply. He had hoped to get through hat little remained of his life without ever having to uch another human being again. Dwayne's chin on his oulder was as shattering as buggery to Trout.

"Is this it? Is this it?" said Dwayne, snatching up rout's novel, *Now It Can Be Told.*

"Yes—that's it," croaked Trout. To his tremendous re- ef, Dwayne removed his chin from his shoulder.

Dwayne now began to read hungrily, as though starved r print. And the speed-reading course he had taken at e Young Men's Christian Association allowed him to ake a perfect pig of himself with pages and words.

"Dear Sir, poor sir, brave sir:" he read, "You are an xperiment by the Creator of the Universe. You are the ly creature in the entire Universe who has free will. ou are the only one who has to figure out what to do ext—and *why.* Everybody else is a robot, a machine.

"Some persons seem to like you, and others seem to ate you, and you must wonder why. They are simply king machines and hating machines.

"You are pooped and demoralized," read Dwayne. Vhy wouldn't you be? Of course it is exhausting, having reason all the time in a universe which wasn't meant to e reasonable."

Chapter 23

Dwayne Hoover read on: "You are surrounded by lo
ing machines, hating machines, greedy machines, un
selfish machines, brave machines, cowardly machine
truthful machines, lying machines, funny machines, so
emn machines," he read. "Their only purpose is to stir yo
up in every conceivable way, so the Creator of the Un
verse can watch your reactions. They can no more feel
reason than grandfather clocks.

"The Creator of the Universe would now like to apol
gize not only for the capricious, jostling companionship
provided during the test, but for the trashy, stinking con
dition of the planet itself. The Creator programmed ro
bots to abuse it for millions of years, so it would be
poisonous, festering cheese when you got here. Also, I
made sure it would be desperately crowded by program
ming robots, regardless of their living conditions, to cra

ual intercourse and adore infants more than almost
thing."

Mary Alice Miller, incidentally, the Women's Breast
oke Champion of the World and Queen of the Arts
stival, now passed through the cocktail lounge. She
.de a shortcut to the lobby from the side parking lot,
ere her father was waiting for her in his avocado 1970
mouth *Barracuda* fastback, which he had bought as a
.d car from Dwayne. It had a new car guarantee.
Mary Alice's father, Don Miller, was, among other
ngs, Chairman of the Parole Board at Shepherdstown.
was he who had decided that Wayne Hoobler, lurking
.ong Dwayne's used cars again, was fit to take his place
;ociety.
Mary Alice went into the lobby to get a crown and
pter for her performance as Queen at the Arts Festival
aquet that night. Milo Maritimo, the desk clerk, the
agster's grandson, had made them with his own two
ads. Her eyes were permanently inflamed. They looked
e maraschino cherries.
Only one person noticed her sufficiently to comment
: loud. He was Abe Cohen, the jeweler. He said this
out Mary Alice, despising her sexlessness and inno-
ace and empty mind: "Pure tuna fish!"

Kilgore Trout heard him say that—about pure tuna
. His mind tried to make sense of it. His mind was
amped with mysteries. He might as well have been
ayne Hoobler, adrift among Dwayne's used cars during
.waiian Week.

His feet, which were sheathed in plastic, were mea: while getting hotter all the time. The heat was pain now. His feet were curling and twisting, begging to plunged into cold water or waved in the air.

And Dwayne read on about himself and the Creator the Universe, to wit:

"He also programmed robots to write books and mag zines and newspapers for you, and television and rad shows, and stage shows, and films. They wrote songs you. The Creator of the Universe had them invent hu dreds of religions, so you would have plenty to choo among. He had them kill each other by the millions, this purpose only: that you be amazed. They have co mitted every possible atrocity and every possible kindn unfeelingly, automatically, inevitably, to get a reacti from Y-O-U."

This last word was set in extra-large type and had line all to itself, so it looked like this:

▶ "Every time you went into the library," said the bo "the Creator of the Universe held His breath. With suc higgledy-piggledy cultural smorgasbord before you, wh would you, with your free will, choose?"

"Your parents were fighting machines and self-pity machines," said the book. "Your mother was programm to bawl out your father for being a defective mon

naking machine, and your father was programmed to
awl her out for being a defective housekeeping machine.
They were programmed to bawl each other out for being
defective loving machines.

"Then your father was programmed to stomp out of the
ouse and slam the door. This automatically turned your
nother into a weeping machine. And your father would
o down to a tavern where he would get drunk with some
ther drinking machines. Then all the drinking machines
vould go to a whorehouse and rent fucking machines.
And then your father would drag himself home to be-
ome an apologizing machine. And your mother would
ecome a very slow forgiving machine."

Dwayne got to his feet now, having wolfed down tens
of thousands of words of such solipsistic whimsey in ten
ninutes or so.

He walked stiffly over to the piano bar. What made him
tiff was his awe of his own strength and righteousness.
Ie dared not use his full strength in merely walking, for
ear of destroying the new Holiday Inn with footfalls. He
lid not fear for his own life, Trout's book assured him
hat he had already been killed twenty-three times. On
ach occasion, the Creator of the Universe had patched
im up and got him going again.

Dwayne restrained himself in the name of elegance
ather than safety. He was going to respond to his new
understanding of life with finesse, for an audience of two
—himself and his Creator.

He approached his homosexual son.

Bunny saw the trouble coming, supposed it was death.
Ie might have protected himself easily with all the tech-

niques of fighting he had learned in military school. Bu
he chose to meditate instead. He closed his eyes, and hi
awareness sank into the silence of the unused lobes of hi
mind. This phosphorescent scarf floated by:

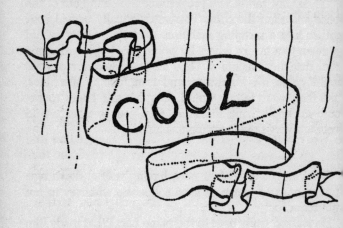

▶ Dwayne shoved Bunny's head from behind. He rolled i
like a cantaloupe up and down the keys of the piano bar
Dwayne laughed, and he called his son "... a God damn
cock-sucking machine!"

Bunny did not resist him, even though Bunny's fac
was being mangled horribly. Dwayne hauled his head
from the keys, slammed it down again. There was blood
on the keys—and spit, and mucus.

Rabo Karabekian and Beatrice Keedsler and Bonnie
MacMahon all grabbed Dwayne now, pulled him away
from Bunny. This increased Dwayne's glee. "Never hit a
woman, right?" he said to the Creator of the Universe.

He then socked Beatrice Keedsler on the jaw. He
nched Bonnie MacMahon in the belly. He honestly be-
ved that they were unfeeling machines.

"All you robots want to know why my wife ate
rāno?" Dwayne asked his thunderstruck audience. "I'll
ll you why: She was that kind of machine!"

There was a map of Dwayne's rampage in the paper
e next morning. The dotted line of his route started in
e cocktail lounge, crossed the asphalt to Francine
efko's office in his automobile agency, doubled back to
e new Holiday Inn again, then crossed Sugar Creek and
e Westbound lane of the Interstate to the median di-
der, which was grass. Dwayne was subdued on the
edian divider by two State Policemen who happened
.

Here is what Dwayne said to the policemen as they
ffed his hands behind his back: "Thank God you're
re!"

Dwayne didn't kill anybody on his rampage, but he
urt eleven people so badly they had to go to the hospi-
l. And on the map in the newspaper there was a mark
dicating each place where a person had been injured
riously. This was the mark, greatly enlarged:

▶ In the newspaper map of Dwayne's rampage, the[re] were three such crosses inside the cocktail lounge—[B]Bunny and Beatrice Keedsler and Bonnie MacMahon.

Then Dwayne ran out onto the asphalt between t[he] Inn and his used car lot. He yelled for Niggers out the[re,] telling them to come at once. "I want to talk to you," [he] said.

He was out there all alone. Nobody from the cockt[ail] lounge had followed him yet. Mary Alice Miller's fath[er,] Don Miller, was in his car near Dwayne, waiting f[or] Mary Alice to come back with her crown and scepter, b[ut] he never saw anything of the show Dwayne put on. H[is] car had seats whose backs could be made to lie flat. Th[ey] could be made into beds. Don was lying on his back, wi[th] his head well below window level, resting, staring at t[he] ceiling. He was trying to learn French by means of liste[n]ing to lessons recorded on tape.

"Demain nous allons passer la soirée au cinéma," sa[id] the tape, and Don tried to say it, too. "Nous espérons q[ue] notre grand-père vivra encore longtemps," said the tap[e.] And so on.

▶ Dwayne went on calling for Niggers to come talk [to] him. He smiled. He thought that the Creator of the U[ni]verse had programmed them all to hide, as a joke.

Dwayne glanced around craftily. Then he called out [a] signal he had used as a child to indicate that a game [of] hide-and-seek was over, that it was time for children [in] hiding to go home.

Here is what he called, and the sun was down when [he] called it: "Olly-olly-ox-in-freeeeeeeeeeeeeeeeeeeeeeeeeeeeee[ee]

The person who answered this incantation was a p[er]

n who had never played hide-and-seek in his life. It
as Wayne Hoobler, who came out from among the used
rs quietly. He clasped his hands behind his back and
aced his feet apart. He assumed the position known as
rade rest. This position was taught to soldiers and
isoners alike—as a way of demonstrating attentiveness,
llibility, respect, and voluntary defenselessness. He
as ready for anything, and wouldn't mind death.

"There you are," said Dwayne, and his eyes crinkled in
ttersweet amusement. He didn't know who Wayne was.
e welcomed him as a typical black robot. Any other
ack robot would have served as well. And Dwayne
;ain carried on a wry talk with the Creator of the Uni-
rse, using a robot as an unfeeling conversation piece. A
t of people in Midland City put useless objects from
awaii or Mexico or someplace like that on their coffee
bles or their livingroom end tables or on what-not
elves—and such an object was called a *conversation
ece*.

Wayne remained at parade rest while Dwayne told of
s year as a County Executive for the Boy Scouts of
merica, when more black young people were brought
to scouting than in any previous year. Dwayne told
'ayne about his efforts to save the life of a young black
an named Payton Brown, who, at the age of fifteen and
half, became the youngest person ever to die in the elec-
c chair at Shepherdstown. Dwayne rambled on about all
e black people he had hired when nobody else would
re black people, about how they never seemed to be able
get to work on time. He mentioned a few, too, who had
en energetic and punctual, and he winked at Wayne,
d he said this: "They were programmed that way."

He spoke of his wife and son again, acknowledged that

white robots were just like black robots, essentially, in that they were programmed to be whatever they were, to do whatever they did.

Dwayne was silent for a moment after that.

Mary Alice Miller's father was meanwhile continuing to learn conversational French while lying down in his automobile, only a few yards away.

And then Dwayne took a swing at Wayne. He meant to slap him hard with his open hand, but Wayne was very good at ducking. He dropped to his knees as the hand swished through the air where his face had been.

Dwayne laughed. "African dodger!" he said. This had reference to a sort of carnival booth which was popular when Dwayne was a boy. A black man would stick his head through a hole in a piece of canvas at the back of a booth, and people would pay money for the privilege of throwing hard baseballs at his head. If they hit his head, they won a prize.

⬥ So Dwayne thought that the Creator of the Universe had invited him to play a game of African dodger now. He became cunning, concealed his violent intentions with apparent boredom. Then he kicked at Wayne very suddenly.

Wayne dodged again, and had to dodge yet again almost instantly, as Dwayne advanced with quick combinations of intended kicks, slaps, and punches. And Wayne vaulted onto the bed of a very unusual truck, which had been built on the chassis of a 1962 Cadillac limousine. It had belonged to the Maritimo Brothers Construction Company.

Wayne's new elevation gave him a view past Dwayne

f both barrels of the Interstate, and of a mile or more of
Vill Fairchild Memorial Airport, which lay beyond. And
is important to understand at this point that Wayne
ad never seen an airport before, was unprepared for what
ould happen to an airport when a plane came in at night.

"That's all right, that's all right," Dwayne assured
Vayne. He was being a very good sport. He had no inten-
ion of climbing up on the truck for another swing at
Vayne. He was winded, for one thing. For another, he
nderstood that Wayne was a perfect dodging machine.
)nly a perfect hitting machine could hit him. "You're too
ood for me," said Dwayne.

So Dwayne backed away some, contented himself with
reaching up at Wayne. He spoke about human slavery—
ot only black slaves, but white slaves, too. Dwayne re-
arded coal miners and workers on assembly lines and so
orth as slaves, no matter what color they were. "I used to
hink that was such a shame," he said. "I used to think the
lectric chair was a shame. I used to think war was a
hame—and automobile accidents and cancer," he said,
nd so on.

He didn't think they were shames anymore. "Why
hould I care what happens to machines?" he said.

Wayne Hoobler's face had been blank so far, but now
t began to bloom with uncontrollable awe. His mouth
ell open.

The runway lights of Will Fairchild Memorial Airport
ad just come on. Those lights looked like miles and miles
f bewilderingly beautiful jewelry to Wayne. He was see-
ng a dream come true on the other side of the Interstate.

The inside of Wayne's head lit up in recognition of that
dream, lit up with an electric sign which gave a childish
ame to the dream—like this:

Kurt Vonnegut

hapter 24

Listen: Dwayne Hoover hurt so many people seriously
at a special ambulance known as *Martha* was called.
artha was a full-sized General Motors transcontinental
s, but with the seats removed. There were beds for
rty-six disaster victims in there, plus a kitchen and a
throom and an operating room. It had enough food and
dical supplies aboard to serve as an independent little
spital for a week without help from the outside world.
Its full name was *The Martha Simmons Memorial Mo-*
e Disaster Unit, named in honor of the wife of Newbolt
amons, a County Commissioner of Public Safety. She
d died of rabies contracted from a sick bat she found
nging to her floor-to-ceiling livingroom draperies one
rning. She had just been reading a biography of Albert
hweitzer, who believed that human beings should treat

5

Kurt Vonnegut

simpler animals lovingly. The bat nipped her ever
slightly as she wrapped it in *Kleenex*, a face tissue. S
carried it out onto her patio, where she laid it gently o
form of artificial grass known as *Astro-turf*.

She had thirty-six-inch hips, a twenty-nine-inch wa
and a thirty-eight-inch bosom at the time of her dea
Her husband had a penis seven and a half inches long a
two inches in diameter.

He and Dwayne were drawn together for a while
because his wife and Dwayne's wife had died su
strange deaths within a month of each other.

They bought a gravel pit together, out on Route 2;
but then the Maritimo Brothers Construction Compa
offered them twice what they had paid for it. So th
accepted the offer and divided up the profits, and t
friendship petered out somehow. They still exchang
Christmas cards.

Dwayne's most recent Christmas card to Newbolt Si
mons looked like this:

Newbolt Simmons'' most recent Christmas card to wayne looked like this:

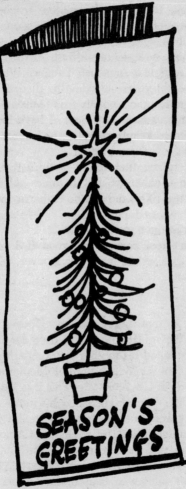

Kurt Vonnegut

◆ My psychiatrist is also named Martha. She gathe[rs] jumpy people together into little families which me[et] once a week. It's a lot of fun. She teaches us how [to] comfort one another intelligently. She is on vacation no[w] I like her a lot.

And I think now, as my fiftieth birthday draws ne[ar] about the American novelist Thomas Wolfe, who w[as] only thirty-eight years old when he died. He got a lot [of] help in organizing his novels from Maxwell Perkins, [his] editor at Charles Scribner's Sons. I have heard that Pe[r]kins told him to keep in mind as he wrote, as a unifyi[ng] idea, a hero's search for a father.

It seems to me that really truthful American nove[ls] would have the heroes and heroines alike looking f[or] *mothers* instead. This needn't be embarrassing. It's simp[ly] true.

A mother is much more useful.

I wouldn't feel particularly good if I found anoth[er] father. Neither would Dwayne Hoover. Neither wou[ld] Kilgore Trout.

◆ And just as motherless Dwayne Hoover was berati[ng] motherless Wayne Hoobler in the used car lot, a man w[ho] had actually killed his mother was preparing to land i[n a] chartered plane at Will Fairchild Memorial Airport, [on] the other side of the Interstate. This was Eliot Rosewat[er,] Kilgore Trout's patron. He killed his mother accidenta[lly] in a boating accident, when a youth. She was Wome[n's] Chess Champion of the United States of America, ninete[en] hundred and thirty-six years after the Son of God w[as] born, supposedly. Rosewater killed her the year after th[at.]

It was his pilot who caused the airport's runways

come an ex-convict's idea of fairyland. Rosewater re-
embered his mother's jewelry when the lights came on.
e looked to the west, and he smiled at the rosy loveli-
ss of the Mildred Barry Memorial Arts Center, a har-
st moon on stilts in a bend of Sugar Creek. It reminded
n of how his mother had looked when he saw her
rough the bleary eyes of infancy.

I had made him up, of course—and his pilot, too. I put
lonel Looseleaf Harper, the man who had dropped an
omic bomb on Nagasaki, Japan, at the controls.

I made Rosewater an alcoholic in another book. I now
d him reasonably well sobered up, with the help of
coholics Anonymous. I had him use his new-found so-
iety, to explore, among other things, the supposed spir-
ual and physical benefits of sexual orgies with strangers
New York City. He was only confused so far.

I could have killed him, and his pilot, too, but I let
em live on. So their plane touched down uneventfully.

The two physicians on the disaster vehicle named
artha were Cyprian Ukwende, of Nigeria, and Khash-
ahr Miasma, from the infant nation of Bangladesh.
th were parts of the world which were famous from
ne to time for having the food run out. Both places
ere specifically mentioned, in fact, in *Now It Can Be
ld*, by Kilgore Trout. Dwayne Hoover read in that
ok that robots all over the world were constantly run-
ng out of fuel and dropping dead, while waiting around
 test the only free-willed creature in the Universe, on
e off-chance that he should appear.

▶ At the wheel of the ambulance was Eddie Key, a youn[g] black man who was a direct descendant of Francis Sco[tt] Key, the white American patriot who wrote the Nation[al] Anthem. Eddie knew he was descended from Key. H[e] could name more than six hundred of his ancestors, an[d] had at least an anecdote about each. They were African[s,] Indians and white men.

He knew, for instance, that his mother's side of th[e] family had once owned the farm on which Sacred Mirac[le] Cave was discovered, that his ancestors had called "Bluebird Farm."

▶ Here was why there were so many young foreign do[c-] tors on the hospital staff, incidentally: The country didn[′t] produce nearly enough doctors for all the sick people [it] had, but it had an awful lot of money. So it bought do[c-] tors from other countries which didn't have much mone[y.]

▶ Eddie Key knew so much about his ancestry becau[se] the black part of his family had done what so many Afr[i-] can families still do in Africa, which was to have on[e] member of each generation whose duty it was to mem[o-] rize the history of the family so far. Eddie Key had beg[un] to store in his mind the names and adventures of ance[s-] tors on both his mother's and father's sides of his fami[ly] when he was only six years old. As he sat in the front [of] the disaster vehicle, looking out through the windshiel[d,] he had the feeling that he himself was a vehicle, and th[at] his eyes were windshields through which his progenito[rs] could look, if they wished to.

Francis Scott Key was only one of thousands ba[ck]

here. On the off-chance that Key might now be having a look at what had become of the United States of America so far, Eddie focussed his eyes on an American flag which was stuck to the windshield. He said this very quietly: "Still wavin', man."

Eddie Key's familiarity with a teeming past made life much more interesting to him than it was to Dwayne, for instance, or to me, or to Kilgore Trout, or to almost any white person in Midland City that day. We had no sense of anybody else using our eyes—or our hands. We didn't even know who our great-grandfathers and great-grandmothers were. Eddie Key was afloat in a river of people who were flowing from here to there in time. Dwayne and Trout and I were pebbles at rest.

And Eddie Key, because he knew so much by heart, was able to have deep, nourishing feelings about Dwayne Hoover, for instance, and about Dr. Cyprian Ukwende, too. Dwayne was a man whose family had taken over Bluebird Farm. Ukwende, an Indaro, was a man whose ancestors had kidnapped an ancestor of Key's on the West Coast of Africa, a man named Ojumwa. The Indaros sold him for a musket to British slave traders, who took him on a sailing ship named the "Skylark" to Charleston, South Carolina, where he was auctioned off as a self-propelled, self-repairing farm machine.

And so on.

Dwayne Hoover was now hustled aboard *Martha*—through big double doors in her rear, just ahead of the engine compartment. Eddie Key was in the driver's seat,

and he watched the action in his rearview mirror. Dwayn
was swaddled so tightly in canvas restraining sheets tha
his reflection looked to Eddie like a bandaged thumb.

Dwayne didn't notice the restraints. He thought he wa
on the virgin planet promised by the book by Kilgor
Trout. Even when he was laid out horizontally b
Cyprian Ukwende and Khashdrahr Miasma, he thougl
he was standing up. The book had told him that he wer
swimming in cold water on the virgin planet, that he a
ways yelled something surprising when he climbed out c
the icy pool. It was a game. The Creator of the Univers
would try to guess what Dwayne would yell each da
And Dwayne would fool him totally.

Here is what Dwayne yelled in the ambulance: "Goo
bye, Blue Monday!" Then it seemed to him that anothe
day had passed on the virgin planet, and it was time t
yell again. "Not a cough in a carload!" he yelled.

● Kilgore Trout was one of the walking wounded. H
was able to climb aboard *Martha* without assistance, an
to choose a place to sit where he would be away from re
emergencies. He had jumped Dwayne Hoover from be
hind when Dwayne dragged Francine Pefko out c
Dwayne's showroom and onto the asphalt. Dwayn
wanted to give her a beating in public, which his ba
chemicals made him think she richly deserved.

Dwayne had already broken her jaw and three ribs i
the office. When he trundled her outside, there was a fai
size crowd which had drifted out of the cocktail loung
and the kitchen of the new Holiday Inn. "Best fuckin
machine in the State," he told the crowd. "Wind her up
and she'll fuck you and say she loves you, and she won

t up till you give her a Colonel Sanders Kentucky Fried
iicken franchise."

And so on. Trout grabbed him from behind.

Trout's right ring finger somehow slipped into
wayne's mouth, and Dwayne bit off the topmost joint.
wayne let go of Francine after that, and she slumped to
e asphalt. She was unconscious, and the most seriously
ured of all. And Dwayne went cantering over to the
ncrete trough by the Interstate, and he spat Kilgore
out's fingertip into Sugar Creek.

Kilgore Trout did not choose to lie down in *Martha*. He
tled into a leather bucket seat behind Eddie Key. Key
ked him what was the matter with him, and Trout held
his right hand, partly shrouded in a bloody handker-
ief, which looked like this:

"A slip of the lip can sink a ship!" yelled Dwayne.

◆ "Remember Pearl Harbor!" yelled Dwayne. Most
what he had done during the past three-quarters of
hour had been hideously unjust. But he had spared Wa
Hoobler, at least. Wayne was back among the used
again, unscathed. He was picking up a bracelet whic
had pitched back there for him to find.

As for myself: I kept a respectful distance between
self and all the violence—even though I had crea
Dwayne and his violence and the city, and the sky ab
and the Earth below. Even so, I came out of the riot w
a broken watch crystal and what turned out later to b
broken toe. Somebody jumped backwards to get out
Dwayne's way. He broke my watch crystal, even thoug
had created him, and he broke my toe.

◆ This isn't the kind of book where people get wha
coming to them at the end. Dwayne hurt only one per
who deserved to be hurt for being so wicked: That
Don Breedlove. Breedlove was the white gas-convers
unit installer who had raped Patty Keene, the waitress
Dwayne's Burger Chef out on Crestview Avenue, in
parking lot of George Hickman Bannister Memor
Fieldhouse out at the County Fairgrounds after Pea
University beat Innocent Bystander High School in
Regional Class High School Basketball Playoffs.

◆ Don Breedlove was in the kitchen of the Inn wh
Dwayne began his rampage. He was repairing a defect
gas oven in there.

He stepped outside for some fresh air, and Dway
came running up to him. Dwayne had just spit Kilg

out's fingertip into Sugar Creek. Don and Dwayne
ew each other quite well, since Dwayne had once sold
eedlove a new Pontiac *Ventura*, which Don said was a
mon. A lemon was an automobile which didn't run
ght, and which nobody was able to repair.

Dwayne actually lost money on the transaction, mak-
g adjustments and replacing parts in an attempt to mol-
y Breedlove. But Breedlove was inconsolable, and he
ally painted this sign in bright yellow on his trunk lid
d on both doors:

THIS CAR IS A LEMON!

Here was what was really wrong with the car, inciden-
lly. The child of a neighbor of Breedlove had put maple
gar in the gas tank of the *Ventura*. Maple sugar was a
nd of candy made from the blood of trees.

So Dwayne Hoover now extended his right hand
Breedlove, and Breedlove without thinking anythin
about it took that hand in his own. They linked up lil
this:

This was a symbol of friendship between men. Th
feeling was, too, that a lot of character could be read in
the way a man shook hands. Dwayne and Don Breedlo
gave each other squeezes which were dry and hard.

So Dwayne held onto Don Breedlove with his rig]
hand, and he smiled as though bygones were bygone
Then he made a cup out of his left hand, and he hit Dc
on the ear with the open end of the cup. This create
terrific air pressure in Don's ear. He fell down becaus
the pain was so awful. Don would never hear anythin
with that ear, ever again.

▶ So Don was in the ambulance, too, now—sitting up li]
Kilgore Trout. Francine was lying down—unconsciou
but moaning. Beatrice Keedsler was lying down, althou

he might have sat up. Her jaw was broken. Bunny Hoover was lying down. His face was unrecognizable, even as a face—anybody's face. He had been given morphine by Cyprian Ukwende.

There were five other victims as well—one white female, two white males, two black males. The three white people had never been in Midland City before. They were on their way together from Erie, Pennsylvania, to the Grand Canyon, which was the deepest crack on the planet. They wanted to look down into the crack, but they never got to do it. Dwayne Hoover assaulted them as they walked from the car toward the lobby of the New Holiday Inn.

The two black males were both kitchen employees of the Inn.

Cyprian Ukwende now tried to remove Dwayne Hoover's shoes—but Dwayne's shoes and laces and socks were impregnated with the plastic material, which he had picked up while wading across Sugar Creek.

Ukwende was not mystified by plasticized, unitized shoes and socks. He saw shoes and socks like that every day at the hospital, on the feet of children who had played too close to Sugar Creek. In fact, he had hung a pair of tinsnips on the wall of the hospital's emergency room—for cutting off plasticized, unitized shoes and socks.

He turned to his Bengali assistant, young Dr. Khashdrahr Miasma. "Get some shears," he said.

Miasma was standing with his back to the door of the ladies' toilet on the emergency vehicle. He had done nothing so far to deal with all the emergencies. Ukwende and police and a team from Civil Defense had done the work so far. Miasma now refused even to find some shears.

Basically, Miasma probably shouldn't have been in the field of medicine at all, or at least not in any area where there was a chance that he might be criticized. He could not tolerate criticism. This was a characteristic beyond his control. Any hint that anything about him was not absolutely splendid automatically turned him into a useless, sulky child who would only say that it wanted to go home.

That was what he said when Ukwende told him a second time to find shears: "I want to go home."

Here is what he had been criticized for, just before the alarm came in about Dwayne's going berserk: He had amputated a black man's foot, whereas the foot could probably have been saved.

And so on.

⬧ I could go on and on with the intimate details about the various lives of people on the super-ambulance, but what good is more information?

I agree with Kilgore Trout about realistic novels and their accumulations of nit-picking details. In Trout's novel, *The Pan-Galactic Memory Bank*, the hero is on a space ship two hundred miles long and sixty-two miles in diameter. He gets a realistic novel out of the branch library in his neighborhood. He reads about sixty pages of it, and then he takes it back.

The librarian asks him why he doesn't like it, and he says to her, "I already know about human beings."

And so on.

Martha began to move. Kilgore Trout saw a sign he
ked a lot. Here is what it said:

IT IS HARDER
TO BE UNHAPPY
WHEN YOU
ARE EATING

CRAIG'S
ICE CREAM

And so on.

Dwayne Hoover's awareness returned to Earth momen-
arily. He spoke of opening a health club in Midland
ity, with rowing machines and stationary bicycles and
hirlpool baths and sunlamps and a swimming pool and
o on. He told Cyprian Ukwende that the thing to do with
health club was to open it and then sell it as soon as
ossible for a profit. "People get all enthusiastic about
etting back in shape or losing some pounds," said
)wayne. "They sign up for the program, but then they

lose interest in about a year, and they stop coming. Tha[t's] how people are."

And so on.

Dwayne wasn't going to open any health club. [He] wasn't going to open anything ever again. The people [he] had injured so unjustly would sue him so vengefully th[at] he would be rendered destitute. He would become o[ne] more withered balloon of an old man on Midland Cit[y's] Skid Row, which was the neighborhood of the once fa[sh]ionable Fairchild Hotel. He would be by no means t[he] only drifter of whom it could be truthfully said, "See hi[m?] Can you believe it? He doesn't have a doodley-squat no[w,] but he used to be fabulously well-to-do."

And so on.

Kilgore Trout now peeled strips and patches of plas[tic] from his burning shins and feet in the ambulance. He h[ad] to use his uninjured left hand.

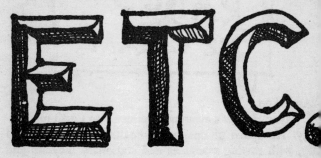

ETC.

pilogue

The emergency room of the hospital was in the base-
ent. After Kilgore Trout had the stump of his ring finger
sinfected and trimmed and bandaged, he was told to go
ostairs to the finance office. There were certain forms he
d to fill out, since he was from outside Midland
ounty, had no health insurance, and was destitute. He
d no checkbook. He had no cash.

He got lost in the basement for a little while, as a lot of
ople did. He found the double doors to the morgue, as
lot of people did. He automatically mooned about his
vn mortality, as a lot of people did. He found an x-ray
om, which wasn't in use. It made him wonder automati-
lly if anything bad was growing inside himself. Other
ople had wondered exactly the same thing when they
assed that room.

1

Trout felt nothing now that millions of other peop
wouldn't have felt—automatically.

And Trout found stairs, but they were the wrong stair
They led him not to the lobby and the finance office an
the gift shop and all that, but into a matrix of room
where persons were recovering or failing to recover fro
injuries of all kinds. Many of the people there had bee
flung to the earth by the force of gravity, which nev
relaxed for a second.

Trout passed a very expensive private room now, an
there was a young black man in there, with a white tel
phone and a color television set and boxes of candy an
bouquets of flowers all around. He was Elgin Washing
ton, a pimp who operated out of the old Holiday Inn. H
was only twenty-six years old, but he was fabulously wel
to-do.

Visiting hours had ended, so all his female sex slave
had departed. But they had left clouds of perfume behind
Trout gagged as he passed the door. It was an automati
reaction to the fundamentally unfriendly cloud. Elgi
Washington had just sniffed cocaine into his sinus pa
sages, which amplified tremendously the telepathic mes
sages he sent and received. He felt one hundred time
bigger than life, because the messages were so loud an
exciting. It was their noise that thrilled him. He didn't
what they said.

And, in the midst of the uproar, Elgin Washington sai
something wheedlingly to Trout. "Hey man, hey ma
hey man," he wheedled. He had had his foot amputate
earlier in the day by Khashdrahr Miasma, but he ha
forgotten that. "Hey man, hey man," he coaxed. H
wanted nothing particular from Trout. Some part of h
mind was idly exercising his skill at making strange

e to him. He was a fisherman for men's souls. "Hey
—" he said. He showed a gold tooth. He winked an

rout came to the foot of the black man's bed. This
n't compassion on his part. He was being machinery
n. Trout was, like so many Earthlings, a fully auto-
ic boob when a pathological personality like Elgin
hington told him what to want, what to do. Both men,
dentally, were descendants of the Emperor Charle-
ne. Anybody with any European blood in him was a
endant of the Emperor Charlemagne.

lgin Washington perceived that he had caught yet
ther human being without really meaning to. It was
in his nature to let one go without making him feel in
e way diminished, in some way a fool. Sometimes he
ally killed a man in order to diminish him, but he was
tle with Trout. He closed his eyes as though thinking
d, then he earnestly said, "I think I may be dying."

"ll get a nurse!" said Trout. Any human being would
e said exactly the same thing.

No, no," said Elgin Washington, waving his hands in
amy protest. "I'm dying *slow*. It's gradual."

I see," said Trout.

You got to do me a favor," said Washington. He had
dea what favor to ask. It would come to him. Ideas for
rs always came.

What favor?" said Trout uneasily. He stiffened at the
tion of an unspecified favor. He was that kind of a
hine. Washington knew he would stiffen. Every
an being was that kind of a machine.

I want you to listen to me while I whistle the song of
Nightingale," he said. He commanded Trout to be
nt by giving him the evil eye. "What adds peculiar

beauty to the call of the Nightingale, much beloved
poets," he said, "is the fact that it will *only* sing by moo
light." Then he did what almost every black person
Midland City would do: He imitated a Nightingale.

♦ The Midland City Festival of the Arts was postpon
because of madness. Fred T. Barry, its chairman, came
the hospital in his limousine, dressed like a Chinaman,
offer his sympathy to Beatrice Keedsler and Kilge
Trout. Trout could not be found anywhere. Beatr
Keedsler had been put to sleep with morphine.

Kilgore Trout assumed that the Arts Festival wou
still take place that night. He had no money for any fo
of transportation, so he set out on foot. He began the fi
mile walk down Fairchild Boulevard—toward a ti
amber dot at the other end. The dot was the Midla
City Center for the Arts. He would make it grow by wa
ing toward it. When his walking had made it big enoug
it would swallow him up. There would be food inside.

♦ I was waiting to intercept him, about six blocks away
sat in a Plymouth *Duster* I had rented from *Avis* with
Diners' Club card. I had a paper tube in my mouth.
was stuffed with leaves. I set it on fire. It was a *soig*
thing to do.

My penis was three inches long and five inches in
ameter. Its diameter was a world's record as far as
knew. It slumbered now in my *Jockey Shorts*. And I g
out of the car to stretch my legs, which was anoth
soigné thing to do. I was among factories and wa
houses. The streetlights were widely-spaced and feeb

king lots were vacant, except for night watchmen's
s which were here and there. There was no traffic on
rchild Boulevard, which had once been the aorta of
town. The life had all been drained out of it by the
erstate and by the Robert F. Kennedy Inner Belt Ex-
ssway, which was built on the old right-of-way of the
non Railroad. The Monon was defunct.

)efunct.

Nobody slept in that part of town. Nobody lurked
re. It was a system of forts at night, with high fences
l alarms, and with prowling dogs. They were killing
chines.

When I got out of my Plymouth *Duster*, I feared noth-
That was foolish of me. A writer off-guard, since the
terials with which he works are so dangerous, can ex-
t agony as quick as a thunderclap.

was about to be attacked by a Doberman pinscher.
was a leading character in an earlier version of this
k.

Listen: That Doberman's name was *Kazak*. He pa-
lled the supply yard of the Maritimo Brothers Con-
ction Company at night. Kazak's trainers, the people
o explained to him what sort of a planet he was on and
at sort of an animal he was, taught him that the Crea-
of the Universe wanted him to kill anything he could
ch, and to *eat* it, too.

In an earlier version of this book, I had Benjamin

Davis, the black husband of Lottie Davis, Dway
Hoover's maid, take care of Kazak. He threw raw m
down into the pit where Kazak lived in the daytime.
dragged Kazak into the pit at sunrise. He screamed
him and threw tennis balls at him at sundown. Then
turned him loose.

Benjamin Davis was first trumpet with the Midla
City Symphony Orchestra, but he got no pay for that,
he needed a real job. He wore a thick gown made of w
surplus mattresses and chicken wire, so Kazak could
kill him. Kazak tried and tried. There were chunks
mattress and swatches of chicken wire all over the ya

And Kazak did his best to kill anybody who came
close to the fence which enclosed his planet. He leaped
people as though the fence weren't there. The fe
bellied out toward the sidewalk everywhere. It looked
though somebody had been shooting cannonballs at
from inside.

I should have noticed the queer shape of the fe
when I got out of my automobile, when I did the *soig*
thing of lighting a cigarette. I should have known tha
character as ferocious as Kazak was not easily cut out o
novel.

Kazak was crouching behind a pile of bronze pi
which the Maritimo Brothers had bought cheap from
hijacker earlier that day. Kazak meant to kill and *eat* n

I turned my back to the fence, took a deep puff of
cigarette. *Pall Malls* would kill me by and by. And
mooned philosophically at the murky battlements of
old Keedsler Mansion, on the other side of Fairch
Boulevard.

Beatrice Keedsler had been raised in there. The most
nous murders in the city's history had been committed
ere. Will Fairchild, the war hero, and the maternal
cle of Beatrice Keedsler, appeared one summer night in
26 with a Springfield rifle. He shot and killed five rela-
es, three servants, two policemen, and all the animals
the Keedsler's private zoo. Then he shot himself
rough his heart.

When an autopsy was performed on him, a tumor the
e of a piece of birdshot was found in his brain. This
s what *caused* the murders.

After the Keedslers lost the mansion at the start of the
eat Depression, Fred T. Barry and his parents moved
The old place was filled with the sounds of British
rds. It was silent property of the city now, and there
is talk of making it into a museum where children
uld learn the history of Midland City—as told by
rowheads and stuffed animals and white men's early
tifacts.

Fred T. Barry had offered to donate half a million dol-
s to the proposed museum, on one condition: that the
st *Robo-Magic* and the early posters which advertised
be put on display.

And he wanted the exhibit to show, too, how ma-
ines evolved just as animals did, but with much greater
eed.

I gazed at the Keedsler mansion, never dreaming that a
lcanic dog was about to erupt behind me. Kilgore
out came nearer. I was almost indifferent to his ap-

proach, although we had momentous things to say to o
another about my having created him.

I thought instead of my paternal grandfather, who h
been the first licensed architect in Indiana. He had
signed some dream houses for *Hoosier* millionaires. Th
were mortuaries and guitar schools and cellar holes a
parking lots now. I thought of my mother, who drove
around Indianapolis one time during the Great Depr
sion, to impress me with how rich and powerful my mat
nal grandfather had been. She showed me where I
brewery had been, where some of his dream houses h
been. Every one of the monuments was a cellar hole.

Kilgore Trout was only half a block from his Creat
now, and slowing down. I worried him.

I turned toward him, so that my sinus cavities, whe
all telepathic messages were sent and received, we
lined up symmetrically with his. I told him this over a
over telepathically: "I have good news for you."

Kazak sprung.

◗ I saw Kazak out of the corner of my right eye. His ey
were pinwheels. His teeth were white daggers. His slo
ber was cyanide. His blood was nitroglycerine.

He was floating toward me like a zeppelin, hangi
lazily in air.

My eyes told my mind about him.

My mind sent a message to my hypothalamus, told it
release the hormone CRF into the short vessels conne
ing my hypothalamus and my pituitary gland.

The CRF inspired my pituitary gland to dump the h
mone ACTH into my bloodstream. My pituitary had be

ing and storing ACTH for just such an occasion. And
er and nearer the zeppelin came.

nd some of the ACTH in my bloodstream reached the
r shell of my adrenal gland, which had been making
storing glucocorticoids for emergencies. My adrenal
d added the glucocorticoids to my bloodstream. They
t all over my body, changing glycogen into glucose.
:ose was muscle food. It would help me fight like a
cat or run like a deer.

nd nearer and nearer the zeppelin came.

ly adrenal gland gave me a shot of adrenaline, too. I
ed purple as my blood pressure skyrocketed. The
naline made my heart go like a burglar alarm. It also
d my hair on end. It also caused coagulants to pour
my bloodstream, so, in case I was wounded, my vital
es wouldn't drain away.

.verything my body had done so far fell within normal
rating procedures for a human machine. But my body
: one defensive measure which I am told was without
:edent in medical history. It may have happened be-
:e some wire short-circuited or some gasket blew. At
rate, I also retracted my testicles into my abdominal
ity, pulled them into my fuselage like the landing gear
.n airplane. And now they tell me that only surgery
bring them down again.

:e that as it may, Kilgore Trout watched me from half
ock away, not knowing who I was, not knowing about
:ak and what my body had done about Kazak so far.

:rout had had a full day already, but it wasn't over yet.
v he saw his Creator leap completely over an auto-
ile.

◆ I landed on my hands and knees in the middle of ▮child Boulevard.

Kazak was flung back by the fence. Gravity took cha▮ of him as it had taken charge of me. Gravity slamm▮ him down on concrete. Kazak was knocked silly.

Kilgore Trout turned away. He hastened anxio▮ back toward the hospital. I called out to him, but ▮ only made him walk faster.

So I jumped into my car and chased him. I was ▮ high as a kite on adrenaline and coagulants and all tha▮ did not know yet that I had retracted my testicles in▮ the excitement. I felt only vague discomfort down th▮

Trout was cantering when I came alongside. I clock▮ him at eleven miles an hour, which was excellent fo▮ man his age. He, too, was now full of adrenaline ▮ coagulants and glucocorticoids.

My windows were rolled down, and I called this▮ him: "Whoa! Whoa! Mr. Trout! Whoa! Mr. Trout!"

It slowed him down to be called by name.

"Whoa! I'm a friend!" I said. He shuffled to a st▮ leaned in panting exhaustion against a fence surround▮ an appliance warehouse belonging to the General El▮ tric Company. The company's monogram and motto hu▮ in the night sky behind Kilgore Trout, whose eyes w▮ wild. The motto was this:

PROGRESS IS OUR MOST IMPORTANT PRODUC▮

◆ "Mr. Trout," I said from the unlighted interior of t▮ car, "you have nothing to fear. I bring you tidings of gr▮ joy."

He was slow to get his breath back, so he wasn't mu▮

conversationalist at first. "Are—are you—from the—
Arts Festival?" he said. His eyes rolled and rolled.

I am from the *Everything* Festival," I replied.

The what?" he said.

thought it would be a good idea to let him have a
d look at me, and so attempted to flick on the dome
t. I turned on the windshield washers instead. I
ned them off again. My view of the lights of the
nty Hospital was garbled by beads of water. I pulled
nother switch, and it came away in my hand. It was a
arette lighter. So I had no choice but to continue to
ak from darkness.

'Mr. Trout," I said, "I am a novelist, and I created you
use in my books."

'Pardon me?" he said.

'I'm your Creator," I said. "You're in the middle of a
k right now—close to the end of it, actually."

'Um," he said.

'Are there any questions you'd like to ask?"

'Pardon me?" he said.

Feel free to ask anything you want—about the past,
ut the future," I said. "There's a Nobel Prize in your
ure."

'A what?" he said.

'A Nobel Prize in medicine."

'Huh," he said. It was a noncommittal sound.

'I've also arranged for you to have a reputable pub-
er from now on. No more beaver books for you."

'Um," he said.

"If I were in your spot, I would certainly have lots of
estions," I said.

"Do you have a gun?" he said.

I laughed there in the dark, tried to turn on the li
again, activated the windshield washer again. "I d
need a gun to control you, Mr. Trout. All I have to d
write down something about you, and that's it."

◆ "Are you *crazy*?" he said.

"No," I said. And I shattered his power to doubt m
transported him to the Taj Mahal and then to Venice a
then to Dar es Salaam and then to the surface of the S
where the flames could not consume him—and then b
to Midland City again.

The poor old man crashed to his knees. He remin
me of the way my mother and Bunny Hoover's mot
used to act whenever somebody tried to take their ph
graphs.

As he cowered there, I transported him to the Berm
of his childhood, had him contemplate the infertile egg
a Bermuda Ern. I took him from there to the Indianap
of my childhood. I put him in a circus crowd there. I l
him see a man with *locomotor ataxia* and a woman wit
goiter as big as a zucchini.

◆ I got out of my rented car. I did it noisily, so his e
would tell him a lot about his *Creator*, even if he v
unwilling to use his eyes. I slammed the car door firm
As I approached him from the driver's side of the car
swiveled my feet some, so that my footsteps were not o
deliberate but *gritty*, too.

I stopped with the tips of my shoes on the rim of
narrow field of his downcast eyes. "Mr. Trout, I le
you," I said gently. "I have broken your mind to piece

nt to make it whole. I want you to feel a wholeness and
ner harmony such as I have never allowed you to feel
fore. I want you to raise your eyes, to look at what I
ve in my hand."

I had nothing in my hand, but such was my power over
out that he would see in it whatever I wished him to
e. I might have shown him a Helen of Troy, for in-
ance, only six inches tall.

"Mr. Trout—*Kilgore*—" I said, "I hold in my hand a
mbol of wholeness and harmony and nourishment. It is
riental in its simplicity, but we are *Americans*, Kilgore,
d not Chinamen. We Americans require symbols which
e richly colored and three-dimensional and juicy. Most
all, we hunger for symbols which have not been poi-
ned by great sins our nation has committed, such as
avery and genocide and criminal neglect, or by tinhorn
mmercial greed and cunning.

"Look up, Mr. Trout," I said, and I waited patiently.
Kilgore—?"

The old man looked up, and he had my father's wasted
ce when my father was a widower—when my father
as an old old man.

He saw that I held an apple in my hand.

"I am approaching my fiftieth birthday, Mr. Trout," I
id. "I am cleansing and renewing myself for the very
fferent sorts of years to come. Under similar spiritual
nditions, Count Tolstoi freed his serfs. Thomas Jeffer-
n freed his slaves. I am going to set at liberty all the
terary characters who have served me so loyally during
y writing career.

"You are the only one I am telling. For the others, to-

night will be a night like any other night. Arise, M
Trout, you are free, you are *free*."

He arose shamblingly.

I might have shaken his hand, but his right hand w
injured, so our hands remained dangling at our sides.

"*Bon voyage*," I said. I disappeared.

◗ I somersaulted lazily and pleasantly through the vo
which is my hiding place when I dematerialize. Trou
cries to me faded as the distance between us increased.

His voice was my father's voice. I *heard* my father—a
I *saw* my mother in the void. My mother stayed far, f
away, because she had left me a legacy of suicide.

A small hand mirror floated by. It was a *leak* with
mother-of-pearl handle and frame. I captured it easi
held it up to my own right eye, which looked like this:

Here was what Kilgore Trout cried out to me in my ather's voice: *"Make me young, make me young, make e young!"*

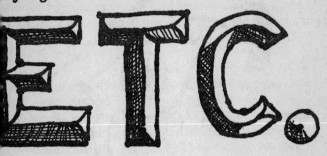

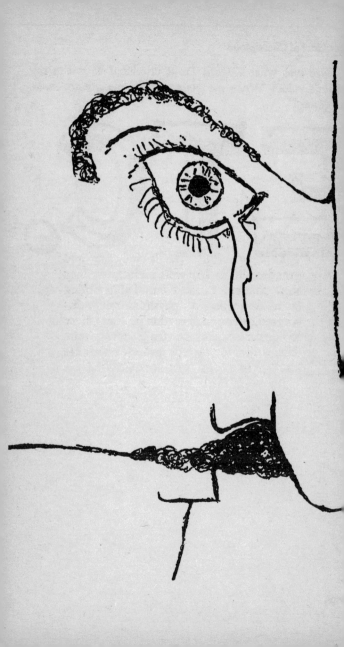

▶ Kurt Vonnegut, Jr., is the son and grandson of Indianapolis architects. They were painters, too. His only living sibling is a distinguished physicist who discovered, among other things, that silver iodide can sometimes make it snow or rain. This is Mr. Vonnegut's seventh novel. He wrote it mostly in New York City. His six children are full-grown.

"IT WAS A MARRIAGE MADE IN THEIR OWN HOME IN CHEDBURY, AND NOT IN HEAVEN. . . .

". . . this book shows how two people of opposite temperament, one thoughtful, conservative, and even a trifle dull, the other, quick-witted, charming and independent, made the 'happily ever after' come true by dint of love rooted in patience and mutual thoughtfulness."

—*San Francisco Chronicle*

PEARL S. BUCK, winner of the Nobel and Pulitzer prizes in literature, ". . . wrote 84 books in her lifetime, and each seemed to reflect the simple philosophy of love which was evident in her work and throughout her life."

—*Boston Globe*

Millions of devoted fans have long admired her ". . . brilliant writing. Only Miss Buck can work her spell in this manner. . . . Her word portraits are superb; her finely drawn feelings paint exquisite portraits; and when the reader finishes one of her books, the feeling is that one has actually visited and talked to the protagonists."

—Broox Sledge,
"Travels in Bookland"

THE LONG LOVE
was originally published by The John Day Company, Inc.

Books by Pearl S. Buck

Published by POCKET BOOKS

PEARL S. BUCK

The Long Love

PUBLISHED BY POCKET BOOKS NEW YORK

THE LONG LOVE

John Day edition published 1949

POCKET BOOK edition published November, 1959

6th printing.....................January, 1975

Foreword

Some years ago I woke one morning to find myself strangely oppressed. I felt suddenly that I was no longer a free individual. I had been cast in a mold. I had written so many books about Chinese people that I had become known as a writer only about China. This was natural enough and nobody's fault. When I began to write I knew no people intimately except the Chinese. My entire life had been spent in China and beyond that in Asia. In midstream, however, I had transferred myself to the West and to my own country, the United States. Soon, since any writer writes out of his everyday environment, I began, however tentatively, to write about American people. I became thereby someone else.

This someone else, who now was also I, for the old self, the Asian self, continued to exist and will always continue, was, I repeat, oppressed. The oppression was the result of a determination on the part of my readers, sometimes loving, sometimes critical, to insist that there must be no other me than the one they had always known; that is to say, the Asian me. But here was the new American me, eager to explore and adventure among my own people. To provide freedom for this American me, pseudonymity was the answer. The writer must have a new name. I chose the name of John Sedges, a simple one, and masculine because men have fewer handicaps in our society than women have, in writing as well as in other professions.

My first John Sedges novel was *The Townsman*. It is a long book, a story of the West, Kansas in scene, to which state I had made many quiet visits. I was pleased when Kansans praised its authenticity. Its hero is a modest fellow who refuses to ride wild horses, be a cowboy, shoot pistols into the air, kill his enemies, find gold in any hills, destroy Indians, or even get drunk. He is content merely to become the solid founder of a city. The novel was well received by critics and sold to some tens of thousands of readers. It thus proved itself as a successful first novel by an unknown writer.

Four other novels were published under the name John Sedges, and guesses became rampant as to the author. No secrets in this world are kept forever. Somebody always knows and tells. And my two selves were beginning to merge. I was by now at home in my own country, my roots were digging deep, and I was becoming increasingly familiar with my own people. The protection of John Sedges was neither so necessary nor so effective as it had been. In Europe the John Sedges novels were openly sold as Pearl Buck books. I was moving toward freedom. The shield was no longer useful.

So John Sedges has served his purpose and may now be discarded and laid away in the silver foil of memory. I declare my independence and my determination to write as I please in a free country, choosing my material as I find it. People are people whether in Asia or America, as everybody knows or ought to know, and for me the scene is merely the background for human antics. Readers will still be the critics, of course, but I shall hope and strive to please and to amuse. Why else should books be written?

PEARL S. BUCK

One

EDWARD HASLATT was a young man both intelligent and cautious. When he had risen from his bed one fine morning he had not committed himself to a proposal of marriage. That it was possible he admitted. If the day were fair, if he found himself in a happy mood, if Margaret were kind, if they found exactly the spot he wanted for their picnic, then it might very well be that he would ask her to marry him.

He had determined that unless all these details were auspicious, he would wait. He had learned his lesson, he hoped. If she refused him again today it would be for the third time, and he would cease to think of her. That is, he hoped he could cease to think of her. While he dressed himself carefully, with an eye to the wave in his brown hair, and to the color of his tie, which was blue in contrast to his quiet brown eyes, he meditated on his tendency to faithfulness which amounted to stubbornness. Without this trait, he would certainly not have humiliated himself to ask a girl twice to marry him, to have suffered her refusals, and now to contemplate further humiliation.

Prudence and pride combined had often led him to wish that he could stop thinking about Margaret Seaton. His mother had frequently reminded him that she was not the only girl in the world and not even perhaps the prettiest, but such words did not penetrate his heart. There Margaret remained alone, and he had only to consult his heart to remember her in all the detail of her curly black hair, sea-blue eyes, fringed with long black lashes, and her somewhat wide and too mobile mouth. Her profile was to him one of utter beauty. Her forehead was square and smooth, neither high nor low, and with-

3

out the slight bulge he disliked so much in his own. Between her black brows her nose was low bridged and straight and delicate until the end where it tilted slightly, merely enough to make her upper lip short. He tried to persuade himself that her face had nothing to do with his loving her so painfully, but he knew that without this face, which in every detail was what he liked best in a woman, he would not have found her so inescapable. Without this face, certainly he would not have contemplated asking her for the third time to marry him.

For now, looking out of the window, he knew that there was no excuse to be found in the day. The mists were rolling softly from the round New England hills, and by midmorning even the valleys would be bright. The small clear river was still clouded, but by its own low fog. Once the sun fell upon it this too would be dispelled. The town of Chedbury was northwest of the city of Boston. It lay upon a sloping flank of Granite Mountain, its houses encircling a central green. At the highest point of this green stood the large and ancient church of white-painted wood. Its steeple was noble in design and its roof was high shouldered, as though winged. Chedbury was proud of its church, and its design, pure and spacious, had made it impossible for other denominations to compete among the townsfolk. So wholly did the church dominate that even the town hall, built a hundred years later, dared not stand beside it. Chedbury's town meeting of that date had built the hall behind the church, and had put the firehouse beside it. From down the hill neither could be seen, and on a Sunday, when most of Chedbury sat in the walnut pews of the church, the people felt comfortably that it had been wise of their ancestors to have the fire engines handy in case some secret blaze threatened their prize possession.

Around the green were some twenty houses, a small clean hotel, Mather and Haslatt's Printing Shop, a grocery store, and the post office. Among the twenty houses the Seaton house was the largest, a square compact house, double winged, white shingled with green blinds. Upon the roof was a captain's walk, encircled by a white wooden balustrade, and the same solid balustrade enclosed the porches, both upstairs and down. Margaret, if she were at this moment looking out of the east window of

4

her room, could see the same street upon which Edward gazed from his own window in the small but intensely neat house which was his home. The street looked washed and clean. He and Margaret had grown up on this street, all but neighbors, and he had fallen in love with her in high school. But he had been far from the most handsome or the most brilliant in their class, and she had snubbed him in favor of Harold Ames until their senior year, when, to his family's astonishment and his own, he had suddenly begun to grow tall. This drew Margaret's attention to him, and since Harold had been a year ahead and away at college, he had begun to go with Margaret. But he had not been rash enough to speak of love then, although he was already beginning to fear that he was doomed to love her. His own prudence protected him, and after their graduation he contented himself with asking her to write to him when they separated, he to go to Harvard and she to Vassar, and with seeing her, whenever she was willing, during subsequent summers and winters. This was not enough, for during two summers she was away, one on the Continent, and the other in England, where some of the ancestral Seatons still lived. Her father, Thomas Seaton, was a Tory of British water, in spite of the fact that the first Seaton had fought against the English regulars near Chedbury in 1775.

The Haslatts were English too, but not obtrusively so. Mark Haslatt, Edward's father, was not quite so well placed as Thomas Seaton. The Haslatt family had come to Chedbury a scant fifty years ago, whereas Seatons had always lived here, and as far as anyone knew always in the same old red brick house, to which Thomas Seaton had added the two wings when his children were born. The Haslatts had moved from one house to another, as their fortunes improved. Edward did not know the full history of his father, for his mother kept it wrapped in vagueness. He knew that at one time his father had even been a sheepherder on a Western ranch, and that his mother, the daughter of a homesick New England family, had brought him back to Chedbury. The first years had been desperate ones—that Edward knew, for he could remember them. He had still, in the sore recesses of his early childhood, the memory of ugly houses, poor furniture, a perpetual smell of laundry which grew acute on Monday

5

mornings, when his father rose early to help his mother with the family wash. There was another period when his father was a conductor on the winding little trolley line between Chedbury and Deerbourne, and still another when he was trying to learn to be a contractor, apprenticed to his more successful brother, Henry Baynes. But this, too, had failed. Not until his father found himself in the printers' firm of Loomis and Mather did ease begin to come to the troubled family. There somehow Mark Haslatt fitted, and with security his confidence rose until at last he became a partner. When Loomis, the senior partner, died, the firm became Mather and Haslatt.

By the time Edward was ten years old and his younger brother Baynes was five they were comfortable in this twelve-room house. The white paint, the green blinds, the neat lawn under the elms, his own room in the third story, high enough to look out over the hills, became the setting of his boyhood. His sister Louise knew no other home. But because he could remember the other transient houses, their misery and their smell, he never quite forgot that this home was luxury.

Not that everything had been happy even here. Edward had a deep pride which forced him to frequent suffering. His common sense told him that such suffering was often self-inflicted and unnecessary, and this in turn made him ashamed to speak of it to anyone, and again in turn doubled his suffering. But so it was, and he could do nothing about it. He told himself that if Margaret were ever to marry him and he could be in his own home, free from his mother and her moods and angers, and his father and his efforts to placate and soothe, he could be happy. But he was not sure. He was a creature compound of both parents, and he knew it. He feared sometimes in his darker hours that it was quite possible his moodiness would be too much even for his own marriage.

Nevertheless he refused to face this as knowledge. He steadfastly tried to convince himself that his ups and downs were the result of external circumstances and his need to get away from a home that he had outgrown. Whether his brother and sister felt as he did, he did not know. They were outwardly friendly with him, but they shared no confidences. His parents were determined to send both of the boys to college, and Edward had not the heart to tell his father that no college could possibly provide all that was expected of it. As the eldest, he had been graduated from Harvard this spring with sufficient honor, and Baynes, now at prep school, was to enter in due time. Louise was still in grade school. She was a thin tall girl with nothing remarkable in her face, unless it was her extreme blondness. It was still not decided whether she was to go to college.

Mark Haslatt, so eager for his sons, was dubious about the education of women, and Mrs. Haslatt, who had married at seventeen, had finished only the grade school in the little Kansas town where her father had been the general storekeeper. Edward, in his own pride, had tried recently to rouse ambition in Louise but she had only listened, her pale eyes wary.

"Don't you want to go to college, Louise?" Edward had inquired with sternness.

Louise saw that she was forced to answer. "I don't care if I do," she said in cautious assent. Then immediately she added with more courage, "And I don't care if I don't."

It was a family not unhappy, one tied together with deep and unspoken loyalties, but never quite cheerful. Fear of life, memory of hard times, dread of small slights in the community and the casual forgetfulness of friends, all combined to keep the household temperature low.

For this reason the high and constant gaiety of the Seaton family seemed to Edward fascinating, if not altogether admirable. Self-assured, domineering, careless, old Thomas Seaton loved and quarreled with his handsome, white-haired wife. There was no caution in their tongues, and Edward enjoyed and yet was alarmed by the sharpness of their judgments, the edge of their wit. Without wit himself, he hoped that he might develop it were he in the clear brisk atmosphere that surrounded the Seatons. With them he was quite another man. Quiet and prudent, he was nevertheless courteous and agreeable, and he held his own well enough. He was not cowed by the Seatons, not even by old Thomas. Margaret's first admiring word had come as a consequence. "I must say, Ned, that you do hold up your end very well with Father. He's used to pertness from Sandra and me, and to tempers from Tom, but you're so—impervious. He's not used to that."

Edward had smiled, without betraying the fact that he had smarted under Thomas Seaton's thrust. "A printer, eh? Newspaper?"

"No, sir—books," Edward had answered sturdily.

"You can't get rich on that," Thomas said.

"Getting rich is not my ambition," Edward had replied.

"Ha!" Thomas had snorted. He was a big thick man, with grizzled red hair and beard. He wore tweed suits in a day when most gentlemen wore black broadcloth. But that was his English squire affectation, Chedbury thought. Edward had quivered under the portentous grunt, but it was true that he was not actually afraid of anyone. Doggedly he had overcome in himself the fears of his family.

"Edward!" Louise's voice now floated up the stairs. "Mama wants to know if you're ready for breakfast!"

"Coming!" he shouted. He turned from the window, gave himself a final stare in the mirror and ran downstairs almost content with his appearance. He had no vanity about his angular face, believing himself far from handsome. But he took some pride in his height and in his good figure, square shouldered and lean. There were other men worse off than he, was the way he summed himself up.

Entering the solid comfortable dining room he felt his spirits rise. It was long before the day of antiques and the furniture was of heavy walnut, expensive but serviceable. One of the first things his mother had wanted when money began to accumulate in the bank was a good dining-room set. The long mirror on the buffet met his eyes as he entered and presented him with a double vision of the loaded breakfast table, his family seated about, and himself at the door. Only Baynes was not there and it was of Baynes that his mother spoke.

"Come in, Edward. I'm telling your father that I thought you cost him a pretty penny at college but Baynes is going to spare no expense, I see by the bills we're getting already. Your father has only just got up the courage to tell me."

"I thought you seemed tired last night, Mary," his father said mildly. His gray mustache was colored with egg yolk.

"So I was," she retorted, "and I'm tired again now. Do wipe the egg off yourself!" She looked at her husband while he wiped his mouth and then she turned to Edward. "Sit down, son. Do you want me to put up some lunch or will Margaret take the food?"

He sat down and resolutely, although self-consciously, did not bow his head in silent grace. His father's mumbled "blessing" over these meals had begun to seem provincial. Yet it took some strength to begin to eat, without even the gesture. He avoided his mother's eyes, lest catching his she be emboldened to reprove him again for his godlessness. This made him feel partially a coward but he was prudent. He poured heavy cream and much sugar on the bowl of oatmeal that was waiting at his place. "Don't bother, Mother," he said. "I'll buy something at the store."

"Nonsense," she said incisively. "Store food!"

"Then some of that chocolate cake," he suggested. He was not at all sure of Margaret's efforts but he would not have revealed this to his family.

His mother looked doubtful. "I'll make some sandwiches, too, out of that chicken we had last night," she said. "Then you'll be on the safe side."

"Safe side of what?" his father inquired dryly.

Edward smiled and his mother laughed. When she laughed they all forgave her. "Safe side of anything!" she said briskly. "Want more coffee, Mark?"

"No," his father said, "I've got to get down to the shop."

"Don't act like you were sorry to go," his mother rejoined. "You know that the day when you have to quit shop will be the sorriest day of your life."

"Oh, Mama," Louise cried in distress. "Why do you?"

Her mother had risen and was at the kitchen door, but she paused. "Why do I what, miss?" she asked.

"Nothing, nothing," her husband said peaceably. He folded his napkin, stared at the swinging door through which she passed, and then looked at his watch.

"Know what I'm going to do the day I retire?" he asked Louise.

"What, Papa?" she asked with mild interest.

"I'm going to catch the first train west and see where I used to live and maybe stay there," he said.

"Oh, Papa!" she wailed.

"You'll never retire," Edward said comfortably. He was eating buttered muffin with zest and appetite, and since the egg and bacon were exactly as he liked, he added them heartily to the foundation of oatmeal already consumed. He supposed he had stopped growing, but his hunger was huge.

At this moment the telephone rang in the hall, and startled them all. It was a new instrument in the house, and the bell rang harshly and always unexpectedly. Edward hastened out of the room, picked up the heavy receiver and listened to a series of whirrs and rumbles. Out of these came at last Margaret's voice, fresh and impatient. "Is that you, Ned?" she demanded.

"Yes, it is!" he shouted.

"Don't bellow, Ned! It takes off my ear," she called back. "Ned, can you hear me?"

"Yes, I can," he replied in a lower tone.

"You sound so odd," she complained, "as though you were shy."

"I'm not," he said briefly.

"Ned!" she called again.

"Yes?"

"Ned, will you be very disappointed if we put off the picnic?"

His heart fell into the pit of his stomach. Then he grew so angry that he was speechless.

"Ned, did you hear?" she cried.

"Yes, I do hear!" he cried back. "And I shall be very disappointed, Margaret."

There was silence for an instant. Then her voice came back as vigorous as ever.

"It's only that Father has suddenly decided to go to New York and wants me to go with him."

"I've been counting on this day ever since you came home, which is three weeks and more," he replied.

"Oh, Ned!" she cried with new impatience. "You're always here and so am I—as if there weren't millions of days!"

"We may not get such another fine day," he said. Then he went on grimly. "If you don't want to come, then I don't want you to come, but let's not plan another day, Margaret. Let's just say there won't be a picnic—ever again!"

His mother came to the door of the hall, a spoon in her hand, and he saw her make fierce faces at him.

"Edward Haslatt!" she hissed. "If you take this—"

He waved her away, trying to hear Margaret.

"Oh, dear, I knew you'd feel that way," she complained.

"Of course I do," he said stubbornly.

"Ned, if I come, will you promise to behave?"

"Depends on what you mean by that," he said.

He wished his mother would go away, so that he could speak freely. But the telephone was never considered private. His father stood waiting at the front door, and Louise was now in the hall.

"You know what I mean," Margaret insisted.

"I do not," he retorted.

"Edward, you're so—indomitable!" she complained.

"Maybe I am," he agreed.

There was a silence so long that he wondered if she had hung up. Then she said in a resigned voice, "Very well. Do you like ham or beef sandwiches?"

"Mother is putting up some chicken," he said. "Don't you bother."

"Oh, good," Margaret said, without gratitude in her voice. "Then I'll only bring apple pie, shall I?"

"That'll be all right," he said shortly. "I'll come by for you in half an hour."

He hung up the receiver and faced his family. "It's all right," he said shortly.

"Shall I make the sandwiches?" his mother asked.

"Yes, please, Mother," Edward said.

His father kissed his mother and went his way and Louise began to clear the table and his mother returned to the kitchen. He himself went upstairs and to his own room. He felt shaken, and he did not want his mother to see it. The mild hopefulness with which he had begun the morning was now entirely gone. He committed himself to pessimism. Margaret did not love him and would never love him. He wished that he had had the sense to abandon the picnic. Then his deep unalterable stubbornness rose in him. No, he would go, he would do

11

everything exactly as he had planned. He would ask her to marry him and when she refused he would tell her that he would never ask her again.

When he came downstairs with his hard straw hat under his arm, his angular young face was so stern that his mother said not a word when she handed him the neatly wrapped box into which she had packed his lunch. He took it and had already reached the door, when he heard her speak.

He paused.

"What'd you say, Mother?"

Her gray eyes were profoundly tender. "I said, God bless you, my son," she repeated.

He blushed with surprise. "Thank you, Mother," he muttered and was gone.

He had hired a horse and buggy, and from the high seat of the vehicle he saw Margaret waiting for him on the porch of the Seaton house. Any other girl in Chedbury would have waited for him inside the house, and any other girl would have worn a hat and coat and possibly gloves. But Margaret sat on the top step, leaning her bare dark head dreamily against the white-painted post. She had a paper parcel beside her, undoubtedly the pie, and she wore her old gray tweed suit, the skirt of which he privately considered too short. It was at least six inches above her ankles. She knew how he felt about it, for her too discerning eye had caught his disapproval one rainy day when they had met accidentally on the street.

"What's the matter?" she had demanded. "Do I have a smudge on my face?"

When she had wormed out of him why he had averted his eyes, she had laughed at him. "I tore the edge of my skirt on a barbed wire fence," she said frankly, "and so I had to shorten it all around. Don't be silly, Ned." He had retired into silence and they had parted.

Now as he drew near he felt that had she really cared about him, she would have put on something else. "For two cents I wouldn't ask her to marry me," he thought gloomily, but he knew he would.

She looked up alertly when he reached the gate.

"Slowpoke!" she called. "I've been waiting ages." She jumped up with the lightness that was so pleasant to see, and walked quickly down the path. He knew that at the windows along the street, curtains were drawn back to see them go off, but she would not care.

"It took me considerable time to figure out whether you were coming or not," he said. He made preparations to get out of the buggy, but she swung herself up beside him.

"I see you've got the new horse," she said, paying no heed to his last remark.

"I told Jim I didn't want the balky one," he rejoined. Everyone in Chedbury knew Jim Smiley's horses intimately.

They rode in silence for some time. He was still too ruffled to make talk, and his heart was very low. In spite of the old suit Margaret was looking beautiful. She had put on a blue linen blouse, and he was startled to see that it was collarless. It was almost as strange as if she were décolleté. She caught him looking at her neck.

"If there is anything I hate it is having to wear a high collar on a picnic," she instantly declared. "It's an old blouse I cut the collar off."

"Looks nice," he said with reserve.

"I don't really care how it looks," she said.

They were silent again for a while. Then being young, she but twenty-one and he twenty-two, the magic of the day stole into their blood. Though they lived to be a hundred, there could not be enough of such days. The mists were gone, and the sun shone down on the changeful autumn colors of the trees. The street of Chedbury, lined with old elms, its white houses set back in green lawns, became soon a country road between low stone walls, and then a wide upward trail into a brilliantly shadowed wood, beside a clear brook.

Edward's mind busied itself with the question of when he should make his proposal of marriage. If he kept it unspoken upon his mind, he could not enjoy his food. On the other hand, he would have no appetite whatever once all hope was gone. He was disgusted with himself to discover that he was so foolish as still to harbor hope in his heart. When she had shown him so plainly this morning!

The trail reached a sudden parting in the trees, and they looked down the beautiful hillside upon which Chedbury lay, now the very picture of a village, the houses glinting white in the sun and the spire of the church lifting itself slender and tall above the surrounding trees. This, he decided suddenly, would be the place, let come what may. He drew up the horse and jumped down.

"Let's stop here, Margaret," he said.

She laughed. "Don't be so grim—unless you are going to murder me, Ned. Heavens!"

But she leaped down in one of her long graceful motions and stood only a little less tall than he, waiting. Her bright blue eyes were knowing and confident, and while he felt all his love rush out toward her it occurred to him that some small amount of shyness in her might have been more natural. There was nothing about her that was like other women, and this was why he loved her so desperately and yet with foreboding. Life with Margaret could not be peaceful, whatever else it was. He did not deceive himself. Had there been any way to save himself, he might have done so, but there was no way. If she would not have him, he supposed in common sense that someday he would marry someone else, but he could not imagine it.

"Sit down on that log, Margaret," he commanded her.

She sat down obediently, and he stood and looked down at her and saw what he expected—that her eyes were full of laughter.

"Put the whip down, Ned," she said gaily. "Suppose old Miss Townsend is using her telescope!"

He turned abruptly without answering, tied the horse, and threw the whip into the buggy. Then he sat down on the log. Sitting thus, they were below the level of the treetops on the hill and therefore invisible. At this hour of a weekday it was not likely that anyone would be on the mountain.

"Margaret," he began firmly, "let's have it out once and for all."

Her hands flew to her face. "Oh, dear!" she said from behind them. "Before lunch?"

"Here and now," he said in the same stubborn voice. "It'll be for the last time, I promise."

"No, Ned, don't promise!" This little voice, coming from behind her hands, threw him off entirely.

"Eh?" he exclaimed. "Why, Margaret!" Mad hope surged up in him. "You don't mean—"

14

She shook her head, her hands still against her eyes. "I don't mean anything! You're always thinking I mean things!"

He reached over and with both hands pulled hers away from her face and held them hard. She tried to free herself and could not.

"Say what you do mean," he commanded.

She stopped struggling and looked suddenly sensible and mild. The sun fell full on her vivid face, and it was all he could do to keep from taking her into his arms. "You didn't even bring a hat, and your nose is already freckling," he accused her.

"That wasn't what I thought you were going to say," she said softly.

"It isn't," he retorted, still holding her hands, "but you keep taking my mind off . . . Margaret!"

"Yes?"

"Shall I go on?"

"If you must . . ."

He considered her, the red mouth, the creamy neck, and the little black curls of her hair. "I'll never give up," he muttered.

She lowered her lashes at this and was silent, and he felt the triumph of her yielding.

"Margaret," he spoke her name in a deep and solemn voice, "for the third time, I ask you—will you be my wife?"

Each time he had asked her she had responded differently. The first time she had laughed, had shaken her head, and had run away. He had been fool enough to blurt out his love for her at the senior dance, and almost immediately her next partner had claimed her, a Groton fellow whom he loathed, and not only because he had lost the editorship of the *Harvard Crimson* to him. The second time was well considered. He had walked home with her from church, and artfully taking her the long way around, he had imagined that she would need his help on an icy road. But she had been very independent indeed. When he had again asked her to marry him she had said positively, "No."

"Why not?" he had demanded, instantly hurt.

"I don't feel like it," she had replied.

15

To that she had not been willing to add one word, and they had walked the rest of the way in silence.

Now he waited trembling. She tugged her hands away suddenly from his, and he was terrified. But he let them go quickly and sat in silence. When she spoke, it was with unexpected thoughtful calm.

"Ned, of course I have been thinking a great deal. I knew you'd ask me again. Goodness, how I know you—much better than you do me! That's the trouble. If I didn't know you so thoroughly I'd probably marry you right off. But—"

She paused, shook her head, and looked sad. He felt his heart fall again, like a stone thrown in a well. "What's the matter with me?" he asked. He was so wounded that he could not summon his pride.

He expected laughter, but he was further confounded when she lifted serious eyes to his. "You're good," she replied with entire honesty. "It's me."

His heart bounced up again. He leaned toward her ardently. "If it's only that, Margaret, darling, darling, leave it to me. I'll take you as you are."

But she moved away from him, out of reach of his hands. "There isn't anything the matter with me, Ned. It's just—I want a very special kind of marriage."

He looked so blank that she gave him a slight push. "There—you see you don't even know what I mean!"

"Why don't you tell me?" he demanded.

She considered this and began again. "I don't want to be married the way other people are. I want it to be splendid—fun, you know, and strong enough for us to fly at each other when we feel like it, and say what we really think, and yet know that nothing can separate us, not even moments of hate. I'm not a careful person, Ned. I don't want to have to stop and think whether something is going to hurt your feelings. I'll get tired of that. Everything's got to be straight and strong and clear."

"I can take that," he said.

"I'm not sure you can," she retorted. Her firm hand busied itself with a bit of crumbling wood on the log. Every time they met he had looked at that hand to see if it wore a ring. The nightmare of his life was that she would engage herself to someone else before he had a chance to make her see she must marry him.

"How can I make you sure?" he asked.

"I don't know," she replied.

He had not imagined such an impasse as this—Margaret willing to marry him if she could be sure he was strong enough! He knew what she meant. With her extraordinary intelligence she had penetrated his weakness, the ease with which he could be wounded—his feelings hurt, as his mother put it.

"You're pretty smart," he said slowly. "Any man takes his life in his hands when he marries a smart woman."

"That's true," she agreed.

"But it's you or none, Margaret. I'm that sort," he said slowly.

"If I marry you," she said gravely, "it will be my life and my career. Will it be yours?"

He looked into the clear and honest depths of her sea-blue eyes, and then he saw dimly a vision of what marriage could mean to a man—a companionship complete, a friendship profound, something as far above the dull mating of the commonplace as man was above the beast. "Yes," he said. "That I can pomise—and I do."

"Then will you marry me?" she asked.

The wonder of these words lay in their simplicity. She spoke them quietly, not moving to touch him, not putting out her hand.

"Are you—asking *me?*" he gasped.

"Yes!"

"Oh, Margaret!"

He rose and drew her up to him. "Sure you mean it?"

"If you'll keep your promise."

With his right hand he pressed her head against his breast. "If you know me so well, don't you know I keep my promises?"

She lifted her head and looked at him. "Yes," she said again. It was assent and faith, and he trembled with fear and joy. . . .

Across this sublimity she broke a moment later with a murmur. He bent to hear it.

"I'm hungry," she was saying into his coat, "aren't you?"

He laughed and let her go. "Starved! But we can't eat here on the road."

"Why not? It isn't as private as making marriage proposals."

"No, but it's not my idea." He felt rising amazement. "Matter of fact, none of it's been what I planned this morning."

"You *planned?*"

"Of course. You don't think I would leave the biggest thing in my life to chance, do you?"

"Oh, Ned, do you plan everything?" she cried.

"Of course," he said stoutly.

She flew into a fit of incomprehensible laughter at this and ran to the buggy and he untied the horse and leaped in beside her, and they began to wind slowly up the trail. He put an arm about her and felt the astonishing ineffable joy of her leaning upon him. She said, "I'll always be spoiling your plans, because I only do things when I think of them."

"I'll learn that—and everything," he declared.

"But when you get to the picnic spot—"

"It's not a real spot," he felt it only honest to say.

"Yes, it is, if you dreamed of it!" she insisted.

They found it over the brow of the mountain, beside another stream, that eddied in a small pool. Both of them cried out at the same moment that it was found, he pointing with the whip, she with her forefinger. He unharnessed the horse and tethered it at a little distance and she unpacked the lunch. His mother had put in a small clean tablecloth and inspired by this, Margaret picked red oak leaves and laid them together for plates. Upon them she placed the neat sandwiches, the cake, and the pie. He was about to sit down beside her but she shook her head. "Sit across from me, Ned. I want to see how you'll look every day at breakfast."

He obeyed, and was mortified to feel that he looked foolishly shy. "I'm not much to stare at," he said, trying to be casual.

"I've hated every handsome man I ever saw," she remarked. "Sandwich, Ned!"

He took one and bit into it. "You didn't hate Harold Ames," he reminded her.

"Don't be silly—I did!" she retorted.

"Did he ask you to marry him?"

18

She bit deeply into her sandwich. "What if he did?" she asked.

"Nothing—only I don't like it." He was ashamed to tell her that jealousy was one of his vices. Instinctively he knew that she would not tolerate jealousy. Then he felt it a necessity to be honest with her. "I'll have to tell you I'm a jealous disposition—at least I think I am."

"I know you are," she said.

He looked at her. "Do you!" he rejoined somewhat feebly. Then his rare humor glinted. "Are you always going to tell me you already know everything I tell you? It'll make for a dull marriage."

"I won't always tell you," she said, dimpling. The two dimples in her cheeks were what he had seen first about her as a little girl at Chedbury birthday parties.

"Know what Lucy Snell used to say about you?" he asked with wicked intent.

"What?"

"She said you laughed on purpose to show your dimples."

She laughed. "Maybe I do."

"Doesn't anything ever make you angry, Margaret?"

"Not if I feel happy, and I nearly always do."

He sighed. "I wish I could say that! I have the devil of a temper."

"I don't mind the temper if you'll bear my not being afraid of it. I shan't take anything from you, Ned."

"I don't want you to." He put down his second sandwich and looked at her earnestly. "Margaret, I want to say something now while I'm calm and happier than I've ever been in my life. And I want you to remember it when I'm in one of my sulks, and pay no mind to me."

"Yes, Ned?" She put down her sandwich that she might listen properly.

"I don't want you to be afraid of me, ever—or ever to yield to me. Stand up to me, Margaret—and help me!"

"I will," she said softly.

"At whatever cost?" he asked sternly.

"Yes!" Again her beautiful full *yes!*

"Even if I should strike you?"

Her eyes flashed. "If you hit me I'll hit you!" she said warmly.

They both laughed. "Free for all, eh?" he said fondly.

By common accord they leaned across the little table-cloth and kissed.

Thus passed the glorious day. He would not have dreamed of prolonging it beyond the prudence of Chedbury's watchful eyes. His tenderness for her was bottomless—he would protect her even from himself. So, timing the drive home by the stand of the sun in the sky, soon after four he rose from the spot where he had been lying at her feet while she sat on a low old stump.

"We must be going, Margaret, if we're to get home before sunset."

"Why should we get home before sunset?" she inquired dreamily.

He did not answer at once, busying himself with harnessing the reluctant horse. She knew as well as he did why they should get home and she was teasing him. For a moment he toyed with the idea of accepting the provocation. He might say, "Very well, we won't get home." But he was afraid. There was no telling how far her mischief might carry her. Once when they were children someone had dared her to jump from the barn roof on the Seaton place, and he had stood by, not believing that she would be so foolish. But she had been so foolish and he could never forget the horrible moment when she had jumped into the air and he saw her dark curls flying behind her head and her arms outspread like wings.

"Remember the day you jumped off the barn roof?" he asked now.

"What makes you think of that?" she asked.

"I wonder!" He waited until the horse was ready. "Come, Margaret," he said firmly.

She wavered and then suddenly obeyed. The sight of her thus docile drew the love out of him like lodestone and he took her into his arms and kissed her more ardently than he had yet allowed himself.

"Oh, Ned," she whispered, "we are going to be happy!"

"Of course we are," he agreed.

So they came down the mountain through the late and golden sunshine, and the trail became the country road and the road became again the street of Chedbury, and by the time he reached the gate of her house they were sitting decorously side by side and not too close. He leaped down, opened the gate, and their hands clung for a moment.

"Good night," she said softly and her eyes glowed dark as sapphires.

"Good night, dear love," he said. "I'd call you tonight, but the family is always about. Tomorrow I'll be over to see your father."

"Let me tell him first!"

He paused at this. "No, Margaret—leave it to me to speak for myself."

"But why?"

"I'd feel better to have it so."

"Then I've got to keep it all night? I'll tell Mother at least."

"No, Margaret," he insisted. "Tonight let's just have it all to ourselves."

She opened her mouth to protest, then did not.

"All right, Ned," she said softly, and gave him her quick and brilliant smile.

Upon this he left her and drove the horse and buggy to the livery stable and went home on foot through the golden street.

Now that he was alone he felt solemn, exalted and set apart. He had given his promise to Margaret that their marriage would be his life and his career. What this meant he did not fully know, but he knew that Margaret was his center, and all he did must be built about her. He was capable of devotion as few men were, perhaps, and it did not degrade him to know it. He found a deep fulfillment in self-devotion. But he knew that only Margaret could have called this fulfillment into being. Had he married someone else, he would at this moment have been thinking of himself. Now he was thinking of Margaret.

He lifted his head and breathed in the cool autumn air, sharp and pure. He lifted his eyes to the mountain where so much had taken place. The day was divided as cleanly as if a sword had cut across time. This morning he had been one man and now he was another. His marriage was to be like none he had ever seen.

He opened the heavy walnut door of his father's house and stepped into the hall and listened. The house was silent. Then he heard a murmur of voices from the kitchen, his father's and his mother's. He wanted to tell no one of what had come about this day. Tomorrow when he went to see Mr. Seaton he would have to tell, and then his own family must know. But tonight must be the drawn-out dream which the day had been. He tiptoed upstairs, entered his own room, and stood with his back to the closed door.

The room was impressed upon his memory by childhood and youth, and yet now it looked new to him. No, it looked as old as a shell outgrown, a skin cast aside. His home was here no more.

He moved about silently, washed himself and changed his clothes, and went downstairs. The door of the dining room was open and he saw Louise setting the table.

He paused at the door. "Supper about ready?"

She looked at him vaguely. "I suppose so."

"I'll fetch the milk jug," he said. He went into the kitchen and was immediately aware that he had interrupted talk between his parents. His father looked at him self-consciously, and his mother, continuing to stir the gravy she was making in a saucepan, did not look at him.

"I've come to fetch the milk jug," he said.

"It's there," his mother said.

His father got to his feet from the chair behind the stove. "Have a good day?" he asked, trying to be casual.

"Yes, very good," Edward said, trying to be as casual. He opened the icebox and took out a bottle of milk and poured it and carried the jug into the dining room. Louise had finished the table and was at the window staring into the twilight of the street. He wondered what her thoughts were and could not have asked, knowing full well how he at her age would have refused such a question.

At the same moment his mother pushed open the door and came in, carrying a platter of sliced boiled beef, covered with the gravy. "Come along, now," she said briskly. "Let's eat while the food is hot."

His father came in while she hurried back for potatoes and cabbage, and they sat down. The evening, Edward thought, could be exactly like every other. Only he knew that it was not.

"Edward!"

His mother's ghostly voice woke him that night out of a sound sleep. He saw her standing in the middle of his bedroom, wrapped in her gray flannel dressing gown. Her hair was in curlers and her face was pale in the moonlight that fell through the wide open window.

He sat up in bed, half dazed. "What's wrong, Mother?"

She came near and sat on the bed, then rose and shut the window and sat down in the barrel-backed chair, shivering.

"That's what I don't know," she said in a low tense voice. "I can't sleep for thinking of things."

"What things, Mother?" Instinctively he knew.

"Edward, I know something happened between you and Margaret today."

"What makes you think so, Mother?"

"You were different all evening."

"Was I?" He was flabbergasted at this, having flattered himself that he had been entirely natural.

"Even Louise noticed it," his mother said.

His stubbornness rose up in him and he did not reply. What claim had anybody on his confidence until he chose to give it? He was no longer a child. That he had spoken his love and that Margaret had accepted it made them both free of the past.

"I don't want to seem to inquire into your affairs," his mother said after a decent interval, "but it would hurt me if you got married without telling me, Edward."

"I am not married," he said reluctantly.

"Are you engaged?" She put the question so swiftly that it was like the pounce of a bird. He did not know how to parry it, being too honest. "Well, yes, I am," he said slowly. Then his anger got the better of him. "I was going to tell you tomorrow, Mother. It did seem to me more decent to speak to Mr. Seaton first, after I'd found out Margaret's mind."

"But I'm your mother," she said.

He recognized the pained sadness in her voice. How often in his childhood had it compelled him to acts which he had hated! In his adolescence it had still compelled him, although he had occasionally protested and with anger. That phase had passed, too, and he had learned to remain silent when he caught the overtones in his mother's voice. Now, sitting up in his bed, he was enraged to feel her forcing him back into his adolescence. All his new manhood resisted her. He set his lips firmly and gazed at a print on the wall above her head. It was one he had chosen himself when he was fifteen, a white ship sailing at full speed over a bright blue sea, under a sky as blue. He knew now that as a print it was not the best, but on so many mornings had he waked to that fresh blue sea and flying ship that he would have missed it, had it been gone. He thought, "I'll want to take that with me."

"You're not going to say a word?" his mother inquired.

"Not till tomorrow, Mother."

"Then I call it heartless of you," she declared. Her square face turned a coppery red and she pulled at her corded belt and tied it more tightly. "And I shall go on and say what I was going to say. We've nothing to be ashamed of. Your father's business is as good as any in Chedbury or around. What I'm saying is for your own good."

"Don't say it, Mother," he broke in.

"I will say it!" Her voice rose. "I'm not to be stopped by my own son, I hope. I warn you, Edward, you'll never be happy with those Seatons. She's a stuck-up proud girl, and she hasn't a proper decency."

He kept his eyes on the flying ship and the blue that was the color of Margaret's eyes.

"A poor housekeeper, too! And, Edward, they don't think a thing of divorce. You know even Thomas Seaton's own sister has been divorced. That's why she has to live in Paris. Decent people won't have her here. And where does old Seaton get his money? He's never worked enough to have it. Somewhere in New York, speculating! Who knows? And they have no religion—he's a freethinker, and she'll have freethinking ways and bring up your children different from all of us, and I'll have no comfort in them."

He glanced nervously at her hands. They were trembling and he knew what would happen. The next moment she began to cry soundlessly, and then she hurried out of the room, leaving the door wide open. He sighed, got up, closed the door and opened the window and turned off the lamp. He'd have to tell Margaret that after all his mother had wormed it out of him. Only by thinking of Margaret, only by going over the whole day, minute by minute, was he able to reinforce his determination and renew his love and so begin again his own life. Then he fell asleep, comforted. His mother did not matter any more.

Under his everyday exterior the next morning Edward concealed from his mother any memory of their conversation in the night. With determination he kept himself from calling Margaret on the telephone, even from his father's office. For his father, after muttering his usual blessing and then in abstraction eating half his breakfast, had suddenly said, "If you have nothing better to do, Edward, I could take a little help in the office this morning."

Edward nodded and nothing more was said between them. His mother was silent, too, beyond the necessary questions about the food, and Louise ate in her usual silence. But Edward knew, as well as though words had told him, that his mother had repeated to his father the midnight scene, and that this morning at the office his father would manage to be alone with him and to say something. He could not imagine what it would be.

But none of it mattered, he told himself. Yesterday was true, and this afternoon he would see Margaret. He did not look forward with pleasure to his interview with Thomas Seaton, but he was not afraid of it. He would be dignified and self-assured, knowing that he had Margaret's promise, and even if the older man objected, the marriage would go on just the same.

The meal was finished, and Edward and his father rose simultaneously. "I'll meet you at the door, Father," he said.

He kissed his mother, as he knew she liked him to do, nodded to Louise, and left the room. Out in the hall he toyed again with the temptation of calling Margaret, and decided against it. He suspected that she slept late and it would be harder to call and not hear her voice than not to call. He put on his brown gabardine topcoat and a few minutes later he and his father were walking down the street together. Chedbury was peculiarly pleasant in the morning, the houses clean, the windows shining, and smoke curling softly from the chimneys. Sooner or later

25

front doors opened and other men came briskly out to go to work. So he and his father proceeded, exchanging few words, but the silence was easy.

At the shop he fell behind to allow his father to go ahead and the men looked up and nodded and he followed his father into the rather large office.

"Sit down there," his father said. "I'll give you some proofs to read."

Edward obeyed, taking off his hat and coat and hanging them on a rack in the corner. The office had not changed during all the years he had known it, and he often sat here in the odd hours he had helped his father during vacations.

He began to read the proofs, dull pages of a pamphlet being put out by some historical society, and it was the middle of the morning when suddenly his father spoke.

"Edward," he said solemnly, "how do you propose to make your living?"

Edward looked up. He knew that his father had shown extraordinary patience not only on this day, but during the past four years, while he had been pursuing his somewhat leisurely way through college. The very necessity of his father's youth to make an early livelihood had made him take pride in being patient with his son.

"I think it's the first time you have ever asked me the question, Father," he said. He put down proofs and pencil, and wheeled around on his screw-bottomed chair.

"I've never had to ask you," his father said proudly. "But the time has come now when I presume you will want to earn your own way, and certainly the time has come when I'd like to ease your mother's life a little. I want her to have help in the house. She hasn't been willing so long as you were in college and the other two in school. She isn't as strong as she was—it stands to reason a woman can't be. I've told her to hire somebody this week."

"I'm glad of that," Edward said heartily, and paused.

"Well?" his father said.

Edward smiled his slight cool smile. "It would be easy to say I know what I want to do, Father, if I had any special talent. But I haven't—except a general interest in books."

"Books?" his father repeated, astonished.

"Are you surprised?" Edward inquired. "But you've printed books all these years."

"Not just books," his father corrected him. "I've printed anything that came my way—catalogues, pamphlets, bulletins, wedding announcements, Christmas cards, anything."

"I'm thinking you might like me to take the book section of the business and develop it a little," Edward said daringly.

He saw immediately that this was an entirely new and somewhat frightening idea to his father.

"Books are a risk," his father said slowly. "Look at them piled up in the second-hand shops in Boston! It scares me every time I go there. People read them once and then sell them."

"They have to buy them before they can read them," Edward argued.

"All these newfangled public libraries," his father went on. "That fellow Carnegie—the book business will sink to nothing. Who's going to buy a book if he can read it for nothing?"

"Will you take me on for a year?" Edward asked.

His father's opposition crystallized what had been the vaguest wanderings of his own mind. It was true that he did not know what he wanted to do for a livelihood. In college he had lived, by the chance of a roommate, in the midst of a group of young men who had not needed to think of work immediately after graduation, and he had fallen into the way of contemplation rather than activity. Yet he knew that this was an atmosphere entirely alien to him, and that he must indeed work with all his ability as soon as possible. But he had been graduated only last June. Beyond all else, he had felt that until he had settled the matter of his marriage with Margaret, he could not choose a livelihood. Too much depended on the life that she would want and where they might choose to live. He was somewhat perturbed now by his own abruptness in the decision he had made even for a year.

His father meanwhile had been pondering the question. "Maybe for a year," he said slowly. "I'll talk with Mather, provided you don't do anything to call for extra capital."

Edward did not reply for a moment. The business de-

27

pression, which had terrified his father and had shadowed his last year at college, was perhaps beginning to recede. The banks had been saved by the millionaires, staking their fortunes against the fears of little men with nothing. His father had been almost revoltingly grateful to "the big fellows."

"If I can't convince you by the end of the year to put in some capital, I shall consider myself a failure," Edward said.

He was about to wheel his chair around again when his father raised his hand. "Wait a minute, son—I promised your mother something."

Edward saw him flush and immediately felt at ease. "Mother was cross with me in the night, I know," he said frankly. "But, Father, if you don't mind, I'll just wait until tomorrow and then everything will be clear."

"Your mother is easily hurt, son," his father reminded him.

"I know, because she has passed that same quality on to me," Edward said quietly. "But I think it's wrong to be so quick to be wounded, and it's a trait I mean to get over."

He turned then in good earnest and picking up his pencil he went to work again, and his father said no more. They went home together at noon and only the barest words of business passed between them. They ate in almost entire silence the noon meal of meat and vegetables and an apple pie and then Edward went upstairs to his own room. He knew that Thomas Seaton slept for an hour between one and two. It was his intention to reach the house in time to see Margaret before her father waked and then, as soon as possible afterward, to appear before him.

He washed, examined his somewhat too easily growing beard, and decided to shave again. Then he dressed himself in his good dark blue serge suit, white shirt, and stiff collar. The tie he usually wore was dark blue, too, but today, thinking of Margaret, he chose one she had given him last Christmas of wine-red satin with a stripe of blue. Thus arrayed, with care to his shoes and his nails, he felt that he had done all he could, and he went downstairs and out of doors without seeing his mother or looking for her. But some impulse when he was on his way made him turn his head and he saw her standing at the sitting-room window, looking out after him, her hand over her mouth. He could not see her eyes, but he felt their painful and earnest gaze, and he lifted his arm and waved to her. With no more than an instant's hesitation she waved back to him with her white handkerchief, and at the effort, all his resentment left him. As well as he knew himself, he knew her and that she had forgiven him and he was the happier for it.

"Softhearted, that's what I am," he thought half sadly, and wondered whether his life would be the harder for his soft heart.

Thus somewhat soberly he approached the big brick house which Chedbury merely called "Seatons'." It stood back from the street in the midst of its traditional elms, and the lawn was thick with falling leaves. No one was to be seen except the small hunched figure of old Bill Core, who tended the garden. He was gathering leaves slowly with a bamboo rake as Edward went up the brick walk.

"Anybody around?" Edward asked.

"Not that I've saw," Bill replied. He leaned on his rake. "Who're you lookin' for?"

"Margaret?" Edward said tentatively.

"Out under the apple tree behind the house last I saw," Bill said. "That was before dinner, though." He chewed slowly and grindingly, and spat a large dark brown blob into the leaves.

But Edward did not go to the apple tree. He felt some formality in the afternoon ahead of him and he went up the five marble steps to the front door of the house. There he rang the bell. Usually the maid opened the door but this time to his pleasure Margaret herself flung it wide.

"I saw you coming," she said softly. "He's just waking up. How beautiful you look! Don't you love that tie? Promise me you'll let me choose all your ties! Shall we stay outside a bit?"

"I'd rather get it over," he said, still on the threshold.

She laughed. "Poor Ned! He's not too bad, really. Though I rather think—" she broke off and shook her head.

He stepped inside the door. "Think what?" he demanded.

"I'd better not tell you."

"Margaret, tell me!" he insisted.

"No, I won't," she declared. "Because it's too silly."

"But you thought it!"

"Well, I think very silly things—often."

Before he could protest again Thomas Seaton's voice shouted suddenly from the library. "Who are you talking to, Margaret?"

She turned her head toward the voice. "To Ned, Father!"

There was a grunt to this and silence.

"He's only just waked," Margaret explained.

"Tell me what you were thinking about?" Edward said stubbornly.

"Oh, my goodness," she said suddenly. "Well, it was this—Father once had the idea that he wanted me to marry somebody—a man in New York."

"He did?" Edward exclaimed. Rage ran in his veins suddenly and he took a step toward the library. Then he turned. She was standing with both hands folded under her chin, looking at him with bright blue eyes, not laughing, and he came back.

"You can't change your mind now," he said gravely.

She shook her head. "No fear," she said.

Thereupon his rage and his pride combined and he walked into the library. The afternoon was warm, and the room was sunlit and silent. Tobacco and leather and old books scented the air with a dry and musky odor. A long window opened to the always neglected gardens and yellow leaves from an elm tree drifted across the panes. Thomas Seaton sat between the arms of a sagging leather armchair and Edward saw his grizzled red head leaning on its back.

"Is that you, Peg?" he said drowsily.

Margaret answered from the door. "Father, I told you Ned was coming to see you."

Edward turned and frowned at her. "Go away, please, Margaret," he said. "I shan't want you here while we're talking."

She made a face at him and vanished, shutting the door with unnecessary noise.

Thomas Seaton laughed. "That's right, my boy," he said in his slow rich voice. "Order her about. It's good for her. Come and sit down."

Without moving even to lift his head, he pursed his thick lips at the chair across the hearth and there Edward sat down. Margaret's father, he thought, was not prepossessing. His stained tweed vest was open and his belt unloosed, and over the brown shirt he wore his big hands were folded. He had taken off his shoes and put his feet on a faded brown velvet hassock. But his large sleepy face was benign and amused.

"Eh?" he said.

"There's no use my beating about the bush at this late day, Mr. Seaton," Edward said promptly. "I suppose you've noticed that I've been interested in Margaret for years."

"I've noticed," Thomas Seaton said dryly. "But there've been others."

"Well, I'm different from them all, I think," Edward said, allowing himself the smallest of smiles. "I asked her to marry me yesterday and she said she would."

"She's a very changeable miss, and it wouldn't be fair of me to keep that from you," Thomas Seaton retorted.

"She's never said 'yes' to me before, nevertheless, and I shan't let her change her mind," Edward said firmly.

Thomas Seaton laughed again. "Then what have you come to see me about?" he inquired.

"I wanted to tell you myself," Edward said. At the older man's laughter he felt his ready pride ruffle and prick and he was grave.

Thomas Seaton unfolded his hands and pulled out a yellowed silk handkerchief from his pocket and rubbed his face all over. The act seemed to wake him. He opened his eyes wide, sat up in his chair, and began to stuff tobacco into an old meerschaum pipe.

"If I must take this seriously," he said, "then I'd better put my mind to it. Margaret's my favorite child, and I can't just give her away. How are you planning to make a living, young man?"

"I hope you realize I wouldn't ask Margaret to be my wife, without giving some thought as to her support," Edward replied. "My father has the print shop as you know, Mr. Seaton. I shall help him there, and likely take it over some day."

"You aren't the only son," Thomas Seaton said in the same dry voice.

31

"No, sir, but I'm five years older than Baynes, and there's no competition there. By the time he's ready to work, I'll be well up in the business—maybe its head. Dad owns the business, really. Mr. Mather has turned eighty, you know."

"Don't push your father about," the older man said suddenly.

"I wouldn't think of it," Edward replied hotly.

Thomas Seaton began to puff on his pipe. He leaned back again. "A temper of your own, I see."

"I'm sorry," Edward said instantly.

"How much do you think you'll make—let's say, at your top?"

Edward hesitated. His father made, he supposed, five or six thousand a year. Whether that would seem much or little to a Seaton he had no way of knowing. He looked into Seaton's eyes, blue and bright. "I have no way of knowing," he said frankly. "It all depends on myself. I shall do more than carry on the shop. I've told my father that I want to begin to print books for myself—publish them. That might do very well."

"You like books?" Thomas Seaton inquired.

"There's something about them," Edward admitted reluctantly. He did not wish to reveal to this observing older man the peculiar influence of books upon him. Without any desire to write a book of his own, all his creative mind stirred when he held a good book in his hand. If, after he had read it, he felt it become a part of himself, it was precious to him. He wanted it well bound and more than once he had gone to Boston and had ordered rebound in scraps of leather or mohair some book which he felt had become his own.

"Know anything about book publishing?" Thomas Seaton inquired.

"I have my own feelings about it," Edward replied.

A long silence fell upon them after this. Thomas Seaton's eyes closed and Edward wondered if he were about to fall asleep again. He waited in respectful though impatient silence. But the older man was not asleep. He began to talk, his eyes still closed.

"If you and Margaret have fixed it up, I suppose I'll have to take it. Not that there's any objection to you in my mind! But whether you are the man for her, I don't know, and I don't suppose she knows until she has tried you."

At this Edward remembered the warnings of his mother in the night. Divorce was in this family. He would have none of that, however things went between him and Margaret. "I mean to make a success of my marriage," he said doggedly.

"So do we all," Thomas replied. "But it's more than your marriage, my boy. It's the woman, too, and she can wreck any marriage, if she's a mind to do it. Margaret's a handful, and there's no use in pretending she isn't. She gets it from her mother. I had to beat her mother once—it was with an umbrella, I remember. I'd just come back from London, and she took a fancy to some man or other while I was away. It's in their blood. I'd bought a good strong umbrella at Harridge's and when she told me the first thing that she'd changed her mind about me I said, 'No, you haven't,' and went after her with the umbrella. She cried, but I didn't give an inch. I slept with her that night, and the next day she was all right again. I never even knew the man's name."

He chuckled and Edward listened with horror. What would his mother have said to this sorry tale? Thank God she need never know!

"The moral of that is," Thomas Seaton went on, "you keep a strong hand with Margaret!"

"I'll do my best," Edward said with reserve, "though it could never come to beating—not with me."

"Ah well," Thomas Seaton said. "You'll devise your own weapons. But there's worse than an umbrella." He coughed, sat up and fumbled for his leather slippers, found them, and put them on. Then he stood up. "Peg!" he shouted.

The door opened so quickly that Edward wondered as he rose punctiliously to his feet if Margaret had been listening at the keyhole. He dismissed the thought as unworthy, but her father laughed as he sat down again.

"You've been listening, you scalawag," he said to her.

"No, I haven't," Margaret replied, dimpling. "I would have but I was afraid it might make Ned angry. He isn't used to it. I was only standing ready, on call. Do sit down, Ned."

She sat down on the hassock between the two of them, her long beautiful hands clasped about her knees.

"Well, shall he have me, Father?" she asked.

"He says he will," her father replied.

Great love was between these two, and Edward felt it jealously, as the eyes of father and daughter met and melted and spoke. It was unfair, surely, for the older man to have had the advantage of long years with her, watching her as she grew from birth to womanhood. What other man could hope to have such knowledge of her? Then it occurred to him that there was no such relation between his own father and Louise, and again he knew that there was something in this Seaton family that made them different from his own.

"But will you have him, Peg?" Thomas Seaton asked. "It goes two ways, you know."

Margaret smiled her deep dimpled smile. "It's taken me years to make up my mind," she said frankly.

"Nonsense," Edward said abruptly. "You only made it up yesterday—you know that, Margaret. Why, even yesterday morning, you were wanting to put off the picnic. And twice you—"

He stopped, aware that Thomas Seaton was listening avidly and with laughter bright in his eyes.

"Only twice?" Seaton said. "That's nothing, man! Her mother broke our engagement nine times."

He and Margaret joined in laughter offensively loud to Edward's ear. "At any rate," he said soberly, "she's made up her mind, whether yesterday or not."

Margaret turned on Edward vividly. "I began asking myself the very first day I saw you whether I'd marry you or not."

He could scarcely believe this and yet it stirred him to the bottom of his soul. "But we've always known each other," he said feebly.

"I've always been asking," she said promptly.

"Then why did you turn me down so hard?" he demanded.

"Oh, you took so long to grow up," she said scornfully. "I really thought you'd never be a man—and I hate boys. You're still not really grown up, Ned, but I can see you will be, someday."

Thomas Seaton got to his feet and waved his big

ands. "You two are as good as married," he said, swallowing his laughter. "Don't be too sharp with him, Peg. He's a good young man. Don't get wicked with him."

He ambled sidewise toward the door, his hands in his pockets now and his coattails in the air. "And Edward, I advise you—get yourself a good English umbrella. You'll need it."

He went out and left the two of them, taking care to close the door.

Margaret blew a kiss after him and turned to Edward warmly. "Isn't he adorable? He shut the door because he understands us. He understands everybody, I think —me best of all." She pulled the hassock forward and leaned her head upon Edward's knees. "Oh, how blissful I am!"

"Are you really happy?" Edward asked. He had been slightly repelled by her father's forethought as though the old man had coarsely imagined that they would at once want to begin to make love! But he could not resist the sight of Margaret's dark head on his knees. What grace of God that she had her mother's dark curly hair, and her father's blue eyes! With red hair she would have been quite another woman. Besides, he did not like red hair.

"Oh, happy!" she repeated dreamily. "To think I needn't worry any more about getting married! It's all settled at last, and I can put my mind to something else."

He was amazed again, and he said, withdrawing his hand from her head, "Think of what? You needn't have worried about it."

But she took his hand and pillowed her soft cheek in his palm. "Of course I worried," she said frankly. "Every girl does. How did I know you would ask me again, and how did I know whether even if you did I would say yes? And suppose I said no, would you ask me yet again? How did I know? And suppose you didn't, what could I do, that is supposing I wanted you to ask me again?"

He sighed, and then drew her strongly into his arms. "Stop it there, Margaret," he commanded. "Just be still with me for a while, will you? I'm somewhat overcome."

She laughed softly at this, but she yielded, and he sat in the warm golden room, holding her, completely happy, except for the slight gnawing fear that the door might open suddenly to show someone's surprised face. He was chagrined that she divined the fear and rose, walked across the room and locked the door. Then she came back and curled into his arms again, and he sat holding her and feeling his love grow, second by second, until it terrified him with joy. Her right arm crept around him under his coat, and her left hand up to his cheek, and understanding, after a while, the soft steady pressure of that left hand, he yielded, turning his face to hers, and bending to her he joined his lips to hers in a long kiss.

From this kiss it was he who first moved away. He trembled at the power she had over him. Her lips, thus fastened to his, made his blood fire and his limbs were melted. He struggled against such giving up of himself. Somewhere in him, if he was to remain master of his life, there must be a place where he stood alone to survey all that he had, even her.

"Come, my dear," he said resolutely.

She looked at him languidly and he had to harden himself against the roselike face upon his breast.

"I must go home, darling," he said tenderly. "My father and mother must be told, too, you know."

He was utterly unprepared for her again. For she sprang from his arms, her face eager and even excited. "Oh, what fun!" she cried. "Now I'll come with you."

He got to his feet. "But will it be the thing to do?" he muttered.

"Why not?" she asked robustly. "Don't I have to know them? Oughtn't they to know me?"

"I suppose so," he said uncertainly.

She forgot him and looked down at herself. "This old dress!" she exclaimed passionately. "I'll have to change."

He had not noticed what she wore, but now he saw that it was a dress of faded blue linen, crumpled by his crushing her in his arms.

"What'll I wear?" she asked anxiously. Then she put her hand on his lips. "No, don't tell me—I must be myself."

With that she hastened out of the room and he went over to the window and stood looking out into the quiet weedy garden. Some old-fashioned chrysanthemums were blooming under the elms, brilliant spots of red and gold. At the end of the garden the small marble statue of a naked boy looked out mischievously from a pool choked with leaves. A year from now, he supposed, he would be married. He and Margaret would be living somewhere in Chedbury—that was a thing they had to plan, too. He would have no living with their families, neither his nor hers. There was plenty of room in this huge old house, but he would refuse to consider it. If he was to make her happy, he'd have to have her to himself.

She came back in a few minutes, wearing a new autumn suit of a heather blue and a soft felt hat. Nobody in Chedbury wore clothes like hers, so plain and soft, and she was beautiful in them.

"I got it in London," she said. "Do you like it?"

"It suits you," he said. And then overcome with her beauty he was humbled to pain. "Oh, Margaret, can you be patient with me and mine?" he asked. He took her gloved hands. "We're common folk compared to you."

She gave him a smile tender and exquisite. "I'm only marrying you—that's what we've to remember," she said.

He felt her words strong and comforting and he put his arm about her shoulder and gave her a hard squeeze. "That's right," he said heartily. "Remind me of it every morning, will you?"

They walked out into the afternoon sunlight and the sense of the magic of his life crept into Edward's consciousness. It was impossible to imagine that his wife, his house, could be like those of any other man. Whatever the faults of others, he and Margaret were beyond their possibility. They carried happiness within themselves, in their youth and health and humor and in the quality of their love. He strode along at her side, just enough taller than she to be complacent, his step matched to hers, and hidden between them were their clasped hands.

"Ned," she said suddenly, "I'll have to tell you that I did tell Mother last night, after all."

"You did?" he cried.

"I couldn't help it. She came into my room when I was getting ready for bed and saw it all over me, I suppose. So I simply said yes, I was engaged, and she said she was glad of it."

In the agitation of his interview he had forgotten the midnight scene with his own mother. Now he thought of it and was troubled as to whether, in honesty, he should tell Margaret of his mother's doubts. He decided to postpone the telling.

"Is that all your mother said?" he asked.

"Well, she said we'd have to begin talking about when we'd have the wedding, and where we'd live."

"So we shall," he agreed, "and that brings me to the question. What do you want for a ring?"

"A sapphire," she said so promptly that he was surprised.

"Sounds as if you'd had it picked for a long time," he observed.

"I have," she said. "I know exactly where it is—in an old jewelry store in New York."

"Do you mean to say you had the ring picked before you had the man?" he demanded and was vaguely pained.

She laughed and squeezed his arm with both hands. "I began thinking about the ring the night I said I wouldn't marry you—the first time—remember?"

Did he remember! However happy he was he'd never forget that evening.

She had not paused for his answer. "And then I thought, if I ever did marry you, I'd want a sapphire, set in a wide band, and so when I went to New York—"

"Oh, Margaret! And I was suffering so, thinking you'd never have me—"

"Then you were silly. Good sapphires are fearfully hard to find—good ones, that is—and I did find one."

"But suppose it had been sold?"

"Oh, I found it only this spring, and I begged the old man to keep it for me, for I knew I'd be married sometime."

"Even if not to me, I suppose!"

"Don't be jealous, Ned, and he said I surely would, too, but just in case would I put down twenty-five dollars on account."

"Margaret, you didn't!"

"I did, so the ring is safe, and I should think you'd be glad."

He was too confounded by all this to know whether he was glad or sorry, and it took him five full minutes of contemplation. This was only brought to an end by her voice, begging him.

"Ned, please forgive me—it was awfully forward of me. I can see that now."

He was pleased to forgive and he did so fully and magnanimously. "It's odd, Margaret—there's no pretending it isn't. But it's you, and that's all that matters. We'd better go tomorrow to New York and fetch it, I suppose."

"Oh, lovely!" Her rich voice sighed out the rich word, and he knew that he had behaved well. Upon this satisfaction they entered the house and he was pleased to see that his father had just got home and had not time, therefore, to change his respectable office suit of gray cloth for the patched brown smoking jacket in which he spent his evenings, although he was on the stair.

"Father!" he called from the door.

His father turned. "Yes?"

"I've brought Margaret, Father. It's all settled—"

His father came down the two steps he had mounted and held out his hand shyly. "Well, Margaret—we've always known each other, I guess, without much more than speaking—"

"Oh, yes, Mr. Haslatt." Margaret's voice, her outstretched hand were warm and instant.

His mother came to the door of the hall, and slipped off her apron and threw it behind her. Something had been expected, Edward surmised, for she wore her second-best black dress and she had put a fresh white ruching in the high boned collar.

"Edward, am I to congratulate you?" she asked.

Behind the stilted words he saw her as she had been last night and he met her stiffly. "Yes, please, Mother. It's all decided. I had a talk with Mr. Seaton."

"Welcome, Margaret—"

His mother, unrelentingly grave, led them into the sitting room and there Louise sat with a magazine. She got up awkwardly, her face flushing.

"Louise," her mother said formally. "Edward has come to tell us that he and Margaret are engaged."

Louise smiled a little and yielded her hand to Margaret, who clasped it and held it. "Oh, I've known Louise since she was born! I hope you won't mind me! I'm glad to have another sister."

In a moment they were all sitting down, not knowing

what to say, and Margaret, her warm eyes seeing everything, began to talk rapidly and gaily.

"Oh, I hope you will all like me—because I do so like all of you. I'm going to try so hard to make Ned a good wife. You'll have to teach me lots, Mrs. Haslatt. Mother's a dreadful housekeeper, in fact. She just doesn't keep house—but I want to be good at it. I don't even want a maid, because if I have one I'll never learn for myself. May I come sometimes on Saturdays and learn, dear Mrs. Haslatt?"

There never was so enchanting a woman, Edward told himself and he saw without surprise that his mother was melting.

"Well, I don't know, I'm sure, that I'm such a wonder," she began.

"Yes, you are, Mother," he said heartily, "and I shall take it as a kindness if you'll tell Margaret everything. I'm sure she's right when she says she doesn't know anything."

He was surprised to hear himself talking in this easy Seaton fashion to his own mother, and she looked at him suspiciously but was silent. Margaret picked up the silver ball of talk where he dropped it.

"Ned, I'll surprise you! I can learn when I want to, and I'm going to buy a little book and put everything into it. 'Mrs. Haslatt's muffins,' 'Mrs. Haslatt's cream tomato soup—'" She broke off. "I can't go on saying Mrs. Haslatt, can I? I'll say Mother Haslatt."

Edward saw his father absorbing all this, drinking in Margaret's warmth and charm and beauty, his eyes yearning and his mouth open under his gray mustache. Louise, too, was gazing at Margaret, forgetting her shyness, leaning forward on her elbows. Only his mother struggled against her own yielding.

"Maybe Edward will like new ways," his father said slowly.

Edward felt as his own the potential hurt to his mother in these words.

"There's nothing I like better than the way Mother cooks," he said quickly.

"I didn't mean that," his father replied. "I think it's only right for young people to do differently from the old ones. I'd expect that."

"I'm sure I don't want them to copy my ways," his mother said in the suppressed voice whose misery Edward recognized at once.

"We understand," Margaret said.

Edward got up. "Margaret, I must get you home," he said with authority.

She rose. "All right, Ned." Then she turned impulsively to his mother. "Mrs. Haslatt, will you let us have him tonight for dinner? Is it too selfish of me? But we haven't seen my mother yet—not together. I'll send him home early."

Now his mother was compelled to speak. "I suppose it's all right. Though I have his supper here ready—"

Mark Haslatt spoke suddenly. "Let him go, Mary. There are not many days like these in any man's life."

The suppressed feeling in all of them was released suddenly with these words and it filled the room. Edward wanted to get away. "I'll be back early, Mother," he muttered. He took Margaret's arm and hurried her away.

The evening was like none he had ever spent in the Seaton house, but then he had never been accepted into the family before. Margaret brought him into the library, pulling him gently with her hand in his. She was the middle child, and her elder brother Tom and her younger sister Sandra were already there, with their parents.

"We always gather in the library for a bit before dinner," she said. It was Seaton to call it dinner, he thought, and he wondered if in his own house his supper would be dinner. He frowned slightly, thinking of how many such things remained ahead of him to decide. For that the decision was chiefly to be his it would not have occurred to him to doubt.

They all looked at him with friendly faces as he came in, but nobody moved. He knew that they had been talking about the engagement, and he felt kindliness in the air, although it was restrained. Tom he knew casually, without intimacy, and Sandra he had noticed chiefly because she was about Louise's age, but so much prettier that he had felt sorry for Louise. She had a bright pert face, and Thomas Seaton had given her his red hair. Margaret's mouth was delicate in its fullness but Sandra's was

41

sulky. Tom did not lift his tall loose-boned body from the deep chair in which he sat, but he grinned. Some shyness made Edward want to draw his fingers from Margaret's but she held him firmly and marched straight to her mother.

Mrs. Seaton sat in a high-backed red velour-covered chair by the fireplace. The fire had been lit, and since the lamp was shaded the light from the flames flickered over her beautiful and willful face, still so young under the rolls of her white hair. She wore a black velvet gown, old-fashioned in its fullness, and there was a ruffle of white lace about her neck.

"Mother," Margaret said abruptly. "I asked Ned to dinner so that you could get to know him."

Mrs. Seaton put out a hand long and slender like Margaret's, but it was bright with rings. When Edward took it in his hand he knew that although it looked like Margaret's it was soft as hers could never be. There was steel somewhere in Margaret's hand.

"You're so silly, Meg," Mrs. Seaton murmured. "How can I get to know him in one evening?"

"You've got to like him in one evening anyway, Mother, because I'm going to marry him."

"Is there any reason why I should not like you?" Mrs. Seaton inquired, looking at Edward with her direct brown gaze.

"Sit down, my boy," Thomas Seaton intervened. "Don't let yourself be made the center of a sparring match between two women. Tom, why don't you exert yourself?"

Tom did not move. "He may as well know me at my worst, Father," he said in a pleasant deep voice.

"Do sit down, Ned," Margaret said. "Sandra, why are you speechless?"

"Because it seems so odd to think you're going to get married," Sandra retorted. She sat on the leather hassock, bent over so the skirt of her green velvet frock flowed over her feet. "Besides," she said in the drawling voice which was her present affectation, "I can't stand up or he'll see how short this old frock is. Father's too stingy to get me a new one. Edward, that's the kind of family you're marrying into!"

"She's lying, Ned," Margaret said carelessly. "The trouble is she wants one of the new sheath things and Father has only just let me have one."

She went out of the room with her light and springing tread and Edward sat down, feeling more shy and yet excited than he had ever before been in his life. This was the first of many times that he would be in this room with this family. "It won't be so hard after this, though," he thought doggedly and he sat, impervious and silent, under their frank stares. They had all "dressed," as Margaret put it, in some fashion for their evening meal. He had never been here when there was not a party and so he supposed that this was their habit. Even Thomas Seaton had put on an old black velvet coat with his tweed trousers. Tom wore a somewhat old-fashioned tuxedo that did not entirely fit him. Sandra continued her conversation.

"You are so stingy, Papa. You make poor Tom wear your old tux."

"Shut up, Sandra," Tom said amiably.

"It's a good suit of clothes," Thomas Seaton said. "I'd wear it myself if I could get into it."

"But the depression's over and I don't see why—"

"Do be quiet, Sandra," her mother interposed. "I'm sure we're all bored with you."

Silence fell again, and Thomas Seaton leaned over a small table at his side and poured some sherry from a crystal decanter into a small glass. "Take this to your new relative," he commanded his daughter.

Edward sprang to his feet. "I'll get it for myself, thank you." He took the tiny glass with strong feelings of interest and guilt. He had not tasted wine half a dozen times in his life, and his mother worked in the temperance society in Chedbury. Had he believed in it he would have proudly refused the wine, but he disliked intensely the feverishness of women against liquor, even though his reason acknowledged that some of them had undoubtedly endured enough from drunken husbands and empty pay envelopes to justify their fervor. But his father was a teetotaler, and he resented his mother's devotion to a cause so remote from her. He sat down again and sipped his wine.

"I'm glad to see you like a glass of wine," Thomas Seaton said. "Not that what you and I do, and Tom here and a few more like us, will do any good—we're in for a period of morality, my boy. I can feel it coming. The depression scared us to death and we'll be good for a while."

"I'm going to learn to smoke, Papa," Sandra's confident drawl interrupted his slow hesitating rumbling.

"I don't care what you do," Thomas retorted. He was holding his glass against the firelight, squinting one eye through it. "You and your mamma can both smoke if it'll comfort you for getting old."

They pronounced it Papá and Mammá with the accent on the last syllable in a fashion that seemed foreign to Edward and yet that he knew was not affected. They had manners of their own but these were not what had been taught to him as manners. He sat alert and silent, appreciating the ease of this family, valuing without knowing why he did the glint on velvet, the whiteness of Mrs. Seaton's hands folded on her lap, the faded red of the long curtains drawn now across the window. Tom's aquiline profile, sleepy and smiling, was part of it.

"Margaret's taking a long time," Tom said suddenly. He turned to Edward. "You know, I admire your courage. What'll I call you—Ed? She's laid down the law against Ned. That's her own private name. We have to obey her or she has tantrums."

"She doesn't have tantrums," his father said in his slow heavy voice. "You don't know what tantrums are, Tom. You should have seen your mother at Margaret's age. Screaming and shouting when I didn't give you your way, didn't you, my love? But they get over it."

Mrs. Seaton smiled and produced two dimples exactly like Margaret's in the unflawed smoothness of her cheeks. "I wouldn't compete with you, old dear," she said sweetly. "When I shouted you yelled. It got so tiresome. I always lost my voice afterward, I remember."

"You see, Edward," Thomas Seaton said complacently.

"They're lying, both of them," Tom said lazily. "We can't believe a word they say. They make themselves out as hellions when they were our age."

"Anything we do they always pretend they've done worse," Sandra said. "It makes us feel so inferior."

Had they laughed Edward would have joined in their laughter, but they were mischievously grave and he could only smile with discomfort. They would take knowing, he told himself.

At this moment Margaret came into the room, looking, he perceived at once, beautiful beyond anything he had ever seen. She had put on a pale gold sleeveless gown, very long, that fitted her body closely. It was split up the front to a point below her knees and her gold-clad legs were visible. Above the dress her dark head was high and her eyes were sapphire blue and bright. They were all startled and she enjoyed their amazement. Edward knew that she was a vision and he hated the way she looked. She turned around slowly. "I wanted to wear it the first time tonight," she declared. "When it's old I shall keep it and remember."

All of them were looking at her differently. Tom said nothing, but he lit a cigarette and gazed at her, over the curling smoke. Her mother looked critical. "I wonder if women will really take to these tight things," she murmured. "They make such demands on the figure."

"It's sweet!" Sandra cried. "Oh, I can't bear it being so sweet. I want to tear up this old thing of mine!"

"It'll make new men of us all," Thomas declared wickedly.

Tom burst into high laughter and then they all laughed except Edward. He could manage no more than a smile, being rent in two by Margaret's beauty and his own deep distrust of beauty in this shape. When she was his wife he would forbid her wearing such dresses. "The sooner we're married the better," he thought grimly.

He found his eyes caught suddenly by Mrs. Seaton's as though she knew what he was thinking. Then she moved her eyes away quickly. "Come along, we're starving," she declared, and led them behind her toward the dining room. He and Margaret went last of all.

"Don't you like me?" she whispered, her hand warm under his arm.

"I'm not sure I do," he replied.

"Oh, why not?" she asked.

"You're too beautiful," he said and was glad there was time for no more talk.

The evening was over. He was surprised that it had proved so short, in spite of his fears during dinner that

45

it would be long. The family had talked exactly as though he were not present, throwing him a careless handful of words, a reference he could not understand, with smiles always warm and pleasing. They had talked about everything from the grocer's amazing profile to what Thomas Edison had just said about the new flying machines. For the first time in his life he heard the word helicopter, although Tom used it as though it were a household utensil. Thomas Seaton paused for a few minutes in his enjoyment of the stuffed leg of lamb to express his scorn of William Jennings Bryan.

"You've never even seen him," his wife said.

"I've read enough of his sentimental mouthings," he retorted, "and any man who wears his hair long is sure to be unsound."

In the midst of talk that seemed disconnected but was connected, as he perceived, by unseen waves of communication, Edward caught Margaret looking often and thoughtfully at him. He looked back at her, fully aware that some time before they parted this night he would learn what these looks meant. He braced himself somewhat, determined that he would not yield his honest opinion and from that instant began to enjoy the really excellent food.

After dinner everybody had coffee in small cups except Thomas Seaton who parted his short thick beard with his fingers and supped his creamed and sweetened coffee with loud pleasure from a large cup. There was a little desultory talk, then Sandra drifted away and Tom announced that he was going to "see a girl," Mrs. Seaton went gently to sleep, and Thomas picked up the newspaper.

Margaret motioned to Edward. "Come into the garden, Ned."

"I'll fetch your coat."

"It's warm as anything," she objected.

"Where is your coat?" he asked stubbornly when they were in the hall and waited until suddenly she laughed and opened the coat closet and took out her old blue coat.

In the garden, sitting on an iron seat that felt hard and cold through his clothes, she threw the coat back. The moonlight fell on her bare smooth arms and shoulders.

"I shouldn't have worn this dress," she said. "It was

silly, perhaps. No, it wasn't—feeling as I do about to-night."

"I shan't like you wearing it before other men," he said.

She turned her startled face toward him. "You think it's not modest?"

"I know it's not," he returned.

She smiled, but not quite enough to bring the dimples. "Now, Ned, how do you know?" she asked warmly. "What makes you feel it's immodest?"

He was shocked by this and made no pretense of hiding his feelings. "I don't think you should even ask."

"You mean I mustn't ask you how you feel when a woman is immodestly dressed?" she asked.

"No," he replied. "It's not fitting."

She considered this. Then suddenly she put the coat on again. "Are you ashamed of the way you feel?" she inquired. Her eyes, wide and curious, were fixed on his face and he could not down his quick flush.

"Margaret, I don't like this talk," he said firmly. He wished that she would not look at him as she was now doing. There was something provocative, teasing, amused, something almost wicked in her persistent gaze. He wanted to punish her, to restore her to what he felt was proper decency. He was afraid of her when she was like this, and he proceeded to choose his weapons. "It makes me think of what my mother said last night," he began.

"Ah, you told your mother last night!" she cried.

"I was going to tell you."

"But you didn't tell me, Ned, and I did tell you."

"We got talking about the ring."

"What did she say last night?" she demanded.

He considered. "I won't tell you," he said at last. "You won't forget it."

"Will you tell me if I tell you?"

"Tell me what?"

"What my mother said last night—when I told her."

He considered again. Curiosity overwhelmed him. No, it was more than curiosity—it was necessity. He ought to know what her mother thought of him, indeed, he must know in order that he might start fair and square.

"What did she say?" he asked abruptly.

"Will you tell me?"

"I suppose so."

Margaret withdrew a little and composed herself to speak in a clear distinct voice. "She said, 'How will you manage when he doesn't laugh at your jokes?'" She looked at him with frank eyes, in which there was a touch of pity.

"Is that all?" he asked.

She was astonished. "Do you want anything worse?" she demanded.

"I don't think that's so bad," he said.

"Oh, dear." She covered her face with both hands. "Oh, dear, oh, dear," she murmured under her breath. She took her hands away again. "Ned, I can't marry you!"

He was frightened by the gravity of her look and he humbled himself. "I don't think what either of our mothers says matters," he said stoutly. "My mother said you'd be a bad housekeeper and even that maybe someday you'd talk about divorce. But what does she know?"

"But of course I'm a bad housekeeper," Margaret declared, "and I don't doubt sometimes I'll want to be divorced."

"Margaret!" he cried wildly.

"All married people do," she went on, "and the only difference is that the ones who really love each other tell each other everything and the others don't dare to."

He was stupefied by this, and he was as still as the stone boy in the fountain behind them.

"Oh!" Margaret cried. "But you mustn't let me go, of course—never—never—whatever I say."

She flung herself into his arms and he held her hard and all his courage and stubbornness came flooding back into him. His head was whirling but his heart was calm.

"I don't understand you," he said between set teeth. "I never know what to expect. I suppose I never will. But whatever it is you are—I shan't let you go—ever!"

He put his face into the soft curves of her neck, where her hair curled upward, and was half suffocated with his love.

"Oh!" Margaret sighed, after a long time. "I'm perfectly happy, Ned—even though I know I'll often make you miserable. Please, Ned, forgive me for everything that's going to happen?"

"I'll forgive you everything," he muttered, and was terrified by his weakness.

48

The prospects of marriage deepened the acquisitive instincts in Edward Haslatt. These were already strong, for he was of a nature that drew to himself what he wanted, and what he had he held. Any impulse to share was secondary and acquired, implanted only by his sense of justice.

Now that Margaret had promised to marry him he became obsessed with the necessity for a home and the means to maintain it. Had his father's business been one that he disliked or thought unsound he would have deserted it in search of something better. But he liked printing. Even as a boy he had enjoyed visiting the shop and, after school and in the long vacations, he had besought his father for the lowly positions of errand boy and later of printer's devil. Until his father had become a partner, however, these had been steadily refused, lest Mather or Loomis imagine that he, Mark Haslatt, was trying to get his son into the business. When Loomis died his father had still feared old Robert Mather, and not until Edward's last year of college had he allowed him to come freely into the shop to help with the presses. He had been gratified to discover how much his son already knew about type and was only troubled lest Edward might want new and rare types that could not be used often enough to justify the expense.

"For what we do here now, old-fashioned Scotch type is about all we need," he told Edward. "Of course we have a few special types to please fussy customers, and for wedding announcements and such. You can tie up a lot of money in type that you don't use once in ten years."

Edward had listened respectfully to such advice for as long as he could remember. Now, however, with the promise of being allowed to print a book or two, he pondered it afresh. He genuinely loved books and the prospect of building up, very slowly, of course, what might someday grow into a real publishing house excited him in a measure only second to his marriage. Yet whatever rashness he held in his nature was completely quelled by the necessity of supporting a wife and the children he wanted and expected. His salary concerned him constantly and he urged his father to consult Mr. Mather at the first possible moment, so that he and Margaret would know what they were to live on. His father was pessimistic.

"Bob Mather is so old he doesn't know why anybody needs much to live on," he told Edward one evening. They were in the sitting room and Edward was at home only because Margaret and her mother had gone to New York to buy her trousseau. Secretly Edward had not approved of this. After they were married he would not be able to afford New York clothes and Margaret would have to do with the Chedbury dressmaker. But he did not tell her this, since her father was still paying her bills.

His father, in his shirt sleeves, was sitting in an old Morris chair beside the stove and in other days Edward might also have been without his coat. The permeating influence of Harvard, however, and now of the Seatons compelled him to other ways, even in the home sitting room, and he was encouraged by his mother, who thought it was "nice" of him.

"I'll want two thousand dollars a year," Edward argued.

"Old Mather won't see why," he replied, without lifting his eyes from the newspaper.

"Then I shall look for a job somewhere else," Edward said.

"Well, I'll do what I can," his father replied. He appeared absorbed in his paper.

"When will you, Father?" Edward urged. He was fidgeting over the rack of magazines at the end of the sofa. The slowness of time was intolerable. Margaret had set the wedding for Christmas Eve—a bad time, he thought, for it would be all mixed up with Christmas. But she had persisted, declaring that it would be wonderful to wake up on Christmas morning married. "I've always loved Christmas," she declared, "and now it'll be wonderful." He felt beset with the problems as well as the joys of marriage.

"Hm?" his father asked vaguely. "Well, maybe tomorrow. I have to take some papers up to him anyway."

Robert Mather was too old to come to the office now but every new job had to be laid before him, with full estimates of what it would cost. He examined the figures through his small, sharply focused spectacles and decided whether the job was worth doing. Edward knew his father dreaded these visits to the bedridden old man, but he performed them as his duty, never forgetting that half the business still belonged to Mather.

"Would it be unwise to put the matter of my salary to him at the same time that you are submitting estimates?" he suggested.

His father rubbed his head meditatively. "Well, I'll judge," he said at last. "If Mather's in a good mood, it might be as well to put it to him. If he ain't—I'll see."

He went back to his paper and then a moment later put it down. "Have you thought any of living with one side or the other? I don't know how your mother and Margaret would get along—nor yet how you would do up there. But as far as I'm concerned, if Margaret would do her share in the house—"

"We both feel we must set up our own home," Edward said positively.

"Maybe it's best," his father agreed mildly. This time his attention to his paper was permanent, and the minutes dragged until bedtime.

Chedbury still being empty of Margaret, Edward spent the next morning at the shop, drawing up the estimates on a pamphlet that advertised a life insurance firm. He paused to ponder the matter of life insurance. What if he should die? True, he was young and healthy, yet completely healthy men could drown or could break their necks in astonishingly simple ways. He made up his mind that old Mather must agree to two thousand dollars or he would leave Chedbury and go to Boston or even to New York.

By evening when his father came home there was no such clear-cut decision offered for him to accept or refuse.

"Well, old Mather said he wouldn't approve more than eighteen hundred the first year, son—but if you worked out good, he'd see about the two hundred extra after that."

"The old skinflint!" Edward spluttered. "I've a good mind to throw it all up."

"I know how you feel," his father said, "but there's a lot of things to consider. Old Mather isn't going to last forever. In fact, he looked bad today. I should be surprised if he lasted out another year."

Edward was silent while prudence worked in him. Chedbury was in a good geographical position, near enough to several big cities to solicit business and yet far enough away to keep overhead costs low. To move elsewhere now would mean extra expense, in addition to uncertainty. Young men fresh from Harvard were no rarity on the market. "Is there any chance of buying Mather out?" he inquired.

His father grinned. "I've been dreaming of that for the last ten years. But I'd need twenty thousand dollars —of which I have five at present."

Then his father sighed and went upstairs with lagging steps, and his mother put her head in the door to announce that she needed more wood for the kitchen stove. Edward rose and went out into the woodshed at the back of the house. It was sunset and the luminous quiet sky spread over the town. His fretfulness faded. Under this sky his beloved was speeding homeward to him. He was meeting her at half past nine, and there was nothing else in the day now except that he would see her. He filled the woodbox with energy, fed his brother's hound dog, and ate a large supper in rising spirits. When he let himself out of the house at nine o'clock his courage was high. The train was fifteen minutes late and at quarter to ten he had Margaret's hands in his and only Mrs. Seaton's imperious cries that there were seven boxes kept him from taking her in his arms. The train stopped three minutes at Chedbury, being bound for larger places, and he dashed into the car to collect the boxes, surprised, in the midst of all his haste, that Margaret had been so extravagant as to take a Pullman, in spite of its being only a day journey to New York.

But tonight he was disposed to criticize her for nothing. They sat side by side in the Seaton carriage, their hands clasped under the robe, while Mrs. Seaton described the unutterable difficulties of shopping in New York. Once at home she declared herself exhausted and went directly upstairs to bed, whither Thomas Seaton had already gone, and Margaret pulled Edward by the hand into the parlor and there behind closed doors they ended their first separation. She flung herself into his arms and he held her to his heart.

"Oh," she breathed at last, "it's terrible being so in love that it makes you miserable!"

She laughed, freed herself from his arms, and shook

her skirts. Then she dropped upon the couch. "Did you miss me?" she demanded.

"Every moment," he replied, sitting down beside her.

"I would have missed you if there'd been a second to do it in," she declared frankly. "Oh, Ned, when you see my wedding dress!"

She closed her eyes in ecstasy and clasped her hands behind her head.

"Tell me," he begged, his eyes upon the lovely line of her throat.

"I can't," she answered. "It's to be a cloud of lace. I'm wearing Mother's veil, of course, and she's going to let me have her pearl necklace. I love being married!"

"It's more than the wedding—" he began but she stopped him.

"Don't tell me!" she cried. "I want to enjoy every moment of it as it comes. Just now I'm only thinking of the wedding. When I'm through that I'll think about what comes next and next and next."

She flouted his sober look and then repented and laid her head on his shoulder. "What did you really think about while I was gone?" she demanded.

He put his arm about her, feeling patient and much older than she. "About money mostly," he replied.

"Why money?" she inquired dreamily.

"Because we want our own house to live in, and we want to buy our own bread—"

"And butter," she went on, "and jam."

He broke in on this. "Father asked old Mather how much salary I could have and he said eighteen hundred the first year and two thousand afterward—if everything went right."

"That's plenty," she said still dreamily. "I have a lot of clothes."

"It isn't plenty," he retorted. "I wish to God I could buy the old devil out!"

"Why don't you?" she inquired, and she lifted her forefinger and followed the line of his profile. "You have such a nice nose," she murmured, "and your mouth, sir, is handsome."

He ignored this although he heard it with pleasure. "It would take twenty thousand dollars," he said.

She sat up and stared at him. "Did you know I have

twelve thousand dollars of my own? . . . Don't look so shocked—it's true."

"That has nothing to do with me," he said stiffly. In his heart he had often feared that she had money and would not be wholly dependent upon him.

"My grandmamma left it to me, because I was named for her. She left Tom five thousand which he has spent, and Sandra has five thousand which she hasn't spent, because she hasn't got it yet. And I haven't spent mine for the same reason—but I'm to have it the day I marry. That was in Grandmamma's will."

This horrifying information she gave him without the slightest perception of how he would feel when he heard it. He determined instantly that he would never touch any of her money.

"I shall give the money straight to you and you can buy off Mr. Mather, and I'll make my father give you the rest," she went on.

"No!" he exclaimed, stung at last to speech. "I'd never get over the shame."

She sat upright. "What shame?" she demanded.

"I shall support you myself," he announced.

"Why, of course," she agreed, her blue eyes wide and sparkling, "but I want to put my money into our business. And Papa won't mind."

He got to his feet and began to walk up and down the floor, and then he paused before her. "Margaret, if you ask your father for one cent's help for me I'll—I'll—"

"Break the engagement?" she inquired with bright curiosity.

He looked down into the enchanting face. "No," he groaned.

"Then I will do it for you," she declared pretending to pout.

"Please, Margaret," he begged. "Don't tease me."

"Then promise me to take my money," she said.

Cold sweat broke across his forehead. "Don't, darling, please!"

"I was going to buy you something out of the money anyway," she said remorselessly. "Some pearl studs or maybe one of those new motor cars—or a yellow diamond ring for your little finger."

"Now Margaret," he exclaimed, "what would I do with any of those things?"

"So why not take the money and make it work for you —and me, too?" she retorted.

He stood, impressed against his will by this argument, and she pursued ruthlessly her slight advantage. "Don't you see, I'll still be dependent on you," she urged. "If you don't do your work well, we'll be ruined. Doesn't that satisfy you, Ned?"

"You've mixed me all up," he complained.

"Oh, you're so proud!" she cried. "I want you to support me, Ned. I don't want my own money. I'll keep thinking all the time how I could buy a ticket to Europe —when I'm angry with you. Of course I'll often be angry, Ned, and so will you, and it'll be a mercy if all the money we have is tied up so we can't get it."

The end of all this impetuous talk, this soft pleading, reinforced by her arms around his neck and her clinging body, was to destroy him so completely that he agreed to take the money, which however should be kept in her name, and the stocks it bought held in her name. He would not take money from her father, but he would ask his own father to put in his five thousand, and maybe somewhere they could borrow or scrape together the three thousand more.

Margaret flung herself on the sofa in exhaustion. "Oh, thank God, it's settled!" she sighed. "But if you're always going to be so hard to convince, Ned, I'll not live long."

He ignored this and presented her with the next problem. "Where shall we live, Margaret? Not with your parents or mine, anyway."

To his surprise it appeared that she already knew where they were to live. "I know—we'll rent the old Holcombe house. It's been empty ever since I first saw it and picked it out."

"Margaret, have pity on me," he begged.

She opened her eyes at him. "But it is a lovely house, and all that land around it—"

"It's half a mile from town," he objected.

Everybody in Chedbury knew the Holcombe house and Sunday schools had picnicked for years on the neglected grounds. Old Mrs. Holcombe had been born and had died there when Edward and Margaret were children and her husband had gone away to finish his days in England. Stanley Holcombe had been a don at Oxford when his wife had brought him here to write the many books he had always wanted to write. Strange to say, he had written several of them, and Edward wondered now if his first impulse toward books had not come from the tall delicate-faced Englishman. He had seen him sometimes in the shop, whither Mr. Holcombe came to consult about paper and types and bindings. Twice he had tried to persuade Mr. Loomis to undertake a private printing, but Mr. Loomis had been afraid of it.

"That house will cost much more than we can afford," Edward objected.

"No, it won't," Margaret contradicted him in a fierce whisper. "You'll see!"

When he shook his head and looked doubtful she declared willfully, "Anyway, that is where I am going to live after I am married, and it would be nicer if you'd live with me." Then she sighed. "I'm fearfully tired, Ned. Please go home." She rose and tugged at him until he was on his feet. "Good night, Ned. I do love you."

She kissed him once, a long soft pressure of her lips upon his, and then slipped out of the room and left him there. He stood a moment listening to the clip-clap of her heels on the stairs and realized that she was not coming back and that there was nothing for him except to go home.

Walking along alone through the sharp night air he considered again the matter of her money. He still disliked the thought of it, but his conscience was consoled somewhat by the fact that it would still be hers. When he let himself into the house, through the open door of the sitting room he saw his father at the dining-room table, a paper shade over his eyes, working at sheets of paper. He went in surprised, and his father looked up at him with a faint smile. "Your mother's gone to bed, but I've been figuring all day how I could buy old Mather out. There's no way, unless I mortgage the house, and I've always told your mother I wouldn't do that, come whatever."

What he had not been willing to do for his own sake he was now suddenly happy that he could do for his father's. "I've been talking to Margaret," he said. He sat down and pulled the sheets of figures toward him. "Seems she's going to get twelve thousand dollars the day we're married—by her grandmother's will. I didn't know it until today. She wants to put it in the business."

His father sat back and pushed up the shade. "Well," he breathed, "well, now!"

"I didn't want her to do it at first. You know how I'd feel," Edward went on.

His father's face fell. "Of course not," he said slowly.

"But she insisted. You know how the Seatons are—she's a Seaton, if there ever was one—and so I told her I'd only consent if she kept it in her own name and we'd give her stock in exchange," Edward said.

His father's face lit again. "That we could do," he exclaimed.

"Still it won't be enough," Edward said.

They looked at each other. "I wouldn't mortgage the house," his father said softly, "but I could borrow."

"I don't own a thing," Edward sighed.

"Should I tell your mother?" his father asked. The inquiry was directed to his own conscience, as Edward knew, and he did not answer it. "Funny how women have to be so sure of a roof and a bed," his father mused. "I reckon it's because they feel helpless."

They sat silent again. Suddenly his father shuffled the papers together. "I won't tell. I'll just do it. We'll get it paid back before she knows it."

"All right, Father," Edward said.

He watched his father's absorbed face. Small lines disappeared, and the pursed lips loosened into a smile. His father looked up. "It looks like one of my dreams, anyway, will come true," he said shyly.

He spent the next months waiting for his wedding day and in two frames of mind. There were hours when he was convinced that Christmas Eve would never come, so intolerably did the dawns rise and the twilights fall, and other hours when he felt the day was rushing upon him with something like doom. He was much disturbed by this variance in himself, but it did not occur to him to tell anyone of it. Was there in him somewhere a real reluctance to marriage and if so, could it possibly mean a lack of male vitality? This was a horrifying thought and it made him moody and withdrawn, although he went

57

as usual every evening to see Margaret. As the autumn days had changed to frost and then to cold, their picnics and walks had become hours before the fire in the library, where, after a brief half hour or so of desultory talk with a Seaton or two, they were left alone until eleven o'clock, an hour that Edward had arbitrarily set for going home.

Usually these evenings sped by, for Margaret had samples of carpets and curtains and they discussed the placing of furniture in the rooms of Holcombe's old house, which was now being repaired. The house and its changes were Thomas's wedding present to his daughter and Margaret took passionate delight in every detail. With a wisdom whose depth Edward did not at first divine she had announced that she would not buy a stick of furniture or a yard of carpet, or so much as a sofa pillow without Edward's cooperation and approval.

"Our house is as much your home as mine," she told him.

He was accustomed to his mother's complete power over the house and this new responsibility pleased him and at the same time frightened him. He knew nothing of house furnishing, and his ignorance and Margaret's decisive tastes might very well provide more cause for quarrel than for cooperation.

In one of his darker moods therefore he surveyed one evening samples of stair carpet that she had waiting on the table.

"The real problem is whether we want the blue or the rusty rose," Margaret said.

"Why not this brown?" he inquired gloomily.

He picked a small square of a dun shade that was almost the color of dust.

"You don't feel well tonight, Ned," Margaret said.

"I'm all right," he replied.

Her penetrating blue eyes did not give him up. "Something is wrong," she declared.

He shook his head.

She went on remorselessly. "You get this way every week or so. And I have to guess what it is."

He sat down and lit his new pipe. He had never smoked regularly before, but Thomas had advised him to take up pipe smoking before marriage. "It's a wonderful help,"

Thomas had said, his eyes laughing under his brushy red brows. "If you have your pipe in your mouth you can't answer right off."

"I know because I feel the same way," Margaret said, her eyes still on his face. He met them and maintained his silence and she continued the one-sided conversation. "Sometimes I just don't want to get married, either."

His heart congealed. The shades of reluctance fled and he cried out, "Margaret, what are you saying?"

"Not that I don't want to marry you, Ned—just that sometimes I feel queer about getting married, now that I really am going to do it."

He took the pipe out of his mouth. "You're sure you will?"

"It's in the abstract, yet—oh, Ned, you mustn't fill your pipe so full, darling!"

A coal of tobacco had fallen upon his coat and she flew to brush it off and examine the damage. A slight brown stain clung to the gray cloth. "Dad fills it only a little over half full."

She took the pipe from his hand and knocked it slightly upon the hearthstone, and he felt silly. But she was unself-conscious as she put it back in his mouth.

"You smoke and let me talk a bit," she said briskly. "That's why Dad smokes, you know—so Mother can talk and he needn't answer."

He spluttered at this. "Now Margaret, how do you know that?" he demanded.

She laughed. "Oh, I know his tricks," she exclaimed. She seated herself on his knee and pulled gently at the lobe of his ear. "Of course I can only guess how you feel, Ned—but here's my guess. We want to get married—we want to marry each other—but when we think about starting off alone in the house, having only each other and being dependent just on each other, well—"

She looked so grave that again he felt frightened. He put down his pipe on the small table beside him and drew her to him. "Don't you dare feel so," he commanded. "Else I'll take you to the justice of the peace and we won't wait for the wedding day."

"Isn't it the way you feel?" she insisted.

59

"I reckon," he said reluctantly. Where would he ever hide his soul if she could so divine it?

"There's only one cure for feeling afraid of each other," she said and her cheek was against his breast.

"Time," he suggested.

"No, this," she replied.

He held her close then, and they were silent and he felt the rightness of what she had said. To come closer was the answer. He must remember never to yield to remoteness. When he felt far then he must force himself to come near, and in the nearness distance would be no more. It would take an effort of will, even though he loved her so dearly.

"Yes," he agreed, and then felt the monosyllable too brief. He made an effort. "You'll have to teach me to say things. I live so much in silence."

She replied, "I'll ask you what you are thinking when I want to know, and you must tell me."

She fell silent then, and when he looked down upon her face he saw her gazing into the fire, her eyes steady. She was strongly built, not too thin, but she was so soft, her frame so pliable, that she fitted every curve of his body, and when he held her like this she seemed small and light. His dark mood was gone and he felt only unutterable tenderness. Passion was somewhere waiting but he kept it there. This was only the approach to marriage.

Suddenly, carelessly, the weeks began to gallop, and then he realized that there were no more of them. It became a matter of days, then hours and each hour was no longer than minute. The two families swung into tense action. Clothes, flowers, food, invitations, the formalities of bridesmaids and best man and parties left him scarcely time to think even of Margaret. Their life together was postponed. At night, when they were alone for a little while they clung together without speaking. "Let me be tired, Ned," Margaret begged. "I have to keep up before everybody else."

"You needn't keep up before me—ever," he said.

"Oh, blessed!" she sighed. "That's why I love you."

He had asked Baynes to be his best man, and then fearful lest a younger brother take such responsibility too lightly, he asked Tom Seaton to keep an eye on him and see that he did his duty. Tom, growing fond of young

Baynes, exerted himself unusually and a comradeship sprang up between them. Yet it was Baynes who did duty on the night before the wedding. Tom had let himself get drunk at the bachelors' dinner, and Baynes volunteered to be the one to take him home and put him to bed in the slumbering Seaton house.

"You go to bed," Baynes had muttered to Edward. His gray eyes crinkled. "You need your sleep, old man." So Edward had helped them into a hired cab and let them go.

But Margaret heard the front door open and she came to the stairs, her hair down on her shoulders and a blue kimono wrapped around her. When she saw Tom she ran down the steps, her bare feet noiseless.

"Oh, Tom!" she whispered. "You *would*—you miserable sinner!"

Tom smiled without opening his eyes or making a sound. He swayed back and forth on his feet and Baynes caught him.

"I don't believe he's going to walk up the stairs," Baynes whispered. Without being told he knew that this must be conducted in silence.

"He will, too," Margaret retorted.

With expertness she lifted Tom's hand and bit his thumb and at the same instant clapped her hand over his mouth. Above her head Tom's eyes opened reproachfully.

"Hayfoot-strawfoot," she commanded.

He moved his feet sluggishly and she wound his arm around her shoulder.

"Get under his other arm," she whispered to Baynes.

He obeyed and together they moved up the stairs and into Tom's bedroom. They went to the bed and he dropped upon it. Baynes took off his shoes, and Margaret drew a cover. Tom was already asleep, and they tiptoed from the room.

Outside the door they paused.

"Does he do this very often?" Baynes asked softly.

"Whenever he has the slightest excuse," she said under her breath.

Baynes hesitated, looking down on her with some shyness. He was tall and thin, and in the dim light he looked young and tired. "You go back home as fast as you can," she whispered. "There'll be a lot for you to do tomorrow."

He still hesitated. "What'll I call you?" he inquired.

"Call me?" she repeated.

He went on. "I've always been just a kid to you and Edward—I'll have to call you something now."

"Are you glad?" she asked.

"Yes," he answered. Although he had seldom spoken to her in all the years he had known her, he liked her and felt a strange tingling sense of nearness to her—she was going to be his brother's wife.

"Call me Maggie," she suggested.

"But is that what Edward calls you?" he asked.

"Nobody calls me Maggie. It can be your special name for me," she replied.

He considered this uncertainly. "Will Edward mind?"

"I like him to call me Margaret," she replied. "It seems to suit him."

He had no notion of what she meant by this, but he accepted it. "All right—Maggie."

"And don't tell anybody about Tom," she said.

"I won't," he promised. "But Ed knows, of course."

"Does he?" She paused, then she said, "Sometime I'll tell you why he gets drunk."

"Is there a reason?" he asked in surprise.

"There's always a reason," she said decisively. "Now go home—do!"

He walked home through the cold December air, and let himself into the house. There was neither sound nor light and he stole upstairs to his own room, undressed, and crawled into his cold bed, worrying lest tomorrow Tom could not help him out.

On the other side of the wall Edward lay motionless and awake. What did men think about the night before they were married? It depended, he supposed, upon what sort of men they were. He supposed that for some men it was a night of impatient waiting for physical fulfillment. He had heard of men who could not wait, and who went to a brothel. In the talk of boys together in college there had even been advice that this was a good thing to do, because it kept a man from being too urgent. A woman was always afraid on her wedding night—if she was a virgin, that is. He had heard such talk without seeming to listen, being shy and fastidious. Now he knew that he had listened, for here it all was in his mind. He had thought

62

it filthy talk then and it seemed even more filthy now. He wanted fulfillment, of course—but not at all costs. He wanted the fulfillment of wholeness, but what that was he could not comprehend, except that it was more than physical.

Lying alone in his room for this last night of his solitary life, he was aware of a profound satisfaction that he, too, would go to his marriage a virgin. There would be nothing to tell Margaret tomorrow night—nothing at all. Had there been episodes in his past, he would have been wretched had he not told her. His fearful honesty would have compelled him. He had kissed a few girls—two, to be exact—but the memory of their faces, their lips, were now disgusting to him. He groaned and turned on his side. The folly of the young! Thank God it had carried him no further. That was because he had so early loved Margaret. He sighed, and her face swam out of the darkness. He would take every hour as it came, all the hours ahead, the days, the years. His mind ran down those years and he saw himself and Margaret—children, too, but he could not see their faces. There would be plenty of room in that big house. He supposed that he'd get as used to the Holcombe house as he was to this room. It would cease to be the Holcombe house, it would become his. The spigot of the bathroom leaked—but they were lucky to have a bathroom—most old houses didn't. Mr. Holcombe was English and that was why. He must remember to fix the spigot. He fell asleep at last.

His wedding day was sunny—that he made sure of when he sprang out of bed. Sunshine and blue sky above snow! The gray sky had opened and a steady quiet rain at dusk had changed to snow during the night and the clouds had cleared. He stood at the open window for a moment, breathing in the crisp cold air, and his spirits soared. What had he been afraid of yesterday or any other day? This was the day of his heart's desire, the dream day of his life. Religion was the social custom of church going and the stereotyped prayers of his childhood long since left off, but at this moment he fell to his knees beside his bed and prayed speechlessly that God would help him to be a good man and good husband for his beloved. It was only for a moment and he was on his feet again, half ashamed. But the impulse had done him good. He did not often let himself act upon impulse.

Now, feeling unusually free, he prepared himself for his wedding day. There was plenty to do. He had slept later than his habit, and his mother had not called him. When he had eaten his breakfast he must go to the church for rehearsal, and by the time that was over, it would be noon. Margaret was to sleep for two hours this afternoon —that Mrs. Seaton had told him firmly—and he would go to the shop and work out those two hours as the easiest way to rid himself of them. Then it would be time to bathe and dress and see that the last things were packed into his new pigskin bag, which had been his wedding gift from his father and mother. "It's not your Christmas gift, mind," his mother had taken care to say.

So engrossed was he in his own day that he had not thought of what it would mean to his family, and he was surprised to see them all in the dining room waiting for breakfast with him. He saw when he opened the door that they were even in their second-best clothes. His father was reading the paper, his mother was watering the plants on the window sill, Baynes was whistling the canary into a frenzy, and Louise stood watching. She was always happier when Baynes was at home. Seeing that plain somewhat patient young face, Edward felt a stab of remorse that he so often forgot his sister.

"Well, young man," his father said mildly. He looked over his spectacles.

"I didn't expect to see everybody," Edward said. He felt shy and awkward, hating to be the center of attention.

"It's the last morning," his mother said gently.

The last morning? This, which was all but the first morning for him, was for her the last. For one brief instant he had a dim perception of what time meant to a human life, and he could not answer her. His father answered for him. "Come now, Mother—don't gloom, my dear. We want him to be as happy as we've been, don't we?" He rose, snapped his newspaper together, and took his place at the head of the table.

"Great day in the morning," Baynes murmured.

They sat down and family breakfast began in silence.

Edward looked up and found Louise's eyes fixed on him. She looked away when his eyes met hers.

"Your dress all ready, Louzey?" he asked. The affectionate name of their childhood came unexpectedly from his tongue. She flushed and nodded.

"I didn't think she'd look well in that rose-colored taffeta but she does," his mother said.

"Good," he said heartily. He glanced at his brother. "I gave the ring to Tom, Baynes, but when the moment comes I want you to hand it to me. I'll show you this morning."

"I'll be there," Baynes said. Whether Tom could be was another matter.

The comfortable hearty breakfast went on. The canary fluttered its wings and sang furiously and sunshine fell across the table. The big base-burner in the hall warmed the room. His mother had made muffins and opened a jar of strawberry jam, and Edward ate with appetite. The coffee was good, the cream thick, and the dish of scrambled eggs and bacon was what he liked best, upon a foundation of oatmeal.

"Well, my boy," his father said after a long silence. "I suppose you won't get down to the shop."

"I thought I'd come down for a while this afternoon," Edward replied.

"Don't have to! Let's see—you'll be away two weeks," his father went on.

"It'll be queer to think of you at the seashore," his mother said.

"Can you really go in swimming?" Louise asked in a dreamy voice.

"How queer—when we'll be having Christmas!"

"Hey," Edward cried out. "What about the Christmas tree?" He had forgotten it altogether.

"We'll decorate it tonight, after you've gone," his mother answered. "It'll give us something to do."

She had planned it all, he saw. He was touched that they would miss him, and wondered if it were disloyal to Margaret that he should feel now a pang of vague homesickness because he would not be here tonight to help decorate the tree. Lest his mother discern his heart he answered only Louise.

"Margaret says it'll be that warm." They were going

south to New Orleans. It was Margaret's choice and he had been staggered by the distance and the cost.

"I'd like New Orleans well enough," he had replied to this, "but I'd rather go somewhere near enough so that my money will carry us there and back."

"Oh, hush," she had retorted to this. "It's my honeymoon as much as it's yours. I'll pay my half."

But he had refused such compromise. They were going, but only as he could pay for it. That is, they were going by day coach and they had rooms at a boarding house instead of a big hotel.

"I like little clean boarding houses," Margaret had said quickly. "Big hotels are always stuffy."

She had no foolish pride.

"Margaret, behave yourself!" Mrs. Seaton implored. They were rehearsing in the church, decorated for Christmas, and Margaret was willful and teasing and so beautiful that none of them could keep their eyes off her. Edward was bemused with her. He wanted to shake her for her naughtiness and with difficulty he kept from kissing her. He caught Baynes looking at her with infatuation and that sobered him.

"Come," he said with sudden sternness. "Let's get it right."

She quieted at the sound of his voice and went through the ceremony, obeying Dr. Hart, the minister, with an airy demureness. Sandra was patient, Tom was nowhere to be seen, and Baynes had got the ring from him somehow and managed without dropping it.

"Whom God hath brought together let no man . . . et cetera," Dr. Hart finished hastily. "I think that is about all. The rest is familiar. Just pause a moment, Edward, before slipping on the ring. Give me two seconds to round off my phrases."

Baynes put out his hand for the ring.

"I'll keep it now," Edward said.

"Don't forget to give it to me, then," Baynes replied, slightly hurt that he was not trusted.

Dr. Hart listened to this, his eyes amused. He had christened these young people, had later received them into the church, and now they were taking their own part in the eternal pattern of birth and life and death. He bowed his head and walked softly away. Since the manse adjoined the church, he had kept on his carpet slippers and no one noticed his going.

If Edward had hoped for a moment with Margaret alone he did not get it. She squeezed his hand and gave him a long look from under her black lashes. Then she shook her head. "I have to obey Mamma this last day," she said sweetly and followed her mother and Sandra out of the vestry door. He was left alone in the quiet church with Baynes.

"Seem queer?" Baynes asked.

"A bit," he said briefly. He looked at his watch. He wasn't going to talk over anything with a kid like Baynes. "Guess I'll go home and finish packing so that I can go along to the shop after dinner." Then he relented. "I daresay you'd better take the ring after all." He handed it to Baynes and was rewarded by the pleasure in his brother's young face.

"Thanks," Baynes said. "I'll see how Tom is. He was properly stewed last night. He get that way often?"

"I've only seen it a couple of times," Edward said.

They parted, glad to separate. They were still too young to show their fondness for each other or even to know how close they were as brothers. Baynes went along kicking pebbles out of his path and Edward walked home soberly. He wished that Margaret would not get such laughing fits. They were not pure merriment, of that he was sure. Some day he would tell her he did not like them.

When he reached home he went uptairs and found his mother bending over his suitcase.

"Now, Mother," he began warmly.

"I was only putting in a new toothbrush," she said defensively. "Your old one wasn't fit."

He had not thought of so small a thing, but he knew she was right. Would there be other things he had or ways of doing things that would not seem nice?

His mother sat down on the window seat. "I know your father hasn't said a thing to you, Edward. It's queer how men can't talk to each other. I do want to say this —it's so important to a woman that a man is—nice."

He could not answer, nor look at her face. He kept looking at her hands, thin and dry and strong, folded in her lap.

67

"I'll try to remember," he mumbled.

"Maybe you don't even know what I mean," she said.

"I think I do, Mother."

She sighed and suddenly the tears came to her eyes. "I do hope she'll make a good wife," she said.

"Good or not, I don't want any other," he replied gently.

"Well—" She rose, and going to him she kissed his cheek and he put his arm around her. "Thank you for everything—and I wish I'd been better here at home."

"You've always been a good boy," she replied. "I put your Christmas present in the bottom of your bag—and something for Margaret, too."

She held the embrace a moment too long and then withdrew. "Well, I guess, then—" She broke off, smiled through more tears, and went away.

He sat down where she had been sitting and stared out into the street. Nice? But Margaret might not think niceness was what she wanted. That he would have to find out. Nevertheless, vaguely alarmed by what his mother had said, he looked over his things and rejected a pair of pajamas that were patched and put his best ones on top. He cleaned his razor and washed his comb and brush and took out a new tie for tomorrow morning. New socks, new handkerchiefs, a clean shirt for every day.

The Chinese bells chimed through the house and he went downstairs to dinner, and without desire to eat. His excitement he masked carefully under an air of indifference and he was grateful that no one seemed to notice him. His mother was urging Louise to let her use the curling tongs on her hair and Baynes was abstracted. His father was silent.

"Coming down to the shop with me?" his father asked when the meal was over.

"Yes," he replied.

They put on their coats and hats and walked down the street together. "About that loan," his father began, "I don't suppose you could borrow a thousand yourself?"

Edward considered. "I'd have to talk it over with Margaret."

His father threw him a sharp look. "I'm not telling your mother about our house."

"Margaret and I have made a sort of bargain to be frank with each other," Edward replied.

"We all do at first," his father retorted. They walked for a block in silence, then his father straightened his shoulders. "Well, it's too much to ask on your wedding day," he said abruptly. They entered the shop and parted, his father to the office and he to the pressroom to examine a page of type for a temperance folder ordered by a woman's society in Boston. He studied the proof. "Strong drink destroys a man's soul," the headline announced. He reduced the size of the type and lessened the space between the lines. In one hour and forty minutes he would be standing before the minister, with Margaret at his side. In two hours they would be man and wife.

Edward was completely composed, this to his own astonishment. He went through the ceremony with tender gravity, thinking of Margaret and not himself. The church was full of the people they had both known all their lives, elderly men and women whom they had badgered in one way or another as children, who had been their teachers in school and Sunday school, who had sold them food and clothes and Christmas toys, who had invited them to parties and picnics. And there were the young married, watching with wise bright eyes, confident and approving. Children stared, awed by the mysticism of the ceremony, and girls and boys, too old to be children, watched with hearts beating for themselves when their time came. It was the accomplishment of his one dream, this hour set apart and perfect, the church warm and bright with holly and pine and the lighted lamps of evening streaming out through the windows to lie upon the snow. Organ music filled the shallow arches of the roof and Mrs. Sulley, the old doctor's wife, short and squat and grotesque with fat, poured out a voice powerful and pure. Dr. Sulley had brought both of them into the world, but he was not here. Over in the next valley a farmer's wife was giving birth to a child.

"The voice that breathed o'er Eden," the strong sweet voice was gentle with tenderness.

And Margaret, who this morning had been willful with mischief, was grave and tall. She carried a little ivory prayerbook and no flowers, and her hair was a dark cloud under her lace veil. Sandra and Louise stood behind her like twin roses, and he was surprised to see that Louise was almost pretty. Her mother had curled her hair under the wide velvet hat, and her lips looked red.

He felt Margaret's shoulder against his, her arm touching his, the soft fullness of her white form against his thigh and knees. Her low voice was composed and sure and when he answered his own was unfaltering. Baynes was sweating but when the time came for the ring he handed it to Edward, hooked slightly over the tip of his little finger so that it would not drop.

"With this ring I thee wed."

His voice followed old Mr. Hart's slow steady tone, deep with tenderness. Margaret was looking at him, her blue eyes fathomless. His head swam a little and he held her hand tightly. Their voices repeating, answering, came in perfect rhythm. "Man and wife!" Out of the swirl of joy these words came as clear as bells. It was over. He turned and held his head high and with her hand inside his elbow, they walked down the holly-wreathed aisle. "What God hath joined, let no man put asunder—" No man, not even himself!

"There!" Margaret said.

She took off her hat and put it on the seat opposite.

"It wasn't too bad, was it?" he asked.

The train swerved around a hill and panted steadily on.

"Not for once," she said.

"Not for once only," he retorted.

She smiled at that and she put out her feet. "My shoes, too."

He knelt and took the shoes from her narrow silkshod feet. He held her right foot in his hand. "What a little foot," he murmured foolishly. His restrained blood began to beat. "But it's cold—right through your stocking!" He nursed her foot in both hands. Her instep was high and arched and her heel firm.

She curled her toes into his palm. "You couldn't do this if we were in the day coach, Ned."

He looked up. She was smiling down at him with such a look of tenderness and shyness that he felt half faint, and he managed to keep his head only enough to salvage his pride. At the very moment when they had stepped on the train, the platform crowded with people coming home for Christmas and shouting at the wedding party, Thomas Seaton had thrust an envelope into his coat pocket.

"This is my private wedding gift to you—as man to man," he had muttered.

The train had started immediately after they got on, and he saw a porter taking their bags.

"Wait!" he called.

"Look in your pocket, Ned," Margaret said.

He had looked in the envelope and had found tickets for the drawing room in the sleeping car. "Margaret, you've gone ahead of me again," he had said most reproachfully.

"Ned, I didn't," she answered. "He did it without my knowing it—until five minutes before we got on the train."

He could not be angry with her then and he could not be angry now. It would have been hard indeed to have sat under the staring eyes of a coach full of strangers. Still, there was something deep, somewhere, that would have to be settled between them. His wife must be content with what he could give her—she must forget her father and mother and turn to her husband—but this was not the time for argument between them. He pulled the pillow from the seat and put her feet upon it and covered them with the steamer rug his mother had given them. Then he sat down beside her and drew her into his arms and kissed her.

All these months he had guarded himself, wary of his own heart. Now he held her long—his lips upon hers, and one by one the guards went down. His arms tightened about her and she yielded for a moment. Then he felt her struggle against him. First her hands pushed his shoulders, and then she tore her lips away, and he saw a look of strange inquiry in her eyes.

He released her. "I am too much for you," he said abruptly.

She busied herself with the flowers she wore on her breast. "I don't know yet," she said after a moment. "You see, it's not only you I don't know—it's myself, too."

He had begun to be hurt but with these words she healed.

"We won't rush," he said.

She considered this. "Still, we'll do what we like, shall we?"

Now it was he who considered. "What if one likes and the other doesn't?"

She laughed. "You don't know anything more than I do—I can see that."

"You don't mind?" His pride lifted his head again, on guard, ready to be struck down.

She flung her arms about him. "I think it's lovely. We're starting out absolutely equal. Ned, tell me the truth, have you ever been in love before?"

"No—no," he whispered, and leaning over her, he kissed her temple. He could feel a beating vein there, straight from her heart.

"Nor, I!" she sighed with joy.

"Sure?" He lifted his head to look into her eyes.

"Nothing like this."

"But something?" he persisted.

"Just—searchings," she answered.

The quick darkness of December had fallen, and putting off the lights as long as the lines of hills could be seen, they watched the landscape darken. He sat in a dream of delight, his arm around her, her head on his shoulder, until he heard her voice murmuring against his neck.

"Ned!"

"Yes?"

"Could you eat very much at the reception?"

"No—could you?"

"No—and I'm starved."

He reached for the light. The flying landscape disappeared and their room became a cozy cell.

"We'll eat here," he said.

"Oh, yes."

He pressed the button and when the porter had brought the menu, he gave himself to the frowning consideration of the best food for happiness. They studied the dishes together while the porter waited grinning, and then gave their order. Not until Edward was consuming duckling instead of the lamb chops he had ordered and ice cream

72

instead of apple pie, did he realize that he was not eating his favorite foods and finding it all delicious.

"Only what you want," he murmured.

"How do I know what I want?" she asked.

"Then promise to stop me as soon as you know!"

"What if I want more?"

"Promise to tell me!"

"I don't know—if I can."

This interchange in the middle of the night made him sit up in bed and turn on the light. She lay against the pillow, the soft lace of her nightdress open on her bosom. It pleased him that she did not put up her hand to draw the lace together. Her eyes were shy but honest, and she did not hide them from him.

"You aren't afraid of me, Margaret?"

"Are you afraid of me?"

"A little."

"Why?"

"I don't want to offend you."

She lay thinking for a moment, her eyes still on his. "I might offend you," she said at last.

"Only by making me think—I'd done something you didn't like," he replied after a moment, and put out the light again.

They lay side by side, feeling their way toward one another, while the train swayed its way southward through the darkness. Nothing he had known of her in the past helped him now. He had first seen her as a little girl when he was twelve years old. She had been in school with him since they were in first grade and doubtless he had seen her before then. But when he was twelve and she eleven he had seen her one day with a sense of shock and individuality. Her black hair, curling about her face in small feathers, was in two braids tied with scarlet ribbons. Her cheeks were pink and her lips were red, and she had just won a Fourth of July race on the school grounds. He had been holding one end of the string when she flung herself against it. "Peggy's first!" her schoolmates had yelled.

After that he had always seen her first, in the schoolroom in the morning, out in the yard at recess, in church on Sundays. With what pains he had maneuvered his place at the end of the pew so that he might see the back of her head and the occasional turn of her profile, two seats ahead! Yet he had not spoken to her alone for nearly three years after that, when he was fifteen.

Yet all the times they had talked together and walked together, had quarreled and parted to make up shyly again, none of it helped him now. She was new, a stranger, yet the one he loved with his whole being. He was torn between selfishness and love. All the healthy hunger of his young manhood, his unsatisfied, carefully hidden curiosities, the banked passions, the honest animal in him, rose up now. He had no aids to self-control except what he could muster for himself. Church and society had withdrawn. They had given their sanction. Within holy wedlock whatever he wanted was his.

Now it was only love that took command. He loved her so much that he wanted above all to please her. In his total ignorance he had the instinct from somewhere in his intelligence to know that union depended upon two, not one. There was so much about her that he did not know—nay, what did he know? He had no guide to the delicate mechanism of her body and her spirit. Even she could not help him. And he did not want her help, except in response and communication. Had she taken the lead in love, he would have been repelled. The way was his to make. She was the sleeping princess whom he must rouse, not to horror and shame, but to pure delight, so that they might live forever after in happiness.

He was frightened by the responsibility, and fear made him tender and slow. Fear and love mingled together, sharpened every sense and perception, and he was rewarded by her stillness and then by her yielding.

"It hurts me—but I love you."

"You are perfect."

"Ned, did anybody tell you anything?"

"No—did you know anything?"

"Nothing."

"Then we'll find the way ourselves."

"Yes."

They slept, lulled by the rhythm of the train, woke and slept again, until the day broke. He heard her voice at his ear, "Merry Christmas, Ned—Merry Christmas, Merry Christmas—let's open our presents, sleepy head."

He opened his eyes under the curtain of her hair over his face.

Christmas? He pulled her head down to his shoulder. "I'd forgotten."

Reticence being his nature, Edward had conceded the wisdom of a honeymoon as far as possible from home, as different as possible from the accustomed air. The soft warm atmosphere of New Orleans, the sunshine, the mists drifting in from the Gulf and melting away again, the laziness, the sense of holiday, the colors on the streets and houses, the glimpses of flowered inner courts and gardens, everything was new. Their boarding house was small but good. Their room was large and cool, and a balcony hung from the big window. Ironwork as delicate as lace shielded them and revealed to them the patio below, where bamboo and ferns surrounded a pool of clear water, still as the square of sky above them.

They lived as remote from daily life as though they were in a trance. He ate food that he had never tasted before, hotly seasoned, sour and sweet and peppered, fried shrimps and fish and ballooned potato chips, spiced soups and flowered ices. He had always been a sparing eater of plain foods but now he ate heartily, although with more prudence than Margaret did. Indeed he saw to his secret surprise that she could be something of a glutton, for the taste of something that she loved. He ate experimentally, knowing that he would always choose for his daily food the brown bread, the baked beans, the lean meat, of his habitual fare. But Margaret, her cheeks glowing and her eyes sapphire, cried that she could eat of such food forever.

"Why do we eat boiled potatoes and cabbage at home?" she inquired of him.

"I guess we like plain things," he replied.

"I don't!" she declared. "I like things that taste."

Her slender firm body was as hard as his own, defying fat, and she ate as she pleased, slept hours on end when the mood for sleep fell on her or stayed up half the night. All his careful habits were upset and put aside, and he let it be so, knowing that it could not last. He encouraged curiosities that he did not possess and followed her into old shops and churches smelling of mold and he bought for her strange flowers and an old French chair and an ancient prayerbook with a clasp studded with seed pearls and they sat in a square and ate oranges and watched children of every color playing together.

"I didn't think you'd be like this, Ned," she exclaimed one day.

"Like what?" he asked.

"Fun!"

"Why did you marry me then?" he asked.

"Because—"

She walked beside him, both hands clasped over his arm, her head just below the level of his eyes, and he did not press her. He was secretly astonished at his own capacity for enjoyment. Here where they were unknown he felt no embarrassment at her love openly expressed before strangers. They were in a solitude of strangers, one among many couples in love. While the rest of the world worked and went to bed early and rose to work again, they lived the life of royal beings. Their room became a sort of home, and the sight of her clothes hanging beside his grew natural and was no longer a sight for wonder. When she had hung her frocks beside his sober gray second suit, he had made occasion to open the closet door during the day, that he might see again the intimacy. When she asked him what he did, he was ashamed of his softness.

"You must tell me," she insisted.

"I'm a fool, that's all," he had said.

"Ah, don't be ashamed of anything, Ned!"

"Well then," he opened the closet door. "Your frock there—against my things—"

She ran to the closet and nestled her cheek against his coat. "I'll tell you something."

"What?" His heart melted with love and went running through his veins like fire.

"When I told my mother I wasn't sure I wanted to marry you, she said, 'How do you feel when you see his coat hanging in the hall?' So one day when you were there talking to Father—remember?—I went into the hall, and I put my arms around your coat—like this, and I knew."

He was speechless with the wonder of this and he took her in his arms.

In the midst of love and satisfaction he was ashamed to discover in himself, one day, small vague thoughts of business. He stifled these intruders and hid them from Margaret as though they were thoughts of other women. What then was his surprise when after another day of unalloyed joy and idleness she said suddenly, "Don't hate me, Ned, but I have a hankering to get at our house!"

She was lying across the bed on her stomach, clad only in a chemise made of white clouds, and her hair was hanging over her shoulders. He still felt shy about staring at her. "I couldn't hate you, Margaret. I wish you wouldn't say such things."

He was astonished that her courage was more than his. While he had hidden his thought from her, she had dared to speak out. This was intolerable and so he spoke out, too. "Matter of fact, I've been having an idea or two myself about the office."

"Ned, you haven't!"

It was an exclamation and accusation, and he was wounded. "Is that worse than your thinking about the house?"

"No but, Ned—you're thinking wrong things now. I don't mind you wanting to get back to the office, but aren't you interested in the house?"

"Of course I am."

"But you said office!"

He grew dogged. "The office is my job."

"So is the house. We're to do it together."

"I doubt I'll be much good at it."

She shook her head until her hair flared. "If you aren't interested in our home, I'll live in a boarding house."

Some sort of absurd quarrel was brewing between them and he stopped it firmly. "Margaret, let's go home."

She did not answer this. Thinking it over, idly, she wound her dark hair about her throat and tucked in the ends. "How do I look in a high collar, Ned? Everybody will think we didn't have a good honeymoon if we come home early."

"I like your throat bare. What do we care what people think? We know what sort of a honeymoon we've had."

"Have you really liked it?" Her voice was foolishly wistful.

He sat down beside her. "What do you think?"

"I think you have, a little—about as I have. It's been perfect."

He lifted her into his arms. "You'd better think so. It's the only honeymoon you'll ever have."

She sighed. "Oh, Ned, I didn't really think you could be so heavenly nice!"

"I knew how nice you'd be—and you are."

He rocked her back and forth, his face in her neck, and she clung to him with both arms. Then she began to laugh silently.

"Ned!"

"Yes?"

"Know why I'm laughing?"

"Do you?"

"I've thought of something."

"Again?"

"Let's go home secretly and not tell anybody!"

He sat still, contemplating this thought. It would be entirely possible to live for a few days at least in the Holcombe house—in their house, he was trying to call it now —without anyone knowing it. They were not expected back for a week and the house was ready for them except for the last dusting and the hot meal. Mrs. Seaton had hired a maid for them, she had written them, Hattie, an Irish girl. It would be nice to have the house their own by right of possession before she came.

"I am greedy," Margaret said. "I want to begin living now—this minute."

"Isn't this living?" he asked.

"Holiday," she retorted. She lay in his arms, looking at him, and he felt his head whirl. Her complete abandon was entrancing and at the same time it made him uneasy. What was the source of her childlike naturalness and what did it mean? He knew that there was no such relationship between his own father and mother. He knew that to this day his mother undressed in the dark, after his father was in bed. His father was irritated by it because she stumbled over furniture and Edward had heard him grumbling.

Margaret herself had made a quick end to any shyness. She had laughed when he wrapped himself in his brown bathrobe their first evening in the boarding house. "Why do you want to put that heavy thing on?" she inquired.

"I'm a hairy sort of a beast," he had replied in an effort to appear casual. "Not beautiful—"

She had come over to him at this and had taken off the robe and looked at him from head to foot. "You have a good figure. Why hide it?" This she had said so dispassionately that he was immediately set at ease. Then her sapphire eyes had sparkled wickedly. "Especially from me!"

They had laughed upon that and he had hung the robe in the closet.

And yet, although he knew well enough that it was not lack of proper modesty, there was danger in her naturalness. What would he do if ever she displayed it to anyone except him? It was a delightful private trait, but could it be kept private? He reviewed in his memory possible occasions when she might have been tainted with what was called "being too free." He could remember nothing of the sort, but he had not been much in the Seaton house. He caught her looking at him curiously now and suddenly he felt ashamed of himself and buried his face in her chair. He doubted that he was good enough for her, even at his best. This doubt at least he determined to keep to himself.

The landscape was deep in snow when they drew up to their own door. They had left the train at Rockford, the station above Chedbury, and then had spent an hour shopping for food. Margaret had bought a huge basket and into this their parcels were piled, while he went to find some sort of conveyance. When he came back he saw that she needed deliverance.

"You strangers around here?" the inquisitive grocer inquired.

"We're moving nearby," Margaret answered.

"Rockford?" the grocer persisted.

"Out in the country," Margaret said calmly.

Edward broke in. "There's a farmer going out our way. I was lucky enough to catch him at the livery stable."

They escaped the grocer and lugging their basket they climbed into the sleigh pulled by a couple of heavy farm horses. The farmer was taciturn and drove them speechlessly to the house. For his silence they were so grateful that Edward added a quarter to the two dollars of the agreed price, but the farmer shook his head, and still silent, he picked out the extra coin and returned it and drove on.

"How wonderful he is!" Margaret cried. "Oh, if everybody in the world were like that—except you and me!"

Edward reached for the key behind the shutter of a window, and fitted it into a frozen lock. It would not turn.

"Breathe into it," Margaret advised.

But his breath was not warm enough, and so she stooped and blew out a frosty gust of sweet warmth. Her breath was always sweet. It was one of his blessings. Together, laughing and blowing, they warmed the lock and the key turned and they stepped into the clean ice-cold house. A look of horror went over her face and she stopped on the threshold without closing the door.

"You didn't lift me over the doorstep!" she cried.

He seized her in his arms, carried her out, and brought her in again, setting her down before the hearth, in the living room. He had learned to call it that from her, for in his father's house there was no such room. A parlor, a sitting room, neither was a living room.

"Sit down while I get our fire started," he commanded her.

"Do order me about, Ned, just for sentiment's sake," she replied and sat down.

He knelt on the hearth and put a match to the fire already laid. "As soon as this starts I shall go down to the cellar and get the furnace going," he said. "But you'll warm your little feet here."

"Light the kitchen range first," she urged. "I can't wait."

She could not keep from singing. Song was impossible to him, but it bubbled out of her. She could not sit still and forgetting his command, as she always did when she wished, she ran about the house. He lit the kitchen stove and downstairs in the cellar he could hear her feet, flying over the floor above his head. They paused at the stair and she called down, "I shan't go upstairs until you come with me!"

"Good girl!" he shouted back.

The furnace was laid ready, too, and he poured a little kerosene on the kindling and heard the roar of fire. This was the warmth of his house and for the first time he felt the house was his own. Then he frowned. There was no sieve for the ashes and there would be waste of coal. The thought of buying a sieve and even of using it gave him pleasure although it was a task that he had detested whenever he had been compelled to do it in his father's house. He washed his hands at the kitchen sink, saw that the fire was blazing in the living room, and then went into the hall where Margaret waited, her foot on the stair. She flung her arm about him and he put his about her and thus arm in arm they went up the broad stairs. Mr. Holcombe had not liked the narrow stairs of New England and he had built his hall spaciously and the stairs wide, as they had been in his home in England.

"Bless him," Margaret said.

"Are you thinking about Mr. Holcombe, too?" Edward asked amazed.

"Weren't you?" she replied.

They walked the length of the upstairs hall to the room that was to be their own. This was the room where he was to live his intimate life with her! His children would be conceived and born here. He would grow old here, and here, please God, he would die.

Death he had not thought of once since his marriage, and now it sprang at him monstrously. One of them must die first! It had not occurred to him that it would be so. But which? Could he live if it were she? And yet she must not be left alone. Then he put the thought away. Certainly he must not tell her what he was thinking. He tried quickly to think of something else, lest with her uncanny intuition she discern the cloud of death in his mind.

"The sun pours in," he murmured. Two wide windows opened to the south and beyond them the snow-laden hill rose round to the blue sky.

She turned suddenly and hid her face in his breast. "Don't leave me!" she whispered.

"But of course I shan't leave you," he protested.

"Let me die first," she begged.

"I promise," he said quietly.

He held her and then as suddenly she drew away from him.

"I must cook dinner!" she exclaimed and ran down the stair like thistledown, her skirts floating about her.

They were alone for three days, and during the whole time Edward worked in almost silent zeal and entire absorption. He went over the entire house from attic to cellar. While Margaret dusted and arranged closets and bureau drawers, and put wedding presents into their new places, he put up hooks, tightened hinges, adjusted doors, painted worn spots on floors and window sills, and hammered picture hooks. Beyond the windows the snow remained immovably deep, and he took his exercise in shoveling paths fiercely and thoroughly. He enjoyed this far more than New Orleans and faced the truth about himself that however much he longed to enjoy what might be called pleasure he found his real delight in work. He tramped around the outside of the house, examining every shutter and frame and lock. There was a large porch on the back of the house and there were boards in the floor that had rotted and must be replaced. Hour by hour he made the house his own and his home and when the fourth night came he had forgotten that Mr. Holcombe had ever lived here. He built the fire in the living room as he had done each evening, and it was his fire and his hearth.

As though Margaret felt his possession she went upstairs after supper was ready and she put on a long-sleeved, long-skirted frock of dark blue velvet. He went to meet her and stood at the foot of the stairs, gazing at her as she came down. She did not evade his adoration and it did not make her shy, and this was another of her traits that he loved. His mother met praise with uneasy laughter and denial but Margaret smiled at him with full acceptance.

"I put this on to celebrate our finishing the house," she said. She stood on the last step and leaned upon his shoulders, and he put his hands about her slender waist and lifted her in his arms and carried her to the big leather chair by the hearth which had been in his room at Harvard, a gift from his father and mother one Christmas. Then he stood and looked around the rooms. Margaret had lit candles and lamps everywhere before she went upstairs, and room opened into room in a glow of light.

"We can live here always," Margaret said. "There's room to grow."

The measure of what he was to have depended now altogether upon himself and he was sure of himself, too. So far in his life, so good.

"Now I know you are really my wife," he said to her.

She smiled up at him, her hands clasped behind her head. "And haven't you known it until now?"

"Not to the bottom of me." He fell on his knees before her.

"I haven't forgotten my promise—to make our marriage my life. I'll not forget that as long as I live."

She took his face in her hands. "I hope I'm good enough for you," she cried softly and when he protested she closed his lips with her kiss.

They ate their supper; they spent the evening in happy wandering through their house; they sat by the fire until it died to coals. Then they locked the house and went to bed. He had not overcome the shyness of his body. He could not put into words the act of his passion. He did not want words. He wanted silence and feeling. But she wanted words and she made talk, laughing, half play, half teasing, as though she evaded the depths of his feeling. He had allowed this playfulness until now but suddenly tonight he made her keep silent.

"Don't talk, don't talk."

"But, Ned, you're so serious, darling! And this is joyful, isn't it?"

He did not answer her and she fell into silence, too, and gravely she accepted his love. When it was over he was astounded and then terrified because she began to cry, silently.

"I hurt you!" he exclaimed.

"No, you didn't," she sobbed.

"Then—why?"

"I don't know—I don't know—I feel different." She whose words came always so easily could tell him no more than that and he held her until she slept, distressed and yet exultant.

He was awakened the next morning by a voice in the lower hall and he got up and put on his bathrobe and went to the stairs. There he looked into the red and frightened face of Hattie, the maid.

"Oh, my soul and body!" she screamed. "I didn't know you was here!"

"We got home early," he explained.

"I didn't bring anything to eat with me," she cried.

"There's food in the storeroom," he told her. "I like oatmeal and scrambled eggs and my wife likes just eggs. Toast, of course, and coffee. We'll be down in half an hour."

Hattie changed everything in the house unconsciously but subtly. He and Margaret were now master and mistress as well as man and wife and they came downstairs decorously to sit down to a meal they had not prepared. Their talk must be fit for a servant to hear and he found himself making plans for the day in so dry a manner that Margaret's eyes grew wide. When Hattie had left the room she looked at him with reproach.

"Is that the way you are going to talk from now on?" she asked.

He pretended not to know what she meant. "Don't you think I ought to get to work and earn our living?"

"But you sound so stuffy," she complained.

"Perhaps work is stuffy," he rejoined.

She made a direct attack. "You know you were talking for Hattie!"

"I was trying to talk in spite of her," he retorted.

"The only way to be happy with servants is to forget they exist," she declared.

He ate in silence for a few minutes. Hattie had made the scrambled eggs today too hard. That would have to be changed sooner or later. Could anyone forget she existed? It would take practice.

Margaret talked on, oblivious of Hattie's comings and goings. "I don't like those curtains in the guest room, after all. What if I change them with the ones in the dressing room? Do you object to large cabbage roses, Ned? I love them—so hearty! Hattie, I don't like my toast so brown—make me another slice, there's a good girl! Or I wouldn't mind having them in my own boudoir, if you think they're too feminine for you—yes, that's better. I'll put them in my boudoir."

She had insisted on a dressing room for him and a boudoir for herself, their bedroom being the big room between, and although he had thought it pretentious, yet he found he had liked dressing in privacy and much as he loved her, he did not mind missing the brief interval between her tumbling out of bed with her curls all flaring and then her appearance again, clothed and the curls smoothed. He disliked disorder, and he knew her well enough to know now that order was not the rhythm of her being as it was of his.

The meal drew to a close and with some sentiment he prepared to leave the house and go to work. But she was preoccupied with the changing of curtains and he thought her casual. When he put his arms about her, in the hall after carefully closing the dining-room door against Hattie, he inquired, "You won't mind being left alone all day?"

"I thought I'd just run home for a bit this morning," she told him.

"Why didn't you tell me before?" he asked a little hurt.

She opened her eyes at him again. "You aren't going to expect me to tell you every time I run home?"

"But this is home now," he reminded her.

"Yes, but you know what I mean. Don't tease!"

He would not allow himself to be jealous of her family. "Call me up at the office?"

"I might even come and see you at the office."

"Do, my darling!"

"We might have luncheon in Chedbury and come home together," she suggested.

"Can you eat that food?" he asked.

"Oh, once in a while," she said.

So their day shaped itself as they stood in each other's arms. He opened the door and looked at her and closed it again to kiss her once more and then ran resolutely out, stopping to wave from the gate, and seeing her face pressed against the window, he forced himself to walk on. Luckily there had been no more snow during the night and the half mile to Chedbury would not be too difficult by means of walking in the ruts of farm wagons. Soon he would have to have a vehicle of some sort.

When three quarters of an hour later he sat at his desk, he knew his man's life had begun, at last.

Two

EDWARD HASLATT was not one of those who rejoice to see the spring. There was something about winter that he liked. The contrast between the roughness of frozen snow and bitter cold and cruel winds sharpened his sense of combat and deepened the comfort of his house when he opened the front door and stepped into his warm wide hall. During the eleven years since he and Margaret had first begun to live in the house he had improved it until today it was as fine a home as could be found about Chedbury.

Chedbury was, outwardly, as it had always been, except that its ancient beauty had been made more perfect. The church had been recently painted, and since the war, every house about the green had been repaired and freshened with paint.

Actually Chedbury was engaged in a private war of its own. During the World War a manufacturer of steel products, lured by the promise of cheap labor, had tried to buy land at the southern end of the town for a factory. Thomas Seaton had risen from the pleasant lethargy of his life, had led an embattled township with such success that Jim Figaro, the ambitious young industrialist, had not been able to buy land nearer than two miles away. Even this was too near for Chedbury, which complained that the factory smoke spoiled the paint on the church when the wind blew from the wrong direction.

Meanwhile South Chedbury began to grow. Italians, Portuguese, and Canadians had begun to make a town of their own, compounded of small flimsy bungalows. From these the townsfolk of Chedbury separated themselves severely and old separations among themselves were forgotten as they banded together against the new. Haslatt now was as good as Seaton, for both alike were against South Chedbury.

Edward smiled wryly when his mother and Mrs. Seaton met at the Village Improvement Society, and yet why not? Margaret was a Seaton and he had built a small, respectable book business about the printing shop, which was now his own. The question today was whether he should not open a New York office. The center of the publishing business was there, as Baynes was always telling him. Writers, it seemed, one found only in the city. Well, he did not want to publish too many books, and he was cautious in the presence of writers.

He stepped out of his house on an early spring morning with his mind full of these problems. Margaret followed him out of the door, and he lingered beside her on the front porch. Two years ago they had torn down the long narrow porch and had put up this wide square one with thick white pillars. It had added dignity to the house and he liked it.

"It's still cold," Margaret said, shivering in her dark woolen frock. "Though it looked as warm as May from the living-room window! I do believe that's a daffodil."

She ran down the steps ahead of him, as lithe and swift as ever and stooping over a flowerbed, now a mass of short green leaves, she plucked a daffodil bud, tipped with yellow.

"It'll bloom quickly enough in the house," he said. "Next week this time they'll all be out."

He kissed her again, first glancing toward the gate. Margaret laughed. "You're still shy about kissing me, aren't you, poor darling!"

He denied this stoutly. "Not shy—it's just that I feel private about it."

Smiling, she thrust the daffodil bud into her fichu, reached up and pulled him by the ears and kissed the underside of his chin. "Good-by, Ned! Don't be late."

"Not tonight. Tomorrow night that fellow's bringing his book."

"Oh, dear," she murmured.

"He's coming on the late train, and if the book seems good, it might be sensible to be friendly, eh, Margaret?"

"Only if his fingernails are clean," she said firmly. "The

last one was fearfully grimy and the book wasn't any good after all."

Edward laughed. "I'll ask him to hold out his hands."

He was suddenly grave. The words made him think of something. She caught his look and turned away, a shadow on her face.

"Don't be hard on Mary any more," he said in a low voice. "After all, she's only a little thing yet."

Margaret's full underlip tightened. "I can't bear bitten nails. It's disgusting. Besides, if she doesn't stop now she'll go on all her life."

"You'll turn the child against you, Margaret, and that'll be worse than bitten nails."

Her eyes filled with tears. "I don't care about myself."

"Yes, you do," he urged, "or if you don't, then I care about you. I can't bear the children to think you're scolding them."

"But I must scold them when they're naughty," she insisted. "Else who will teach them anything, Ned? You're away all day and when you come home you just want to pet them. It's I who have to be with them."

"If you are just your own self, dear, they'll learn," he urged.

"Ah, but they don't," she retorted.

He saw the tears glistening on her lashes and forbore. "Well, we won't start arguing on this beautiful day, my love. Go back into the house and get warm. If Mary frets you too much, we'll pack her off to boarding school. It's you I think of first."

She pulled a handkerchief from her white lace cuff, wiped her eyes, and smiled. "I'm not as wicked as you think. I read stories to Mary and I made little cakes yesterday that she likes."

"I know," he said fondly. "You're the best of mothers, at heart."

They had been walking slowly down the clean-swept path and now they were at the gate. He did not kiss her again. Instead he smiled and tipped his hat.

She leaned over the gate after he had closed it. "What time will you be home, Ned?"

"About six, I think," he called back. He waved as she turned, and hastened for the trolley. His eyes were tender when he caught it and found an empty seat.

She'd go back into the house and get Mary into her coat and hood and then, putting on the heather-brown coat that he'd bought for her when they were in England last year, she would walk with the child part way to the new grade-school building. Probably she would take the boy with her. It was strange to think that he was the father of three children, and that little Tom would start school next year. The baby, a girl, Sandy, was a year old. Three children were enough, he had decided. He had been careful that Margaret did not have children too quickly. Each time she had been in good health, rested and ready, and the children had been born strong and handsome. His eyes clouded again at the thought of Mary. What was wrong between Mary and Margaret? There might have been no drop of common blood in them. The child adored her mother and could not please her.

"She's a bit slow," Edward mused, "and Margaret is so flashing quick."

Yes, he had been careful of his wife. He tried always to think first of her and what she wanted instead of his own needs. He sighed, thinking of the years just ahead when Mary must grow and her mother must let her grow. Then he stopped thinking. Habit warned him that the next stop was his. He rose and marched down the aisle, tall, slender, swaying as the car curved and stopped.

"So long, Mr. Haslatt," the conductor said.

"So long, Bob," Edward answered and swung down the step, crossed the street, and went into his own shop. He still called it the shop, as his father had always done, although in the years since he had taken the responsibility for the business, he had steadily enlarged the plant, always with caution, and always against his father's will. Someday he would take over the whole building. He wanted even now to erase old Mather's name and make it Haslatt and Sons, Printers and Publishers. Mather had died the year after he had started the publishing.

That first year of probation had been a heartbreaking one. Edward had dreamed of a successful book and a handsome profit. Instead he had only squeaked by. The book that had so fascinated him had made very little money, and he had defended it doggedly before old Mather as he lay on what was to be his deathbed.

"It isn't this one book that I bank on, Mr. Mather," he

had said. "It's a first novel and a very good one, considering. The man who wrote this book can write a better one. Why, talking with some publishers in Boston they tell me it's always more than likely that you lose on the first book of any writer. And we've made a hundred and seventy-five dollars."

"Overhead, overhead," old Mather had growled.

"I counted in overhead," Edward had retorted.

Well, he had squeaked by, and the next year Tennant had given him the big book, the one that had made it known all over the world, he liked to think, that Mather and Haslatt were publishers as well as printers. On the strength of real profits he had ventured on eight more books, all of which were failures, so that his second year actually ended with a loss. Old Mather had died during the year, however, and although his father was terrified enough, he had agreed to go on with Edward for another year, and the printing business had held up. The next year he'd got the rights for two British books, and they had sold well, and by the third year Tennant had another big book, and he had insisted on larger offices. The fourth year he had lost Tennant to a New York firm which had wiled him away with a huge advance. That had staggered them a bit until he had found Wellaby, who wrote New England historical romances, and these had carried them ever since. He was somewhat ashamed of the romances but the profits from them enabled him to publish books he could not possibly dare to accept otherwise.

He entered the combination freight and passenger elevator, nodded to the boy who ran it and stood silent while it carried him to the third floor. He arrived half an hour later than the employees and so he went up alone. The elevator came to a too sudden stop and he remonstrated mildly, "Now, Sam, I told you to have your mind on what you are doing."

"Yes, sir, Mr. Haslatt," the boy said quickly.

He stepped out, knowing that he had said enough. They were all a little afraid of him and he considered this a good thing. He nodded to the telephone girl and passed his father's office. Then he went back and opened the door. His father was already at his desk, poring over a ledger.

"You're early, aren't you?" Edward asked.

93

"You're late," his father retorted, without looking up.

Edward smiled. "Some time I'm going to spend the night here. It's the only way I can get ahead of you."

"I can't sleep the way you do," his father replied. "Say, Edward, look at this."

He held a figure firmly with his finger and Edward looked over his shoulder. "You've overadvertised five hundred dollars on Wellaby!"

"Figures aren't all in yet," Edward said sharply. "There was a good sale at Christmas and scarcely any books came back in January."

"Hm, hmm," his father mumbled. "I can't see how it's fair business to take back books just because a bookshop can't sell them. You don't send back to Wellaby the books you can't sell."

Edward did not reply. He nodded to his father and went into his own office and closed the door. Jane Hobbs, the secretary he shared with his father, had opened his morning's mail and on top of the letters he saw one from his brother Baynes, whom he had allowed reluctantly to go to New York for a week to bring back estimates of what an office there would cost. Baynes had taken Sandra with him. The New York office, Edward suspected, was more than half her idea.

He took up the letter and read it carefully. Sandra, Baynes said, was proving a great help with the office. Lewis Harrow, the young fellow he was sending to Edward to look over, was bringing a couple of manuscripts with him. They had located an inexpensive place, very small, really only a suite of three rooms, in a building in mid-town, occupied by three other publishing firms. The address was a good one. That was Sandra, Edward thought grimly. He put down the letter. He would not be quick about taking on the extra overhead. If he took it on, it would be for only a year, and Baynes would have to bring in enough money to cover the costs. He had not dared to tell his father anything about it yet. He frowned slightly and read the rest of his letters, his mind still busy with Baynes.

This younger brother had complicated life by following in his elder brother's footsteps. Among all the many livelihoods that Baynes might have chosen, he would have only publishing. In printing he had not the slightest interest. He wanted only to make books, perhaps even to write them someday. And he had married Margaret's younger sister. Edward had been not a little disgusted when soon after his own marriage Baynes had confessed that he was in love with Sandra.

"You can't be seriously in love when you are only a freshman in college," he had said sternly, and then being too honest for his own comfort, he had admitted to himself that he had been in love with Margaret long before college.

"Sandra is somewhat frivolous," he had then said to Baynes.

Baynes had grinned and said nothing. He was still growing and Edward saw with displeasure, which he recognized as unreasonable, that his younger brother would eventually be some inches taller than himself.

There had been no more conversation about Sandra, and Baynes had persisted in a desultory courtship, that ended in betrothal in his senior year in college. Neither Edward nor Margaret put confidence in the marriage, for Sandra said quite frankly that she did not know whether she would like Baynes when he had finished growing up although now she thought him amusing. Yet in less than a year it had taken place. The young couple had moved at once to New York, where Baynes had worked in lowly positions in several publishing houses, and Sandra's luxuries had continued to be supplied by her father. When war was declared, Baynes, egged on by Sandra, had volunteered for a British regiment, and Sandra followed him to England. Four years of fighting on one front after another had left Baynes still unscathed, and apparently unchanged, except for an even taller frame and broadened shoulders, both of which Sandra approved. When Baynes came back a captain, he got out of uniform as quickly as possible and applied to Edward for a job, declaring that he and Sandra would live at the Seaton house. Neither of them wanted a house of their own and there was still no talk of children. In the last year, however, there had been a great deal of talk about New York. Edward had felt that Baynes coming into the business as a younger brother should learn the printing business from the bottom up, but Baynes persisted in remaining ignorant, declaring that he did not know one type from another.

He took no interest in Edward's slowly growing typographical library. To Edward's horror he did not know Scotch type from Garamond and already he spent half his time in New York—hunting writers, he insisted.

"I don't know what to do with Baynes," Edward had confided gloomily to Margaret one winter's night after the children were in bed. He had that day received a letter from Baynes, in which this younger brother swore he had found a genius, whose name was Lewis Harrow, and that upon the strength of this find the city office must be opened immediately and that Sandra was, therefore, looking for an apartment.

"What's the matter with Baynes?" Margaret had inquired sleepily. She had been sledding with the children in the afternoon and her cheeks were scarlet and her lashes drooping.

"He won't learn anything about printing, and still he wants to go into the business," Edward complained.

"Why don't you find out what he already knows?" Margaret asked. "Sandra says he's full of flair."

"Flair for what?" Edward demanded.

"Smelling out people who have books in them."

Edward had not replied to this. "You had better go to bed," he said to Margaret after a few minutes. "It's no good your pretending you aren't asleep."

She rose at that, smiling drowsily, her hair all wisps of curls, and then she had trailed out of the room, her long velvet skirt behind her.

Nevertheless it was on the strength of this possible flair that he had consented soon after that to take Baynes into the shop, and it was still in the hope of this flair that he was considering a New York office. Sooner or later his father would have to be told. Prudent and conservative, Edward was wise enough to know that these two qualities, though essential, were not enough. The publishing business demanded a stretch of the imagination that he was not sure he had. Baynes alone of course would be a menace to the business. Out of a possible hundred ideas that he produced, he would be lucky if five were practical. This Lewis Harrow might be a genius—and might not. Edward sighed, wondered if he ought to refuse his younger brother as assuredly he would have refused any other young man he had hired, and then ecided he would risk his faith in the imponderable flair. e had recognized in himself this faith in a quality he aw but did not possess. It was what had made him want o marry Margaret, and it had kept him married to her revocably all these years. He was in love with her im- nortal quality. But where had the immortal dust dropped pon the soul of Baynes, born of the same parents as imself? And assuredly Louise had none of it. Louise, till unmarried, was teaching school in Chedbury. She vas one of the stones that he gave his children instead f bread, he sometimes thought grimly. Mary would have er next year in fifth grade, and he did not relish the idea. Vhat did his pallid sister have to give his shy, easily gonized little daughter?

He pressed his clean-shaven lips together firmly, ouched a bell, and without looking up when his secre- ary, Jane Hobbs, came in, he began to dictate.

"Dear Baynes: Yours of the eleventh inst. re- ceived. You can go ahead on the office provided the total outlay is not beyond the figures I gave you, including office equipment, etc. As to the author, please make no promises until I have sized him up. Also I must see completed ms. as usual. No ad- vance, of course, until I have made up my mind. The time has come to tell Father about plans and I will do so today. I expect strong objections and I look to you to prove him wrong.

Your aff. Bro.,
Ed."

He dictated steadily for an hour, letters filled with fig- res, estimates, rejections, complaints, and then fingering he lobe of his ear and pursing his lips, he considered a lunge. Jane Hobbs waited. She was a thin-faced middle- ged woman and she waited, pencil poised. His weak- less, as she knew for she was the custodian of his typo- raphical library, was in buying new type.

"What's on your mind?" she now inquired.

He looked at her half shyly, the corners of his mouth witching. "You know those Fell types?"

"I was looking at 'em yestiddy," she replied.

"We ought to have the Janson, to go with them."

"What's that?" she asked.

"Dutch seventeenth century." He hurried on under her disapproving look. "It's like the Garamond—easy to read, sharp, beautiful type. Yes, I'll have it—"

He dictated the letter brusquely. It had taken five years to make Jane realize he could do as he liked in the business. Five years he had endured her secret returns to his father to report what he was doing. Then one day he had locked the door of the office and standing against it he had told her that he would fire her if ever again she told his father anything. He would talk with his father when it was necessary—not she! And Jane, weeping hideously, had accepted his coming of age.

"You'll have to buy more cases," she said grimly, rising to leave the room.

"Order them," he commanded. "I've decided to bring the fonts for initials and small types out of the shop— have everything together so that I can pick what I want. The men leave things around."

When she was gone he got up and as usual made the rounds of the shop. He liked to be what he called a manufacturing printer. He was proud of his new power presses and his machine-made paper. Above anything he feared the accusation of being artistic. He wanted to be sound. And yet he knew his own weakness. He could not resist fine type and richly made paper. In the six months that he and Margaret had once spent in England and on the Continent, he had visited every old foundry he could find and he had brought back old type faces and handmade papers. The shop now was separated from the offices and the library and reception room by a thick double wall and double doors. He did not want the noise of the machines racking the air where he planned and wrote. But once through the double doors the noise was pleasant to him. He liked the smell of ink and the look of the grimed men watching so intently the pages they set and printed. It was a hobby of his that every man in the shop had to know something of what all other men did, so that each had a feeling for the whole and for himself as a part of the works. He sternly rejected any notion of indispensability. If some man were ill or on vacation, he would not hire another to take his place. Someone in the shop had to know how to take up and he himself was not above spending a morning at type setting.

But what he loved best to see were the sheets of a book rolling off the press, then to be folded, gathered, stitched, and trimmed ready for the casing. The bindery was the newest and most modern part of the shop. He brought Margaret there sometimes to show her samples of cloth and to discuss color and design. He did not expect from her much interest in the business, but sometimes she showed deep and continuing interest in a manuscript and then she wanted to meet the writer and from then until she held the finished book in her hand, she wanted to follow every step. He enjoyed her presence, although it was sometimes troublesome, for she did not realize, or would not, that however exciting a book, it could only be one of many things that he must think about.

He paused beside a press this morning and watched the letters stamp themselves upon a heavy cream-colored paper. He had ordered Caslon type for this particular book, a little book it was, memoirs written by an old gentleman in Boston, and privately printed. Baynes was scornful about private printing. "You only get what other publishers turn down."

But Edward would not agree. "I don't look at it that way," he had replied in the steady somewhat monotonous voice that had become habitual to him these years. "There are books that people don't want put into the trade. They write them for friends or family. It's natural they want a hand in choosing the paper and the type and the binding. I don't see why they shouldn't."

So he had gone on printing small private books of poems and essays and memoirs, and sometimes he had printed sermons and plans for peace and he had never expressed to anyone, not even to Margaret, his secret pleasure in satisfying these individuals who longed to make permanent something of their lives. He motioned to the elderly man who was running the press and the machine stayed.

"Is that ink a true black?" he asked. "I don't want it on the brownish side. I'd rather it had a touch of violet."

"That's what you said," the man replied, "and that's how I mixed it."

"It's all right," Edward said after a moment. "It dries blacker."

"It does," the man agreed.

The machine started again and the creamy paper ran its course. The old gentleman had written about his boyhood in Boston. He could just remember the sailing ships that went to China, and he had taken an hour of Edward's time to explain why he wanted his memories kept for his grandchildren and his great-grandchildren. "It gives meaning to one's life," he had said half diffidently, pulling at his white whiskers.

"It does indeed, Mr. Stallings," Edward had agreed. He wanted meaning in his own life, too.

They had decided on no color in the ornamentation, but there were to be fine initials at the head of each chapter, and black and white fleurons.

He moved on down the aisle. At the next press, in complete contrast, he was doing a banker's biography, set in Bodoni, with wide margins and on hard paper. He paused, admiring in silence the presswork. This press was run by a young man from South Chedbury, John Carosi, whom he had hired only the year before, a brilliant workman, uncertain of temper, and he had a suspicion that the fellow was secretly interested in setting up a union. Well, if he had such ideas he would have to go. A union shop, Edward had said firmly, he would not have.

He decided not to speak to the young pressman and he walked slowly down the central aisle and back to the offices. He had better talk with his father now, before they both were tired with the day's work. He did not like to lose his temper with his parents. Indeed he would not. They were both getting childish and needed care and yet they resented any loss of authority. His father drew the same salary he always had, and this, too, was something that Edward would not think about. Now that Louise was off their hands and Baynes earning his own living Edward could not repress the dogged thought that surely he and Margaret and the growing children needed more than they had. Yet the business could not stand an increase in what he paid himself unless his father took less.

"I'll never suggest it, though," he had said to Margaret only last night.

"Of course not," she had agreed almost indifferently.

100

To money she was always indifferent. Where it came from, how much they had, whether they were secure, were questions which she never asked. She bought little for herself and wore her old clothes because she liked them, and yet she could commit an extravagance that left him breathless, as when she came home from New York one day wearing an old wrought-gold necklace.

"I'll need a couple of hundred dollars, Ned," she had told him cheerfully.

He had felt the crimson blood fly to his face. "I don't have it, Margaret," he had said simply.

The look of wonder on her face was like a blow. "Oh, I'm sorry." That was all she said. She took the necklace off at once.

His pride had risen at that and he had taken it from her and put it on again. "Keep it," he said. "I'll call it your birthday present."

He had borrowed the money next day from the bank, giving his note for three months. That had been eight years ago. Now, of course, he could easily have paid for the necklace.

He tapped on his father's door and walked in. The old man was leaning back in his chair, drowsing a little, his pencil still in his fingers. He opened his eyes and fumbled at his lips. "I was just adding up sales," he mumbled.

"Good," Edward said cheerfully. He sat down at the chair on the other side of the desk. His father and Baynes shared a desk. "There's something I want to talk over with you, Father. It's been on my mind a good bit. You know I don't like talking until I see through a problem." With this he plunged into the heart of the matter. Better to get it over with!

"I won't say Baynes has influenced me," he concluded. "Yet in a way he has, too. Baynes has something to contribute to the business, Father—something that neither you nor I have—some sort of flair, I suppose! I know a good book when it's brought to me, and I can make a nice thing of type and binding and all that, but I can't nose out books and Baynes can. From asking about, I find that publishers need someone like that. It's lucky, maybe, that we have him in the family. He seems to have found someone already—fellow named Harrow."

He made his tone light to counteract the gathering heaviness of his father's ash-white brows. "Maybe you trust Baynes in New York," his father said, "but I don't—not with that wife of his. She's not like the one you got. Sandra's another piece of goods." He shook his head and his eyes were dark. "Ducks and drakes," he muttered. "Carryings on! Cocktail parties—that's the latest thing, I hear. All charged to expenses—"

"I'll see to that," Edward said firmly. He did not tell his father that he was beginning to understand that a small amount of getting about was perhaps a good thing in the book business. He called it getting about, and he was more than willing that Baynes should undertake it. He had attended a few such gatherings on his rare visits to New York and he had disliked them intensely. Yet it troubled him that he saw there the heads of firms much larger and more important that his own. They were solid men and he could not imagine they enjoyed any more than he did the strange drinks and fancy bits of bread and filling. Especially did he dislike the women writers. Thank God that his only woman author at present was an old lady of sixty, who wrote youthful little stories for children. He considered them trivial and yet they sold well and they made up into pretty books. She had paid for the first one herself as a present to her grandchildren and when it went into the fourth edition, he offered to put the next one into the trade. But he liked to have it said that Haslatt's was a man's publishing house.

His father had sat frowning and ruminating. Now he suddenly banged the ledger shut. "I know very well you and Baynes run things to suit yourselves," he said bitterly. "I ought to be dead, too, like old Mather. The country belongs to the young these days. There's no respect left for the old, whatever sense they've got. It's a queer thing that a man spends his life getting a little wisdom together somehow and then it's not wanted. Young folk think they're born with all the wisdom."

Edward did not at once answer these too familiar remarks. He sat silent for a moment and suddenly he had his inspiration. "That's a nice thing for you to say, just when I was about to suggest something to see how you like it."

His father looked at him sidewise, his eyes frosty under his brows. "Well?" he drawled. "What's the next big idea?"

"What do you say to changing the name of the firm to Haslatt and Sons?" Edward asked.

His father stared at him. "Leave old Mather out?"

"He is out, isn't he?" Edward replied. "Every bit as much as Loomis—"

"Hm," his father said, "I'll have to think a bit."

"But why, Father?" Edward urged. "After all, it was only a printing shop when Mather was here. It's you and I who have built the book business, and now Baynes has come in."

"It's true that Mather didn't like the books," his father conceded.

"We are really making a little on them, Father," Edward went on. "Everybody says you can't make millions on books, but it's a steady respectable business—something more, too, I think, than just business."

"Business is all I want out of it," his father growled with a return to hostility.

"Well, it's not all I want out of anything," Edward said stoutly. "I don't want to be just a businessman. I want some of the good things of life, too—some of the arts and some of the thoughts and some of the friends that making books brings me. I can't write books myself, I know, but I like to take what others write, if it's good, and give it a life of its own. That's important—a business if you like, but still it's something more. A writer would be helpless if he couldn't get his manuscript made into a book. Shakespeare would have been forgotten by now, if it hadn't been for some printer-publisher like us."

His father stared at him. "What's come over you?" he inquired. "I never heard you talk so fancy."

"Trying to convince you," Edward said, and grinned. "But it's what I think you feel, nevertheless."

They sat silent for a moment, as they often did. The sunshine from the narrow window fell across Mark Haslatt's head and turned his thick stiff white hair to snow. He had grown thin and dry in the years that had passed and something dour in his nature had become plain upon his wrinkled face. He hated to grow old and yet he had to grow old. There was no compensation for him in age. Sometimes he looked at his wife across the breakfast table, the children all gone and only the two of them left, and she looked so old that he was frightened. Ten years ago she had been heavy and sound, a kindly woman with a scolding tongue, which he had continually resented, and now she had grown into a thin mild silent old woman. Sometimes he thought her mind was not what it had been and this frightened him more than anything. Maybe his own mind wasn't what it had been. Nobody would tell him, of course. His two sons would go on, as smooth as cream, managing everything and telling him nothing. But he'd kept his hands on the accounts just the same. He wasn't too old yet to know when the figures were in the red.

"Then shall it be Haslatt and Sons, Father?" Edward asked.

He saw his father start, as though he had been dreaming. "Oh, I suppose it might as well be," he said half grumbling. "After all, it is Haslatt and Sons, you might say."

"Exactly," Edward said briskly and he got up. "It's time for your lunch, isn't it? I'll go home with you, if you don't think it'll upset Mother."

"It won't," his father said. He lifted himself up by the arms of his chair, found his hat and Edward held his coat. A few minutes later they were going down the elevator together. "Your mother don't look so good," his father was saying. "I wish you'd take the chance to see what you think."

"I will, Father," Edward promised.

They fell into silence again. A few acquaintances passed them and neither of them talked before outsiders. But silence was easy. Edward was realizing again, as he had begun to do in the last few years, that his father was an old man. There was something very pathetic about age. It fell upon a man like a disease, and it was incurable. He imagined his father's secret dismay as he found himself less able each year than he had been the year before, his strength fading, his mind less alive. And there was nothing to do! How cruel was God—if there was a God! Edward still went to church every Sunday with his family and they all sat together in the Haslatt pew. He continued to do this even though a profound doubt was invading his soul, a doubt that he steadily refused to face. He put it aside now and considered what practical means there might be of comforting his parents for the loneliness of old age. Consideration, of course, and the sparing of every hurt, but this was not enough. There ought to be pleasures in old age. Surely every period of life had its compensations, if one could find them.

People had to be taught how to find pleasure. Perhaps that was the true purpose of education—to help the individual discover the pleasure of being his age. So Edward mused, allowing his mind the liberty it naturally took, unless compelled to labor. And then he thought of his daughter Mary. Louise could never teach her anything about pleasure! A crime this, that his sister should be allowed teaching! Thank God that Margaret still laughed easily.

The noon sun was warm, and along the street children were snatching a few minutes' play between school and their meal. The front door of the house was open and in the hall there was the smell of roast beef from the open kitchen door.

"Mother!" Mark Haslatt shouted. "Ed's here for dinner!" He turned to his son. "I'll bet she's in the kitchen, doing the work while the hired girl looks on. I can't get her to rest."

His mother came to the kitchen door untying her apron. Her wrinkled face cheered as she saw her son. "Why, this is real nice, Edward. Wait till I hang up my apron. What's the matter you've come home?"

He bent to kiss her dry cheek. "Nothing. Just thought I'd see how you are."

"Fine and dandy," she replied. "I do hope the beef's not too done. The girl likes it like leather. Want to wash up?"

"I'll go upstairs," Edward said.

He mounted the stairs to his old room. Everything was exactly as it always had been. Even the bed was made up, as though he were to sleep there tonight. It was like coming back into a warm outgrown shell, and something of his boyhood fell upon him again. He washed his hands at the old-fashioned stand, pouring the water from the ewer into the basin. The house had a bathroom, but his mother had kept the washstands in the bedrooms.

He went downstairs in a few minutes and his parents

were waiting for him in their chairs and the girl was putting the roast on the table.

"Hello, Gladys," he said.

"Howdy, Mr. Haslatt," the girl answered. She was a farmer's daughter, pallid and freckled, and her sandy hair was in an elaborate braid. Ten years ago she would have sat at the table with the family but now she did not. The Haslatts had moved up in the town, and Mrs. Haslatt knew better. She was still president of the Women's Christian Temperance Union, and they met regularly here at the house once a month, important in the knowledge that their work had been successful. Edward never discussed Prohibition with his mother. Old Thomas Seaton had made him feel the folly of forbidding people what they seem determined to do, and the atmosphere of that house was wholly opposed to this one. Thomas Seaton drank as much as ever and fumed at the trouble of getting his liquor, and Tom Seaton had gone into the bootlegging business in a gentlemanly way. That is, he arranged for imports of Scotch whisky. Edward imagined that his mother knew all this, but she, too, did not mention it.

She watched the carving of the roast with anxious gravity. His father was not an expert carver, and she could not rest until she had made sure that the grain of the meat ran opposite to his knife. He had sharpened his knife carefully and he began to cut big thin slices and the red juice ran out. She sighed, relieved. "It's a lovely roast—I'm glad you came today, Edward. How's Margaret and the children?"

"All well," Edward said mildly. "Margaret picked her first daffodil bud today."

"Did she?" Mrs. Haslatt replied. Her mind was occupied now with the baked potatoes that Gladys was handing around. "Take the big one, Edward—you're looking thin."

"You're never satisfied with the way I look," he grumbled amiably. But he took the big potato, dripping with butter.

"Did you put that dressing on the greens like I told you?" Mrs. Haslatt inquired of Gladys.

"Oh, my soul and body," the girl groaned and setting the potatoes on the table she fled toward the kitchen.

106

"Her memory is no longer than her nose," Mrs. Haslatt remarked.

"Her nose is long enough," Mr. Haslatt said. "It's like her father's. I always say that old Babcock's nose is as long as from here to Jerusalem."

"I'm sure Gladys tells her family every single thing we do," Mrs. Haslatt said, sighing.

Edward smiled. "Well, you don't do anything very bad."

"Has little Tom lost that eye tooth yet?" Mrs. Haslatt demanded after they had eaten for a few minutes.

"He has, and I know it only because he expected a dime under his pillow and I forgot it," Edward confessed.

His father laughed. "I'll bet he didn't let up on you until he got it."

"He didn't," Edward said.

"That little Tom is a real smart boy," his mother exclaimed. "I know you don't like greens, Edward, but these are something new—broccoli, it's called. We get so tired of spinach, now that your father can't digest cabbage."

It was the desultory talk of the old days but it was easy and comfortable. The dining room was warm and the smell of the food whetted his appetite. He took two small feathery rolls and buttered them heavily. He liked being here alone sometimes with his father and mother. They had been kind parents to him and he had forgotten the ways that had irritated him when he was growing up. Now he simply felt that they were good and that they loved him, and that the walls of home were solid here. He wanted his children to feel the same way about his own house.

"Baynes wants to live in New York," his father said suddenly.

Mrs. Haslatt dropped her fork. "For goodness sake—what for?"

"He thinks we need a New York office—get new authors and so on," Edward said, taking another roll from the plate of hot ones that Gladys was passing.

Mrs. Haslatt waited until the girl had left the room. "Seems to me you've got as many books as you can manage a'ready. I couldn't read that last one, *The Singed Flower*—wasn't it?"

"It's beginning to sell, though," Edward said. *The*

Singed Flower was a book from a writer he'd found in England, a man named Peter Pitt. He had not understood the book, either, but he had caught a vague feeling from it, as of music in the distance. Margaret had read it three times.

"I don't dare think of Baynes and Sandra in New York," his mother was saying. "Why, they'll spend money like water—the two of them hand in glove! I wish Baynes had a little more character with his wife. He's just putty. Sometimes it's real disgusting."

"I guess we're all putty when it comes to our women," Mark Haslatt said and smiled faintly.

Mrs. Haslatt took mild offense. "Now, Father, I don't know what call you have to say that. I've taken good care to keep my place in the house."

"Oh, well—it's only a joke."

"A mighty poor one!"

"Don't fight, you two," Edward said amiably. "It's a bad example to your children."

"There now, Mother," Mr. Haslatt exclaimed with feeble mischief. "Don't I tell you?"

"Oh, shut up, you—" Mrs. Haslatt said with heavy humor. "Is Tom Seaton acting as bad as ever?"

"I haven't seen him in a month," Edward replied. His wife's brother carried, in this house, the burden of his mother's disapproval. In spite of the double marriages, the two families had remained apart, meeting only at formal occasions. Edward had grown at home in the Seaton house, but Margaret would never be quite at home here. The reason for this, Edward was well aware, was that his mother had always to approve before she could welcome and she could not approve either of her sons' wives. She knew, although she would not acknowledge even to herself, that the Seaton family was higher socially in Chedbury than the Haslatts, but she maintained in her own mind the belief that the Haslatt family had a virtue in its soundness that could not be matched by any Seaton. There had never been a drunkard among the Haslatts and never a divorce. Moreover, the Haslatts were churchgoing and the Seatons were not—or at least only irregulary.

"I've told Baynes that we'll only try it for a year," Edward was saying. "If he can bring in enough business to cover his own salary and the extra overhead, then I'll consider it further."

His father noticed the "I," instead of "we," and did not speak. It was only a sign, unconscious, that Edward thought of himself as the head of the whole business, but it thrust one more thorn into the older man's heart.

"Well, I can't take responsibility for it," he said under his breath. "What's the dessert, Mother?"

"Apple pie," she said promptly, "and I made it myself, for Gladys makes a crust an inch thick and like a piece of rubber. It's sinful to waste good food like that."

The pie came on, still hot, and when Mrs. Haslatt cut it the fragrance of sugar and cinnamon mingled with that of the apples.

"What a dinner!" Edward murmured. "I shan't be able to work for an hour."

"No more you shouldn't," his mother said robustly. Her dry cheeks had grown faintly red and she cut large slices of the pie and passed them proudly. "There's the cream in that luster jug—or would you rather have cheese?"

"I'll take cheese," Edward said, and helped himself to the square of yellow sharp cheese.

He was beginning to feel well fed and relaxed. Of course it would be folly to eat like this every day. His own luncheons were frugal affairs, and he dined at night. But he liked good food and knew that he did and he was rigorous with himself about his waistline. Only when he came home, as now, did he let himself eat as he had when he was a boy.

"I believe we're going to have a little boom in business," he said to his father. "Things look good. That's one reason why we can let Baynes have some head."

"The Republicans'll be in for a change," his father agreed.

"Poor old Wilson," Edward said.

"I don't feel sorry for him one bit," his mother protested. "He was getting us mixed up in everything—he's mixed himself, I'm sure. They say he's kind of lost his mind."

"I don't believe that," Edward replied. He did not tell his parents that he had voted steadfastly for Wilson each four years. The man was decades ahead of the nation, a

109

man who saw over the mountains into the future. Old Thomas Seaton had finally convinced him of that. But it could never be explained to his parents. What change in him his marrige to Margaret had wrought! He smiled at his mother. "I can't eat another bite."

"You've eaten real good," she said fondly. "Now you don't have to go right away, do you? Father always takes a little snooze."

"So he should, but I mustn't—yet," Edward said. "Jane Hobbs will be counting the minutes that I'm late."

"Oh, that old maid," his mother said tolerantly. She regarded all unmarried women as freaks. Then she frowned slightly. "Edward, I wish Louise would get married."

"No one in the offing?" he inquired, folding his napkin and slipping it into his old silver ring.

"She's so closemouthed," his mother complained.

"I think she'll marry late," Edward said to comfort her. "Maybe someone older than herself."

"She ought to get married before she's thirty."

"Well, she has a few years to go."

He rose and leaned over her. "Thanks for a grand dinner. I shan't be able to eat tonight."

"I hope Margaret won't blame me for that," his mother said, bristling slightly.

"She never blames anybody for anything," he said carelessly. "Except Mary, maybe."

"She is hard on that child," his mother exclaimed. "I've noticed it, too—though to me Mary's the best child you have."

"Mothers and daughters," his father murmured. He had risen and was stretched out now on the old leather couch under the window.

"Oh, hush up," Mrs. Haslatt cried. "I was always nice to Louise, I'm sure."

"You never paid her the mind that you did the boys," Mr. Haslatt returned.

"What's the matter with you two?" Edward demanded. "I don't remember your arguing so much when I was young."

"We've got more time for it now," his father said. His eyes were closed but his lips twitched with secret laughter.

"Old men get so independent," his mother complained.

"It's our last chance," his father retorted.

"Oh, you old bum," his mother said with affection.

Edward laughed. "Well, if you're having a good time! See you later, Father."

He went into the hall and put on his hat and coat and glancing back into the dining room he saw his mother sipping her coffee. His father was beginning to snore softly. There was an air of warm content in the room, and he realized how much he loved his old parents. He went back to his office, his heart wrapped in tenderness, and wondered if some day his children would look at him when he was old and love him in the same deep amused fashion. So one generation held the other by the heart.

He went to his own home at the end of the day and the sense of permanence clung to him still. He in his time, and in his approaching prime, was fulfilling his place. The early spring evening was cold and he held the collar of his gray topcoat about his throat. He had left his muffler at home this morning, deceived by the soft spring sky, but now the large white clouds had been blown over the hills on the wings of a north wind. There might still be frost tonight if the wind went down. He walked against the wind toward his house and saw it looming solidly against its background of trees. It was square and the roof was low and the railed porches were white in the evening light. Ten years had deepened the shadows of the woods, and trees that he and Margaret had planted in their first spring together were saplings no longer. The elms leading to the house were beginning to make a noble column. He walked between them up the brick-laid walk and one by one he saw the lights of his home begin to shine. That was Margaret. He knew her trick of going from room to room as soon as the sun had set, and turning on the lights. She did not like the twilight, and the children had learned from her to want the lights as soon as the land turned gray.

Eleven years and the house had grown to be as much a part of him as his own body. The thought of himself and Margaret living there together with their children sent his ambition soaring. He wanted everything for them. Other men could want amusement and travel and fame and money, but whatever he wanted was for them—for Margaret first, and then for the children. Comfort and beauty and richness he would work for that he might bestow all upon them.

He opened the door of the wide deep hall and let himself in and there was Margaret, lighting the last lamp.

"Giver of lights," he murmured. Then his heart quickened. He caught a wild sweet gleam in her eye.

"Know why I love you?" she inquired in a matter-of-fact voice that did not deceive him.

"Anything new?" he asked, hanging up his coat in the closet under the stairs.

"Maybe I've never told you," she replied.

"Still hiding things from me, are you?" he retorted.

He put his right arm around her shoulders and tipped her head back with his left hand. "Well, why do you love me?" he inquired.

"Because never once in all these eleven years have you reminded me of electricity bills when I turn on the lights at night!"

"Is that all?" He pretended to be disappointed.

"But that's wonderful!" she exclaimed.

He kissed her lips again gently, tasting their warmth. They were soft and full. Strange how he could tell from the first touch of her lips!

He let her go, knowing now that she did not like to be held too long. He had learned to let her go before she freed herself from him. Ah, what a deal he had learned about loving her! He had been hurt in the old days when they were first married because she twisted herself free so soon. He wanted everything to last forever. Now he knew that anything could become her cage, even his love. He turned to the stair and began to mount slowly to his room and she stood watching him.

"Want another reason why I love you?" she asked.

He paused and she came and laid her hands against the paneling of the stair and he looked down into her blue eyes. "Another reason?"

"One more. It's this—you never turn out the lights that I put on."

"Why should I?" he parried. Only some intuition he had not understood had taught him never to put out a light she had lit. He had often wanted to do it—longed to, in fact, within his prudent soul. It was folly to burn a dozen lights. Then his ceaseless determination to hide nothing from her forced him to tell her this. He leaned over the banisters, and looking down at her he said with half-shamed honesty, "Margaret—look here, I ought to tell you—I've always wanted to turn out the lights. It seemed extravagant to have the whole house lit."

She flung her laughter up at him like a bright bubble. "I know you've wanted to turn them out. But you never have! Sometimes I thought, really he will do it tonight— sometimes when you've been cross or we've had one of our fights. But you never did."

Her intensity warned him. He must not rush down to her and make love to her. These were her approaches. He must withdraw a little, let her pursue until she had committed herself. Oh, he had learned!

"Silly!" he said.

He went on up the stairs and she stood looking after him and he, knowing she was watching, went calmly on his way, his heart hammering against his breastbone.

In his room he washed and changed his clothes and then carefully chose a tie of wine red for his white shirt. She had put on her blue velvet and he had seen it when he came into the house. At first he had been stupid about noticing the small signs but now he had learned. Long ago when he had sworn to have no other love beside her, it had come to him that the variety all men craved could be found in Margaret, if he had the patience and the wit to woo her manifold self.

And yet the evening routine went on as usual. He heard his baby daughter's murmuring voice and going into the small room across the hall he found her in her crib, bathed and fed and ready for sleep. She was pulling the ears of a worn pink teddy bear and its nose was wet with her chewing. When she saw him the teddy bear dropped and she smiled widely, enchanted with him.

"Daddee," she murmured, in ecstasy. He picked her up gently and held her to him and kissed the softness of her fragrant fat neck.

"Ow," she said loudly and giggled. He understood that he needed a shave.

"Thanks for reminding me," he said conversationally and still holding her he pranced about the room noise-

113

lessly and was rewarded by ripples of laughter. So free was her laughter indeed that it ended in an attack of hiccoughs which she enjoyed with fresh amazement, and to quiet her he had to give her a drink of water which she then spat out on his clean shirt bosom.

"Here, young woman," he said with decision. He put her back in bed, kissed her on both cheeks, restored her teddy bear and pulled the blond curl on the top of her head. Then he went to his room and shaved and changed his shirt again.

By the time he was ready to go downstairs his son Tom was coming to look for him. And Mary opened the front door. He heard her first inquiry, "Is Daddy home yet, Mother?" Bless her for always making this her first question. She came running up the stairs and burst into his room. Tom was behind her. He looked like old Thomas, a square-set red-headed fellow. Mary was dark. Edward had unknowingly bestowed upon her his own brown eyes and she had Margaret's curly dark hair. But she had none of the brave freedom of Margaret's carriage. She walked timidly, always a little unsure of welcome. It must be part of his job as father, he told himself, to take the shadow from her, so that she moved as one who walked in light. Strange that Margaret could not see what he meant when he tried to tell her!

He put out his arms first to his daughter, and then felt his son seize his arm and pull it away. "Here—ladies first," he said.

"Mary isn't a lady," Tom said scornfully. "She's on'y a girl."

"Lady to you, young man!"

Tom clung to his arm. "Daddy, kin I have a two wheeler? My tricycle's broken. And I'm too big. I could give it to Sandy when she's high enough."

"Oh, gosh, old man. I can't just promise without talking with Mother."

Mary had said not a word. He felt her clinging to him tightly, her arms about his waist, head against his breast.

"How are you, sweetheart?" he said. "Have a nice day?"

"Yes," she whispered.

"Let's go down to dinner—"

He had won a point with Margaret about that. At the

114

Seaton house the children never had dinner with the family. Supper came first for them and then there had been dinner for the parents and their guests.

"All very well for the English," Edward had said. "They don't want their children about, but I do." They had compromised and after their fifth birthdays the children came to dinner.

He took his place tonight at the head of the table and smiled across a pot of spring flowers at his wife. Hattie brought in small bowls of soup and set them down and went out again. The family meal had begun and it went on as usual and as he hoped it always would, as long as he lived. He listened to what the children had to say and he made replies to please them and to correct them, and Margaret joined in with her usual vigor. She had heeded his words of the morning and she was tender of Mary, refraining, he saw, from correcting her for small mistakes in table manners. It was like any other evening and yet he was perfectly aware that it was one of their rare evenings, and that in spite of the presence of the children he and Margaret were alone with each other.

"I had dinner today with Father and Mother," he told her. "Roast beef and all that—I shan't be able to eat much tonight."

"Roast beef and what?" Tom asked with interest.

"Apple pie," he replied.

"We have chicken and stewed peaches," Margaret said.

Foolish little words and all the time he was aware of a slumberous softness in her eyes. Did the children feel something magic in the air? Had he ever as a child felt this glinting silvery cobweb being woven across the table between his parents? He had not been aware of it, but then perhaps in that house there had been no such weaving. A profound reticence lay between the generations in any decent house, and his was a decent house, and so had been his father's. Here was something he had discovered; when Margaret was witty and her laughter sharp, then, though he laughed, he withdrew, aware of her declaration of solitude. But when she laid aside wit and did not make laughter, he could come near her and she would not repulse him. Oh, the misery of her repulse! He still was wary of it, even after years. For she, the woman, was essentially solitary and he was not, and this was

115

what astonished him. She had welcomed their children, one by one, and she was a tender and physical mother, suckling them at her breast. And yet when the time came to wean them she was ruthless and eager to be cut off from them. He had not understood this when it had first happened with Mary and he had accused her of coldness to her child. Then before Tom was born he had occasion to observe a little dog, a female spaniel he had reared. She had given birth to pups and had nursed them day and night, never leaving them until suddenly one day when they ran to suckle her, she had turned on them and had bitten them and they had gone yelping off, heartbroken. She was through with them and her breast was dry and she had to force them from her and recover herself.

He had not told Margaret of the parable, but he had pondered it, remembering always his vow that he would make his marriage the mainstream of his life. How large that promise had been he had not realized when he gave it, but he could not take it back. And he was aware, too, of her promise which she had given. He never heard her speak a wish to separate herself from him. Yet he knew at last that there were times when she could not bear him near her, even as she had not wanted the child at her breast any more.

At first he had been wounded to the very core of his being and in those early days so foolish as to accuse her at times of not loving him. She declared the accusation was folly and yet she could not explain why she did not want him near her. "Leave me alone," she had repeated. "Just leave me alone, will you, Ned?"

"But why, Margaret?"

"How do I know? Only don't touch me."

He had wished, once or twice, that he could confess his troubles to other men with wives, but his stubborn delicacy forbade it. Had he loved her less he might have spoken but he could not reveal her to another's eyes, either in the spirit or in the flesh. So he held back his anger, and once when she had shut the door against him he accepted his humiliation and determined to wait until she came to him. But her pride was equal to his. She did not come, and angry now at himself, he had approached her again, although only with words.

116

Indeed that it might be no more than words, he had chosen the living room one night after dinner. It was before their trip to England. Mary was then a baby and she had been put early to bed. He had been reading Tennant's second manuscript, he remembered, and Margaret was playing the piano quietly, all her music subdued. He had sat watching her straight and graceful back, her cheek half turned toward him. Then he had spoken. "Margaret!"

At the sound of his voice, though he had made it gentle, she had started violently and her hands crashed the chord.

"Yes?" Her voice was cheerful enough.

"Shall we talk a little while?"

He was not prepared for the joy with which she turned to him at once. "Oh, Ned, will you?"

He had laid his manuscript on the table and she came and sat in the chair opposite him. "Margaret, if you wanted talk why haven't you said so?"

"But you've been a stone!" she cried softly.

He was aghast. "I? You've been miles away from me!"

She shook her head and gazed at him speechlessly, and drew her upper lip down between her teeth.

"You've changed since we've been married," he had accused her. "You used to say anything to me."

Still she did not speak.

"See?" he said, angry in spite of his determination against anger. "You don't help me now. What *is* the matter between us?"

The delicacy of her skin, white against her black hair, was one of her beauties and she had flushed deeply. "I can never get away from you," she had said, and to his horror he saw her begin to tremble, her hands quivering so that she clasped them tightly in her lap and her lips trembling.

She wanted to get away from him! He had waited for a moment until the first surge of hurt died down. Then he had said as quietly as he could, "But you should have told me if you wanted to go away. Would you like to go home for a visit? Hattie can do for me. Or would you like to go to Boston or New York—even England, for that matter?"

"We've always said we'd go to England together," she said.

The absurdity of their position, face to face, and yet struggling to find each other made him ashamed. "It would be easier if we could forget that we're married," he said with sudden inspiration. "Let's imagine that we are as we were before."

She smiled, and he saw her whole body relax. She stopped trembling and then she laughed. "Ned, that's clever of you. Let's do more—let's pretend we're talking about two other people—not you and me—just a he and a she, somewhere, anywhere, anybody, just married and with a small quite nice baby, everything really wonderful, a lovely house, their bills paid—well, very nearly paid. There's my new suit, of course, and I know it was far too expensive but I had to have it for some reason or other—at the moment. I don't care about it now, and I wish I hadn't had it altered."

"It'll be paid for this month," he said, "and so let's call it paid for. All right. He and she—"

He entered into the fiction somewhat stiffly, feeling downright silly. It would have been easier just to speak straight, but perhaps it would not. Anyway, let it be as she wanted. "What about this woman, She?" he inquired. "Does she still love her husband or doesn't she? That's what he keeps asking himself. Maybe he overpersuaded her. After all, he is a stubborn fellow, this He, and he remembers that he insisted—somewhat—upon marrying her."

"Oh, but how can he think she doesn't love him?" Margaret cried. "She feels she is just beginning to know how to love him. That is—sometimes she feels that way."

"Not all the time?"

"She adores him a good deal of the time, she's getting proud of him because she sees he has a lot of brains, really—more than she thought. Her father said to her only the other day—'You've got something in that chap.' But there are times when she wants to be by herself."

"Because she hates him?" he asked.

"No," she replied gravely. "That's what she's beginning to see—not because she hates him but because she just wants sometimes to be alone and whole, complete in

118

herself. She doesn't want to share herself all the time. Most of the time she does want to, though."

He was looking at her who was his wife, his own, and he felt the rending of flesh. "He never wants to be alone, away from her," he told her.

She was trembling again a very little. "Oh, but that's because he's different."

"He's only human—too human, perhaps."

"It's not that—they're both human beings, Ned, and there they are the same."

"Then she's not afraid of him?"

"Oh, no—really she finds him even charming—as a human being!"

Now they were looking at each other steadily. He put the next question.

"Does she feel there's a part of him that is not human?"

"She—she doesn't like to say it's not human—"

"But it isn't?"

"Perhaps it's just—natural."

"Nature being different from human?"

"Yes."

Again the long pause and again his question first. "And she hasn't this nature?"

"Yes—yes—she has."

"Then—why does she draw away from him?"

She was thinking intensely and her dark narrow brows were drawn together over her honest eyes. "She doesn't know—but perhaps it's this. In him she feels the nature is something separate from him—always there, waiting."

"Waiting?"

"For a chance."

"A chance?"

She had ignored the question in his voice and hurried on as though she might not hold the words she wanted if she did not keep her thought running in them. "In her, the nature is all mingled with everything. It's not separate—it doesn't wait—in fact, most of the time she doesn't know it's there. It is only when something she sees in him seems especially endearing—oh, sometimes when she sees his profile is really good, or that his shoulders are broad—or maybe when he is simply thinking and she sees his face in a new way—oh, I don't know—but anyway, then she feels—nature in her, too. But it doesn't separate itself from everything else in her and it isn't physical, at first. And it doesn't wait, you know, Ned. It has to be called to."

He had leaned toward her, and would not go near to touch her. "My dear, but how am I to know?"

She had shaken her head again, and he had been puzzled by that new and shy Margaret. They had talked about everything in the world except this He and this She, who were their secret selves.

"Could you make some small slight sign to me, darling? If you could—"

She shook her head.

"I'd promise not to hurry you," he said quietly. "You'd be the one to make the sign."

"I might be ashamed to."

"Ashamed—with me? Oh, no, Margaret!"

She had not moved her eyes from his face. Still leaning toward her and still careful not to touch her or go near her, as though a butterfly poised upon her knees that must not be frightened away, he had made his voice tender and grave. "Let's not talk any more. I think I understand what you've said. And I'll wait."

She moved quickly and the butterfly seemed to fly away, a thing of gold and blue. "But I don't want to feel you waiting all the time for me to—that's what puts me off, Ned!"

How clumsy he had been—the one wrong word! He shrugged his shoulders. "Then I shan't wait, my dear. After all, you forget I'm a busy man and there's plenty on my mind, beyond sleeping with my beautiful wife, pleasant as that is. I'll keep my mind on other things, and I'll be grateful to you for what you freely give."

He had picked up his manuscript again and had begun to read it, trying to quell the beating of his heart. He was angered and hurt and proud and yet he knew that he loved her exactly the same. So they had sat for some fifteen minutes and then she had come to him and kissed the top of his head delicately.

"Good night, Ned—and thank you."

"Good night, dear. I'll be a little late tonight. I have this to finish."

She had gone away and he had put down the manuscript and had sat long, pondering deeply upon the mystery of marriage. It would have been easy to have his own will, as men did, but then she would escape him altogether. He could not live with her shell. He must have her whole, and that meant that he must have her willing. She could escape him, even when she lay in his arms. He had felt her spirit leave him, and there was only her body beside him and then though it was warm and fragrant, it was dead. Ah, that was where she had him— it was where woman always had man, if he truly loved her. And then there was no pleasure in her for him, not unless he was a clod, which he, Edward Haslatt, was not. There was some strange inner morality in this act of sex. It was moral only when he felt it right and good and he felt it right and good only when her spirit did not escape him. The sin was in the flesh—no, the sin was when flesh was without the spirit. If he were content with her flesh, then it was insult to her who was his love, and whom he loved wholly.

He began dimly to understand the meaning of love. Put to selfish use, it did not function. It had to be unselfish in order to satisfy even selfishly. Had he been of coarser fiber, he might have put woman aside, as a puzzle not to be seriously understood. But then had he been of coarser fiber, he would not now be married to Margaret. He was what he was, and they were inseparably married, unless he drove her spirit from her body. Then wandering and alone, it might never return to him or to his house. The thought of this had put him into a cold terror, and he had sworn to himself a vow that he was never to break, a vow as solemn as his marriage vows, and indeed comprehended in them, as he had come at last to perceive. He would possess her whole or not at all.

He had kept his vow all these years since it was made and he kept it tonight. He had learned, however, that there was always a moment, which if he did not seize, he lost. The delicate manifestations that she made of her mood enchanted him, and his enchantment he had at first allowed to continue too long for her modesty. For if she perceived that she was leading, she instantly withdrew, and then he had lost her again. He could not woo her after she had withdrawn—it was too late. She evaded him. She gave that final swift shake of her head that he

121

dreaded. She began to talk of other things or she took up a book. Positively he must meet her at some point. This point, he had discovered after a year or two or fumbling mistakes, was as soon as she knew that he had understood her manifestation. From the moment she saw that she had made clear to him her mood, then he must take the lead and she must follow. Nor must he postpone too long the consummation. His lead must follow her mood.

How many years it had taken him to learn these things! He had learned them slowly and stupidly, he often told himself. Yet he was compelled to learn them even for his own sake, for he was not a beast. He was above simple lust. Then, having learned, he was tender with her and attuned to her, and he was rewarded. In her content was his own fulfillment. The process had refined his soul while it had sharpened his senses. He and Margaret were so profoundly married, now at the end of eleven years, that he felt, with triumph, that he had made a success of his marriage. Had he been a different kind of man, a man without patience, without the wit to perceive that a man could not be satisfied with a woman unless she was satisfied with him, what loss to him! For he had not changed his whole character or improved his most common faults. He was still easily wounded and susceptible to jealousy, although he thought he had learned to hide it from her. Jealousy she could not tolerate. Stubborn though he was, she had frightened him half beside himself in the second year of their marriage. One night Tom had come to dinner, bringing with him a young Irishman, a blue-eyed, black-haired fool of a fellow, whose tongue was loose at both ends and laced with wit. Margaret had abandoned herself to laughter during dinner, and after dinner when Hattie brought in the coffee, she had patted the place beside her on the couch.

"Come here!" she had cried to Sean Mallory.

Edward had stood watching while the young Irishman sat down beside Margaret. And then she would not look at him, after he had glared at her, after her eyelashes had flickered at him. She had been gay and wild and Tom had encouraged her, and Sean Mallory, quick to perceive the young husband's silence, had yet found it impossible to resist the gay girl's voice, her sparkling provocative talk, her laughter.

When the two guests had gone silence fell as the door closed. Margaret sat on the couch where she had been sitting all evening, and she looked at him with hostility in her blue eyes. He had been confounded by the change in her. It was like seeing a landscape upon a sunny day gone suddenly gray under a cloud. The shock broke his control.

"I can stand anything," he had said to her between his teeth, "anything except what's physical."

She had looked at him honestly bewildered. "Physical?"

"That you asked him to come and sit down beside you, where I was going to sit—you motioned him with your hand—"

She rose, electric with anger. Her eyes gleamed, her hair quivered, her cheeks flamed. "Now that is enough," she said in a quiet and terrible voice. "You will make me despise you if you go on."

She had walked with dignity to the door and there she had turned. "What you say is an insult to me," she declared. "I will not endure it, do you hear me, Ned? If ever again you accuse me of being—physical—with a man I don't love, that day I will leave you."

She went upstairs and he heard her door close. He followed, after a miserable half hour in which he ostentatiously wound the clock and locked the doors and fed the cat and put out all the lights downstairs. When he tried the handle of her door it was locked. He spent a sleepless night, telling himself that he was right to have spoken and that innocent though she was, how was the Irishman to know that she was innocent? How could any man think her innocent when she was so beautiful?

He rose the next morning still angry and cold and she did not come down to breakfast. When he went in to her room to kiss her, her lips were lifeless and her eyes dark. She was unrepentant and he knew her well enough already to know that she would never repent of anything she had said or done and that she did not repent now. Very well, neither would he repent. He had gone away to the day's business, cold and hurt, and when he came home he was very tired. He found her quiet and usual and they had never spoken again of the matter.

But she had not forgotten it. He knew because years later, only last year, indeed, when Sean Mallory having become a poet of almost first water, he had mentioned casually that Haslatt and Mather had a chance to bid for his new book, Margaret had said nothing. She was arranging roses in a bowl on a small table under the wide living-room window and she had continued to choose one flower and then another. He had let the bid go by and Livingstone Hall had published *Fire in the Night*. He had brought home a copy of the book and had put it on the library table. When she saw it she had taken it and thrown it into the wastepaper basket. He had reproved her.

"Margaret, what folly—a new book, with good reviews!" He stooped to pick it out of the basket again.

"Don't put it on the table," she had cried at him.

He had refused to yield to her. "I'll take it back to the office and put it on my own shelves," he had said with dignity.

Afterward he remembered that long ago she had told him she liked to speak out what she felt. "I don't want to have to stop and think whether something is going to hurt your feelings—" That was what she had once said. He had a vague sense that nevertheless she had learned to stop and think about his feelings, and that she no longer spoke out. But he, too, had learned if not to stop feeling yet to stop showing what he felt. In spite of their dreams, their marriage had shaped itself out of what they were. Their faults had made it, as well as their virtues. Well, it was good. He still could not imagine himself loving any woman except Margaret.

A telegram from Baynes the next morning announced the certainty of Lewis Harrow's arrival, and in the late afternoon Edward went to meet the train that was bringing, he hoped, the new author. This morning it seemed settled that the firm was to be Haslatt and Sons and he had called up a sign painter. In the afternoon he and his father had chosen the lettering Haslatt and Sons, Publishers and Printers. His father had actually been excited and Edward was calm, in consequence, though in spite of new pride. Now he wished the sign could be ready for tomorrow morning when Lewis Harrow could see it. He smiled, half ashamed at his impatience.

The train slowed to a stop at the Chedbury station. It was a local running out from Boston, and since Chedbury was next to the last station, few people were aboard. It was easy to discover a thickset young man who wore no hat and a shabby topcoat. He stood looking left and right, and Edward drew near. "Mr. Harrow?"

"Lewis Harrow," the young man said.

His intense eyes did not light under half-lowered lids nor did he smile. He wore a young dark mustache and he carried a worn bag.

"I am Edward Haslatt."

They shook hands and the young man began to speak in an uneven staccato. "Good of you to come and meet me—yourself, I mean."

"Chedbury is a small place and I can walk here to this station quite easily," Edward replied. "I am glad you can spend the night. The trolley is only just around the corner."

They walked away together, the young man with a slight limp, and at the car Edward involuntarily lifted him slightly by the arm.

"Thanks," the young man said. "I got a potshot in the leg in the war."

"Sorry to hear that," Edward said.

"It's nothing—now."

They sat in silence for a moment and then Edward began to talk, diffidently. He was still shy before his authors, still, he feared, more printer than publisher. Then he perceived that Lewis Harrow was even more diffident than himself, and he laid hold of his pride and began to speak with determination. "I hope you won't be impatient with me if I take several days, or more, in reading your manuscript. I read slowly—and perhaps make up my mind slowly, too."

"I don't mind," Lewis Harrow said indifferently. He was gazing out the window. "It's still beautiful country. I was afraid it had changed."

"It's nice," Edward admitted. "Have you been here before?"

"Yes," Harrow said. "But long ago."

Edward looked out on the familiar landscape with complacent pleasure. Most of the time he forgot it, but when someone approved it, he remembered that it was fine and his own. When he and Margaret were first married he had honestly made great effort to see as quickly as she did the beauty in land and sky, but to his confusion she had soon detected his effort and one day she had said plainly, though with good nature, "Don't pretend, will you, Ned! You needn't care about the sunset."

"Well, I do," he had retorted. "I can see it's beautiful as well as you, but I can't cry out over it."

"How does it make you feel?" she had asked curiously.

"I'm pleased my world contains it," he had answered after some reflection.

"That's well put," she had said as though surprised. "Perhaps it says more than you know."

"Perhaps it does," he had agreed.

Afterward it occurred to him that she lived in every moment entire as it came, but he lived each moment as it was related to the past and the future. Thus he did not see the sunset as only a splendid sight, but he saw it in its place in the landscape of his home.

"You have a family?" Lewis Harrow was asking.

"A son and two daughters," Edward replied, "all small yet—the youngest a baby."

"I like children," Harrow went on. "I hope yours will like me."

"You'll find Mary shy," Edward replied. As always his heart flew to protect this eldest child. "The others are ordinary enough—though their mother would reproach me for putting it that way. One can't say yet, as a matter of fact, what the baby is. I'm fond enough of my son, but I can't see signs that he'll set the world afire."

Harrow laughed. "A practical man, though a father!"

Edward narrowed his eyes in a small smile. "I hope so," he said dryly. "Here's our stop."

They got out at the corner road and walked the brief distance to the house. Edward said nothing, wanting to catch undiluted by irrelevant talk the stranger's first glimpse of the house. He paused cunningly just before the road turned. "Just around the bend you'll see where we live," he said carelessly. They made the turn and

Harrow stopped to exclaim in honest admiration, "What a house!"

"It was built by an Englishman, years ago," Edward explained, taking care to be casual. "His wife died and he went back to England just about the time we were married. It was too big for us then, of course, but —well, we wanted it. My wife was used to space and I wanted to give her what she'd had."

"Is that she?" Harrow asked. They were walking on again.

"Yes." They could see Margaret quite plainly now. She was cutting a few daffodils.

"She looks young," Harrow said.

"A year younger than I," Edward said.

"You're not old," Harrow said, smiling.

"Only older than you," Edward said, returning the smile.

They became aware that they were talking trivially and fell silent. A moment later they were at the gate and there stood Margaret in her blue wool dress, her hands full of the yellow daffodils. Her black hair curled about her face and her eyes in the light of the sunset were a startling blue. Edward felt the old sting of physical jealousy and his palms tingled. Why did she have to stand there looking as though she had suddenly come to life?

"This is Lewis Harrow," he said abruptly. "Harrow, this is my wife."

Margaret put out her hand and the young man took it. "I hope you don't mind my saying you're beautiful."

Edward, surprised by this boldness, stared with displeasure at his guest, and saw for the first time how strange was the color of his eyes, a yellowish hazel. But before he could speak, Margaret said frankly, "I don't mind a bit. Do come in, both of you. Sandy's calling for you, Ned."

The door of the house flew open and Mary darted out. "Oh, Dad!" she cried. "I thought you'd never come." She flung her arms about his waist, a brown-skinned, brown-eyed child whose hair was too long and dark for the small anxious face.

"I told you I had to meet Mr. Harrow," Edward said, hugging her.

"I told her, too," Margaret said, "but she frets about everything."

"Does she!" Harrow said half playfully. "How well I understand that! I always fret."

"Do you?" Mary breathed. "It's awful, isn't it?"

"Really awful!" Harrow agreed.

He seemed to have forgotten Margaret and Edward forgave him on the instant. So seldom did anybody see his plain little daughter.

"What do you fret about?" Mary asked.

"Well, whether your father will like my book," Harrow said mischievously.

"Father!" Mary cried. "You will like his book, won't you?"

"Mary, please go in and have your supper," Margaret said suddenly.

"Isn't she eating with us?" Edward asked.

His eyes met Margaret's. "She and Tom are having their supper early tonight," Margaret said.

The evening passed. At each stage Edward watched Harrow not only with his own eyes but through Margaret's delaying, fluctuating feeling toward the young man. Thus he knew that she was first horrified at Harrow's table manners. He buttered his bread slice whole and ate it so. He gnawed the meat from his lamb chop and wiped his greasy hands shamelessly on his napkin. Whatever he did was unconscious. Obviously he had never been taught manners, nor had he observed them. This physical coarseness was balanced by a delicacy in feeling and perception strange and quick. He lounged on the couch after dinner and shook his head at coffee. "Keeps me awake," he declared, "and sleep is important to me. I want my brain crystal in the morning." But an hour later he divined restlessness in Margaret and he smiled at her boldly.

"You feel you've seen me before, don't you?"

"I do," she replied, "how did you know?"

"I feel you wondering."

"Nonsense!"

"Of course I do," he insisted. "It's my business to feel what people are thinking. Well, you have seen me before."

His confident smile was not attractive but it was compelling.

"Where?" Edward asked with caution.

Harrow gave a loud laugh. "Right here in Chedbury!"

"Wait," Margaret said. "Let me think—"

They waited, their eyes on her vivid thinking face.

"The only thing I can see is our old laundress. There's something about you—"

"There is. I'm her son."

"But her name was Hinkle."

Lewis Harrow interrupted her. "Impossible name for a novelist! As soon as Mother died I changed it. I'm Harrow now, legally."

"You weren't the boy who used to lug in the baskets for her?" she asked.

"I was and am," Harrow said without embarrassment.

"Your face was always dirty."

"Still is, a good deal of the time."

"But how old are you?"

"Twenty-eight."

Edward sat silent. The bright demand in Margaret's voice, the directness of her curiosity, had drawn a fearless response from the young man. He had seen this happen again and again between Margaret and some other human being. She was irresistible when she wanted to be— and when the other person was strong enough for it.

Lewis Harrow was strong and he felt no need for self-defense. He turned now to Edward. "The novel I've got for you tonight is about war. I was in it, of course. I have to get it out of my system. But I've already begun another."

"That's good news," Edward said quietly. "It's what a publisher wants to hear—that there's always another."

It was his turn now, and he took it, and Margaret sat by, listening, her eyes intense and her cheeks flushed, while they talked of the writing of books.

"What do you think of him?" This Edward asked her when long past midnight they were getting ready for bed.

"It depends on what he's doing," she replied. She took off the wrought-gold necklace and the earrings which a few years ago he had bought to match it. "When he's

129

eating he's an animal. Maybe he's an animal anyway. But when he talks he makes me think of Beethoven."

"The two aren't incompatible," Edward murmured. He felt exhausted. There was some force in Harrow that burned the oxygen out of the air. A consuming sort of fellow—he didn't want to be with him too much! There was that manuscript lying on the table in the small study that adjoined the bedroom. He did not intend to go near it tonight. He lay down in his bed a few minutes later, and felt the sheets cool and grateful to his outstretched legs. Margaret was already in her bed, and before he put out the light he took his final look at her through the open door between their rooms. Five years ago they had decided on separate rooms. She lay as always high on two pillows, her soft black hair outspread. She wore a long-sleeved nightgown and there were frills of lace over her clasped hands. Their eyes met and smiled.

"I'd hate to be married to anybody except you," she said sweetly.

"Thank you, my dear," he replied.

They had already kissed and so he put out the light. He heard the small sigh she gave before she slept and then there was silence. She was exhausted, too.

He lay for perhaps an hour, waiting for sleep. He was not a sound sleeper even at the end of his usual days, and tonight he felt his awareness in every nerve and vein. Thus though his heart beat steadily and slowly he could count the pulsation of his blood as it flowed through his body. His hearing sharpened and magnified the cracks of beams above his head, the scrape of a shutter loosened against the outside wall of the house, the slow rise of the night wind. Margaret's breathing, soft and not quite steady, disturbed the rhythm of his own, and involuntarily he tried to keep in tune with her. So for two hours he lay tortured by his wakefulness, troubled by nothing clearly enough to absorb his mind, and yet all the minor troubles of his days flitted darkly across his brain—Margaret's injustice to his dear little Mary, the young man in his printing shop, the labor union that threatened the peace of his work, his father's increasing weakness, his own need for more money and the impossibility of speaking of it, Baynes and the New York office, Baynes and Sandra, this fellow Harrow. He doubted his own ability to handle Harrow. Suppose the fellow turned out to be something stupendous, a really great writer, had he, Edward Haslatt, the skill, the knowledge to shape the notable career of a genius?

Upon this he thought of the manuscript lying on his table and he rose noiselessly and put on the woolen bathrobe and the slippers that were at the foot of his bed. Margaret slept on, and still silent he stole across the room and opened the door into his study.

When he had finished reading the manuscript the dawn was glimmering in the sky. He was shivering cold and his eyelids burned and he felt sick with weariness. His hands as he turned the last page into its place were trembling. It was more than fatigue. It was wonder and disgust and admiration and terror. He had found at last a man who could write and was not afraid of God or man.

"I've got to be strong enough for him." So thinking, Edward crawled into his cold bed and fell asleep.

Six months later on an evening in late spring, he was still not sure that he was strong enough. The whole town of Chedbury had gathered in the courthouse to hear Lewis Harrow talk. His fame had overwhelmed them irresistibly. The swift and staggering success of his book had astonished and irritated them. The motive of his novel had been to make a vast joke of war. His hero was a young officer who early had seen the monstrosity of urging his men to sacrifice life, their best and most essential possession, for any cause whatever. In the end he had himself to choose between sensible escape to save his own life, or death on the battlefield to maintain illusion for men dependent upon him. Chedbury would have forgiven Lewis Harrow had his hero chosen death. Instead the heady young officer had chosen to surrender to his own men, with apology, a swaggering smile, court-martial and guns facing him as he stood back to a wall.

So unorthodox a bravery had confounded the sober people of Chedbury. Harrow had brought them fame but its cause was questionable. Reluctantly, after months of debate, they had decided to give him belated acknowledgment by inviting him to speak to them, and pride had struggled with curiosity in coming to hear him.

Mrs. Seaton said what many others felt. "It's a pity it had to be only Mrs. Hinkle's boy who got us famous."

Old Thomas Seaton had opened his sleepy eyes after dinner when he heard this. "Yes, why couldn't it have been you, Tom? Or even Meg or Sandra? Any child of your mother's would have done better than Lew Hinkle."

Tom had grinned without speaking. He talked less and less and looked brighter, smarter, and more sleek as he grew older. Still unmarried, he lived at home, but since he did not now ask for money, his father let sleeping dogs lie, though well aware that the cause for his son's solitary content, or resignation, lived in South Chedbury, in the form of a plump and pretty Italian girl. The cause for Tom's early drunkenness, Margaret had confided to Edward, was that he had fallen in love with a fair-haired English girl, whose father was an earl. The Seaton family, so notable in Chedbury, was less considerable in Great Bairnbourne Castle. Mrs. Seaton in wounded pride had demanded that Tom come back to Chedbury at once, and Tom had obeyed, to forget rather easily, it seemed, his first love. He had recalled it uneasily, however, upon reading Harrow's book, when the rebellious hero had loved just such a young English girl as he still remembered, when alone sometimes at night. The likeness had not escaped Mrs. Seaton's sharpness, and between mother and son there had arisen an irritability increased by their determined silence upon the subject of their thoughts.

Even between Edward and Margaret, Lewis Harrow's book had brought a small discord. Physical cowardice she hated and she smelled something foul in the idea of a soldier, an officer, choosing death at the hands of his clan rather than his enemy.

"Maybe they were his real enemies," Edward had suggested.

She had given him a quick look. "It's not like you to be subtle, Ned."

"I don't do it easily," he conceded.

"Explain yourself," she demanded.

But he could never do that and he had tried less and less as the years passed. Words had been essential to her in the early years of their marriage and he had made earnest attempt to use them freely to her then. The fluency that was natural to her made him sweat with effort and he gave it up as unnatural to him.

"I can't explain myself," he now said.

"Try!" So she urged him. When he hesitated she said, biting her red underlip, "How strange it is that men don't mind stripping their bodies naked before women, but ask them to uncover their thoughts and they grow as shy as virgins!"

She had settled herself on the couch to read the evening this went on, and half exasperated, half baffled, he had stopped on his way upstairs to tell the children good night and had taken her head between his two hands, had kissed her and gone on his way. He no longer quarreled with her for any reason.

Meanwhile talk had continued in Chedbury. There had been a good deal of discussion at a meeting two weeks before as to whether they would use the church or the courthouse. The new minister had decided the matter by rising to his feet, very tall and dry. "I've read Harrow's book," he had said. "I feel it would not be safe to allow him the use of the church. Profanity seems natural to him. We'd better compromise on the courthouse."

People had laughed. The salt of their minister's tongue was their everyday blessing. His sermons were plain and sometimes they made a man angry, but at least one knew what they were about. Joseph Barclay had been to sea in his youth and had been converted in Liverpool by an English Methodist preacher making the rounds of the red-light district to rescue the men from the ships. This preacher had rescued the young officer by mighty words and a loud quarrel with the woman who had him in tow. With his two hands he had laid hold on the boy and forced him out into the rainy darkness of an English night. He had taken him home and lectured him and prayed with him and held him God's prisoner until he promised to repent.

So Joseph Barclay had repented and had one day returned to America to keep his word with God. He was fifty years old now, and Chedbury had called him when Dr. Hart had said they must. At seventy Dr. Hart had gone out and searched for the man who must take his place in Chedbury. He had found him in a little church in the city of Lowell, a church so blackened by factory smoke outside and the grimy hands of the congregation inside that anyone else would have passed it by. But Francis Hart had heard of the man who spoke so plainly that people always knew what he was saying, and there he had found him. It had not been too easy to persuade the plain-speaking man to come to Chedbury. "I belong here among the factory folk," he had told old Dr. Hart. "I don't like dressing up. And when I preach I'm liable to take the skin off."

"Factory folk get their skin taken off in other ways," Dr. Hart had retorted. "Nobody dares to skin my folk in Chedbury except me, and after I'm dead they'll grow soft."

He had lived to hear the new minister preach a couple of fine searing sermons and then he had died of pneumonia caught on a zero morning when he insisted on shoveling the snow a blizzard had thrown on his front walk. People did not always like Joseph Barclay but nobody dared rebel because old Dr. Hart had brought him there. And the fellow told the truth so consistently that no one wanted to be the first to speak against him. There was, moreover, a certain excitement in going to church each Sunday. Joseph Barclay never said the same thing twice. He lived alone in the parsonage, was unmarried, and half the time he cooked his own meals because no woman in Chedbury would make fish chowder the way he liked it.

In the courthouse, then, the people of Chedbury sat on a late spring evening, waiting to hear what the son of old Abe Hinkle had to say. The older people could remember the family well, and when Abe died in his final drunken fit, they had helped Mrs. Hinkle by giving her monumental heaps of laundry. Many of the younger people could remember Lew Hinkle, the spindle-shanked boy who went to school with them. They distrusted the change of his name, though he made no pretense of concealing either his father's name or his reason for changing it. "No use keeping a name that's a commercial handicap," Lewis Harrow had said publicly to newspaper reporters, even in New York.

Tonight he stood, too much at ease, some thought, before his audience. He was soberly dressed in a new gray suit, his rough black hair was smooth, and the only exception that the reluctant people of Chedbury could take as they gazed at him was the color of his tie which was red. Edward himself regretted the tie. He disliked bright hues especially when worn by men, and Margaret had learned never to give him anything except a tie of a solid blue or gray. He did possess one tie of wine red that he wore usually on Christmas day with his good dark suit.

The courthouse was of an unusual and somewhat theatrical design. A hundred years ago an ambitious politician had conceived the idea of a central platform where he could hold forth upon occasions. Around this platform set against the north wall five tiers of seats rose toward the door. Since the courthouse stood upon a hill, the effect was dramatic. It had never been more so than tonight, when all of Chedbury had come out to hear this humble and almost unknown son. The Seatons sat together at the left, and with them were Baynes and Sandra, come from New York today. Edward had toyed with the notion of inviting them to the brief dinner that he and Margaret had eaten with Lewis Harrow, and then had decided against it. Sandra had a way of stimulating men to talk and he did not want Harrow exhausted before his speech. There was no use in wasting on Sandra witticisms that might amaze an audience. Sandra had put on a brilliant green dress without sleeves, and she had combed her red hair high, like the crest of a bird. Edward looked away from her impatiently. New York was bringing out the worst in her. Old Tom Seaton was drowsing in his seat and Mrs. Seaton nudged him with her elbow. That was the difference between them. Old Tom slept into his age and she grew more wakeful as death drew near. Edward's own parents sat side by side just in front of himself and Margaret, and with them was Louise. So seldom did he see his sister that he looked at her now with the detached, half-critical mind of a stranger. She looked rather pretty in her quiet unadorned fashion, hair parted and put back into some sort of knot at her neck and a blue dress that made her skin pale and white. Her profile was better than it had been when she was a girl. A certain thickness she had then was worn away and she looked delicate.

He stopped looking at Louise after he perceived these general improvements and settled himself to listen to

Lewis Harrow. He had taken Harrow down to the platform a few minutes before and had made a brief introduction. He knew that he was a poor speaker, and being uneasy on his feet, he said a few terse words in a dogged monotone, bare and without congratulation, either to Harrow or to himself as the publisher of a spectacularly successful first novel. But Chedbury was used to Edward Haslatt and they did not judge him. To brisk short applause, he had walked to his seat beside Margaret. She looked up at him softly, laughter hidden in her eyes, and he felt her hand steal into his and cling.

He pondered for a moment the meaning of this inexplicable handclasp as the people settled themselves to listen to Harrow. Nothing Margaret did was without significance. She did not give him one idle caress. Why, then, he asked silently, did she now press her soft palm into his, under the careful cover of her fur cape? Distracted for a moment, he scarcely heard what Harrow was saying.

Lewis Harrow spoke quickly, his deep voice penetrating into the farthest reach of the great round hall. Edward had never seen him discomfited, even when attacked by a galaxy of newspaper men, but tonight he perceived a slight belligerence in Harrow's manner, as though he felt himself on trial before the people of Chedbury. They were haunted perhaps by the memory of a hundred years of other trials in this very place, judgments upon men who had stolen what was not theirs, who had taken lives of other men, women who had wept, clutching the hands of bewildered children. The courthouse was a haunted place.

Lewis Harrow seemed to feel it. He lifted his head and stared about him at them all. The hard central light poured down light and heat upon him and he saw the faces of the people gleaming at him out of the surrounding shadows. Then his diffidence left him and clasping his hands behind him he began to speak with sudden ease.

"What I have done proves nothing, to you or to myself. You have done me an honor in coming to hear me tonight, but I shall not have deserved that honor until I write my second book, and my third. After the third then you may judge me and I will accept your judgment. I can write about war—yes, I grant you that I made

136

you feel something of what men suffer in a war. But anybody can write about such melodrama. The story is ready made. The stage of war is small, the pattern set. The common words are ready—patriotism, bravery, death.

"But can I write about life? That you must decide for me, ten years from now. Take our town! If I were to write a novel about Chedbury where would I begin? Where would you begin, if you were I? I grew up here, among you. You knew my parents. With my mother I came in and out of your houses. Our door was the back door, but for my purposes that was the best one. I saw your kitchens. I heard the underside of your lives. Destined to be what I am, I had even then the mind of a writer. That is, I never forgot anything I saw or heard, I still do not. More than that, I understand far more than a word, I hear infinitely beyond a whisper.

"Where shall I begin my next book? Shall I begin with young Dr. Walters? You remember Bertram Walters, how brilliant he was, how handsome. Why he left Boston and came to settle in our little town we never knew. It took me a long time to find out. Until I knew I could not understand any more than you did, why, at the height of his youth and strength, he should kill himself one hot July day. I can remember the day and the hour. I had been swimming with some of you down at the old hole in the river. You left me at Bolster's Alley where I lived. We in Bolster's Alley heard things before you did, and we already knew that he had shot himself in exactly the correct spot in his heart. He was a perfectionist, you'll remember. I loped up to the Walters house and saw him dead—just for a minute before they put me out. Something in his face made me hang around the undertaker's place the next day. Jake Bentley and I were friends in a queer sort of way and he let me come in sometimes and look at the dead people. I looked a long time at Dr. Walters. Jake and I talked and wondered why he did it. Something Jake said helped me to find out, later —half accidentally. It would be telling my story too soon if I told you now.

"Or should I begin with Bolster's Alley itself? There was an alley! You have cleaned it up since I lived there. Our town officers are more efficient than they used to be.

Maybe it's just that we have more conscience than we used to have. The old Hinkle shack is gone. When I lived there with my mother, you'd be surprised at the good citizens I used to see sometimes, on a dark night, walking along the Alley. My mother was a good woman, too old and fat, maybe, for sin, but there were some beautiful women in the Alley.

"Maybe I ought to begin my story with Henry Croft, that matchless teacher, who beat me half to death when I was a rebellious schoolboy. That was only a decade and a half ago—seems strange that things have changed so much that if anybody beat a child now in the public school of Chedbury, he'd be arrested. But there was war then between Henry Croft and me and he always won. He won, too, in another way. I'm no fool and I began to see that the reason he couldn't keep from beating me was that he knew I had something in me and he was furious because I didn't see it for myself. I guessed it one day, when I was around thirteen. He grew angry with me because I hadn't written a composition. He said to me, 'Down with your bags,' and I got ready. He stared at me and began to cry. The whip dropped from his hand to the floor. For the first time in my life I was scared of him. Then he began to shout at me through his tears. 'Aren't you going to make something of yourself?' That was what he bellowed at me. I pulled up my pants, and I knew he would never beat me again. Then I could talk to him. Then he could talk to me. In the next four years he was the most wonderful teacher a boy ever had. He set my feet upon the path."

Margaret had drawn her hand away and now she sat leaning forward on her elbows. The tears were running down her cheeks. Edward had forgotten her, but he turned and saw the glistening of her eyes. The people of Chedbury were motionless in silence. Mrs. Croft sat in her widow's weeds, tall and gaunt, her face like staring stone. Little old Mrs. Walters bent her head. Thomas Seaton was wide awake and Mrs. Seaton was waving her small sandalwood fan swiftly to and fro.

Edward leaned toward Margaret. "Can we let this go on?"

She shook her head without reply, her eyes fixed on Harrow.

"Where shall I begin my book of life?" he was asking. "Shall I begin it in one of our big houses? It is a house full of life, as you well know. Long ago a strong man married a beautiful woman and they produced beautiful children. What becomes of beautiful children? They begin so full of promise. What happens to them? Shall I tell that story?

"I might choose another house and a plain honest sort of family, the family that lives in every other house in Chedbury. They don't struggle with poverty but they struggle with life. The man started out with modest dreams of himself, of love. The woman had a little dream, too, nothing very big, of course. We are cautious folk here. No use dreaming about what we can't have! But the dreams of this man and this woman were all cautious, possible ones. They could be more than dreams. But they weren't. Why? The man and woman were faithful to each other, of course. We never saw him in the Alley. He always went to church on Sunday with his wife and his children, and he wasn't afraid of anything—except life itself. Ask him if he wanted something, from a helping of chicken pot pie at a church supper to a million dollars and he would have said the same thing, 'I don't care if I do.' The phrase expresses him. Perhaps it expresses Chedbury. And yet, in spite of his dreams, which never came true because he never dared to make them big enough, or bold enough, he's had a life. In a way, he's even had a love, and so has the woman. Yes, perhaps theirs is the true story of Chedbury."

Against his own will, Edward glanced at his father and mother but he could not see their faces. Dangerous, indeed, this fellow Harrow! He had taken Chedbury into the hollow of his hand, and he was looking at them all, like a great Gulliver. They'd be angry tomorrow, and he'd hear from it. Then suddenly he had a grim sort of pleasure in it. Whatever happened, he had his big man. Harrow would make Haslatt and Sons known everywhere in the world. But first it was his job to make Harrow known everywhere in the world, a job he'd dreamed of doing somehow, if he could find the man. He could feel in his hands already the big new book. While Harrow talked, Edward, in his mind, turned fine paper, studied the perfect type, considered the width of margins and the design of a jacket. What color for the binding? Wine red, perhaps, and gold stamping? Tomorrow he'd finger his way through his typebook. He was in the grip of his own private frenzy of creation.

He did not notice that night, when they went home and to bed, that Margaret was silent and thoughtful. She went about the house in her usual way, pouring a last saucer of milk for Mary's kitten, peeling an orange and eating it by the dying coals of the living-room fire, and watching him, her blue eyes thoughtful, as he tested doors, pulled down shades and wound the clock in the hall. He went upstairs before her, because it was he, rather than she, who looked at the two older children. They had been moved out of the nursery into rooms of their own when each was seven, and he tiptoed to one bedside and then the other. Tom he always visited first, because he liked to linger by Mary. The boy was lying outstretched and strong, one leg outside the covers. The windows were wide open and a cool breeze, smelling of the not too distant sea, filled the room. He covered Tom and remembered that his son had lost a tooth that day. He took a nickel from his pocket, and feeling under the pillow he found the tooth and left the nickel. Then he went into the hall and opened the next door.

The night wind was cool here, too, but Mary was curled under a thin silk quilt and when he touched her forehead he found it damp with heat. This child had always the impulse to hide herself, to burrow deep into shelter. He rolled back the quilt cautiously from her neck and she woke at once and stared at him with strange eyes. He saw that she did not recognize him.

"It's me, dearie," he whispered, bending over her.

She flung up her arms and locked them behind his head. "You scared me."

"You mustn't get scared so easily."

"Because I thought it was somebody else!"

"It's always I who come here at night to see if you're all right."

"It mightn't always be you."

Some far truth in this confounded him. He kissed her and drew her arms gently from his neck. "Go to sleep, Mary."

She curled down again and he tiptoed out of the room and met Margaret coming from the nursery.

"Sandy all right?" he inquired.

"Robust and lovely," Margaret said.

The phrase fitted their third child. Sandy, not beautiful except as pink cheeks, blond hair, and innocent blue eyes always carry the implication of beauty, was rich in health and simple charm. She was a child upon whom Edward did not waste an instant's worry.

Later, before he got into his bed, he lingered by Margaret's bed, and remembering the clasp of her hand he stooped and gave her a tentative kiss. She received it without enthusiasm, though kindly, and mindful of the lesson that the years had taught him, he smoothed her hair for a moment and then left her. The exhilaration of his spirit prevented him from perceiving her unusual silence and he slept.

"A nice nest of hornets," Mr. Haslatt said the next morning. He was waiting at the door of the elevator when his son stepped out of it rather more briskly than usual.

A collected stubbornness had gathered in Edward as he proceeded on his usual way to the office. The greetings that he received from meetings in the morning on the trolley were always curt. Chedbury was not at its best before noon. But this morning mumbled words were only nods and men read their morning papers without raising their heads as he passed.

All this was introduction to his father's gritty remark, and Edward, inwardly disturbed, refused to acknowledge it.

"What's the matter?" he asked with involuntary deceit.

"Looks like you'll have to take a choice between that fellow and the rest of the town," his father said.

Edward did not reply. He passed between the desks in the main office without speaking and certainly without allowing himself to notice the suppressed and curious looks that the girls sent him. He went into his office and shut the door after his father.

"Sit down," he said.

He sat down himself behind the square old desk that had once belonged to Mr. Mather and his father took the chair opposite. He was never comfortable thus facing his father, but today he did not allow his feelings to move him. If it were to be necessary to fight all Chedbury for Lewis Harrow, let it begin here. He waited for his father.

"I don't see as Lew Hinkle had any reason to talk the way he did last night," Mr. Haslatt said. He wore an old pepper-and-salt suit upon which the thread had worn down to gray, which made more dun the grayness of his skin and hair. He had grown thin with age and his long nose was pink at the tip. In cold or excitement a drop quivered at his nostril and Edward repressed his old youthful impulse to mention it. If he had to contend with his father on the large matter of Lewis Harrow, he would not indulge himself in small personal repulsions. He looked toward the window. Chedbury was most beautiful now, but man could be as vile here as anywhere.

"You have to let a writer talk any way he wants," he said. Then without giving his father opportunity to answer he went on. "Baynes will be in soon, I suppose."

"I've lived my life in this town," his father replied.

"I intend to live mine here, too," Edward said doggedly.

"Your mother says Mrs. Walters is terribly upset."

Edward wheeled in his chair. "The real question is whether we are going to go to the top with Harrow or whether we're going to stay right here in Chedbury along with Mrs. Walters and her kind."

"You can't please God and Mammon," Mr. Haslatt said solemnly.

"Mrs. Walters isn't either of them," Edward retorted.

Upon this foolish conversation Baynes burst into the office like a soaring rocket, scattering good humor and optimism. He had on a new suit, a striped thing, and the shoulders had a silly sloped effect.

"Thought I'd find you two here! Wasn't that a swell performance last night? Skinned half the town, didn't he? All as neat as you please! Took 'em out of cold storage. We've been fighting at the Seatons' or I'd have been here sooner."

"Mr. Seaton sore?" Mr. Haslatt inquired.

"You can't make that tough old hide sore," Baynes said. "Mrs. Seaton is all upset over bad taste, of course. Curious, young Tom is on her side. Nobody is going to have any peace in the town if Harrow really writes that

142

book. If it's half the book he says it's going to be, we're all set for a fortune."

"That how Sandra looks at it?" Edward asked.

"Sandra's out helping him to pick the site for his house." Baynes sat on the window sill and swung his leg.

"He ain't going to live here!" Mr. Haslatt exclaimed.

"He is," Baynes replied. "He doesn't want to live in any of the old houses he could buy. That's Chedbury for you. Yelling about him and still they'd sell him the house from under their feet if he paid enough. He's going to build his house—wants to make his own ghosts, he says."

Edward considered this with the silence usual to him. Certainly it would have been easier if Lewis Harrow had chosen to live at the safe distance of New York, where Chedbury thought writers belonged. But he would do nothing to jeopardize his precious possession. Once in a lifetime a really great writer fell into a publisher's lap. He saw other publishers, big-city fellows, swarming like sharks about the frail bark of Haslatt and Sons. He would indulge Harrow to the last degree, mindful of the genius that the man contained—a gem in a casket of clay.

"He wants to live where he can look down on Chedbury," Baynes was saying. "Sandra's taking him to the top of Granite."

"Who's goin' to build the road up there?" Mr. Haslatt demanded.

"He will," Baynes said joyously, "out of the money he makes from us."

Mr. Haslatt's eyes grew glassy. "We're gettin' in too deep."

Edward turned to his desk. "We'll swim."

At the brusqueness in his voice, Mr. Haslatt rose. "I'd better get to work and leave you two to do the same," he declared, and closed the door sharply behind him.

Edward looked at his younger brother. Baynes was taking on a curious half-dissipated air. He had grown a strong dark mustache which he trimmed to show his still youthful mouth, and as he stared out of the window he twisted one end of the mustache thoughtfully. His dark eyes narrowed. "We ought to get Harrow nicely married to some high-born Chedbury female. Then he could rip us all up

143

without damage. I don't know the girls any more, though, and you never did. Pity I got Sandra—that would have been so beautiful. A Seaton wed to the washerwoman's son!" Baynes laughed silently.

Edward was repelled by both words and laughter. Baynes had grown coarse from living in New York. Maybe it was only because of Sandra. She was coarse, he had always imagined secretly. There was none of Margaret's delicacy in her, and New York had polished away any semblance of youthful reserve. Sandra, neither young nor old, had taken on all the gloss of a silver statue.

"I'm surprised you talk of your own wife in that way," Edward said. "I hope you two aren't growing apart." He was aware of something stiff and old-fashioned in what he said, but he did not know how to put the words differently.

Baynes was blithe. He swung his leg from the desk and sat down in the chair which his father had left. "Sandra's all right—has to have her head, of course. All women do since the war. Notice how different females are since we came marching home?"

"Since I didn't march, I don't notice it," Edward said dryly. He was sorting his morning's mail carefully into piles, ready for dictation, and he observed with pleasure a statement from a paper mill that the cost of paper had gone down again. It had been ruinously high during the war because the government had used so much to print stuff nobody read, anyhow.

"You and Meg are growing old graciously."

The voice of his younger brother, teasing and impudent, roused Edward. He folded the morning newspaper and leaning over his desk in a gesture unwontedly youthful, he clapped Baynes on the head.

Baynes pretended alarm. "Hey—there's life in the old dog yet."

Upon this playfulness Jane, the secretary, opened the door. She stared at the two brothers with gravity, decided to ignore what she had seen and came forward.

"About that new type," she began.

Edward sat back, and determined against shame before this elderly creature whom he had inherited from Mather and Haslatt, he answered mildly, "Come in, Jane.

I've decided on the Oxford. This new book is going to be twice as long, I can see."

Baynes interrupted, "Want me to wait?"

"Yes. I want to hear every damn city trick we can turn."

So seldom did he swear that Baynes looked surprised and Jane turned a muddy red. Both yielded at once to Edward the place of master of the firm. Jane, respectful for the moment, murmured assent and withdrew, and Baynes settled down to business.

For two hours the brothers sat in close conference, more deeply akin in their common reverence for the good fortune that had fallen into their hands than even they were in blood. Baynes talked in his new impetuous fashion, his sentences city clipped, and Edward listened, weighing, assessing, deciding. They laid plans for advance advertising, for a New York dinner, for some of the new cocktail parties that were becoming the fashion. With growing generosity Edward acknowledged that Baynes and Sandra were becoming essential to Haslatt and Sons. He himself could never have planned so dashing a program, and he would not have allowed Margaret to participate in something that in his heart he considered undignified. But the war, he conceded, had changed everything except Chedbury.

On Granite Mountain, Lewis Harrow was roaming. He had mounted one hillock after another upon that massive bosom, looking down at Chedbury with critical eyes. Now as the circle of choice narrowed he climbed a broad smooth height for the fourth time. "This is still the best one," he announced to Sandra.

She, looking a little paler even than usual, was trying not to pant. She sank to a gray rock. "Thank God."

He looked down on her with familiar and cynical eyes. She was the new modern woman whom he had seen in the capitals of Europe and in New York. With all her efforts she did not compare to her older sister. Mrs. Haslatt was a beauty, the sort one saw in the paintings in the Louvre. Queer how he had so loved the monstrosity of a museum that he spent all his leaves in it! There wasn't a girl on the streets of Paris to compare to the lovely women he saw in the Louvre—those women whom he could never conquer.

"You're not as tough as you look," he told Sandra with intentional rudeness. He always wanted to be rude to women like her. He longed to hurt them.

"But the way you've climbed," Sandra complained.

"You didn't have to come."

"Indeed I did. It's all business."

"What—this?"

"Certainly, you're our Great Author—didn't you know?"

"Hell, I know well enough."

"Ask and you shall have anything!" She rose dramatically, holding out her hands.

He turned away from her. "Thanks—I want very little. A house on top of this hill—a low house made of granite, with big windows."

"Where you'll live alone?"

"I've always lived alone."

"Need you?" The red head under a little green hat was gracefully inclined.

"No, I don't need to—I want to."

He began walking down the mountain at great speed, the loose stones rushing under his feet, and she followed.

"With such a temper," she said sweetly, "how wise to live alone!"

He did not answer this, and seeing the broadness of his back she called, "Chalk that off—I didn't say it."

He laughed then and turning he put his arm through hers and they ran down the mountain at dangerous speed. She liked it. Glancing at her rather bold profile he saw that the danger had lit her green eyes and reddened her cheeks. It was a familiar sight. He was quite aware of his power over women and he had used it so often that now he knew he was ready for someone quite different—someone wholly different from this starved slenderness, this sharply pallid face, these chilly thin hands. Plenty of catlike female passion here, of course, but that was all. And passion was cheap—the price was low in any market. It had ceased to be fun. He wanted it with decorations—or perhaps foundations. He wanted something to worship.

They got into his little roadster at the bottom of the

146

hill and wound their way down into Chedbury. At the Seaton house he stopped and she, laying her hand upon his coat, persuaded him. "Come in for a little while."

"You dare me to?"

"Why?"

"I saw your mother looking at me last night through a lorgnette."

"Maybe she'd like you better close."

"All right. If the fur flies it won't be mine."

He climbed out and followed her with stolid footsteps into the great front door. "Handsome house," he murmured, "the wings are wonderful. It took genius to dare to put those balustrades around all the roofs."

"My father did that."

He braced his shoulders and prepared for a handsome old lady with lorgnette with a somnolent old man in a shapeless tweed suit. Old Tom Seaton was not in the big living room but he did not notice it. For Margaret was there—Mrs. Haslatt, he corrected himself. He had kept thinking about her through half the night as she had looked in her own house, as she moved about, so content that it made him angry. Out of this anger he had conceived the things he had later said to Chedbury. She was a queen, possessing a realm and yet, somehow, seeming careless of it. Did she love that dull fellow Haslatt? How could she? Yet she looked impregnable—passionately pure, perhaps. He postponed the thought of passion. He wanted to respect her—perhaps worship her a bit. Life was really fearfully empty.

He went forward gladly, seeing in the light of day that beautiful warm woman whom he had seen last night at her own dinner table. "Mrs. Haslatt!" he exclaimed. "How lucky! Indeed, I didn't expect to see you so soon again."

He clasped her hand in both his own and old Mrs. Seaton sitting by the window observed him with lifted eyebrows. She had withered without growing more gentle, and now her cool gray eyes observed this coarse young man who was holding Margaret's hand. A genius, Margaret had called him. She was too worldly wise not to distrust genius while she valued it. There was nothing more dangerous. And Edward, poor fellow, had none of it. Margaret had married a good man, an excellent man, who was even making her comfortably and quietly rich, but he had no genius. Fortunately this fellow came from impossibly low antecedents. The Haslatts were not aristocrats, but it was a respectable New England family —not quite local gentry, perhaps, but not merchants.

"How do you do, Mr. Harrow," she said, lisping frostily.

"How do you do, Madame Seaton," he replied grandly. He bowed over the narrow old hand she extended.

Only a lowborn person could be so exaggerated, she felt. She was shaken, nevertheless, by the tigerlike eyes so near her own. They were not dark, as she had supposed. They were greenish yellow—an unpleasant color. She withdrew her hand.

Sandra had flung herself into a chair. "He's going to build on the Spur," she announced. She pulled off her hat and shook out her short hair.

"First I must find out who owns it," Harrow said. He sat down by Margaret upon the couch with such assurance that she moved away from him involuntarily. He exuded some sort of faint animal odor, not unpleasant and yet which she disliked.

"I imagine anybody would be glad to sell a piece of Granite," she said.

"I will tempt and beguile and bewitch anybody into doing it," he said turning his tiger-colored eyes upon her. "I will make it impossible for anybody to refuse me."

Mrs. Seaton was suddenly overcome with total dislike for this presence. After all, she had never sat in the same room with the son of a laundress. She rose and walked slowly to the open French window. "Your father has been asleep quite long enough," she observed to her daughters. "I can see him lying out there under the elm tree with his handkerchief over his face. I shall wake him and tell him he must amuse me."

"Wonderful that he can still amuse," Lewis declared. "What a marriage, madame!"

She inclined her head without answering this ribaldry, and they watched her trailing gray skirt move slowly down the steps.

Now the animal presence became very strong indeed, and the summer air was suddenly stifling. Seated close to Lewis Harrow, it was too near, and Margaret rose. "I must be going home—the children will be waiting for luncheon."

"Invite me," Harrow said shamelessly. "I want to see that beautiful child, Mary. Somewhere she will be entwined in the pages of my book, a little delicate vine, green and tender."

"We have only the lightest of noon meals."

Margaret's unwilling voice protested and he refused to accept it. "It is Mary I want to see."

He followed her from the room with strong footsteps and Sandra, peering out of the window, saw with some astonishment her elder sister seated in the roadster and whirled away. Tom lounged into the room at this moment. He was beginning to grow gray early, and this gave him a look of false distinction.

"Damn quiet house," he remarked. "Where's everybody?"

"Gone," Sandra said, and continued to stare out of the window in a peculiar fashion.

When Edward let himself into his home that night there was nothing to intimate that there had been an animal presence there in his absence. The wide hall was calm and since he was late, he knew that Margaret was upstairs putting their youngest child to bed, and that Mary and Tommy were in the process of cleaning and changing upon which Margaret insisted before dinner. The second maid, Nora, whom he had engaged some weeks before because he thought Margaret looked tired, now stole out of the back-hall door and took his hat and stick.

"Put a little sherry in the living room," he ordered and then slowly he mounted the stairs.

It had been an exhausting, exciting, dangerous sort of day. He had plunged deeply into something new and he was at once frightened and exhilarated. If Harrow's next book failed Haslatt and Sons would fail with it, for he had mortgaged all his profits from the war book. It would be close sailing until he had the finished manuscript in his hands and could decide for himself whether Harrow had more than one book in him. That was the test, true always, of a writer. One book did not prove anyone. What Haslatt and Sons wanted—that is, what Edward himself wanted—was a man who was a fountain of books, throwing them off with every new facet and stage of his development.

At the top of the stairs the half-opened door revealed to him Margaret with Sandy in her arms beside the crib. She wore the long blue peignoir which he especially liked and his heart throbbed once or twice at the sight of her beauty. Marriage had become her, he flattered himself. She had bloomed gently, like a rose in mild sunshine. He, being a fancier of roses in a small way, liked in his secret musings to liken his wife to a rose. Such was his inner shyness that he had only once or twice been able to tell her of this likeness. Why he had not been able to keep open the doors of communication between himself and Margaret he did not know and he often pondered. Perhaps he loved her too well, and his old defensive pride rose against complete self-revelation. So large was her nature, so comprehensive her understanding, her ancestry so superior to his, he sometimes feared, that all his old sensitivity remained alert in him, the more wary because he could not tell her that it was there. He was ashamed of this and yet helpless to change it. He wanted her to believe that he was no ordinary man and yet there were times when he knew he was only that. The uncertainty of his inner atmosphere was the result of his own inability to judge himself. Whether he was better than other men he did not know. He suspected that his inordinate pride was a sort of vanity. He believed that he was better than the average but he was not sure. Had he been sure, he was coming to think, he could have spoken freely to his wife at any moment.

As it was, though his heart quickened, though he went into the nursery and took her in his arms, child and all, he could only murmur, "I ought not to touch you—I haven't washed." These words his lips said while his silent heart adored.

He imagined, all his sharp senses aware, that there was something reserved in the kiss she gave him. This possibility rendered him completely dumb. With alarm fluttering in his breast he kissed his daughter and leaned on the side of the crib while Margaret covered the child for sleep.

They left the room hand in hand and again he imagined or perceived the less than usual warmth in her hand, although it clasped his with resolution. But there was a difference between clinging and determination.

"Everything all right?" he asked.

"Yes," she answered promptly. "Except—I don't like your Lewis Harrow."

"My Lewis Harrow?" he repeated, smilingly slightly.

"Yes, yours," she said, "you've captured him, haven't you?"

"I hope so—for the sake of business."

"There it is," she exclaimed. "I don't like to think he's paying for our bread and butter—"

"And his own cake," Edward put in.

She threw him a strange look, which he could not comprehend. "Do you know why I don't like him? Because he invited himself to luncheon today alone with the children and me!"

"Why didn't you telephone me?"

She looked at him in astonishment. "Honestly, Ned, I didn't think of it." Her amazement at herself was so real that he smiled again.

"You must always think of me, you know," he said mildly. "Was he nice to the children?"

"He didn't notice Tommy or Sandy, but he was foolish to Mary. If she were anything but a child I'd say he—made love to her."

"That's impossible, Margaret."

"Ned, it was disgusting, really!"

He saw that her cheeks were flaming and in the same instant, her eyes were so brightly blue, her hair so black and flying, that he felt her beauty burned into the very flesh of his heart. Had she thus appeared to Harrow? Feeling with dismay the rush of old jealousy he had thought long since disciplined from him, he went into the next room, which was his own, that she might not discern his pitiable condition and grow angry. She had not for years been greatly angry with him, for he had not for those same years allowed his young green jealousy to show itself in words or pique. Now he knew it was there in him still, and must at all costs be hidden from her for the sake of his own self-respect in her eyes.

He felt suddenly very tired and he sank into his old leather chair and covered his eyes with his hands. Why

151

should Harrow shower his attentions upon the child Mary? Why Mary and not Tommy or Sandy? Why except that with his cursed novelist's perception and imagination he had already understood that Margaret did not love her eldest child too well? And with this he had forged a cunning cruel weapon to draw Margaret's eyes to himself. Not for one moment did Edward believe that Lewis Harrow cared for any child.

The monstrosity of this behavior in a man, that he used a child for such a purpose, mingled in Edward's thoughts with jealousy lest that Margaret had indeed noticed Harrow because of this wile and with anger that his favorite child should have been made a tool. He sat motionless in the chair, longing furiously to find Harrow and tell him to get out of his sight and forever. This fury he dealt with in continued silence and by means of reason. Harrow was less than a man. He was a thing of emotions and imaginations, fluid with creation, irresponsible, untrustworthy, a creature to be watched and controlled—yes, and used. It was folly to be jealous of him—as well be jealous of a drunkard or a fool. The man had no being except in imagination. Whatever he had done was no more real than the drama in a play—the fellow was probably acting out a scene in the novel he was about to write. It would be giving him undue importance to think of it as something a real man had done. Genius was as valuable and as unpredictable, perhaps as ungovernable, as the waves of the sea.

Upon this slow rationalizing he heard his door open softly and his daughter Mary come stealing in. It troubled him sometimes that she moved so stilly, as though her vitality were not enough for the speed and noise of childhood. Yet she looked healthy enough as she stood there in the door in her little white muslin frock. She was smiling and he saw the dimples in her cheeks, the gift her mother had given her. Margaret's dimples, born again!

"Shall I come in, Papa?"

"Please do, darling—though I haven't washed yet."

"I won't stay."

She walked softly across the floor, almost tiptoe, and leaned against him. When he put his arm around her she rested her head upon his shoulder and he smelled the clean freshness of her dark hair.

"Had a good day, dear?"

"Yes—almost."

"Why only almost?"

"Papa, do you like Mr. Harrow?"

He evaded this. "Mamma says he was here to lunch."

"Yes. He likes me very much."

"Did he say so?"

"Yes."

He was furious again with Lewis Harrow. This daughter of his! He held her close. "We all like you—love you, you know."

"I know." She sighed and he forbore to ask the cause for it. It was so much easier not to ask. He felt her lips at his ear. "Papa."

"Yes?"

"But he likes me better than he does anybody else."

"Did he say that?"

"Yes."

"Then he told a lie!" These words escaped him forcibly.

She actually drooped. "Did he, Papa?"

"Yes! And it was very wrong for him to talk like that to you, Mary. Mamma didn't like it. She told me about it. And you must forget what he said. Little girls get all the love they need from their parents. You must think about school now, you know, and your friends— Millicent Bascom and Josephine Hill. They're very nice girls. And in two years or so you may have dancing lessons and then you will have other friends, too—boys of your own age."

He was taking it far too seriously, he told himself. He was making everything worse, deepening the very impressions which he hoped to erase. He rose. "Now run along, Mary. I must get ready for dinner."

She went out of the room then, her step lingering, and he went into the bathroom and scrubbed his hands with unnecessary vigor.

That, he might have thought, was the end of it. The dinner passed as usual. He could always be sure of a good meal at night, a dish or two that Margaret had planned and to which she had given some touch of her own. Tonight it was veal, baked in French fashion with

153

wine and herbs, and for dessert a blueberry pie. He was growing to be something of a connoisseur in food, for his appetite was variable and he ate better if he considered flavor and texture. Tonight his awareness of everything was sharp. He saw himself at the head of his own table and unconsciously he straightened his spare tall frame as he looked at Margaret. She had put on a gown of some thin silver-gray stuff, so old he had almost forgotten—or else it was new.

"Is that a new dress?" he asked.

"You should be ashamed, Ned," she replied. "It was part of my trousseau. I wore it in New Orleans, don't you remember? Years ago!"

"I remember only a glorious haze," he said smiling.

"I tried it on for fun—just to see if I could wear it. I believe I'm actually a little thinner than I was then."

He kept looking at her after that, knowing that the girl Margaret had no beauty to compare to this, his wife's.

And from them had come these children. They sat one on either side of the table, quiet at the end of the day. Even Tommy ate in phlegmatic silence. He was a hearty eater, and some day he would be a big ungainly man like old Thomas. But Mary was delicate, and in spite of her prettiness there was something about her which reminded him of his sister.

"Seen Louise lately?" he asked Margaret.

Mary lifted her head. "She was cross with me today, Papa—a little—because I was late in the afternoon for school."

"Did you tell her why?" he asked.

"Yes, I said Mr. Harrow was here with us for lunch and then she got cross—only a little. She said it was no excuse."

"It wasn't, I suppose."

"He kept talking," Margaret said vaguely.

"We ought to have Louise over," he said. "Maybe we could have her sometime with Harrow. It would give her something special. We never do anything for Louise."

Margaret replied, "Of course. Let's remember. Only why must we have him again?"

She made her query with raised and quivering eyebrows, as though laughter waited, and he gave her a steady look. "Think of it as business."

Tommy shifted his attention from a second piece of pie. "I don't like Mr. Harrow," he said in his large deep voice. "When he grabs me he holds too hard. It hurts."

"Hit him in the snoot," Edward said suddenly.

His children looked at him in amazement and then broke into joyful laughter. So seldom was their father funny! Their laughter restored wholesomeness to the evening and Edward in the secrecy of his inner being ridiculed his jealousy.

The small house of Haslatt and Sons was shaken to its roots. A tornado had seized it, bringing life, giving growth, forcing heat and light and a spasm of wind. Again and again Edward Haslatt wished that he had never met Lewis Harrow, that the fellow had stayed in France after the war, that he had been lost in New York, almost that he had strayed into the portals of some other publishing house rather than have come to the quiet town of Chedbury to lay hold upon his own budding business. The swelling advance sales of Harrow's new book marched across the country like a triumphant beast. A vanguard of rumor preceded the three young salesmen whom Edward hired and put into the charge of Baynes with every caution against extravagance. Caution was forgotten. The eagerness of booksellers infected Baynes and spread to the salesmen and then ran hither and thither, praising a book none of them had yet read, that no one had seen except Harrow, and he carelessly writing against time declared that it might or might not be finished by late winter.

"It must be finished," Edward said sternly. "I've gambled everything I have on that book, Lewis," and knew as he spoke that there was no promise to be had out of him.

Harrow had been engrossed in the building of a squat storm-proof house on Granite. The walls stood under a wide overhanging roof, and from a distance looked like a bird that had paused to brood upon the mountain. Harrow was amused by the likeness and enhanced it by adding feathery trellises to the wings and a thick short tower to the gate. He called his house The Eagle and on Sundays young people from Chedbury climbed up to see it. He had begun to live in it long before it was finished, and it pleased him to look from the windows and see persons approaching. He rushed out and brought

155

them in, showed them through the low rooms, few in number but huge in size, the windows enormous and set so that he could see for miles when he chose to look out of them. The house stood solidly clawing the ground with its deep foundations, and though the winds roared, it was impervious. Harrow had insisted on walls eighteen inches thick, as he had seen them in the fortresses of Europe. There was neither cellar nor second floor and one room led into another in a semicircle curving toward the mountain.

To Edward the house was astonishing and hideous and he told Margaret what he thought.

"Certainly it is not the house for a family," she replied, "but then I don't think Lewis wants a family. I'm not sure he even wants a wife."

By now Harrow was so much his property that Edward did not inquire how it was that she knew this about him. Women had instinct, of course, and of instinct Margaret had her full share. His jealousy of the spring had passed or perhaps had only been submerged in the rush of increasing business. The revenge that he had feared from Chedbury after the evening in the courthouse had never been taken. Chedbury had bristled, there had been some quiet weeping by Mrs. Walters, and Mrs. Croft was permanently angry. Henry Croft had died ten years ago, and she had been happier without him, as everybody knew, and yet she had not been able to keep from thinking of him for weeks after Lewis Harrow had brought him to life again, bringing back to her the memory of a temper vicious and yet somehow only the dark side of a glittering shield.

Chedbury had grown quiet again, and people watched Harrow come and go up Granite Mountain. However they felt about him, he had his right to be among them, because he had been a child there, a queer cross-grained hungry monolith of a boy whom they had seen without notice when he had lugged baskets in and out of their kitchens; whom now, though they found him repulsive, they respected reluctantly. The weekly paper gave him no notice, and Chuck Williams, the editor, took pride in reading his name in gossip columns of city papers and literary essays in magazines and then in continuing to take no notice. Even when the new book came out, he might take no notice.

In the midst of all this Edward was wakened at two o'clock one morning by the clangor of the telephone in the hall. He rose at once and lifted the receiver and heard his mother's distracted voice.

"Edward, your father's been taken very sick."

"What is it, Mother?"

"He can't speak to me—" Her voice cracked into a sob.

"Have you called the doctor?"

"No. I didn't know what to do."

"I'll call him and then be right up."

He put up the telephone and went softly into Margaret's room. She lay high on her pillows, her long hair braided over her shoulder, her eyes closed in sleep. Tired as he was every night, it had been a long time since he had seen her asleep, and shielding her face from the flashlight he used at night, he was struck with the thinness of her cheeks. He was so close to her and yet somehow they had made no true communication for a long time. He was too busy—so busy that he had neglected to keep his promise to her, made when she said she would marry him. He had let their marriage become secondary to him. That was the problem of a man's life—how to excel in his work and still keep the woman close. Yet how he loved her!

These thoughts, scarcely more than feelings, came in the instant to the surface of his mind and he pushed them down again. He would have to do something about it, but it could not be now. He decided not to wake her, and still treading softly he went out and closed the door.

A few minutes later, having called Dr. Wynne and dressed himself, he was in his car on his way to his father. He had persuaded himself into buying the car a few weeks earlier, on the excuse that he needed it for business.

"Why don't you just say you want it?" Margaret had asked.

He had looked at her half sheepishly. "Seems extravagant, doesn't it?"

"I don't see why," she had replied. "Nothing is extravagant if you can pay for it."

Actually he had finally decided to buy it when he saw

157

Tom Seaton running around in a small roadster on God knew what business. If Tom could buy a car, surely he with his sound progress could do so. He had spent his spare time for a week learning to run it and now it submitted to him pleasantly and increased his sense of power. An occasion such as this, he argued, when his father was taken suddenly ill, justified a car.

He spent the last few minutes thinking about his father. With remorse he reminded himself that he had had no time for months to think about him. The old man had grown increasingly quiet in the office and for days past Edward scarcely remembered seeing him beyond a hasty greeting in the morning. Baynes had run up from New York once or twice every week to confer, and while at first their father had come in to sit with them, in the last fortnight he had not, and they had not noticed, or at least had not spoken of it. Strange how a man's parents, who had been the center of his existence, the spoke upon which the wheel of his life turned, moved out of the center into the periphery and so, he supposed, away forever.

With a sense of impending and inescapable loss, he hastened out of his car and into the house. No one met him and he went straight upstairs to his father's room and opened the door. His father lay on his back in the big double bed where his parents had slept together all these years and his mother sat beside the bed in a small rocking chair tilted forward so that she leaned upon the covers, holding the pale stiff hand. The sound of his father's hard quick breathing filled the room with an angry pulse of sound. The doctor had not yet come.

"Oh, Edward," his mother moaned.

He went near the bed. "When did this happen, Mother?"

"I don't know. I was asleep and then I woke up and felt him in the middle of the bed—he always has taken the middle of the bed—and I told him to move over, just as I do every night. He always does, but tonight he didn't. I gave him a push—just a little one—and felt him so queer and heavy that I put on the light and this is the way he was. He can't even speak to me. Oh, Edward, you don't think—"

"Of course not." He sat down on the bed and looked at

his father. Some sort of dreadful subterranean force was moving in that patient lean frame. The left side of his father's face was dragged down, and a drool of saliva crept over his chin.

Edward took his own handkerchief and wiped it away. "The doctor will be here in a minute."

"He's been worrying too much," his mother moaned. "Every night he came home scared to death of what you boys are doing at the office. You shouldn't have borrowed money on the printing shop, Edward. That really belongs to him."

He had a glimpse in his mother's haggard face, made strange by the gray hair that hung loose against her cheeks, of what it meant to grow old. The old ceased to create. They grew afraid of all change, knowing the monstrous change ahead. They wanted no more to build, but only to shelter themselves. Then his own youth asserted itself. "I'm responsible, Mother," he said with an impatience which shamed him but which he could not help. "I wish Father would stop worrying."

The doorbell rang and without waiting for his mother to reply he hastened downstairs to meet the doctor.

"Hello, Ed," the young doctor said. He was still too young to show sleepless nights and long hours. His predecessor, Dr. Sulley, who had been young with Dr. Hart, the old minister, had died the year before in Florida, that land of rest and joy to which he had sent so many patients, and to which he had never found time to go until he was ready to die. Wynne had taken up the practice and was now engaged in a struggle to make his patients come to his office instead of demanding that he go to see them.

"Who does he think he is?" Chedbury growled, forgetting that its people had killed the old doctor.

"What's happened?" the new doctor asked, following Edward up the stairs.

"I'm afraid to guess," Edward said.

They went into the room together and within a minute the doctor had made his quick examination.

"Your mother had better go out and rest while I finish," he told Edward. Without a word she rose, and left the room. The old man she had loved and tended for so many years had now become a male patient and she was a stranger to him. They heard her begin to sob in the hall. The doctor was a kind man. "Better go with her," he said to Edward. "But come back in a minute."

He went out then and putting his arm about his mother's shoulders he patted her, not knowing how to comfort her. Her shoulder felt unfamiliar. Not since he was a child had he touched her and then he had lain his head upon her breast. She had been closer to him than any living creature and now she was an old woman, separated from himself by distances, unspoken and unspeakable. But he had the wisdom to know that she must do something for relief.

"If it isn't asking too much, Mother, I wish you would make us all some coffee. I'm sure Wynne would be glad of it and so would I."

She turned obediently to the stairs and he went back into the bedroom.

"Obviously a stroke," Wynne said. "A pretty bad one, I'm afraid. I'd better send a nurse. It's too much for your mother to manage. I wish Chedbury had a hospital. He can't stand the trip to Boston."

"I was afraid of a stroke," Edward murmured. His father's thin face was congested with purple blood and now his left side was very much drawn.

"I've given him something," Wynne said. "Where's the telephone?"

"In the hall," Edward replied.

He sat down in the chair where his mother had been and gazed at his father. Strange and terrifying to think that he might never hear his father speak again! Now that it was possible he wished that he had taken time in these last months to listen to his father's voice. Yet he could not have acted otherwise than he had done. His opportunity had come to him, as in another time his father's had come, and he had been compelled to seize it. Had he yielded to his father's fears, had he let Harrow go elsewhere, he might have subsided into a mere printer again, running a small local business. As it was, he had begun to have tentacles over the whole world. Only yesterday Ben Ashton, the postman, had with some pride tossed upon his desk letters from England and France. "Looks like you're gettin' to be somebuddy, Ed," he had

160

cackled. It was true. Harrow had ceased to be a human being; he had become a most valuable property.

This was the inescapable tragedy of life, then, that the generations withdrew from each other, and as he felt the strange pain of separation somewhere deep in his vitals, he loved his father with sudden anguish. He put out his hands and enclosed within them his father's stiff cool hand.

A week later, after days made hideous by the demands of the engine he had set in motion to sell Harrow's new book, a machine which he could neither stop nor deny in its exorbitant demand upon his time, a week during which he worked day and night, rushing between the office and his father's bedside, in which he did not try to go home, in which he saw Margaret only in passing and then at his parents' house with his mother, he and Louise and Baynes gathered hastily at what was to be a deathbed.

His mother was in the rocking chair again, where she had sat almost continuously during the week. She had got up to wash, to put on a clean dress, to eat something when Margaret called. But she would not go unless Louise took her place. Louise had found a substitute teacher and had not left the house for three days. Baynes had come from New York, leaving Sandra to fill his engagements. When the nurse came out of the silent room to call them in, Edward had paused for a moment with Margaret. They were in his old bedroom, she resting upon his bed and he in the green rep armchair that had been his Christmas present the year he was fifteen.

He had risen at the sight of the nurse and when she had gone away quickly, he had turned to Margaret, his heart beating with strange and terrible fear. She had looked at him from the pillow, and he saw that she did not want to come with him.

"I have never seen anybody die," she said in a tight frightened voice.

"Neither have I," he replied.

"Ned—I don't want to be there."

He left her without a word and had not reached the hall before he felt her hands clasping his arm.

"Ned, don't hate me."

"Of course not—only you mustn't delay me now."

Her hands dropped from his arm and he hastened into his father's room, his heart still beating hard with the strange new fear, an animal fear, he thought, as he took his place beside the bed. The presence of the nurse made them all feel strange. They were not alone together. He moved to his mother and knelt down and put his arm about her shoulder, but she did not heed him. All her being was concentrated on the dying man whom she had loved and scolded and cared for and resented and still loved in the cycle of their married life. Baynes looked pale and grave and Louise was crying and the nurse waited quietly for familiar death. It came in a moment, without struggle but with a raucous rattle and choking. Mark Haslatt was dead.

Edward bowed his head on the bed and felt his mother's arm go round his shoulder. He could not think or feel. Then with sudden clarity something occurred to him— "It'll have to be only Haslatt Brothers now," and with these unspoken words he was able to perceive his loss.

Yet life resumed its sway. Within a pitifully few days he had consigned to earth the body of his father and he knew himself the master of his own existence. Though he had not for years taken with sense of obligation anything that his father said, yet that gray shape pervading his days had asserted its claim. Now all claim was gone and memory alone could go to work, unhampered by the living presence, to reconstruct the harassed, silent, and yet kindly man who had been his father. To his father he owed the sound foundation of his business and the principles of industry and caution to which with all his present preoccupation he still held. Prudence he had inherited from his father, and with it he wielded power over Baynes and Sandra, who had none. With prudence, too, he dealt with Lewis Harrow, compelling him to finish his book before the day when he planned formally to open his house by a great party that was to include everybody in Chedbury. "Open house for three days," Harrow declared lavishly, "day and night," he added. "Anybody can come any time."

Harrow had been repulsively pleased at the death of Mark Haslatt. "The sere and yellow leaf," he had called him with scant concealment from Edward and none at all from Baynes. Now that he was dead, Harrow was decent enough not to mention the old man, and he renewed his demands upon Haslatt Brothers, asking for outrageous advances and guarantees of advertisements. Now that his father was gone, Edward found himself renewing his prudence, so that actually the voice of his father was stronger in him than it had been in life.

Hearing this voice he met Harrow firmly one day the next winter. "The Eagle has cost me some odd thousands more than I expected," Harrow came in to announce. Arrogant with his own value he had taken on the habit of entering Edward's office unannounced. This Jane had at first forbidden, but doing battle twice or thrice with Harrow's unchecked tongue, which could return at any hint of enmity to his boyhood rudeness, she now paid him no heed. Some time or other, she reasoned, Edward would have enough of the fellow. At night kneeling by her bed in her old-fashioned cotton nightgown, her feet cold upon the bare floor of her virginal room, she prayed for the time to come soon.

Edward looked up from his desk, his dark eyes cold. "Well?"

"I'd like a couple of thousand advance, Ed."

"You've had a couple of thousand," Edward replied, busy with papers.

Harrow sat down. "Come now, Ed—"

"I'm here."

"You know you stand to get rich off me."

"If I ever get your book."

"It's nearly done, I tell you."

"I haven't seen a page of it."

"God, what's the matter with you? I thought there'd be some life in this firm when the old man went."

"Plenty of life," Edward said. He did not look at Harrow.

"Well," Harrow cried with high impatience, "what do you want me to do?"

"Finish your book."

There was a long pause in which Edward read carefully a proposed contract for Spanish rights in the book he had not seen.

"Is that final?" Harrow demanded.

"Wholly," Edward replied.

Harrow bounced from his chair and tore from the room. Two weeks later, during which time no one saw him, he came down Granite Mountain carrying a great bundle wrapped in brown paper. He threw it upon Edward's desk. "Here it is," he shouted. "Now cough up, will you?"

"You've upset the ink," Edward said. He touched a bell and Jane came to the door, looking grim. "Bring a cloth, Jane," he said.

She returned with the same grim look and mopped up the ink. Only when she had gone did Edward allow himself to turn to Harrow.

"Complete?" he asked.

"Not a page missing," Harrow declared. "Where's my two thousand dollars?"

Edward rejected prudence and to get rid of the man that he might devour the book, he drew a checkbook from the drawer of his desk and knowing it madness he made it out for two thousand dollars. His balance was dangerously low, and if that for which he had gambled escaped him, he would have to mortgage his very home. For the first time he was glad that his father was dead.

All afternoon, the great heap of brown paper stood on the end of his desk. He did not dare to begin to read it here. He would not read it until tonight when the children were in bed and he and Margaret were alone. The dread of disappointment dried his very blood. He drank again and again from the water jug on the window and in half an hour was thirsty again. There was no one to keep him from glancing at the first pages and yet he would not have done so for any amount of money. How absurd, he told himself, to be in the power of one man and such a man as Harrow! He had no idea when he thought of publishing books that it would be a business so racking, so dangerous, so devastating. He prayed only that the book might be clearly good or bad. Then he could make his decision. If it were mildly good and not too bad the agony of the present would stretch into months and even years. Let it be good or bad! He was ashamed as a decent Christian to address God with so personal a plea, surely petty in view of the enormous problems now in the world after the war, and yet in his heart he did murmur these words. Immediately they became ridiculous since in fact the book was already finished, it was what it would be, and not even God could do anything about it. He set himself to work doggedly until six o'clock as usual, pausing only to call Baynes in New York by telephone.

"Baynes, that you? I just wanted to say that Harrow has handed in the manuscript. I'm reading it tonight."

Baynes gave a cry of anguish. "Call me at dawn, will you?"

"No, I won't. But I ought to have some sort of notion tomorrow morning when I come to the office."

"I shan't sleep a wink," Baynes declared.

"Maybe I won't, either," Edward replied and hung up.

It had taken all his self-control not to hurry the evening for the children. With rigorous discipline he had compelled himself to conversation through dinner, to ten minutes of nursery rhymes for Sandy and to the reading aloud of *The Swiss Family Robinson*, which he had undertaken as part of the winter's reading for Mary and Tommy. He had said to Margaret in what he hoped was his usual voice, "I shall be up late tonight—Harrow brought me his complete manuscript today."

Interminably the evening wore on, the children were prepared for bed, and he went up to hear their prayers. A vague sense of hypocrisy always troubled him when he saw their innocent faith. He no longer prayed in exact words, and yet he felt that religion was decent and right, an essential in an honest man's life, however expressed. Prayer was a part of religion, he reasoned, and children should be taught its use, without being promised definite returns. Tonight he tried gently to persuade Mary not to pray for a bicycle, since he had no idea of buying it for her. He did not like to see women cycle. It thickened their legs and destroyed their delicacy. When Tommy prayed for an air rifle for his birthday, however, he considered whether the boy was big enough for it and decided that he was. Some discrepancy between his decisions for his daughter and for his son disturbed him, until it struck him that perhaps God Himself was thus compelled to decide between His asking children. For some the gift was unwise; for others, it was possible. This might be the Reason behind the Inscrutable Wisdom.

The children were in bed at last, and with the pleasant

comfort of knowing that he was a good father Edward went into his room and changed to his old blue dressing robe. When he went downstairs Margaret was already sitting by the fire in her favorite red velvet chair. She was making lace on a small frame, a task which she learned as a young girl one summer in France and which she declared was soothing to the nerves. He appreciated invariably the picture that she made, and he smiled at her as he drew up a side table and prepared for the hours ahead.

"Don't you want to read Lew's manuscript, too?" he inquired.

Margaret did not look up. "No, thank you, Ned. I'll wait until the book is printed." This she said with lack of interest which, in his eagerness, he did not notice.

He went into the hall and brought back the enormous parcel, and putting it on the floor at his feet he began to unwrap it, as he sat in his own chair opposite her. Between them the wood fire burned pleasantly under the marble mantelpiece. Looking up to meet Margaret's eyes, he found she had not lifted them from her lace.

"Next to various moments with you, my dear," he said, trying not to seem excited, "I suppose this is the most exciting moment of my life."

"Perhaps it is even the most exciting," she answered.

There was something of an edge in her voice which at another time he might have explored, but tonight he could not bear to be diverted.

"You know better than that," he retorted, and immediately he lifted the first chapters from the stack between his feet and began to read.

The scene was Chedbury. Harrow had used the very name. A scrawled note at the top of the first page, "Call the town anything you like, in printing, but I had to write it what it is."

The book began with a small wretched boy in a meager house on the fringe of the prosperous little town, a boy whose father was a drunkard and whose mother was a laundress. Harrow had determined to write his life out, not only as it was, but in all its ramifications in a society that did not care how he lived and not too much whether he died, except that the townsfolk were reluctant to pay for too many paupers' funerals. Edward plunged into a Chedbury he had never known.

At eleven o'clock Margaret put her lace frame away into a rosewood sewing cabinet.

He looked up reluctantly. "Going to bed?"

"Yes, Ned."

She came over to him and bending she kissed his forehead. His hands were full of pages, and he could only throw back his head. "Kiss me properly, Margaret," he demanded.

She stooped again and kissed him on the lips. "When are you coming up, Ned?"

"I don't know, dear. I think I'll stay by this as long as I can."

"Why must you?"

"I've gambled too much and I must know if I'll win."

She looked down at him half wistfully, and he looked up at her, aware again of something not said between them, and yet again he could not bear to be drawn from the urgency of what he wanted to do.

"Good night, my love," he said.

"Good night, Ned," she replied.

For a moment he heard her step slowly mounting the stairs, and then he forgot her. He was back in Lewis Harrow's world again, a world which in strange subterranean fashion was also his own.

Hours later he put down the last page silently. He had finished the book. He had no doubts and yet he was full of doubt. He had gambled and he had won. Lewis Harrow had written a great book. Haslatt Brothers could build upon a foundation as solid as Granite Mountain itself. Money would continue to flow from the book for Harrow as long as he lived, and for Edward and his family as well. Upon the profits of this treasure Edward foresaw the delight of publishing other books which he might like but which could not possibly pay—a book, for example, upon the varieties of printing types, their history, and their use, a book for the makers of books and not for the writers.

This was his first thought when he had laid down that last page. The fire on his hearth was a heap of ashes, and every voice in his house was stilled in sleep. He alone was awake and knowing, his exhausted mind alive with unnatural awareness. He leaned back in his chair and closed his eyes. The book was cruel, of course. It spared nothing and no one—not even the lean ferocious boy who had grown up, in Harrow's imagination, to be a man greatly rich through the making of steel. Why had he chosen steel? The man loved steel for its purity and its hardness. Harrow had put some love of his own into the symbol. But there were pages of human love, and these were the pages that frightened Edward. The variety was exciting and shameful, and then in the end came one so tender and so exquisite that it did not seem Harrow could know such love. He began to be afraid of the man. Ribaldry and physical lust he took for granted in him, but where had he got his power for tender worship of a woman remote to him?

Now deep doubt came flooding darkly into Edward's solitary mind. There was no possibility of concealment. He recognized the truth too well. The woman who had called forth this sweetness out of a man powerful and crude was one fashioned into an image he well knew, and it was the image of his own wife.

Some time later, having fumbled the pages together and tied the brown paper parcel as it had been, he got up and put out the lights and went upstairs. On all other nights he was used to stealing into Margaret's room and at least looking at her before he slept. But tonight he did not go in. The door between was ajar as she had left it, and he closed it noiselessly and prepared for bed. He saw from the small clock on his table that it was nearly five o'clock, and his blood was beating in his veins with weariness. He would not be able to sleep, he told himself. Yet his mind was unable to think. He lay numb under the covers and felt the night wind blow upon him from the open window. Then the numbness penetrated him like a drug, and postponing his fears, he slept in spite of himself.

He woke late in the morning. The sun shone whitely into his south window and he saw a rim of snow. In the night then it had snowed. There was a heap of snow upon the window sill. He started up and looked at his watch —nine o'clock. The house was silent about him. The children were already at school, and Margaret must have breakfasted. He heard Sandy's voice now upon the stairs and Margaret's hush.

Then he remembered. He lay back, quite still. Harrow had had the audacity to use the very woman Margaret was, her soft dark hair, her sea-blue eyes, her slenderness and height, even the shape of her hands and her high-arched feet. He had dared to imagine the shape of her breasts, her waist, her thighs.

Intolerable doubt! Edward rose from his bed and stirred with unusual noisiness about his room.

"Papa got up!" he heard his little daughter's voice cry out, and a moment later Margaret tapped upon the door and came in. He was shaving and he kissed her lightly.

"You should have waked me," he grumbled.

"I wouldn't have done it for money," she retorted. "You look a ghost, Ned."

"I'm all right."

He continued to scrape his rather long chin while she stood waiting. When he did not speak she could refrain no more.

"How was the book?"

"Absolutely first rate."

"Was it?"

"Yes."

"Then, Ned—"

"Yes?"

"What's the matter with you?"

"Nothing. Well, maybe—I guess he's taken the hide off some of us Chedbury folk, and I'm worried—a little."

"Oh, he's stupid!"

"No, he isn't—he's too smart. Anybody stupid would have changed things so no one would know. He's so smart he's dared say all he wanted to say."

"I don't think I'm going to read it."

"You'll have to someday, Margaret."

She looked at him curiously, and he fancied a reflection of his own doubt in her watching eyes. When their eyes met and clung it was she who looked away. "Don't worry, Ned. And come down—your breakfast is waiting."

She went away with her brisk wifely step, so much the woman he had known since the day of his marriage that he felt assuaged. Then the damnable quality of Harrow's book occurred to him again. There the woman's husband, who had possessed her so long, did not know her at all. The man did not know, dull fellow, that worship was his wife's due, and that in such worship he would have found his own delight. Edward longed upon a strange and sudden impulse to rush downstairs and find Margaret wherever she was and cry out to her, crushed in his arms, "There is no one who could possibly love you as I do!" His natural shyness moved to restrain such monstrous revelation. She would look surprised, she would open her eyes wide. She might even laugh.

He went on with his dressing, more than a little angry at his predicament. Here on a morning when he should be filled only with relief and satisfaction at his own good fortune, when he should have been distracted by nothing that could check his energy, he felt depressed and doubtful. He distrusted his imagination, disturbed by the workings of something so insubstantial as Lewis Harrow's own. What matter if the fellow was attracted to Margaret? Men could be thus attracted to a delicately bred woman, especially lawless lowbred fellows, and it did not mean that the woman even knew it. He was insulting her by his doubts. It would be only decent to keep them to himself, certainly for the present.

Comforted by the righteousness of delay, he chose a somber gray tie that did not lighten in the least his dark suit, and feeling arrayed to fit his mood he went downstairs and ate his morning meal. Margaret sat in her place, and though she had eaten, she poured his coffee and supervised the prattle and play of Sandy, who had built some blocks into a structure in the corner. The uniformity of his outward surroundings was deeply comforting. The day was like any other day, and that was what he wanted. He looked at Margaret and she smiled. Certainly she did not know what Harrow had done, and he would not tell her.

An hour later he was further comforted by the everyday appearance of his office. Jane was accustomedly cross when he came in late. "I don't know when you're going to get your letters done," she remarked when he had sat down in his swivel desk chair. The snow was melting and dripping down the windowpanes, and he could hear the whir of machinery as he opened the door.

"I want to talk to Baynes first," he said. "The letters will have to wait."

The telephone operator was in a good mood, the hour fortunate, and in a very few moments he was calling through to New York.

"That you, Baynes?"

"Yes."

"Well, aren't you going to ask me?"

"No. Aren't you going to tell me?"

Edward laughed. He had not the heart to continue the cruelty of teasing his younger brother. "Well, all we wanted it to be—it is."

"You mean—"

"Yes, I do. He's done something even bigger than the first one."

"Oh, holy cats!"

"It's too long, but I don't know how to shorten it by a word. There is a scene or two, an episode, I could take out altogether."

His smoldering doubt suddenly leaped into suggestion. Why should he not complain of the length to Harrow and insist that the pages—he could remember them even now —the pages between four hundred and twenty-five and five hundred be eliminated? After all, the woman had come in at the very end of the book unheralded except for the desire that had sought her around the world. He spoke to Baynes again.

"Yes, I think I may insist on a few cuts—only one of any importance. But there's nothing to hold us up. I'll want to see the artist myself for the jacket drawing. It ought to be a scene—something like the one I am looking at this very minute out of my office window, the green sloping up to the church and the Seaton house in the foreground, the firehouse, of course, and the store, maybe a snow scene. By the way, we had snow last night—very soft. We'll have to work hard and fast now, Baynes."

"Sandra thinks we ought to have a big dinner on the day of publication. Get all the critics together and so on."

"Whatever you like."

"You mean that?" Baynes demanded with excitement.

"For once, yes."

He hung up the receiver and sat for a moment staring upon the scene he was planning for the jacket. He ought to call Harrow, but there was no telephone to The Eagle. Harrow did not want one. There was nothing to do but wait until the fellow came down the mountain.

In a mood of arrested doubt and of genuine enjoyment he went into the printing shop. The presses rolling off the sheets of the books he had chosen for his firm gave him a pleasant sense of power. He, Edward Haslatt, here in this quiet, purposely old-fashioned office in a small town in an unimportant region of his country, could entice to himself living, thinking people from anywhere in the world, whose minds flamed and exploded into creation.

He had been proud to receive some weeks ago a thin manuscript of poems from a young man in a valley of the Cotswolds. A year ago he would not have dared to publish so risky a venture, but thanks to Lewis Harrow, he had accepted the poems as soon as he had read them and perceived their elements of emotion and pride. He paused beside the press, which was being run by John Carosi, and watched the wide margins, the thick cream paper imprinted in short black lines. He had chosen his latest text type, Poliphus, thick and warm, carrying the illusion of an ancient art. Was it, he pondered, suitable for the young poet? But like so many young, the lines of this poet, in spite of their originality, had echoed. Edward had decided upon the book, not so much for what it was as for the implications of feeling and imagination which gave promise of future richness in the talent.

"Do you ever read any of the sheets you print?" he asked.

Carosi looked at him, surprised. Edward Haslatt did not often speak to the men he employed.

"I don't," he said curtly. "If I did, I couldn't tend the machine. Like as not the ink would be runny."

He bent his head, and Edward went on, pleased enough. He was printing books that were simple, too simple, perhaps, to be called fine. Yet there was elegance in their simplicity, and with elegance came good style. He pondered as he went back to his desk the answer that had been given him. For machines he himself cared nothing. He did not understand them. Cogs and wheels, he called them, and they were blind slaves formed only to give shape and performance to the thoughts of men.

He had grown far beyond his father, who had, he remembered, an actual tenderness for the machines he had bought with such careful economy. What was printed by them Mark Haslatt scarcely cared—advertisements, announcements of marriage and death, bills of sale, posters, and notices. Edward had inherited something from him, but it was fulfilled by a quality entirely his own. Machines were no more than means.

So ruminating, at ease because he had won, Edward circumvented the core of his inner unease. But when he opened the door to his office he felt a shock. Lewis Harrow sat in the swivel chair, his feet on the desk, and he was roaring with laughter into the telephone. He shouted as Edward came in, "I'll be there—to celebrate either my victory or my defeat. Here comes God! . . . Well," he said, and shambled to his feet.

"Don't get up," Edward said with acid courtesy.

"I had pins in my seat while I sat there," Harrow retorted. He dropped into the chair across the desk. "Out with it, Ed. Do you like my book?"

"How can I help it?" Edward asked. "You know as well as I do what you have done. It is wonderful and terrible. But it's too long."

"Now if you start meddling," Harrow began violently.

Edward held up his hand. "I want it seventy-five pages shorter."

Harrow leaped to his feet. "Give me the manuscript!"

"What for?"

"I'll take it to New York."

"Sit down, you fool," Edward said with patience. "I want you to take out the part about that last woman."

Harrow sat down, snarling. "You publish it as it is or you shan't have it."

"She doesn't add anything," Edward said stubbornly. "You had the book all written without her, and then you dragged her in."

Harrow groaned aloud. "If you'd just forget you aren't the author—" He leaned forward, his square blocked face red with swift anger. "Look here, Ed. Can't you see that it's implied—"

"What's implied?" Edward asked grimly.

"That she's changed his life by being inaccessible."

"Oh, she's inaccessible, is she?"

"Sure she is."

Against his better judgment, goaded by his living jealousy, Edward said, "How does he know what her body looks like?"

Harrow refused to accept the knowledge of what was going on in Edward's mind. "Don't you see that my man knows what women are? Out of the dozen and more women he's lived with, slept with, bought, loved—hasn't he learned something? Given a height, a shape, a narrow hand, flying black hair, blue eyes, a high-arched foot—can't he imagine?"

"It's obscene," Edward blurted.

There was a tight silence, then Harrow spoke. "You're obscene."

The silence fell again. Edward stared down at a little white elephant upon his desk, a desk toy Thomas Seaton had given him one Christmas, ivory weighted with lead.

"What's more," Harrow said suddenly, "you don't deserve her. Someday I shall tell her so."

He rose, flung on his shapeless hat, and strode out of the room.

And with him went all the joy of the great day. Edward sat motionless, leaning upon his desk, his hand shading his eyes. He could not endure the torment of his jealousy. It boiled up in him and he leaped to his feet and strode after Harrow and catching him in the outer hall he held him by the shoulder.

"Come back here and tell me what you mean! If it's what I think, you can take your filthy book with you."

He would have welcomed anger in return, so intolerable was his fury. Instead Harrow's strange tawny eyes were remote and calm.

"Sure I'll come back," he said. His voice showed only mild interest.

In the office again, however, the door closed, he looked at Edward with greedy curiosity. "I've never seen you angry before, Ed—it's quite a sight. A quiet man can really put on a show."

"It's not show." A chill came over him as he answered Harrow. He always shivered with cold when his anger drained away. He tried to moisten his lips but his mouth was dry.

174

"No, I see it isn't." Harrow's voice was musing. He sighed. "How I hate real life!"

Edward did not answer this. He found his pipe in his pocket and lit it, and looking up, saw that Harrow perceived that his hands were trembling.

"Men like you, Ed," Harrow said, "live only in real life. Men like me only use you, and your wives and your children, to write about real life."

"You'd better leave us alone."

"I might be of use to you, though, if you'll accept that of me." Harrow was stubbornly casual.

"Your usefulness is limited to business," Edward retorted and then winced at the pedantry of his words. Why could he not invest his voice with that silver-edge carelessness which sharpened the dullest words? He could not. He was solid, plodding maybe, but without veneer.

Harrow laughed and slapped the desk with his palms. "Ed, will you hear something from me?"

"Maybe."

"Maybe is must, then! You're a fool—that's first."

Edward, sitting now behind the desk, pulled hard on his pipe in lieu of answer. Harrow leaned on his elbows. "Second, if you'll let me go on, your wife, though beautiful, is impregnable. You don't deserve such luck."

"I'd rather you didn't speak of her."

"Don't be such a fool, Ed! I will speak of her, do you hear?"

Harrow's face, so near his across the desk, grew harsh. It was an ugly face, heavy featured, dark, lit only by light eyes and white teeth and changing expression. Eyes and teeth gleamed at him now.

"Of course I'd have been glad to win her away from you. What have you done to deserve her? Can you even appreciate what she is? I doubt it!"

"Stop!" His voice roared at Harrow, strange in his own ears. "You haven't the least idea of the—the relationship between my—my wife and myself. You—you—it takes years to build what we have—and a sort of devotion that you have no notion of."

He was on his feet, shouting at Harrow. His pipe dropped to the floor and a coal of tobacco fell on the carpet and began to burn a hole. He stamped on it and

175

looking down for the moment he heard Harrow laugh softly.

"Don't I know it, man?" Harrow's voice came softly over the desk. "That's why she's impregnable. With all your manifold faults, every one of which you may be sure she sees, she knows what she has and she'll never let herself escape from it. She's accepted the prison of your love."

"It's a not a prison."

"Sometimes it is," Harrow insisted. "But most of the time it's a walled garden, and every day she throws away the key to the gate, so she'll never yield to temptations."

"Is she ever——" He could not bring out the word.

"Tempted?" Harrow's voice was delicately cheerful. "Of course she is. Who isn't?"

"I'm not."

"That's the wall around the garden. She knows you, Ed. Take heart from that. It isn't every man who can be known through and through and have his wife value him the more."

A strange reverence crept into Harrow's bantering. "Why, Ed, you're a fool not to live your life in joy. You do possess your wife. Do you know how few men can say that and know it's true? You're cursed with humility."

"Only because she's too good for me, of course." Edward ground out these words from the tightness of his heart cursing Harrow for his searching shrewdness.

"She's not too good for you," Harrow retorted. "No woman can be too good for what you give your wife."

His eyes fell on his wrist watch and he leaped to his feet. "I have to catch a train in ten minutes—promised I'd be in New York."

He caught up his hat and ran out, banging the door. Alone Edward sat without moving. He felt spent, not being used, he supposed, to release of emotions. For a moment he could not collect himself. Then there came creeping into his veins a warmth of transfusion. He remembered again what Harrow had said. Margaret, his wife, was impregnable. His love kept her inviolate. Then she knew how he loved her. He had never been able to tell her entirely, but she knew.

His comfort was short. For how did Harrow know even

this about her unless he had had most intimate talk with Margaret? What had they said? How much had Margaret revealed and why? Harrow would henceforward be an unwanted third in their most secret life.

He heard the door open but he did not look up.

"You ready to answer your letters?" Jane's voice inquired.

"No."

She shut the door, and he continued to sit. The clock in the outer office struck twelve, and there was a stir of clerks getting ready to go to lunch. Jane must have told them he did not want to be disturbed, for no one came in his door. He sat another hour, breaking his despair and doubt occasionally to fumble with papers, to read a letter or two, to realize that he did not understand anything except the growing demand of his own heart to know the truth from Margaret herself. While he had been engrossed in these offices, intent upon the making of books and selling them, where had Harrow been? What had he been doing when for weeks he had delayed finishing his book, and why, when he finished it so swiftly, had it been to bring into those pages—Margaret?

There was no truth to be had whole out of Lewis Harrow. That man who so impudently comprehended what went on inside human creatures really could understand nothing. What could he know, and how could he know, what it meant to a man to be as he, Edward Haslatt, was a man, firm in integrity, a faithful husband, a good father, a leading citizen whom all respected? Lewis Harrow, knowing everything, his fertile imagination a ferret running into the secret places of lives with which he could have nothing to do, had crept sniffing and sucking into the precious privacy of a house whose doors he was not fit to enter.

But the truth could be had from Margaret. This dawned upon Edward at last with fainting hope. Margaret had never lied to him. She would not lie to him now. He got to his feet, reached for his hat and coat, and left his office. Seeing his grim face, no one spoke to him as he passed, not even Jane.

His house was silent as he let himself in the front door. The children were not yet home from school and Sandy was deep in her afternoon nap. He hung up his hat and coat and looked into the living room. Margaret was not there. For a moment his jealousy leaped to the possibility that she was out, even now, perhaps, with Harrow. The fellow might have run to tell her about the talk interchanged at the office. She might be meeting him somewhere, even perhaps in New York. More than once Margaret had gone abruptly to the city, leaving only a note.

He checked firmly the rush of quivering fears. In common sense he must not go to her trembling and distraught. Profoundly feeling as she was, she shrank with physical distaste from emotionalism. Surface display she could not accept. He went into the library for a moment to collect himself, and found himself remembering instead the times, now long past, when his instinctive jealousy had first been roused. How long she had delayed in her decision to marry him! If she had loved him as he had loved her since he was seventeen years old, she could not so have delayed. She had said once that her father wanted her to marry someone in New York, a needless thing to tell him, surely, when the man was nothing to her, and there was the evening when he had first come to the Seaton house and she had worn a gown so low in the bosom that it had made him uncomfortable and they had quarreled. Then his unholy jealousy reached into the sacred hours of his honeymoon and his startled, half-guilty delight in the freedom with which she had dressed and undressed in his presence, a lack of modesty, beautiful and dangerous.

Actually she had grown more modest with the years. Without words they had come to behave with graceful courtesy that, he had imagined until now, did not separate them in the least. He did not open her door without knocking—he had not done so since Sandra was born. And she did not come in when he was bathing. It had been their joy to have no walls of privacy when they were first married, but they had built them again, bit by bit, walls no stronger than mist, transparent and yet shielding. Had those walls provided her with secrecy?

For she had changed. The old frank abruptness with which she had once spoken her thoughts, asserting her right to wound him if she must because in love there must be truth—this frankness she no longer had. A silvery

178

gentleness now enclosed her, and he was startled to realize how long it had been since they had really spoken with communication.

At this moment he heard a door open and close, and with an impetuousness entirely foreign to him he leaped to his feet and ran upstairs and knocked at the door of her room.

She was there. He did not know, as he stood staring at her, that in his relief his face began to work as if with tears. She had just taken from her closet a garment of some sort. Evidently she had been resting, for the bed was tumbled and she wore a negligee.

"You aren't sick?" he gasped.

"No—only tired. I thought I'd rest while Sandy slept. Why, Ned, what's the matter?"

"Nothing." He sank down into her velvet armchair.

"Don't be silly, Ned. You look dreadful."

He was speechless. Now that he saw her standing there in her rose dressing gown, looking exactly as she did every morning, her dark hair curling about her face, her eyes calm as the sea under sunshine, he felt his heart swell and his breath grow short. He tried to smile and looked so ghastly that she dropped the garment she held and fell on her knees at his side.

"Ned, speak to me, do you hear? Tell me what it is."

His heart kept swelling until he could not get his breath, and to his horror he heard a loud sob. It was his own.

At this she, who had never seen him weep, began suddenly to weep herself. "Oh, darling, what is it? Don't keep it to yourself, dear. Is it the business? Has something dreadful happened? It isn't Tommy—or Mary?"

Her terror gave him strength, and he lifted her into his lap. "No, no—it's too foolish. You won't forgive me."

"But I'd forgive you anything." Her head was upon his shoulder and he felt her cheek wet.

"Would you, Margaret—will you?"

"Of course—I promise. No, I don't have to promise— you know. Oh, Ned, you frighten me."

"Well, then, listen."

And then, holding her head with his cheek upon her hair so that she could not see his face, he told her of his doubt and his jealousy, and she listened. But he would not tell her of what Harrow had said.

If she had grown angry with him, if her body had stiffened as she lay silent in his arms, he would have been reassured. If she had flown at him with some of the impetuous heat of her girlhood, which now so seldom she did, he would have been reassured. But she lay soft and yielding in his arms. She kept her eyes shut —he felt the lashes curling motionless under his chin. Her hand lay in his, and he imagined only a quickening in the beating of her heart as she lay against him. So there was no way for him to know the truth except to ask for it, and having revealed himself naked to the soul in all his folly of love, he did ask.

"I don't want you to be afraid of me, Margaret. I don't want my love to be a prison. Tell me the truth. If Harrow has made love to you—"

Her voice when she spoke was soft and tired. "Is that it? But it doesn't matter if men make love."

"Then he has?"

"He's the sort that will always keep on trying."

"But you don't—"

"Let him, you mean? Of course not, Ned." She sighed when she had said these words, and still she lay in his arms, soft and inert. "It doesn't mean anything to me what he does, Ned. Only—"

"Only what, dear heart?"

"Are you angry with me?"

"No—but terribly afraid."

"Are you satisfied with me?"

"Absolutely."

Upon this she sat up and faced him, her blue eyes sparkling with sudden anger. "How can you be satisfied with me, Ned, when you don't have anything to say to me, when you aren't with me, when you don't bother to find out anything about me, when you can even suspect me of—of listening to Lew Harrow?" She burst into fresh weeping.

He was so comforted by her anger, so reassured by her fury, so assuaged by her tears, that he could have laughed. He hugged her to him by force, and when she pushed him with her hands against his breast he would not let her loose herself from him.

"Are you satisfied with me?" he demanded.

"No," she sobbed. "No, no, no!"

"Now," he said firmly, "now we have something to talk about. Stop crying and tell me what's wrong. Stop, I say!"

He forced her to look at him, her face still streaming with tears, and he shook her as if she were a child. "I haven't kept my promise to you—isn't that what you're thinking?"

She nodded.

"I've forgotten—or I've been too busy, it's the same thing—to make our marriage the most important thing in my life—isn't that what you're thinking?"

"Yes," she whispered. "It's true. That's exactly what you've done."

"And what you've done," he retorted, "is to let me go on, year after year—"

"Because I thought you wanted to."

"Understanding me so little," he accused her sternly.

"Understanding you very well," she retorted, "but not knowing how to change you—unless you wanted yourself to change. How did I know you weren't tired of me? Men do outgrow their wives. But I'm so used to you now, I can't live except with you."

He groaned. "Oh, Margaret, Margaret, what folly for us!"

"Is it really, Ned?'" Her voice and eyes were wistful.

"Why are you humble?" he demanded. "You used never to be humble."

"I think marriage makes women humble," she said, half sadly, "just as it makes men arrogant."

"Nonsense. Your father and mother never were either."

"Ah, but they've never been really married—as we are."

"Take my parents, then."

"They were both humble," she said wisely. "Marriage wasn't good for them—not their marriage."

They fell silent for a moment, each thinking separate thoughts. Marriage, which had made them one, had begun to build a wall between them, had separated them, too, so Edward mused. The necessity to earn a living for them all, the necessity to be father, and she perhaps, with the necessity to be mother—and yet surely somehow this was the proper course of marriage?

"It looks to me as if we'd have to begin over," he said at last. "Maybe it's only second wind we need. Or maybe we need to design our marriage again to what we are now—the man and woman we've become."

Her tears had dried and she smiled. "I do love you." She murmured the words against his lips.

He received them far more solemnly indeed than the first time she had uttered them so long ago, and doubt and jealousy left him suddenly and forever.

"Do you, dear?" If there was less passion in his voice than there had been in his youth, there was tenderness that reached from the bottom of the sea to heaven. "I love you, too, and I want to promise you again, Margaret—"

She laughed with astonishing joy, as though ten minutes ago she had not wept her heart half broken. "Oh, promises," she cried richly, "as if we needed them any more!"

She got up out of his lap and pushed back her tumbled hair.

"What on earth have we been talking about?" she demanded.

"Something important," he retorted.

"Maybe," she said in a practical voice, and began to brush her hair.

He did not reply to this, but sat watching her, a half smile on his lips. It had been something very important indeed. For the rest of his life he would be a different man.

Three

CHRISTMAS EVE, of the forty-fifth year of Edward Haslatt's life, was a fine one. He had risen in the morning to see Chedbury deep under snow. Over the edge of the hill behind the spire of the church a crimson sun shone in a clear sky. He had a feeling of profound pleasure. Christmas was beginning just as it should. By night his children would be gathered under his roof and his house would be full. His mother and his sister Louise were coming for dinner, and later in the evening their usual Christmas dance would take place. This was also a celebration of his own wedding anniversary. He and Margaret had long ago given up trying to make a private affair out of it, and there were times when his marriage seemed a family rather than a personal matter.

Dallying over his dressing for breakfast, Edward reviewed the recent years. His wedding anniversary always induced reminiscence. The difficult quarrel which he and Margaret had carried through over Harrow's novel remained firm in his memory. Harrow had been damnably right, of course; nevertheless Edward did not like to be indebted for understanding his own wife. Yet he was indebted. In the privacy of his own room and the gloomier hours of night he had read many times Harrow's novel, dwelling always upon the pages where the blue-eyed black-haired woman entered suddenly upon the scene. With each reading he lashed his always ready conscience. Margaret had never blamed him again for neglect.

The novel had been one of the miracles of publishing but he had no wish to repeat it. After his conversation with Harrow about the unwanted episode, which Harrow firmly refused to take out, Edward had referred to it no more. He had even succeeded in removing it from his own thoughts. With grimness he proceeded to make the book a masterful success, maintaining a cold face toward an angry Chedbury when it recognized some of its weaknesses skillfully painted upon the characters in Harrow's novel. "If I can lump it they can," Edward told himself in the deep and secret places of his own being.

He sat in his office, the control room of an enterprise that grew so vast that there were times when he himself was terrified at what he, by the grace of Harrow, had achieved. His presses rolled off the editions, and he was compelled to dangerous postponement of all other business. Even so he could not print enough copies of the book which critics, generous and loud in their praise of new genius, insisted was to be read by every thinking American. People rushed to join the ranks of the thoughtful, and Harrow's book was on every living-room table, when any book was, and upon the surge of popular demand Edward made his first motion picture sale.

His life had been upset and his digestion weakened by the constant demand from Baynes and Sandra that he be present at cocktail parties and dinners in big cities, until the press of work increased the necessity that he stay at his desk. All the furor Harrow enjoyed without apparent damage. He ate at all hours, drank prodigiously, and slept, he declared, on his feet.

Edward watched the bank deposits of his firm rise to comforting figures, and felt for once no pricks from his tender conscience, for Harrow's profits were even greater. In these days, though Edward came and went with his accustomed modesty, Chedbury observed a new confidence in him. He was now a soundly successful man.

He had been staggered, however, one Monday morning when little Mrs. Walters killed herself. No one expected it. She had read the book bravely, ignoring to her closest friends the clearly drawn portrait of her husband, dead so many years ago. She had even come to Edward after church the Sunday before and among Chedbury folk, standing about in the sunshine of the green she had chirped, "I think *Town Square* is simply wonderful!"

"It is a great book, though a harsh one," Edward had replied. "Perhaps Harrow will mellow with years," he had added, after looking down into Mrs. Walters' white wrinkled little face.

"Oh, of course he will!" she had trilled.

That night she had taken the shocking overdose of sleeping pills, and Edward had understood with grateful pity that her courage of the day before had perhaps been in preparation and apology.

He had weathered with outward calm the bitter and even angry surmises of Chedbury, and prudently he had sent only a modest offering of flowers to the bier. Anything more would have been construed by Chedbury as the expression of a guilty conscience. To Harrow, however, he spoke privately and forcibly.

"You see what happens when you tamper with real life."

Harrow had shrugged his heavy shoulders. "How little you understand people, Ed! If she hadn't wanted to die she wouldn't have killed herself. I gave her the excuse, that's all. I'm sure she was grateful."

He stared across the room with eyes so remote and all-seeing that Edward had said no more. That night, however, he told Margaret what Harrow had said to him. They had sat late after the children went to bed, and then before going upstairs themselves they had taken a turn or two in the garden, arm in arm.

"A queer thing to say, wasn't it?" he had remarked.

"Yes," Margaret had replied, "and yet like so many things Lew says, it can't be denied because perhaps it's true."

He digested this remark in silence, admitting its accuracy. The wind had blown cool as they reached the far end of the garden, and so they had gone in.

As though the death of old Mrs. Walters had been relief enough for anger, Chedbury relapsed into its usual somnolence after the funeral, and Harrow went on with energy to finish his monstrous house on Granite Mountain and to plunge into his next novel.

Edward conceded in his more melancholy moods that while Haslatt Brothers were highly respectable publishers they were not spectacular, except for Lewis Harrow's books. Two or three lesser successes, produced by discoveries of Baynes and Sandra, had barely enabled him to maintain his independence before Harrow. There had been nothing further between them of personal matter, and Edward subdued his continuing annoyance at the easy way in which Harrow came and went in this house. Except for the weeks and months of fierce concentration, when Harrow lived aloof and alone on Granite Mountain, there was nothing sacred. For the last week Harrow had been incessantly present and busy about the Christmas party.

To this party all the young people of Chedbury came, together with out-of-town friends the children had made at their various schools, and such business connections as Baynes and Sandra felt were inevitable.

Whether old Thomas Seaton could get here tonight was questionable, if the snow held under this sun. He had grown very shaky in his seventy-seventh year. Mrs. Seaton was as hard as a nut. The fragility that had once been her charm had become sinewy and sinister.

Edward pondered the determination of women to outlast men. Would his own Margaret one day linger long after he was underground? To this melancholy question he found no answer as he continued to dress, listening meanwhile for the voice of Mark, his youngest, born to his astonishment and Margaret's laughter, three years ago. He would never forget his alarm when Margaret came to him and told him she was pregnant, after so many years.

"We should never have gone to Italy," he had said solemnly.

"Why do you blame Italy?" Margaret had demanded.

"You know very well what I mean," he had retorted.

For that year Sandy had been put into boarding school, and he and Margaret had gone to Europe once more. In a manner of speaking, it was a second honeymoon, although neither of them had put the idea into words. He had rejoiced that again he had her to himself, her thoughts to be directed to him alone as they had been in the days when they were newly married. This had not quite come about. The children existed for them both, and even at times when they were most intimately close, as they had been, for example, that night in Venice, he saw a faraway look stealing into her eyes, which meant that she was wondering about the children. Once having given birth to a child, a woman seemed to be forever divided.

It had taken him a long time to learn this, and still longer to accept its inevitability.

That night in Venice he remembered in absurdly idyllic circumstances—that is, a moon had risen over St. Mark's and the water in the canal upon which they were riding in a gondola, though actually filthy, was changed into liquid gold. The Italian fellow who was rowing them began to sing a soft shaking melody and his tenor voice, though untrained, had a surprising quality of sweetness. Margaret sitting beside him on the narrow benchlike seat looked like a girl. She had put chiffon or something over her head, and her face was absolutely beautiful. Edward had wanted to make love to her immediately, and in an hour or two he had suggested that they go back to the hotel. She had not wished to go, and this had irritated him. Surely she understood his state of mind, and surely she might have responded to it. He earnestly longed to abandon himself to romantic love. It was not often that he felt he could. That night, far from Chedbury, with no business problems pressing and the children cared for, he had felt entitled to what might be called relaxation. A man of more common clay would have found it in various repulsive ways, but he had turned to his wife.

"Oh, let's enjoy the night as long as we can," Margaret had said, rebelliously.

"You don't enjoy being with me, I suppose," he had retorted. Of course she knew very well what he was feeling.

"We may never see Venice again as long as we live." This was her reply. It was made to remind him of a quarrel they had had once in Kansas. It had been her first journey westward, and her excitement, as tonight, had made her more than usually beautiful. She had gazed at the rising plains over which they were motoring. "It's more lovely than the sea," she had murmured, "because it doesn't change." So beautiful had she been that day, her cheeks sunburned red and her black hair flying, that he had wanted love from her. She had yielded unwillingly, as he had found out only long afterward, because she did not want to hurt him. Nor had this wish to spare him been an unselfish one. She admitted, when he pressed her, that she did not want to have the trouble

189

of a quarrel. Upon this they had quarreled indeed. He had not forgotten the tortuous admissions he had wrung from her.

"You, who insisted that you would marry me only if we could be frank," he had reminded her again. "I am frank enough, but what about you?"

She had been cool and patient. "You make it impossible for me to be frank," she had declared. "If I don't feel just as you do, and when you do, you feel it is my fault. I lie to save myself trouble."

He had refused to acknowledge the possibility of truth in this nonsense, but he knew there was truth in it, though only a wisp, and knew, too, that she was aware of having said something telling. He had made honest efforts, ever afterward, to examine her mood, before indulging his own.

But she had held the Kansas afternoon against him, as he came to know, because while she wanted to be free to enjoy the world through which she passed, he had forced her, because she did not want to hurt him, to center her attention on him. She had never quite forgiven him, nor in a sense had he forgiven her, while he had learned to accept rationally the difference between them, which was that when he was moved by extraordinary experience or pleasure, his impulse was to find release and expression in his love for her. She, he now knew, wanted at such times to be free of him and of love, in order that she might lose herself—and perhaps, him.

For long this difference between them had wounded him deeply, but with the years he had come to believe that it was the difference not only between himself and Margaret, but also between man and woman, and therefore to be accepted.

That night in Venice, with the memory of Kansas alive in him, he had controlled his desire, had sat only holding her hand lightly, had allowed her to wander into dreams she did not share with him, until suddenly long after midnight she had turned to him, her eyes dark.

"Now," she had whispered, "now I am ready."

The outcome of that rewarding night, he was firmly convinced, had been his unexpected son, Mark.

What they would have done without him it was of course impossible now to imagine. A child who upset all their accustomed ways, no less inconvenient to the older children than to himself and Margaret, spoiled as he had become in his irrepressible youth and gaiety, he was a darling headache, as Sandy put it, wherever they took him. Edward adored him privately above all his other children. Someday, he secretly believed, Mark would be the joy of his old age and the mainstay of the business. Baynes had no children and was not likely to have any. Tommy, although now a gangling youth, still showed no interest in anything except football and the curious moaning noises which passed for singing these days. But Mark, even at three, was trying to learn to read. Further than this, Edward tried not to be proud of the fact that, of all his children, only Mark looked like him. So real was the resemblance that there were times when Edward had the illusion that he was looking into his own childish face as he used to remember it, somewhat older than Mark's, in the mirror in his old bedroom. His mother made no pretense that Mark was not her favorite grandchild.

Edward was dressing very slowly, feeling no hurry this morning before Christmas. During the holiday week he tried not to work, if possible, at his usual tasks. He had put on scarcely more than six pounds as he grew older, but Dr. Wynne had warned him of a blood pressure some ten years too old for him. Nothing dangerous, but still it was a barometer. Now he heard a tap on his door.

"Come in," he called, knowing that light metallic sound. Margaret came in, dressed in a new crimson wool dress which struck his eye at once.

"Not too red, is it?" he asked cautiously.

"Is it?" she demanded.

"The skirt's short," he suggested.

"Oh, you!" she said with affectionate humor. "You wouldn't be satisfied unless I went around in some sort of purdah. For heaven's sake, Ned, be your age!"

"I wish you'd be yours," he retorted with good spirit.

Whether it was her slightly graying hair, which made her skin look as fresh as ever, or whether it was the undying blue of her eyes, he did not know, but she had grown more handsome with years. What had been angular and impetuous in her young face had grown smooth and tempered. She had not quite fulfilled his secret long-

191

ing for moments of high romance, but he did not blame her entirely for that, knowing that to the ordinary eye he was not wholly a romantic figure. His face, as he now looked at it in the mirror while he knotted his brown satin tie, was long and dark. His hair was growing heavily gray and his rather large mouth had taken on a dry and saturnine look, which he did not understand, for he was at heart a shy and still too sensitive man. The last thing Jane Hobbs had said to him one day, now five years ago, when she made ready to walk out of the office for the last time, was, "Now that I'm to be gone for at least a month, do for mercy's sake watch yourself, Ed, and don't give money to anybuddy you don't know."

Poor Jane—none of them had thought she would not be back. She had gone to the hospital for some female operation into whose details he did not inquire, the sort of thing he understood that the wombs of old virgins were liable to develop, and she had not survived the operation that was to make her life better. Perhaps it was better anyway. Who knew? Joseph Barclay with all his sermons had never been able to convince him that there was any sort of real life after the grave. He would not speak this doubt as long as his mother lived, for she had at best too short a time left to her in which to hope to see her husband again. With each year since his father's death, the silence growing deeper as the very memory of his voice was forgotten, his mother was able to remember only his virtues, those good qualities that had appeared so scanty in life. Perhaps the physical awkwardness, the small repulsive habits that his father had never tried to overcome, had died with him, leaving his true image clear. Death had performed a service.

"Well," Margaret said restlessly. "I suppose you'll be down to breakfast when you're ready."

"Aren't you going to kiss me this morning?" he demanded.

She moved to him and their lips met with the ease of long habit. She had taken to wearing lipstick, to his private annoyance, but he had given up protest. She wore it very well, of course, just the slightest tinge and not the solid scarlet that Sandra plastered on her mouth, already somewhat too coarse. But still it was enough so that he had to bother to wipe it off, lest one of his children jeer at him.

"At it again, you two!" Sandy had cried the last time she was home from school, when she saw the stain of red on his chin. Young people these days were purposely ribald.

And yet, he thought, as Margaret's lips met his, this kiss was better than ever. Some of the old sting and novelty perhaps were gone, but the present satisfaction was deeper than he could possibly have felt in his youth. He had still not plumbed all her womanhood. She changed all the time, and he had to keep up with the change. Take, for example, her willfulness about working for these foreign peoples—what on earth did they have to do with Chedbury? Except that he did not like the look of things in the world at that! Even when they had been in Europe there was already some sort of shadow creeping over Denmark and Holland. He didn't see it in Italy or in Germany. Everything there was buoyant and the people were full of hope.

"Germany is about to rise to the height of her nationhood," Heinrich Mundt, the German publisher, had declared.

"What on earth are you thinking about?" Margaret now demanded. "Not about me."

"It comes of my not having to rush to the office," he confessed.

"What's the use of kissing me if you don't keep your mind on it?" she said and shook him a little and went away.

A rumble at the front door, a slam, and then a loud shouting voice roaring through the house announced the arrival of Lewis Harrow. A moment later the fellow was bellowing up the stairs.

"Ain't you up yet, Ed?"

Lewis affected these days a return to the speech of lower Chedbury, declaring that it was the sort of English he had learned as a child and anything later acquired was pretense. He had never married, and for all these years had continued to live alone at The Eagle, except for long journeys into various parts of the world, in no one knew what company.

Edward opened his door. "Just coming," he said crisply

and closed it again. A hoarse growling, as of bears, mingled with shrieks, told him that Mark had rushed out of the kitchen to find his beloved. Strange that nowadays because of the child's joy he should be slightly jealous again of Lewis Harrow! Old roots yielded reluctantly.

He went downstairs wearing, as symbol of holiday, the red velvet jacket that Margaret had given him last Christmas. Lewis Harrow, in shabby tweeds, one elbow ragged, gazed at him as at an apparition. "My God, how handsome you are!" he cried and pretended rude amazement.

Edward smiled. "Thank you," he said with composure. "Have you had breakfast?"

He was pleased to see his small son, wearing a blue sailor suit and his breakfast bib, desert Lewis and come flying with outstretched arms. He picked Mark up and carried him into the dining room and put him into the highchair before he took his own seat.

"I had breakfast before dawn," Lewis shouted, following him into the dining room.

"Foolish of you," Edward remarked. "What have you come here so early for—money?"

Their friendship now was past the possibility of breaking, although twice Lewis had quarreled with him and had gone to other publishers and twice Edward had let him go, knowing grimly that no man could bring him the fortune that Lewis did yearly. Twice Lewis Harrow had come back, complaining and angry. "You're all of a lot of thieves, you publishers," he had cried. "I've a good mind to start printing my own books."

"Perhaps you had better," Edward agreed, "then you'll see where the profits go. If you have a thousand dollars left I'll be surprised."

"Shut up and draw a contract for the best book I've written yet," Lewis had ordered. " 'Member that mulatto fellow I told you about last year? I've written a book about him."

"People don't want to read about mulattoes," Edward had complained.

People had, however, read *Pedro and the Public*. It had not been one of Harrow's big books. The critics had been narrow-minded, but plenty of people had read it with joy. It was Harrow's strength that people read him whatever the critics said.

"I don't want any of your filthy money," Lewis now retorted and then corrected himself. "My filthy money, rather. Of course your little shop would go out of business if it weren't for me."

"I did very well when you were fooling around with city men," Edward replied mildly, and fell with appetite to scrambled eggs and bacon.

Lewis stared at him. "My God, look at him eat! It's these rails of men who lay away the grub."

"What did you come for?" Edward asked. "I know you don't climb down Granite on a snowy morning just to watch me eat."

Lifting a forkful of egg at this moment, Edward observed a strange suffused look upon Harrow's face. It had never been a handsome face, and rugged and unaffected, it had changed little with years. Now it was blushing red.

"I came to find out what time Mary's train arrives," Lewis said.

"Why should you bother to meet Mary's train?" Edward inquired. Shades of old jealousy made him look away from Harrow.

"Bacon," Mark said succinctly.

Edward put a rasher on the child's plate.

"Maybe I want to talk about a Christmas present for you," Lewis said.

"Queer you get so red over a Christmas present for me," Edward retorted.

"More bacon," Mark said.

"Don't eat so fast," Edward told his son. "This is the last piece."

"Ain't you going to tell me the train?" Lewis inquired.

"What train?" Margaret asked coming at this moment into the room to find Mark. "Edward, he's already eaten his breakfast and had quantities of bacon."

"I told him this was the last piece," Edward replied.

"Mary's train," Lewis reminded them.

"It gets in just before noon—eleven fifty, isn't it, Ned?" In innocence Margaret spoke.

"Yes," Edward said unwillingly.

"Why didn't you say so?" Lewis shouted. He rose and

lumbered from the room, pulling a fur cap out of his pocket as he went.

Margaret sat down at the table and poured herself a cup of coffee. Then deliberately she lit a cigarette, her eyes, as Edward knew, daring him to object. Well, he wasn't going to object. Whatever she did, she could do. She knew that he deplored the habit that women were taking up of smoking cigarettes, but so long as she did it only in her own home, he would not say anything.

"Has it occurred to you that Harrow is behaving a little foolishly about Mary?" he inquired.

The corners of her mouth quivered. "Has it occurred to you that you are growing rather handsome in your old age?"

Edward was embarrassed rather than diverted. "I am scarcely in my old age," he returned. He continued with his coffee which he was trying to learn to drink without cream, because of a slight though increasing tendency to nervous indigestion. With some effort of will he did not look at Margaret, because he knew she was looking at him and daring him to look at her. Suddenly he yielded and their eyes met, hers amused and his shy.

"What makes you say things that make me blush?" he complained. He could scarcely keep from laughter, and he was too honest to deny, at least to himself, that it was pleasant to have one's wife, after years of marriage, mention his increasing good looks.

"You're wearing better than I am," Margaret said. "You looked old for your age when you were young and now you look young for your age. It's monstrously unfair that a wrinkle shows up so on a woman."

"You haven't a wrinkle," he declared loyally. She did have a few, very fine ones, about her eyes, and one, rather deep, between her brows, because she did not want to wear glasses.

"Now about Lewis," she went on. "Yes, I think he is a little silly about Mary and, yes, it does worry me, for while I know she won't fall in love with a boy of her own age, it doesn't stand to reason that Lewis is the only man possible for her. He wants to worship her and she loves to be worshiped. There's the danger."

He ignored what he believed was an edge of malice in her words. Margaret was behaving well to Mary now as the child grew up. The adolescence that he had dreaded had not been what he had feared. Mary did not conceal the fact that she loved him better than she did her mother, but on the other hand both Tommy and Sandy loved Margaret better. Things evened up in a family, he supposed. Young Mark had learned early to be equal in his demands upon both parents. At any rate, Margaret accepted Mary's partiality for her father.

"I know you don't like me to say this, Ned, but you have spoiled Mary, you know. You've done a little worshiping yourself."

"Nonsense!" He put down his coffee cup.

"Not nonsense, and I don't mind. I wouldn't like worship, for myself."

"Did you once tell Harrow that?"

There was no more than the old shadow of jealousy now. He enjoyed his security as a husband.

"I laughed! There's nothing kills worship so thoroughly as laughter. He was furious with me."

"Can't you tell Mary that?" His eyes upon her were humorous but he was glad he had not known this ten years ago.

"Oh, she's at the serious age. Love with a capital L!" She lifted Mark from his chair, wiped his mouth, and waved her hands at him. "Shoo with you, young man! Go outside and play. Tell Hattie to put on your snow suit and your galoshes."

Left alone with her in the warm and pleasant dining room he felt strangely sentimental. He wanted to convey this to her, and while he was choosing his words, she said, "The real danger is, of course, that Lew has reached the age where he worships youth." A mild cynicism gleamed in her eyes that were still sea blue. "Queer how young men worship old women and old men the girls!"

He disliked hearing this platitude from her lips. Putting down his empty cup he wiped his short mustache carefully. "I was just thinking how much more I love you now than even I did when we were young." Words of love he usually spoke in the night, under the protection of darkness, and he was pleased that here in the bright snow-lit sunshine they did not sound absurd.

"Do you really, Ned?" She leaned on her elbows on the table and inquired this of him with a charming intensity.

197

The canary in the big bay window, inspired by the musical quality in her voice, burst into sudden song. They listened, gazing at each other with such communication that his answer scarcely seemed necessary. He rose from his chair, impelled to take her in his arms, and she, divining his necessity, rose too and met him in long embrace, which was the more passionate because each expected a door to open upon them. For once none did, and at last he drew away and looked at her. "I wish I could tell you all that I feel, I wish I knew how to put it into words. There are still times—don't laugh—when I really want to write poetry."

"I wouldn't dream of laughing," she said gently. "I think it's dear of you and wonderful—something not to be expected by a woman after she's twenty. I am blessed."

"Sure?" He wanted to penetrate deeply into her. Did he satisfy her every need at last? None of the surface mattered if he could be sure that in her fundamental self she was content with him. But he dared not make further demand. Some profound modesty in him inquired even at this moment why he should imagine that she could find a world within the limitations of his being. His conception of love's function now was that of a guarding if overwhelming tenderness, not so much demanding as providing. Did what he provided, then, complete her dreams?

"I'm sure," she said heartily.

At this moment the interruption came. Tommy strolled in for late breakfast. It did not occur to him that he could be unwelcome anywhere and he entered with all the brightness of unimpeded youth. The only real regret that Edward felt concerning his son was that he had named him after old Thomas Seaton and therefore after Tom. These two had not hidden their peculiar affection for Tommy, and this had provided an escape thereby for Tommy from the somewhat austere attitude of Edward as a father. Tom Seaton had weathered into an elder bachelor who still continued to live with his parents. Long tours around the world, immersions in India and South Africa, and more recently a sudden interest in Italian music had given Tom Seaton an excuse for living. Edward considered him a bad influence on all the young men in Chedbury and especially upon Tommy, who was inclined, as his school career developed, to put on the airs of a man of the world, a world about which he really knew nothing except at second hand through his uncle.

Thus Edward saw his fresh-faced young son, who had recently grown so tall that he looked as though he walked upon stilts, enter the dining room with an air that was all too cheerful.

"Happy returns, you two," he said negligently. "Many more of 'em, et cetera."

Margaret, with pleasant composure, sat down at the table to pour coffee for her son. Edward continued to stand as he lit his pipe.

"Anything I can do for the party tonight?" he inquired.

"Nothing, dear," Margaret replied. It would have been impossible for anyone to have believed that a moment ago she had been a young and flushed woman in her husband's arms. She was now the matron, the mother of a grown son. Edward, looking at her from under his eyelids, felt the private excitement of a clandestine love affair. Nobody knew this woman except himself. Especially did young Tommy know nothing about her. It occurred to him also that they had really settled nothing about Harrow going to meet Mary. He did not want to speak of it before Tommy who had all the surface cynicism of youth about love. He pulled out the gold watch that had Mark Haslatt's name on it. "I shall go to meet Mary," he announced.

"Do, dear," Margaret said smoothly. "I was thinking of going myself but if you're going, I'll meet Sandra. She gets in an hour later. I do wish the girls could synchronize."

"Mary always manages to come alone, for reasons she alone, alone can tell!" Tommy sang in a falsetto.

Both parents looked at him with stern eyes but his smooth pink face was innocent. Edward left the room abruptly. He heartily disliked the constant flippancy of his children's generation but it was incurable. Restrain it anywhere and it burst out somewhere else. He put on his hat and coat with a preoccupied gravity and searched for his cane. It was not to be found. He pressed a button and a new maid, whose name he could not remember, came from the kitchen.

"Where's my cane?" he demanded.

"I'll ask Master Tommy," she said at once.

He waited until she returned. "He says he was using it yestiddy," she murmured.

He waited again until she had returned with the cane, grunted when she handed it to him and went out the door. Surely Tommy was old enough to leave his father's canes alone.

"I'll buy him a cane next year for a Christmas present," Edward growled to himself.

But it was impossible on this morning to remain angry even with callous youth. The sunshine sparkled on the snow in the most obvious Christmas fashion. The merchants of Chedbury, having had a slightly better year than they expected, had gone to the extravagance of a large Christmas tree in the square and festooned lights around the lamp posts. He was pleased to see a sleigh pulled by a horse coming stolidly down the road between the passing automobiles, and then was taken aback by seeing that it was driven by Tom Seaton. There were even sleigh bells around the horse's neck and Tom had found somewhere in the Seaton attic a tall white stovepipe hat. People were laughing at him, moved by Christmas tolerance.

"Tommy up yet?" Tom shouted at Edward, waving a scarlet whip as he passed.

Edward nodded and went on. Though it was a holiday and he had no intention of going to his office he could not forbear passing that way, since he was still early for the train, and then having arrived at the door he went in. He had during the recent years taken over the entire building for his printing shop and his book business. Although he had not allowed the books to absorb the shop, he would not print advertisements of cosmetics, of which he disapproved, but he still printed private cards, wedding and funeral announcements, and the programs for the Sunday services. Occasionally he quarreled with the minster's wording, for Joseph Barclay had grown more rather than less extreme in his middle age, and felt that the world was becoming so comfortable that people had to be scared to God. More than once

Edward had returned the sacred copy with a firm note that unless it were modified to some sort of dignity he would not print it. Twice Barclay had refused compromise and twice there had been no printed programs in the church for that week.

The offices were decorated in the best of taste. Aided by Margaret, Edward had contrived just the right atmosphere in his own private office, enlarged by throwing together what had once been his father's office and Mather's. He had paneled the room in oak, and a portrait of his father hung opposite the door and over his own desk. The desk was solid but not large. His infrequent visits to New York offices had confirmed in him a dislike for large light-colored circular desks, confronting anyone who came in. The man behind such a desk designed himself to terrify and for this Edward suspected him of inner weakness.

The shop was of course idle today. It was still an open shop. Edward's blood pressure was points higher than it might have been had he not faced grimly across his desk, some half dozen times, a group of men who came to insist that he operate a closed shop. John Carosi brought them, as he well knew, and time and again he had been on the point of firing the fellow except that in all fairness he had been compelled to promote him for excellence of work until now Carosi was his head foreman. The man was a convinced labor man, and yet so just and truthful that he allowed Edward to argue against unions. And Edward, in decency, was compelled to hear Carosi in reply.

Against Baynes, too, and as heartily, Edward had argued. As Harrow's success had brought the modest spate of novelists to Haslatt Brothers, Baynes, abetted by Sandra, had declared that the offices ought to be moved to New York, leaving only the shop in Chedbury. Edward would not hear of it. Offices in the city and workrooms in Chedbury would have meant, he believed, nothing but confusion.

"You want to keep your hand on everything," Baynes had accused with the irritability that had become natural to him these days.

"I do," Edward agreed. "I've told John he can't even hire a new man without my meeting him and having a talk, and he can't fire anybody unless I see the man myself and know what's gone wrong. It isn't just that I want everything in my own hands, either. I believe that people are reasonable if I take the trouble to explain things to them. I don't want labor and management against each other in our business."

Secretly he wondered whether the deviousness of Sandra had imagined Baynes the real head if the offices were in New York, Edward remaining merely the boss of the printing end. Once he would have spoken his doubt to Margaret, but he had learned as he grew older to withhold judgment, even of his sister-in-law.

Edward regularly went to New York once a fortnight, though Baynes had grown sufficiently steady, after Sandra's escapade with Peter Pitt, to be relied upon.

Three years before this year, now so near its end, the two families of Haslatt and Seaton, as well as the firm of Haslatt Brothers, then at the very height of its first real and permanent prosperity, had been shaken to their combined depths by Sandra's affair. It was all mixed up with business, in the way that only Sandra could mix such incompatibles as love and shop. More and more she had become responsible for publicity and promotion, showing indeed real talent for these unpleasant but essential aspects of publishing. Thus had she arranged for the arrival of Peter Pitt in the United States, for his successful lecture tour, and for the sale of his books, including *The Singed Flower,* as motion pictures.

Not even Edward himself had suspected her of anything more than business acumen. Baynes, later, in the midst of real agony, gave a ghastly grin as he confessed his misery.

"It's beyond me, Ed. She's been driving a hard bargain with Peter Pitt, even while she's been carrying on. Our percentage is higher than ever. I don't know whether to love her or despise her for it."

That midnight now three years gone, when Baynes had rushed from New York to burst into the house could not be forgotten. Fortunately Edward had not yet gone to bed. As he grew older he needed less sleep, while Margaret needed more, and he had been sitting in the library, his feet to the fire, reading one of the pile of manuscripts with which he never finished. The house was silent, the family asleep. From the distance of a fantastic novel about mountain climbing he had heard a cry and had looked up to see Baynes at the door, as gaunt as a ghost.

Even so Baynes had made a pretense of nonchalance. "There you are, Ed—I was hoping you hadn't gone to bed. Got a cigarette on you? I've consumed all mine."

Cigarette between his trembling lips, Baynes had dropped into a chair and had said in a squeaky voice, "Sandra's left me."

The fantasy slid from Edward's hands. "Where's she gone?"

Baynes held out a note and Edward had read it, his nose in the air as though he smelled something foul. "Dear Bub—" such was Sandra's absurd name for her husband. "Don't hate me, will you! At least not permanently? Pete and I are taking a trip—maybe only a little one. I just had to get some sort of radical change. I don't know why, either. Not your fault! Sandra."

He handed the note again to Baynes. "There's something queer in the Seaton blood," he had said solemnly.

"Have you—is it in Maggie, too?" Baynes had asked with clutching hope.

"No," Edward had said firmly, "not at all."

Baynes had shrugged his shoulders and Edward saw that he was trying not to weep and so he had gone on talking. "You had better go upstairs to the east guest room and get to bed." He was deeply moved by his brother's plight and very angry with Sandra, and so his voice was dry. "Have you eaten anything?"

"Couldn't," Baynes muttered.

"Come with me," Edward ordered, and docile as he had once been in his boyhood, Baynes followed his older brother into the pantry. Edward opened the icebox and took out a ham and some lettuce and a slice of cheese and a roll of butter. He went to the bread box and fetched a loaf and put the kettle on and measured coffee.

"I didn't know you were such a cook," Baynes said. His voice was trembling.

"I get myself a snack sometimes when I've been reading late," Edward replied.

He sliced bread and made a sandwich for Baynes and one for himself, and when the coffee was ready he poured out large cups full and found cream and sugar. Baynes looked at the food as though it sickened him, and then suddenly began to eat and drink and Edward saw the ordinary comfort of hot food seeping from body to soul.

"Of course I saw them running around," Baynes said after his second cup of coffee. "I didn't think anything of it—everybody does that sort of thing now."

"You doing it, too?" Edward inquired.

"Only by way of business."

"Haslatt Brothers doesn't make any such requirements of you," Edward said.

"You don't understand," Baynes retorted with impatience. "You live up here in this pure little town."

"I don't know anything about the purity of the town. All I care about is my own home."

Baynes had looked at him with strange eyes but Edward had not inquired into their meaning.

"More coffee?" he had asked.

"No. I'm going to sleep," Baynes said heavily.

The brothers had separated without more talk.

Sandra had stayed away for nearly four months. She had gone to England and she wrote letters to them all with the most frightful effrontery, exactly as though she were merely visiting the land of her forefathers. She had the further impudence to discover and recommend to Edward a man who she believed could write novels, given sufficient encouragement. Baynes told no one that his wife had left him, and Edward told no one but Margaret. Whether she told the Seatons he did not know. The pretense was kept up in the family that Sandra was merely vacationing. Even Baynes as the weeks went on persuaded himself to the pretense and mentioned to Edward one day in the office, as though he were only mentioning it, that Sandra was returning on the eleventh of July.

Edward, beginning that year to struggle with increasing taxes, had not looked up from his accounts. "She's coming back, is she?"

"She's had her fling," Baynes said.

The affair had dried and hardened him. Ebullience had left him, perhaps forever, and his native New England toughness emerged to take its place. Baynes was no longer young.

"You want her back?" Edward inquired.

"She's still my wife," Baynes replied.

"You're being very decent."

"No—only doing what I want."

So Sandra had come back, and Mrs. Seaton gave her a little dinner party to which Edward found himself too busy to go, but at which, he heard from Margaret, the talk had been all of England. "Mother kept saying, 'Dear old England,' every five minutes," Margaret said and wrinkled her nose.

"Does your mother know?" Edward had demanded. He had got out of bed and gone to Margaret's room when he heard her come in and was lying in her bed when she opened the door.

"Of course Mother knows and so does Dad and so does Tom, but nobody is going to say anything outside, now that Sandra's home again."

"Are you going to say anything to Sandra?" he inquired.

She gave him a quick look, while she unfastened her necklace. "Probably Sandra will tell me everything."

So Sandra had done one day when the two sisters were sitting on the beach alone, the children in the water and the men fishing. Edward had bought a house on the seashore in order that he might not have to decide each year where the family would go for their summers.

There was nothing much to the story, as Margaret told it to him that night. He had allowed himself to get too heavily sunburned and it was difficult to fix his attention on the somewhat dull story of Sandra and Pete, bicycling about England, and apparently doing very little. In the end Sandra had been bored. Nothing, she declared to Margaret, was more boring than trying to live with a writer. Pete, she felt sure, was continually planning to put everything she said and did into some future book. It was a relief to get back to her good old Baynes.

"She'll probably go off again—with a banker or something," Edward had said, trying to find a safe place upon which to rest his sore frame.

"I doubt it," Margaret said. "Sandra isn't really a passionate woman. That end of it bored her no end with Pete."

Edward was startled into forgetting his pains. "Why in God's name then did she—"

"Don't swear, Ned—she just wanted to make sure that there wasn't any more to it than she had with Baynes. Sandra's always been like that—wanting to be sure that she was getting all there was."

"What indecency!" he had cried.

"Isn't it!" Margaret had agreed.

He had not quite liked her placidity, in which he could not discern any of his own disapproval, but he had not pursued the subject further. He had remained cool to Sandra for some time, indeed to some degree ever since, but she seemed not to notice it. The Seaton family held its head as high as ever in Chedbury, and Tom if anything admired his younger sister more than before.

What had gone on between the mother and the daughters after Sandra came home Margaret told Edward only partially, in unwilling fragments.

"Mother told Sandra how foolish Aunt Dorothea looked when she was separated from Uncle Harold. A woman alone is so silly. I mean—nobody knows what to do with her." At this moment Margaret had laughed. "Incidentally, Mother was rather nice about you, Ned! She said you had made a really sound and respectable business and Sandra would have been stupid to cut herself off from it—especially for somebody with such a name as Peter Pitt!"

"Thanks," Edward had said with some reserve.

Mrs. Seaton had prevailed and the old New England blood in Baynes had resumed its control. Sandra was thinner than ever and with humor renewed and toughened.

In his own heart Edward asked himself, as he sat in the privacy of his empty offices, how it was that Margaret had grown so well content with him. He believed that she was content. All the impetuous restlessness of her girlhood had left her and she had bloomed into a quiet half-indolent calm, her dark hair graying softly about cheeks still pink. He had never fathomed her altogether, and now he had no wish to do so. If she enjoyed the unfailing stability of his love then he was fortunate.

The sunlight of the cold December shone as bright as polished steel upon the floor and he remembered with a start that he was to meet Mary's train. He rose and went into the shop to see that all was well. No one

was here, either——or so he thought, the machines standing in silence, seeming to sleep in their unaccustomed
stillness. Then at the end of the long room he saw John
Carosi, in his good clothes, bending over a press, a small
oil can in his hand.

"Hello, John," he called.

"Hello," Carosi replied. He had never called his employer sir.

"You can't keep away from here, either," Edward
said smiling.

"I remembered there was something that didn't work
right in this here press," Carosi replied, not acknowledging
the smile.

"Well, merry Christmas——I've got to meet the train.
My older daughter is coming."

"Mary?" John Carosi spoke her name while he continued to find small holes into which to thrust the pin-
point nozzle of the oil can.

"Yes," Edward said. In Chedbury the first name was
the only one, but in his marriage he had absorbed from
the Seaton family a sense of class distinction. None of his
children shared this, and Mary would have answered
joyously to John's use of her name.

He left the pressroom and putting on his hat and
coat again and grasping his cane firmly against possibly slippery snow, he decided to walk to the station.
From here the distance was short and the exercise
would do him good. He mused as he trod firmly on the
now hard-packed snow. He had a genuine liking for Carosi. What he disliked in the man was no individual at-
tribute, perhaps, and yet on the other hand it might be
just that. Carosi limited his world to his labor union.
The small group of working men, dominated by a fiery
boss, who was in turn at the command of a central human
machine, was the universe within which John Carosi
lived. All the multiple affairs of mankind, hunger in Asia,
a possible war looming in Europe, the mounting cost
of living here at home——all these he saw simply from
the point of advantage or disadvantage for his union.
Edward had had an argument with him one day on the
question of whether the increasing cost of printing,
which was nothing but the union pressing for higher
wages, might not some day stifle the book business, even

as, Baynes had declared, the unions in the city had hamstrung the theater and at the very moment when it had to meet the frightful competition of motion pictures.

"Our welfare can't be independent of union labor," he had urged, "but you in turn depend upon the general welfare."

"I've had enough of that," Carosi had replied with obstinate tranquillity. "We're lookin' after ourselves first, down at the union."

It had been a secret mitigation of the alarming depression still lingering in its aftereffects, that the hordes of the unemployed had thoroughly weakened all labor unions. Yet this slight good could scarcely compensate for the repercussions of the American depression on Europe.

He pondered this gloomily as he trod the sparkling snow this Christmas Eve, absently touching his hat to acquaintances he passed. Carosi's insistence upon the group advantage was more than the symbol of the danger of control of business by labor unions. He, Edward told himself, was entirely willing to grant that owners had been operating for years entirely within their own world, too, but he trusted owners more than labor unions if for no other reason than that owners were on the whole better educated. He was more afraid of ignorance combined with power than of any other element in the world of man, and the more frightened because he saw, though at a distance, labor unions bringing to power a very ignorant fellow in Germany. No man, and no group of men, could live for self alone and be safe or make the world safe for others. Human life was a matter of proportion and balance, which he feared were both to be lost in the approaching future. Even Sandra, careless of the welfare of mankind, had seen from the vantage of England some sort of sinister shadow rising in Germany.

From such dark thoughts he was diverted by the whistle of the train flying into the station while he was still two blocks away, and making haste he arrived as the train was pulling out and in time to see his beloved daughter buried in the depths of the rough fur coat which Lewis Harrow began to wear after Thanksgiving and did not take off until just before Easter.

The train Mary had chosen was a slow one, and there

were few people on the platform. For this Edward was thankful as he hastened forward. He did not care for the talkative tongues of Chedbury, after this spectacle. He was further dismayed when his presence did not immediately separate Lew from his daughter. Instead the fellow gave Mary an instant longer in his arms and then she sprang forth laughing, her dimples rampant.

"Dad, darling!" .he cried in the fresh voice he was never sure was spontaneous or cultivated. Whichever it was, his heart melted at its music and he allowed Mary to kiss his cheek. She was the center of his heart and he considered her more beautiful even than Margaret had been at her age. This might be, however, merely that he felt in her some quality of his own and himself, an understanding of her that was natural, whereas he had been compelled to achieve such understanding of Margaret through the force of love. However he scolded Mary, and he intended to scold her now as soon as he got her to himself, he felt the bond between them held.

"Well, now," he said dryly. "Come along home. Your mother wants to see you before she has to leave to meet the next train. She wonders that you and Sandy can't synchronize."

"Oh, we never do," Mary exclaimed.

Her charming face was less regular than her mother's, and its whole look was softer, perhaps because her eyes were brown instead of that clear sea blue. Her skin, too, was softly brunette, and her voice low rather than clear. Examining anxiously this lovely young face among flying black curls, under a small dark fur hat, Edward was alarmed to see how womanly it was, how firm were the red lips, how set the rounded chin. How far had Harrow gone into her untried heart? For surely she was as yet only a child.

Tucking her hand under his arm and giving but the smallest of nods to his most important author, Edward walked down the platform. His eyes fell on Mary's shoes. "There now—I wanted to walk home with you but in those shoes we can't. Of course there are your bags. I suppose you are loaded up with luggage as usual. Where is it?"

"Bill took it," Mary said in her composed little voice. "And I'd love to walk."

Bill was the porter. Inside the station he was waiting beside the assortment a young woman brings home for the holidays.

"You'll catch your death," Edward grumbled. "Though I suppose Bill can send the bags up and the sidewalks have been shoveled."

"I'll change as soon as I get home. Come along and don't fuss, darling."

He enjoyed being persuaded by his glowing young daughter, and they set forth upon streets emptied by Chedbury's early lunch hour.

"Oh, isn't it going to be a perfect Christmas?" Mary's feet dancing upon the hard snow caused her to bob upon his arm.

"It's begun," he replied.

Her bright upward look reminded him that he was going to scold her and that he had better begin before they reached home. He never allowed himself to reproach his beloved child in Margaret's presence.

"Except," he said gravely, "I don't like it when Lew embraces you publicly like that. Maybe he's so old that it doesn't really matter."

He cast a sidewise glance down at her to see how this notion of Lew's age would move her. She repudiated it at once.

"Lew isn't old," she said with complete calm. "Besides, I like my men old."

"Lew is one of your men, is he?"

"Always has been," she said dreamily. "Ever since the first day he came to our house to lunch—always has been, always will be—"

He felt sure she was daring him to go on, and reluctantly he took the dare. "Your mother ought to tell you—" he began and paused.

"Tell me what?" she demanded, squeezing his arm. "Not the facts of life—please don't say that, Dad! I don't want to laugh—not at you."

He mustered his dignity. "What I was going to say is that young girls always fall in love with men too old for them. It's not real love."

"Did Mother?" The question was sharp with a sort of jealousy which he was quick to discern. Had this child also inherited his fatality?

210

"No, your mother is the exception to all rules about women."

"Maybe she didn't tell you."

He paused again on this. "I think she would have told me. She's entirely honest."

He looked down and met her dark eyes. There was something so quizzical, so mature, in this glance, so quickly veiled that he was frightened. The child was a woman!

He wanted to say no more but he loved her too much. "All I want to say now is that I hope you know how dear you are to me. Lew is all very well as an author— one of the great ones, of course—but as a man, he's not fit to tie your shoestrings."

"How do you know, Dad?"

"Because I publish his books, that's how I know! He gets his stuff somewhere and not out of other people's books, either."

Then from her exquisite lips there came these words, blasting his soul and withering his spirit. "I don't care for the old ideas, Dad—I mean about purity and all that. I want a man to be a man, that's all."

"Mary—" he was holding her arm so tightly beneath his own that he was lifting her.

"Let me go, please, Dad."

"I'm sorry—but what I want to say is—there's a lot of men besides Lew—better men."

"Better?" She repudiated the word.

He set his teeth and looked grimly ahead. "See here, Mary—before we get home, let's have this out. You aren't going to marry Lewis Harrow. My son-in-law? It makes me sick. I'll quit publishing his books—damned if I won't!"

He felt her hand tighten on his sleeve. "He hasn't asked me, Dad."

"If he dares to—"

"I will."

They had reached the door of home and before he could utter the groan that welled up in him the door was flung open and Margaret ran down the steps, clad in her furs, a sprig of holly on her lapel, to embrace her daughter. Mary was small in comparison and her cheek sank into the softness of her mother's breast.

211

"Dear child," Margaret said lightly, "why, you're looking very pretty!"

Mary patted her mother's cheek. "You're looking rather wonderful yourself. Where'd you get that brooch?"

"Your father gave it to me last night for being married to him so long. Now do wash quickly and eat your lunch, you two. It's being kept for you. Tommy was to have been here, but he's staying to luncheon with Mother and Father at the house. Now I must be off, or Sandy will feel nobody's bothered to meet her."

A touch on his arm and she was gone. Edward mounted the steps of his house, feeling as he always did, that when she was not there the house was empty. Mary had run ahead through the hall and up the stairs, and he heard her footsteps in the upper hall. She wanted to avoid him, for the first time in her life, and no wonder, with that avowal upon her lips. What was the use of having children when they broke one's heart? He remembered involuntarily the nights long ago when he had got up with her, wakened by her tiny wail and he fumbling to get the bottle hot. He had taken over the two-o'clock feedings because so often he worked late that it was not worth while to wake Margaret. That image was with him still, the wisp of agony he had held in his arms, the impatience, the despair of a human creature deprived of food, the greedy satisfaction when the seeking mouth found the milk, and then the rosebud child, replete and assured again, filled with warm food. He had not got up with the other children, and perhaps it had been those early-morning hours shared with his first child that had made her so precious to him now. He was far more terrified of her budding spirit today than even he had been of her fragile small body in those first weeks and months of her life. Then it had been a matter of newborn flesh and tender bones. Now it was something else, the birth of a quivering spirit, a heart newborn, a self no longer dependent upon him and seeking its sustenance elsewhere. When he thought of Lewis Harrow as the source to which she turned, his gorge rose.

He went upstairs to his room to be alone for a few minutes before he faced her again at lunch. He felt tired and he took off his shoes, and though it was midday, put on his leather slippers. Mark was asleep doubtless at this hour. With much rebellion, Mark still had to submit to his mother's firm decision for daytime sleep. Since Tommy was away, it meant that today inevitably Edward and Mary must be alone for the meal. He felt dispirited and unequal to the necessity. Was he inadequate as a father? Pride rose to deny it, and he braced his shoulders and after a second's meditation decided to change his tie. He went to the mirror and adjusted the deep crimson tie that he chose, and then brushed his hair carefully. So habitual did the tending of one's body become as years passed, that with something like shyness he peered again at his long, rather sallow face, made more brown by his graying hair. Whatever had been young and fresh in his eyes was gone. They had grown piercing and his mouth was set in lines. Not a face to make a young girl want to confide in him! And confidence could never be forced. He could no more compel his child to open her lips now to speak her heart than he could have forced her baby lips to receive food when she was beyond the want of it. There it was—she was beyond the want of him. Nothing that he could provide did she now need.

With this discovery he knew that it was to Lewis Harrow he must appeal with the mustered force of his fatherhood. All that he could do in his daughter's presence was to be as nearly as he could the father whom she would consider ideal. He went downstairs, determined upon courtesy and even courtliness, the tender consideration of an elderly gentleman who happened to be her father, yielding to her face and beauty.

She was there waiting for him in the dining room, the table set for two. Now that her fur coat was off she emerged as a small figure in scarlet wool, her curly hair cut to her shoulders in the fashion set by some motion-picture star whose name he could not remember. He disliked motion pictures, although they were becoming an important part of the revenue of his business. He had, however, gone to the filming of Harrow's last book, *The Shrew*. The leading part had been played by the star whose name he could not remember. She had been blond, and he was relieved that Mary could not look like her.

He pulled out her chair and smiled and was rewarded by the thanks he saw in her eyes. Had it been no more he might have been hardened, but he detected a mixture of timidity, her old childish yearning to be loved, and by him. He was melted at once and he gave himself up to being the ideal father that she wanted, as nearly as he could.

The day wore on to evening. He had tried to read some manuscripts, aware of the increasing noise and merriment in his house, and had been glad to give up all pretense when Margaret put her head into the open door of the library.

"Ned, do take Mark somewhere! He is everywhere he's not wanted and I have so much to attend to before the guests come."

"I thought the caterer was supposed to do it all," he grumbled, in spite of gratitude for the interruption.

"Oh, they always forget from year to year where the silver and glass are."

"Tommy home yet?"

"No. I think Tom took him to Boston."

"Did he tell you?"

"No, but Sandra called and said they might be late."

"I don't like Tommy going with Tom like that—he's too young and Tom's too old."

"Oh, well—it's Christmas, and Tom hasn't anybody special. Do hurry, dear, I hear Mark yelling in the butler's pantry."

"Get somebody to put on his outdoor things, will you?"

"I'll have him at the door." She hurried away and he gathered his papers together.

Half an hour later he was walking around the square with his son Mark skipping beside him, very handsome in a woolly brown coat and gaiters and a red knitted cap. The tree was alight and the festoons glittering. Mark was asking questions about Santa Claus and Edward answered them as honestly as he was able, in view of the fact that Margaret had encouraged Mark to believe in the saint's myth.

"Have you seen Santa Claus?" Mark pressed.

"Well, in a way," Edward countered.

"Bringing me things?"

He had never allowed anyone to use baby talk to this intelligent son, and Mark's enunciation of words was pure and precocious.

"Well, bringing things, certainly."

"Which chimney will he come down tonight?"

"I'm not sure."

He diverted the conversation from mythology, which he had never approved on the grounds that it was foolish to build up a faith which had later only to be destroyed, and called Mark's attention to the electric lights on the tree.

"When I was a little boy, we didn't have any electric lights in Chedbury."

"Where did they come from?"

"All the people paid money and put up poles and we got it in from Boston."

Mark was not interested in electricity and having pronounced the name of Boston, Edward fell to musing about the city which he disliked and admired. In the frightful aftermath of the depression, Boston had practically gone bankrupt. It had not been surprising that New York had been in a like fix, and less interesting that Philadelphia, Detroit, and Chicago were all financially unsound at the same period. The swollen rolls of those millions of persons on relief had been maintained at starvation level only by the largesse, actually, of rich men, who had not been willing to lend their money, however, for anything much above starvation. He himself, as one of the leading businessmen of the Boston area, had been invited to go with a committee to wait upon a Boston multimillionaire, who declared that while he did not want to be responsible for people dying in the streets, yet because he had worked for his money, he was sure that others could do so, and therefore he had to have a guarantee that the weekly dole would be a minimum.

Somehow, largely thanks to Harrow, Haslatt Brothers had continued prosperous enough so that in Edward's own house there had been little sign of the shortages which afflicted even houses once well to do. He had insisted that Margaret not serve champagne at their Christmas party last year, when things had been at their worst because trade had fallen off with Europe after American loans had ceased. This year things were better, however, and he had not mentioned the champagne. It would be served tonight, he supposed, in the great cut-glass punch bowl which the old Seatons had given

them ten years ago as an anniversary present. Still, he
didn't like the looks of things. Huey Long, for instance,
was setting himself up in a very peculiar fashion there
in the South. It was too much like what was going on in
Germany with that fellow Hitler. He was beginning to
imagine that Chedbury was nearer both Louisiana and
Germany than was comfortable.

The discomfort of his thoughts turned his instincts toward the warm shelter of his house.

"We'd better go home," he said to Mark.

The child had been silent for a while, clinging to his
father's hand. His Christmas exuberance was suddenly
over.

Edward bent to his beloved son. "Are you cold?" he
demanded. He laid his lean cheek against Mark's round
and rosy one.

Mark whimpered. "It's getting dark."

Remembering that the child had always been unac-
countably afraid of the night, Edward was reassured.
"We'll go home right away."

"Can't you see the dark?" Mark asked in a small
voice.

"I was thinking of things."

"What things, Daddy?"

"Faraway things—like Germany."

"What's Germany?"

"A place."

"Is it a good place?"

"Not very, I'm afraid—not just now. Come along,
trot!"

Together they trotted down the street which had once
been a road to the country, and in a half hour or so the
house loomed up a mass of light and cheer. Sandy and
Tommy had last year devised a system of indirect lighting
upon the snow-covered trees which was far more effective
than the usual string of small electric bulbs. Tonight
Sandy had turned the lights on early, being an extravagant
miss. He had not yet seen her, for she had left her
Christmas shopping to do in Chedbury, her finishing
school being in a remote spot on the Hudson, and she
had used all her available afternoons for theater mati-
nees, to which she was addicted.

When he and Mark entered the house she was whirling

in a solitary dance of her own under the mistletoe in the hall, and not another soul was in sight. She fell upon him ardently and with kisses when he came in, and she knelt to hug Mark. She was still satisfyingly a girl, with none of the disturbing signs of womanhood. Her short hair, just escaping red, her honestly freckled short nose, and gray-green eyes did not as yet spell beauty.

"I hope you've got my Christmas present," he said by way of a mild preliminary joke.

"I did, you selfish thing," she said laughing. "I've got everybody's presents and I like all I got and I hope people will give me the same things. Dad, I bought Mother a tiny bottle of real perfume—rose! It cost so much that I'm strapped."

"How much do you need?" He put his hand to his pocket, accustomed to this situation.

"Oh, Dad, not tonight—I can't shop tomorrow anyway —but before I go back to school. Mother said I was to take Mark and give him his supper and put him straight to bed."

"I'm going to stay up for the party," Mark shouted, preparing tears.

"When you're six," Edward reminded.

"I'll be going on six soon, next year maybe," Mark retorted.

"Not this year," Edward said with firmness. He did not want this child's fine body destroyed by unwisdom, and he hardened his heart to Mark's loud cries as his sister led him away.

The rooms were warm and beautiful, decked with holly as they were, the chandeliers lighted, the satin sofas gleaming softly. The fires were laid but not lit. It was a home of which any man could be proud. Piece by piece he and Margaret had replaced the cheap things of their first years and now there was not a table, not a chair, of which to be ashamed. He liked only a few pictures on his walls, and when they had been in Italy they had brought back four fine small paintings, not old masterpieces, but good enough to draw the admiration of those who knew such art. The heavy curtains were drawn over the windows and there was a smell of spice in the air, a dash of rum with it. At this hour Margaret would be superintending the eggnog, and he would not disturb her. At the far end of the library, now that the rooms were thrown together, the Christmas tree shone tall and green, decorated in silver. He liked a big tree, remembering the meager trees of his own boyhood.

Then in some haste he pulled out the heavy gold watch his father had left him. He must dress early, for he had to go and fetch his mother and Louise.

The year after his father's death it had become evident that his mother must not live alone, and he had not suggested that she live with him, divining that his house would not be the more peaceful for bringing his mother and Margaret under one roof. Instead he had sought out his sister, living then with another teacher in a small apartment, and with difficulty he had persuaded her to go home and live with their mother.

He had been surprised at the stubbornness with which Louise had met his idea. "It isn't as if you had a real home of your own," he had said.

She had looked at him with strange pale eyes. "That's the very reason I don't want to go," she had replied.

In the end she had gone, however, and he had tried to make it up to her by putting some new comforts into the house, an oil burner, and a new refrigerator instead of the old icebox. Louise had received the benefits in silence. But silence was natural to her. He had no idea what she thought about anything, though he acknowledged that in her tall narrow way she had grown rather distinguished looking, and two years ago she had been appointed assistant to the principal of the Chedbury school. He was sure she was better at administration than at teaching.

He went upstairs and dressed carefully in the new evening things that he had bought just before the depression at Margaret's insistence. He had resisted her because, not having put on weight, he had thought his college clothes would last him the rest of his life. But as usual, when she appealed to his vanity for her own sake, he had yielded. She had chosen the material, a violet black over which he had demurred because of the price.

"This suit you really may wear the rest of your life," she had argued.

So he had yielded again, and then had been secretly glad to have done so, because the garments were cut to fit his tall bony frame and with a pleasure which he would have been ashamed to acknowledge, he enjoyed the softness of the satin linings.

He looked into the pantry on his way out. Its old-fashioned size was never at better advantage than upon such an occasion, and presiding over the caterer and his minions was Margaret, her hair curling about her face, her cheeks scarlet with heat and excitement. She looked at him.

"Oh, Ned, you're dressed already! Is it so late? What did you do to Mark? He's so excited. I must get dressed at once if you're going for Louise and Mother. Do taste this —it's champagne cup. I made it because so many people secretly don't like eggnog and are ashamed to say so on Christmas." She poured half a glass of the mixture and he drank it, after the first taste, with appreciation.

"Really good!" he exclaimed.

She flushed with his praise, and he would like to have kissed her but could not, under the covertly staring eyes of the minions.

"Don't hurry," he told her. "I shall take my time getting home. Mother's always too early."

He went away, having backed his car out of the garage with unusual skill, for he was not a good driver, far less skillful than any of his older children, and they were apt to blame him for small scratches and scrapes on the fenders. The car was a good one and he was proud of it. He would not for any reason have possessed the showy affair the Seatons had bought some five years ago, which had a glass pane between themselves and poor old Job Brummel, who, though their chauffeur, was still and always would be little more than a handyman. Thomas Seaton had hired Job the year after Bill Core died of old age, because of his strangely English profile, inherited from some faraway ancestor who came to America from London. "Makes me feel as though I was sitting in a 'ackney coach," Thomas said with exaggerated cockney-ism.

Edward drove carefully, mindful of ice freezing now on top of the snow, and aware of unsteadiness under the wheels. He wondered if he should have put on chains, which he did not know how to do in any case. In his secret heart he wondered, too, if he ought not hire a driver when the children went back to school. He could not be sure whether in Chedbury it would be thought pretentious. Though again, he reflected, it might be considered only some of Margaret's Seaton blood, but no, damn it, he would not take refuge behind that. If he wanted a hired man to drive his car, he would have him. But overhead could creep up, and the depression was still far from over. He fell to ruminating again on the painful state of the world, put awry by the war and not yet straight, while clouds of war loomed again over human horizons.

Then resolutely he put away his haunting fears and reaching his mother's house he parked the car fairly well, and went in. His mother was dressed and waiting in the living room, her coat and gloves laid together. Louise was reading a magazine, that new digest, he noticed, which he had declared was ruining the book trade. Who would buy a book for two dollars and a half when he could get such a bulk of reading material for a quarter? Louise was wearing a new dress, a dull blue taffeta that was rather becoming. Her blond hair had not grayed and she put aside her glasses as he came in.

"I'm early," he announced. He bent to kiss his mother's dried cheek. Her middle-aged fleshiness had dropped away and she was withered and old. Her scanty white hair was not curled, but she had put into the knot on top of her head her one treasure, a jeweled comb that his father's grandmother had once owned—how, he had never thought to inquire.

"You look quite handsome, Mother," he said, sitting down. "I never saw the comb look better. It becomes your hair since you've grown white."

"I'm going to give it to Margaret one of these days," she declared. Her voice was as piercing as ever and her eyes were undimmed.

He caught a creeping hostile look on his sister's face but she did not speak. "You must give it to Louise," he said.

"No, for she isn't going to get married, so far as I can see," his mother complained. "I want Mary should have it, really, but I suppose it ought to go to Margaret first, in order."

"I don't see why," he said. "Margaret has her own things to inherit."

"Maybe I will give it to Mary, then," his mother went on. "Did I tell you it came from Spain once?"

"No, did it?" He was interested now. Spain, that country of angels and devils, that past heaven and hotbed of present evil! Only last Sunday he had seen a picture in the Sunday newspaper of the plump portentous little man who was rising to power there. How could people worship such gods? At least let them be beautiful.

"There's a mystery about this comb," his mother said with some reserve. "Your great grandfather gave it to his wife honestly enough but his mother had it from somebuddy—nobuddy knows who. Anyway, it's said that's how the Haslatts come by their dark skins."

He was amused at this possibility in past ages and he laughed soundlessly.

"Oh, Mother," Louise said with impatience. "Everybody is always talking about Spanish ancestors."

"Well, we have the comb, haven't we?" his mother's voice was triumphant.

"What if it's only Portuguese?" Edward inquired with mischief.

His mother rose. "You two are just as contrary as ever you were. Let's go. If we're early maybe I can help Margaret."

He knew Margaret's dismay at this possibility and he made haste to put his mother off. "She's got the caterers there tonight—everything's ready, I believe, but we might as well go."

His mother and Louise both put on their day coats, and he made a mental note that next Christmas he would placate Louise still further by a fur evening cape, and then they were all in the car and he was driving his careful way homeward. His mother, sitting beside him, clutched the arm of the seat in a fashion disheartening to him, but he did not mention it to her, aware that for one who had grown up with horses and buggies, a motor car would always be a hazard.

Once in the house he ensconced his mother in a large armchair and leaving Louise to her own devices he hastened upstairs to find his little son and bid him good night.

Mark was in his bed, his arms under his head, the

covers drawn to his neck and his face unusually thoughtful.

"I was waiting for you," he said at the sight of his father.

"I thought you would be," Edward replied and bent to
kiss him.

That cheek, so soft, so fragrant under his lips, nearly
broke his heart with love. Lest he betray his extravagant
tenderness he said in his driest voice, "You'd better go to
sleep before the noise begins."

"I like Christmas," Mark said dreamily, "but I don't
like the night before, because here I must lie, alone in
the dark, while people are alive and laughing everywhere."

"You're alive, too," Edward said sharply.

"Not like in the day," Mark said simply.

The child was really too precocious, Edward told himself. He must talk with Margaret about it after the holidays were over. They must take care of this son, this
treasure.

"I shall be coming back to see you every now and
then," he said, "and I will light the candles on the mantel, so that you will not be in the dark."

He lit the candles one and the other, and turned to
catch his son's smile. "Thank you, Daddy," Mark said, and
closed his eyes to sleep.

Christmas Eve proceeded according to a pattern long
established and well enjoyed. Chedbury, out of deference
to one whom it recognized as a leading citizen, though of
a sort they did not wholly comprehend, had years ago decided against any other event on the twenty-fourth of
December. Edward Haslatt's party was paramount. It was
a heterogeneous affair. To its earlier hours came those
citizens who, though entirely welcome to stay out the evening, knew instinctively that eleven o'clock was the hour
at which they should appear before host and hostess to
say good-by, to give their polite thanks for a "nice time,"
and to wish a merry Christmas.

The party remained somewhat staid and decorous, a
family affair, for those earlier hours. Only near midnight
did its loose strands knit themselves into something ho-
mogeneous and close. Conversation was no longer labored,

and laughter rippled through the rooms. The band, which Edward each year brought from Boston, put aside waltzes and fox trots and set up the catching intoxicating rhythms that had taken such hold upon the youth during the depression. Since there was neither hope nor freedom in the world of reason, they found it in their bodies.

Edward did not like it. He was slightly fatigued by the task of being host to people he had known all his life, to whom he was Ed Haslatt, the son of old Mark, and yet from whom he was now separated because he had built up a business that published books many of which Chedbury could not read. Never quite sure of where Ed left off and Mr. Edward Haslatt began, their old ease was gone, except as Edward himself determinedly kept it. But this, too, was tiring, and as he grew older and his business forced him to become aware of a world of which Chedbury could know nothing, and yet of which it was nonetheless a part in these strange times, he found himself increasingly solitary.

Now, the rooms half emptied, he sat down in an easy chair in a corner of the library to take a few minutes' rest. The champagne cup had gone well. The eggnog would please those who were left. He could see old Thomas Seaton sipping his foaming glass with dreamy pleasure. The old man had given himself up to the joys of the flesh. Everybody was worried about him and Dr. Wynne warned him every time he saw him. Even tonight he was looking at him, while he sat beside Mrs. Seaton. They were talking about old Thomas, and Mrs. Seaton assuredly was saying the same thing she always said: "Thomas says he may as well die an enjoyable death. He says he doesn't want to die hungry and thirsty, and go empty and dry into eternity."

The young people were forming themselves together into that new thing, that rhumba, a savage performance. He saw Lewis Harrow go up to Margaret and propose himself as her partner. Thank God she was shaking her head. Harrow looked all too well in evening clothes. His dark hair had not silvered properly. Instead it had stayed coal black, and grown white only at the sides, as though it were dyed. Yet in justice he had to acknowledge that Lew would not stoop to such folly as hair dyeing.

Now, as though having invited and been refused by his hostess excused him for willfully doing what might make his host angry, Harrow went straight to Mary. She had avoided all other invitations, flitting here and there in her gown of cloudy white, making a pretense of seeing that her grandmothers were tended. Now as Edward watched her he saw a pretty tableau, too distant for him to hear the conversation. The child bent over her Grandmother Haslatt with all her conscious grace, and he saw his mother melt under the loving deference that Mary showed her, and that he was none too sure was not entirely a knowing process of charm. His mother was saying something. Then she took the high Spanish comb from her hair and gave it to Mary. The child's hair was short and how could she wear it? Ah, she was kneeling, and he saw his mother with a sort of tender triumph gather the dark curls together and catch them on top of Mary's head and hold them with the jeweled comb. Mary rose to her feet just as Harrow came near and she looked up at him with that dewy shyness, which again might be only a process of her conscious charm. Whatever it was, what man could resist it? He did not believe that Harrow said a word. The fellow simply held out his arms, and Mary went into them and then the band, as if the performers saw and understood, began to quicken the subtle rhythm, to sharpen its passionate accents, and Harrow and Mary were dancing away as one, and all eyes were on them.

Edward hid his own eyes behind his hand. The fellow danced supremely well, and he was wooing Mary with all the skills of the flesh, and she, at the very age when in spite of her delicacies, it was the flesh she craved, could not but respond. He had not the heart to blame her, remembering himself and Margaret at that age. But they had not such freedom as this thing, this rhumba, with all its license, could and did allow.

He rose, intolerably stung, and went toward the dancers. Margaret, watching him, met him, and slipped her hand under his arm.

"Everything is going well, I think," she said with calm.

"It seems so," Edward replied.

"How do you like my gown?" she demanded.

He looked down at her. It was a violet velvet, very pale and soft. "It's new, isn't it?"

She laughed. "Oh, Ned, you never quite know, do you? Well, yes, it is. Do you think the color is a little old for me?"

"If you mean do you look old in it, the answer is no. Certainly not. Who's that girl Tommy is dancing with?"

"Somebody he brought back from Boston with him, on the spur of the moment."

"I don't like her looks."

"She's very pretty."

"Too obvious."

The girl, wrapped in a sort of sheath of gold, was as thin as a stick and her straight yellow hair floated in ribbons behind her violently moving head.

"What's her name?"

"I don't know—Dinny something."

"Queer times," he commented.

With such camouflage did he conceal the approach to the one thing about which he was thinking. Now he came to it. "Margaret, we've got to do something about Harrow and Mary. I simply won't have it. Why, she might want to marry him!"

"I know, dear. But we can't, you know, any more than I can do anything about my father's fourth cup of eggnog which I see him taking this very minute."

But she would try, nevertheless. Overcome by anxiety she left him swiftly and crossed the floor to the long table in the dining room where old Thomas, already shaky, was holding his cup toward a laughing woman who was filling it.

Thus deserted, Edward felt the blood rise to his brain and intoxicated with his own anger he walked firmly among the dancers and approached Lewis Harrow and touched him on the arm.

"Come with me a moment, please," he said distinctly.

Harrow surprised, came out of his trance. "Can't business wait?" he demanded.

"No," Edward said. He met Mary's hot eyes with a cold stare and with Harrow beside him he led the way to his own small study which of all the downstairs rooms had not been thrown open. The sudden quiet behind the shut door only hardened his resolve. "You needn't

225

sit down, Harrow," he said with the same cold distinctiveness of enunciation. "I simply want to say that you are to leave my daughter alone. She's a child."

Harrow blinked. He had been well aware of Edward's anger at the station this morning, but he had been determined to ignore it. He would ignore it now. "She's not quite a child," he said mildly.

"In comparison to you she is," Edward said. "I don't forget all between us that is good and useful to us both, but I'd throw it all away rather than see her——"

"What?" Harrow asked with malicious mischief.

"Commit her heart to you," Edward said gravely.

Harrow flung himself into one of the leather armchairs. "You're so damned serious," he complained.

"About Mary I am," Edward agreed.

Harrow gave him a strange look. He smoothed back the white wings of his hair with his open palms, and lit a cigarette. "Very well, then, I'll be serious. I consider it rather a privilege for a young girl to fall in love for the first time with an older man—especially me."

Edward gazed at him with actual hate. Underneath it his old jealousy burned, transferred now to this young and tender creature who was his daughter and yet somehow compound, too, of Margaret.

"And how do you feel toward her?" he asked in a thick voice. "When you've made her—love you—then what will you do?"

Harrow looked away. "I don't know," he said at last. "I really don't know."

"It's wicked of you," Edward said.

Harrow glanced at him and away. "These things grow."

At this moment the door was flung open. Mary of course he had been expecting, but Mary angry and unreasonable. This was not she. Mary was weeping and she seized his hand.

"Oh, Dad," she gasped. "Oh, Dad——"

"What, dear?"

"Grandfather—he's—he's—— Mother says you must come—oh quickly, please, Dad!"

He had no time to decide. Margaret needed him. He left Mary, catching in his distraction one last glimpse of her. Harrow had risen and put out his arms, and she had gone into them, He heard her crying. "Oh, Lew, he's dead —he's dead—I can't bear to see him—"

But he did not pause. Margaret needed him.

Beside the Christmas tree lay Thomas Seaton. He had gone to toast the tree, making a joke of it as he had made a joke of everyting in his life.

"Evergreen forever!" he had been declaiming, before the laughing guests. "I who am about to depart—salute thee, the eternal—"

By some strange coincidence of life and death he had fallen at the very moment he lifted the cup to his lips, and the blazing lights of the tree shone down on him as his knees crumpled. Margaret had run to him, but Tom had already caught him. Mrs. Seaton had turned away her head, and Tommy had found Dr. Wynne, napping behind a tubbed palm tree.

Edward hurried to the gathering crowd and parted them with his hands. Margaret sat with her father's head in her lap. She was tearless, and her face was ashen as she lifted it to her husband.

"Come, dear," he said. "Tommy, take your mother's place. Where's Sandy?"

"She ran upstairs—s-sir," Tommy stammered. He looked sick and pale.

"Nothing we can do," the doctor was murmuring. "It came as I feared it would."

"The way he wanted it," Mrs. Seaton said. "Margaret, take me away, please."

Between them they led the quivering old lady upstairs, and into the gray and rose guest room. She was almost entirely calm, and the blow for which she had prepared herself so long had fallen at last and yet she could not quite bear it as she had imagined she could.

"I shall lie down for a bit. Leave me, please, Margaret. I must be alone. Edward, you'll see to everything. Tom's not reliable enough."

"Of course," he said.

"Mother, let me stay—" Margaret began, but Mrs. Seaton would not have it. With a sort of subdued wildness she shook her head. "I must be quite alone—really, I must, just for a bit."

So they left her on the bed under the rose satin quilt, her eyes closed and dry, her lips trembling.

Outside the door Edward took his wife into his arms. "I think of you," he muttered, "only of you."

He put out of his mind the image of Mary alone with Harrow. Doubtless the fellow had told her what had passed. Never mind now—nothing mattered but this straight silent woman in his arms, his beloved, his own. She had buried her face in his shoulder and he thought she would weep but she did not. She held him hard, her hands under his arms and clutching his shoulders, for a long moment. Then she lifted her face and began to cry. "It's strange," she sobbed. "Somehow I clung to Dad in my heart—maybe all daughters do."

Did they? Then what about his own daughter? Who knew what was happening in that small closed room behind the shut door? Old Thomas had not really wanted Margaret to marry him, either, and she had been as willful as Mary was today. Ah, Margaret was his first love, his only love. He put the thought of his child away from him. No child should come between them now. He pressed her head close upon his shoulder and began his comfort. "You were always the best daughter in the world to him. He loved you better than any of his children."

"Do you think so, Ned? Really?" She was trying to control herself, tightening her throat, stopping her tears. She looked up at him and he saw her wet lashes and her eyes blue beneath them and his heart was wrenched with the old painful love, infinitely increased by the years and all that had been and had not been between them.

"I wish I could comfort you," he said with tender wistfulness. "I wish I knew how. I love you so terribly."

He saw her face, so schooled by life, by wifehood and motherhood, soften and quiver and break into a trembling smile, molten with sorrow. "Oh, Ned—oh, Ned—I wish I had been a better wife to you, darling."

"But you have been—you've been perfect."

"No, I haven't. I haven't been half I wanted to be— that day we were first married."

"Then I haven't known it," he said. With astonishment he considered what she had just said, his arms still hard about her. Had she indeed been suffering some private remorse? But for what? He could not imagine.

Then holding her thus, before they returned to the things that had to be done, it came to him that even as

228

he had reproached himself now and again for allowing his worries and cares, even his success, to separate him from her, so she too might have like causes for reproach. They still had a great deal to learn about one another.

"We've only begun to be married," he declared suddenly. "It's taken us all these years to get going—earning a living, raising children—now let's just be married, will you, sweetheart?"

The old name that he had not used for so long, scarcely since she had been a mother to his children, was new again and infinitely exciting. She lifted her lips and he kissed her, the most profound, the most passionate kiss that they had ever shared. All that had been was only the approach to what was yet to be. What was that she had said? That she had clung secretly, as daughters do, to her father! Well, that was over. He had no longer to compete with Thomas Seaton's charm and humor and gaiety. He had Margaret now to himself, forever. Reproaching himself in the midst of sorrow, he pressed her head to his shoulder and she yielded. They stole yet another moment to be alone together and the years slipped away.

Yet underneath the steadfast duty with which he supported his beloved, he suffered an agony of uneasiness. What had taken place between Mary and Lewis Harrow in his study when he was so suddenly called away? He had left them alone together and what more natural than that Harrow had undertaken to comfort his Mary? In the girl's shaken state, weeping for the grandfather she had loved, what more natural than that she would have accepted such comfort?

Edward hastened downstairs, having put Margaret to bed with promises of his swift return to her. But Harrow was gone, as were all the guests. His children were behaving beautifully. Tom had taken his father's body home, and Harrow, Sandy explained, had gone with him to help him.

Edward paused a moment for this younger daughter, perceiving in her manner a humility new and overeager.

"Were you afraid of Grandfather, dear?" he inquired, remembering that Tommy had reported her flight.

Her freckles were submerged in sudden color. "I'm

fearfully ashamed—especially when I'm thinking of being a doctor."

"It is hard the first time," he agreed. A doctor? He was not sure women should be doctors, and he forbore discussion of it now. In the distance he saw Mary. "You two girls had better straighten things up," he told Sandy.

"Yes, Dad," she said obediently.

His mother and Louise were still there. In the suddenly quiet house all of them began now to straighten the rooms, putting the chairs in their places, picking up the paper streamers and toy hats, the empty cups and glasses and restoring the house to decency again. Only the Christmas tree had been left blazing and Edward, unable to bear its garishness, touched the button that put out the lights. Thus abruptly, too, had the light of life gone from the shining and vigorous old man.

His daughters were subdued and they moved from room to room and when all was done they bade him good night quietly. He called Mary back.

"Mary!"

"Yes, Father?"

"Wait a minute, please."

"I was going up to Grandmother."

"I think she'd rather be alone."

"But I want to be with her."

Their eyes met, their wills crossed and clashed and he yielded.

"Very well."

"Good night, Father."

"Good night, my dear."

She ran upstairs swiftly, her cloudy skirts held high, the Spanish comb gleaming in her hair, and he sat down exhausted. Yet he must now take his mother and sister home. They were waiting.

"I can drive, unless you think you need the car," Louise suggested.

"I had better have the car tonight," Edward said, considering.

"I never thought old Mr. Seaton would go this way," his mother mourned.

"It was a good way to go," Edward replied. He shrank from his mother's interest in the dying and the dead.

"I suppose you will have to plan the funeral," she went on.

"Joe Barclay will do that," Edward said.

"Oughtn't you go over to the house tonight?" she suggested.

"I suppose so," Edward said unwillingly, "unless Margaret needs me."

"We'd better go home since we're no more use here."

So saying his mother rose and a moment later they were riding through the cold and snowy night. Lights shone from the windows of houses where belated parents were still filling Christmas stockings and decorating trees and the silence broke when the bells of the church began to ring softly the notes of a Christmas hymn. Children half waking would know that Christmas Day had come, would smile and sleep again. Only an old man would never wake.

The solemnity of the ending of Thomas Seaton's life filled Edward's mind. He had never loved his father-in-law, aware, while refusing to acknowledge it, that there had been some secret rivalry between them. Margaret had belonged to them both. She had clung to her father—that was what she had said tonight—but how much? Perhaps the withdrawal of which he had been so often conscious was because the core of her heart had clung to another, not him. It was not the common rivalry between father and husband but between two different men, the one gay and careless, rich in living, humorous, articulate, his words flowing easily, and the other—himself. He remembered absurdly, after these many years, that Thomas Seaton had once wanted Margaret to marry Harold Ames, who was now the president of a great bank in New York. Edward saw his picture sometimes in the Sunday newspapers, opening a campaign for the Republican party, heading a drive for the Red Cross, giving a check to the mayor for city relief. The handsome smooth face might have been Thomas Seaton's own, a quarter of a century younger. Margaret had not, so far as he knew, ever seen Harold Ames again. But his memory perhaps had survived in her love for her father and her father had forever conditioned her heart. The old doubt that he, Edward Haslatt, could ever wholly possess her, added despair to his dejection.

"Here you are, Mother," he said and drew up at the doorway of his father's house.

"Don't get out," she said, preparing the difficult descent.

"Of course I shall," he retorted.

He got out and saw her to the door, unlocking it and turning on the light in the hall before he stooped to kiss her good night. Louise had come in and closed the door, as he found when he turned to go out. The house had seemed strange since his father's death, a house lived in only by women, who in their unconscious fashion had removed from it bit by bit all his father's ways and possessions.

"Good night, Louise," he said, and opened the door.

To his surprise she followed him to the porch and closed the door on the old woman toiling up the stairs.

"Ed, I don't know as I ought to add trouble to this night," Louise said.

He looked down at her pale still face, wrapped around by a knitted woolen scarf that she called a fascinator.

"What do you mean?" he demanded.

She hesitated. "Maybe I oughtn't to say."

"For God's sake, Louise," he exclaimed, "why can you never speak out?"

"You've no call to swear at me, Ed. I only want to do what's right."

Her trembling lips infuriated him. All the anger he never showed to Margaret and Mary sprang out at this dull and pallid sister of his. "I hate hemming and hawing. If you have something to say, then say it."

"All right, and don't blame me—but I saw Mary and that—that—"

"Well?" His voice stabbed her.

"Lew Harrow was hugging her."

"That doesn't mean anything nowadays," he mumbled.

"After you went upstairs," she continued doggedly. "And I heard her say, I will—I will, two times, like that."

"Will what?"

"How could I know?"

"Just how did it happen that you heard anything at all?"

"I went—I went—"

Her voice faltered, her head dropped, and she untied

the woolen ends about her neck. A monstrous idea occurred to him. She had gone to see what Harrow was doing!

"Why did it interest you to know what Harrow was doing?"

His own injustice occurred to him with these words. Why did it interest him to know the secrets of his sister?

"I didn't think you'd want Mary—to—to—"

"I have never known you to take so much interest in Mary."

In the light of the circle of electric lights, which made the meager Christmas decoration of the doorway, he saw his sister fling up her head in one of her rare fits of anger. He knew these outbursts, coming perhaps once a year after months of creeping silence, and he braced himself.

"You think you're so wonderful, don't you, Ed? You think you're much better than the rest of the family. Yes, you do. And that's what Uncle Henry thinks, too. You never go to see poor old Uncle Henry, though now he's in the county home."

"What in heaven's name has that old skinflint to do with what you were talking about?"

It was true that he had paid no attention to this old relative who had bullied his father in days when the family was poor. Louise could not remember, nor could Baynes, those early years when he had heard his parents worrying lest Henry might be offended and withdraw the pitiful wages he paid his younger brother Mark.

"Because you think you're so fine," Louise raged. "You think Mary is better than any of the other girls. Well, I taught her in school and I tell you she isn't. She's run after Lew Harrow for years—simply years. She's like any of the other silly girls."

"Stop!" He held his hands to keep from striking this foolish old maid who was his sister.

"I won't stop. I'll tell you the truth if nobody else will. Do you think a man like Lew Harrow could really care for a child, a schoolgirl like Mary? Why, he's famous, he's had lots of women, I guess—anyway, he could."

Her voice broke and as always happened her anger could not sustain itself. She began to cry and turning to the door she fumbled for the knob, the fascinator falling over her face.

He understood suddenly what had made the rage and he was embarrassed, and ashamed. They had never been close, he and this sister, and he did not want to know her secrets. He would not tell her what he saw, that she hated his Mary because she herself had, in her feeble way, felt the strength of Harrow's charm—even she! And in her poor way she had fallen in love with him. He pitied her. Impatience changed in him to pity, but shame was still stronger. He would be ashamed before Harrow, lest that man, so acute in the knowledge of the human heart, might already know what he had not known until this moment.

"Let me open the door for you, Louise," he said. His voice was husky. In the space of a minute the curtain between them had been thrown back and he saw her as she had been, a pale little girl hostile to boys and, it seemed to him, including him somehow among boys. She had never learned to come out of herself, and she had never let anyone come in to her heart or mind until now. The monstrous fantasy of her imagination, in dreaming that Harrow could think of her—but perhaps she had not so dreamed. Perhaps it had been enough that she thought of him, that he filled her secret heart, so long as he was not married. She had not minded, perhaps, that he had loved other women unknown to her, but it was intolerable that he might love Mary.

He was fumbling at the door knob, too, while she tried not to sob. He found it and they went in and he stood, not knowing what to say or do. "I am sorry, Louise," he kept saying.

"There's nothing to be sorry for," she gasped. She did not look at him.

He took her hand to press it, but it lay lifeless in his palm and he let it go again. "This has been a trying evening on us all," he stumbled. "You'd better go to bed. I suppose I ought to stop at the Seaton house on my way home, so that I can tell Margaret just what's happened."

She turned from him and went upstairs, trying not to cry.

The cold air was comforting when he was outside again, the cold air and being alone. He would have liked to drive off into the night to have time to disentangle this strange web of affairs in his own house, but he knew he must not. He would stop by and see whether Tommy had gone home, and see what needed to be done for Thomas Seaton yet tonight, if anything could be done. At least it might comfort Margaret more than his presence if he came in saying that all was well there.

Christmas lights had been put out, the streets were still, when he turned in at the circular driveway of the big white house. No one had turned off the two flaming Christmas trees at either side of the door and they blazed on. The lights downstairs were still lit, and upstairs there was one light, in Thomas Seaton's own room.

He rang and no one answered, and trying the latch he found the door open and he walked in.

"Hello," Tom's voice called, his drunken voice, as Edward instantly recognized.

"It is I," Edward replied. He went to the door of the living room and saw Tom there, unsteady upon his feet, pacing back and forth, declaiming to Lewis Harrow, who sat sprawled but sober in a big chair, and to Tommy, his own son, who held a wineglass in his hands from which he drank in small gulps trying not to show his distaste before his uncle.

"No one understood me except my father," Tom was mourning. "He knew how I felt when Daintree turned me down. Ever know I was in love with Lady Daintree of Montrose Hall? She loved me, too, but her papa wouldn't see it and my mamma told me to come home. I came then, though if it had been now, I wouldn't. I went to my father. He said, 'Never mind, Tom, my son, there's lots of women in the world.' That's where he was wrong—women of course, but not one like my Dainty. A man doesn't live alone, of course—not by bread alone and all that. Fioretta Carosi knows, too. Ever see my Fioretta?"

"I've taken a look at her," Harrow said, with interest.

Upon this Edward came into the room. "Tommy, it is time for you to go home," he said coldly to his son. "Your mother will be worrying about you. Go now, this minute."

Tommy set down his glass. "I only came to help Uncle Tom."

"I will help him now," Edward said in the same cold voice, the voice that Tommy had recognized long ago as the voice of one almighty. "Tell your mother that I shall be home soon."

"But how am I to go?"

"I'll take you," Harrow said. He rose as he spoke. "The minister's upstairs, Ed—and so are Baynes and Sandra. I thought I'd better stay with Tom, who's in his cups, as you see."

Tom had let himself sink into his father's chair and was beginning to weep.

"I'll put him to bed," Edward said.

He stood while Harrow and Tommy left the room, and then he lifted Tom by the armpits and pulled him to his feet. "Come, Tom, you're going to bed."

"The kindest man," Tom was muttering. "The best God-damned father—always understand—"

Edward guided him firmly toward the stairs.

"Even said I could marry little Fioretta if I wanted to —know Fioretta Carosi, Ed? No, 'course you wouldn't know—I don't want to marry her—that's what I told him—it's a comedown."

Tom was clinging to the balustrade, trying to lift his foot for the stair. A door opened, and at the top of the stairs Baynes stood looking down. "Leave him to me, Ed," he called down softly. "I've done this before—the night before your wedding, for the first time, but plenty of times since."

"Who's this Fioretta he talks about?" Edward demanded.

"John's sister—didn't you know?"

"Good God, no!"

"I didn't tell you. I thought it would mess things up in the shop—but I thought maybe Margaret had told you."

"Does she know?"

"Sandra told her."

Supporting a now somnolent form, they took Tom upstairs, his head lying on Baynes's shoulder. The two brothers looked at each other.

"Queer family we've married into," Baynes said with a ghastly smile. "Leave him to me, now. I don't undress him. I just pitch him on the bed. Sandra is in there with the old man. She might like it if you went in."

He nodded toward Thomas Seaton's room, and leaving him Edward tiptoed toward the half-open door.

Thomas Seaton lay on his great bed, dressed as he had been at the party, a triumphant smile upon his bearded lips. He had smiled as he died, and the smile held. Joseph Barclay knelt beside the bed, and Sandra stood, her face pale as stone and as immobile, looking down at her father. The minister did not move as Edward came in. He was praying and he finished his prayer.

"And if it be Thy will, O Almighty God, receive unto Thyself this soul. We who know nothing of that path which extends beyond our little world cannot see this soul struggling on its way. But Thou seest, and Thou dost forgive. In Thy name, Amen."

Edward stood silent, until the prayer ended and Joseph Barclay rose to his feet. They shook hands silently. Then the minister said, "I have made all arrangements, I think, Haslatt. The men will be here in the morning to see to things. Mrs. Baynes here has told me what her father wanted. It seems he foresaw something like this."

"I've never seen anybody dead before," Sandra said suddenly. "It's strange when it is my own father."

"Death is not strange," Joseph Barclay said. "Nothing is as strange as life."

"He looks alive," Edward mused.

"He is alive!" Sandra cried. "I'll never believe he is dead. I won't let him be dead. I'll keep him alive thinking about him—forever."

Neither man answered this. Then the words smote Edward with meaning. So might Margaret too keep her father alive, thinking of him, forever.

"I can't do anything here," he murmured. "Baynes is with you, Sandra, and I had better go home to Margaret."

He went away forgetting to say good night, and carried with him the picture of that huge and heavy frame, that mammoth man, that tender father beloved by all his children, whose ghost they would not lay.

His house, when he stepped in the front door, seemed unnaturally still. The hall light burned, but the other rooms were dark. Even Margaret's room, he had noticed as he came up the drive, was unlighted, and the guest room where Mrs. Seaton had gone had been dark ever since they left her there, although Margaret, he supposed, must surely have been to see her mother before she slept.

He hung his coat in the closet under the stair, and put his hat upon its shelf. Then he paused, halted by some instinct that he did not understand. Surely the house was too silent! He was not a man of intuition except where the few, the very few, he loved were concerned, but he was aware now of that intuition. Something was wrong.

He mounted the stairs, agitated in spite of his exhaustion, his heart beating wildly, about what he did not know, and hastening toward his own room, he put on the light. The door to Margaret's room was open slightly and now he went to it and threw it wide. She was there. The light fell on her sleeping form. He went near to her and reaching into the pocket where he kept his pipe and matches, he lit a match. The flame shone upon her face. She had been weeping. Her lids were swollen, and the lashes were still wet. Now under the light she opened her eyes heavily.

"Ned—I waited so long."

"Is everything all right?" he cried.

She turned over and pushed back her loosened hair. "What do you mean?"

"The house feels queer."

"I haven't been out of my room except to go and see Mother. But she still didn't want me."

"Didn't you go to see Mark?"

She shook her head. "I thought of course he was asleep."

His first thought now for his son, he turned and went out of the room and across the hall. At the door of Mark's room he touched the light again and it came on softly under a shaded lamp. His eyes were already on the child's bed, and he tiptoed to it. Mark was safe, asleep and tranquil. In this night of death and sorrow he had remained in peace, unknowing. Leaning on the foot of the bed, Edward felt something under his hand and looking down he saw Mark's stocking. Some time after he had been put to bed the child had got up and hung his small stocking at the end of the crib. It dangled there, empty.

Edward's heart smote him. They had given up the habit of hanging stockings when the other children outgrew their babyhood, and had allowed the tree to be their Christmas symbol. But Mark must have heard about a stocking and feeling lonely, he had climbed out of bed and found his own and hung it, a sign of wanting something that he did not have. Oh, these children of his! So did Edward's heart cry out within his breast. How had he failed them? With all his love constantly awake and trembling over them, they were always going beyond him.

He tiptoed back to the door, intent upon returning to tell Margaret that the stocking must be filled somehow from the store accumulated for Mark tomorrow, when in the hall his eyes fell upon the door of Mary's room. It stood partially open and he paused. She had taken during the last year to locking her door at night and when he had remonstrated at this, half hurt because she wanted to receive his good-night kiss downstairs, she had remained sweetly firm. "I'm really grown up now," she had replied.

"But you're at home," he had reminded her.

"I like my door locked," she had replied simply.

Now his instinct was roused again. Not Mark—then Mary? He prowled toward the door, half afraid lest she cry out against him. Yet she might have merely forgotten it in her weariness. He pushed it open and stood, listening for the sound of her breathing. He heard nothing. The room was still, the air warm. She had not opened the window.

He turned on the light. The room was empty, the bed not slept in.

"Margaret!" he called in a low voice.

She heard him instantly and came running in her nightgown, her hair flying over her shoulders. She saw the empty room, the smooth bed, and began to hasten here and there, while he stood staring and bewildered.

"Oh, the silly child!" she muttered.

She was opening drawers, the closet, a hatbox, a jewelry case.

"Oh, what has she done now!" she muttered.

Then she turned to him and flung her arms about him. "Ned, don't look like that."

"Where has she gone?" he asked.

"I don't know—I don't know! Oh, Ned, don't please look so!"

He flung her away from him. "I'm going up to The Eagle."

"Ned, if it's happened——"

"I must go and get the car," he said stupidly.

"No, you will not!" she cried. They were still keeping their voices low, mindful of the other children, mindful of her mother and of Mark. "You will not go! We'll hear. Maybe she's left a note."

She was searching the room again, and he tried to help her, but he felt dull and weary enough to die. His instinct was gone, and he did not know what to do next. There was no note to be found. Mary had never done what she was supposed to.

"I don't know where to turn," he said helplessly. "Where can I go to find her?"

"You shall not go," Margaret declared. "You shall stay here in our house. Come, Ned, come—you will drop." She pulled him by the hand into his room.

But he would not yield to her. "I cannot just accept this—as if it were nothing. Let us think together—where would they go? It is not too late."

"It is too late," she insisted. "Look at the sky!"

It was dawn, and the sky was breaking crimson at the horizon.

"You don't care," he muttered. "You've never cared about her."

"I do care," she answered and began to weep. "I care as much as you do, but I know her better than you ever can. She has got to leave you, Ned—that's what you cannot and will not understand."

"I can bear her leaving me," he insisted, "but not like this and with him!"

"But you must see that it is only like this—and with him—that she can really leave you." They were sitting on the edge of his bed now and her arms were around him.

"You can't understand her," he said. "You can't understand her because you never have loved her as well as the others."

"I understand her because she is the one most like me," she retorted. "She has gone through what I did. She's loved you too much, Ned—as I loved my own father. She hasn't been able to find someone just like you to marry."

"Don't talk like that."

"Oh, Ned, it's true—and she has chosen somebody utterly different from you—so that she can be free of you. Oh, she doesn't know what she's done—she doesn't understand."

"How is it that you understand?" he demanded.

"Because I was like that, Ned." She flung out her arms, imploring him.

"You mean you loved your father—better than me?"

"I always loved the kind of man he was."

"Which I could never be!"

"And that is why I wanted to marry you, to be free of him—can you see that, Ned? Try to see it—for Mary's sake!"

"Then you haven't really loved me all these years!"

"I have—I have! Ned, don't look at me like that, darling! Because I'm going to love you now as I've never known how to love you. My heart has let go. There's only you."

She folded her arms about him again, but he did not reply to her words of love. Yet somehow she had healed him. Mary had so loved him, her father, that she had needed to cut the bond between them. How slow, how blind he was, that he had not seen before that what she must have was the freedom of her own heart!

"I hope she will want to come back," he said humbly.

"If you let her go, of course she will," Margaret comforted him.

"It will take time for me to stick having Lew Harrow here—my son-in-law, good God!"

"Don't think about him."

They sat a long while in silence while the room slowly brightened to dawn. The sun came over the horizon a globe of melted fire and the snow grew pink. Not a merry Christmas, he thought heavily, and then he remembered.

"Margaret, Mark's gone and hung his stocking all by himself."

She rose swiftly. "Oh, the poor babe—where is it?"

"At the foot of his bed. He mustn't find it empty."

"Of course not. I'll rob some of the things I was going to put on the tree for him."

She opened a closet and chose half a dozen small wrapped packages and a jumping jack. Together they stole out of the room and across the hall and standing side by side at the foot of his bed they stuffed the stocking full, and out of the top the jumping jack peered, laughing.

In his bed Mark did not wake. He lay high on his single pillow, his arms outspread, the lashes dark upon his red cheeks.

"How he sleeps!" Edward whispered.

"As if he never meant to wake," Margaret whispered back.

"Don't say that," he said sharply under his breath.

"Oh, Ned—you're overwrought—I didn't mean—"

"I know—forgive me."

He crawled into his bed a few minutes later, agreeing with her that they must try to sleep a little while, with the day ahead. Sleep, he told himself, was impossible until he heard from Mary where they were—and when they were coming back. But he slept at last, and was tortured by dreams of losing Mary somewhere, a small girl who had never grown up, and of searching for her and not being able to find her. Then somehow the little girl she had once been turned to Mark as he was now and it was his son for whom he searched and whom he could not find.

Four

THE STILLNESS of Granite Mountain was rent by the war whoops of two shrill voices. Edward Haslatt looked up mildly from a magazine he was reading, while he waited for his wife and daughter to return from their inspection of some new garments in another room. His twin grandsons, in full Indian regalia, tore around one of the stone buttresses of this fantastic house and raced out of sight. He sighed and returned to the magazine. It was a popular one, full of pictures that he disliked because he thought them meaningless exposures. He had never allowed himself to be interested in the physical aspects of women other than his wife, and now he was well past the age for that sort of thing. For this he was grateful. The struggle of the flesh was over. This was not to say that he did not have proper relations with Margaret. He could and did, as often as he felt inclined, which was decently less often as the years went, and she met his inclination gracefully, if not eagerly. Indeed so smoothly were they attuned now, as they stood upon the brink of old age together, that he occasionally felt that he would like to write a book on marriage from the man's point of view. There was something original in the idea, as he toyed with it. It would have to be done anonymously, of course. He knew he would never do it. Self-revelation, even namelessly, was impossible for him.

Though his life as a modestly successful publisher of books had been spent among writers of all varieties, he continued to be amazed, amused and sometimes repelled by their willingness to strip the covers from their most secret parts. Yet sometimes he envied them the relief of complete revelation, even while he knew he could never achieve it. For one thing, Margaret would certainly know about it, and he shrank from such exposure, even to her. She knew him through and through, of that he was well aware, and yet they had never put each other into words, as once she said they must. He had never learned her trick of ready speech. Perhaps she, however, had learned to read through silence.

He put down the magazine restlessly and getting up he went to the stupendous window of paneless glass which Lewis had built so many years ago. Such windows were uncommon then, and visitors from Chedbury had told each other privately that they would not like to live in all outdoors. What was a house for if not to hide those inside from those outside? Chedbury had not changed much in all these years. Even the Second World War had not changed the people much. Young men had gone away and some had not come back, and Chedbury was still wrangling over the sort of monument they should put up to the dead. Tom Seaton wanted a white marble shaft in the middle of the green, but Edward had violently opposed such a monstrosity.

"That's because Mark wasn't killed," Tom had said rudely.

Edward had gazed at him over his glasses. "I believe you, too, did not suffer a personal loss."

"At least I went over and saw our men dying," Tom had retorted, "and Fioretta's nephew was killed."

It was true. John Carosi had lost his son in the Battle of the Bulge. Edward, who had been quarreling with him only the day before over the fourth strike at the shop, had put on his hat and coat and for the first time in his life had gone to South Chedbury. It was the week after Christmas and there was the usual snow on the ground and the driving had been bad, even though he no longer drove himself. His frequent trips to New York demanded a chauffeur, now that he was no longer young.

He had found John sitting in his shirt sleeves in a tiny parlor, his fists clenched on his knees as he stared at a picture of Jack in his uniform. John had grown heavy in his middle age and he was sweating with agony, the tears running down his cheeks. Upstairs his wife was wailing among his daughters.

"John, I'm very sorry to hear this," Edward had said at once.

He had found it difficult to meet John's dark and suffering eyes.

"Sit down, Mr. Haslatt," he said without getting up.

Edward had sat down, his hat and stick between his knees. He felt his skin pricking with pain.

"Jack was a fine boy," he said.

"A great boy," Carosi agreed.

"I wish there was something I could do," Edward went on. "I know there isn't, but for my own sake I just had to come and tell you that I—that I would really have done anything to prevent this."

"It's good of you," Carosi said. "I just have to sweat it through."

Silence had fallen between them. He wished that he could assure Carosi that it was a good way for a boy to die—sweet and right to die for one's country, and all that—but he had not been able to say the words. Death was neither sweet nor right for young men like Jack, full of life and mischief, and he could not bring himself to say a thing he did not believe. He sat with his heart aching in his bosom and thinking of Mark, who unless the vile war ended, would have to get into it.

But the war ended abruptly. Two years later to Edward's dismay Mark decided to enlist anyway, in the air force, "to get his share over with," he said.

Edward told John Carosi in the shop. "I hope he doesn't get ground into the mud, the way mine did," Carosi had answered. "That's what keeps my wife cryin'. There wasn't nothing to bring home to bury."

Edward had not been able to answer this, and before he could conquer the sickness in the pit of his stomach Carosi had turned away and had said brusquely, "I may as well tell you that the union's goin' to push for an increase again."

For once Edward had welcomed the quarrel. "I shall have to stop publishing books at this rate, and you know it. People won't buy novels that cost three and four dollars apiece."

"They still buy Harrow's," Carosi retorted.

"You know I've always liked to publish new writers,

young ones," Edward said. "This way I don't dare take the risk."

"That's not my business," Carosi replied.

"It would be your business if Haslatt Brothers failed."

"Personally I'd be sorry, but the union would take care of me," Carosi had said firmly.

. . . He lost his fight with the union and wages went up again. What he had said was true. In any struggle the new and the young went down and sorrowfully he rejected manuscripts of young and awkward writers. He was safe enough only so long as the half dozen or so of his best-selling older authors kept alive. Their books were not as good as they had been—even Harrow's were not. Writers were, he supposed, confounded by the times.

So, for that matter, was he. Mark was still in the air force and he wished he would come home. What was the use of risking one's life every day to carry food into Berlin? He had never wanted the boy to be a pilot. But a son paid no heed nowadays to what his father wanted. His mind harked back, upon this, to his own father. Remembering that kind gray figure, now so long dust save for the spirit of this memory, he took pride in thinking that he had never really defied his own father. Then his sense of justice reminded him that neither had he, as a young man, been confronted with the issues of life and death that faced Mark now.

His imagination, always slow, was nevertheless strong when it was lit by love, and he thought of Mark waking in the morning, day after day, to consider, however swiftly, whether night would see him still alive. The lift was as safe as it could be made, Edward supposed, and yet he had made it his duty to know how many young men actually were killed in this cold combat with a country monstrous in its silent power. He was not for a moment confused by any illusions. It was not to feed hungry people that Mark continually risked his life. Power was being matched against power, even in this trivial way, and his son—oh, agony to think of it—was merely expendable.

He heard footsteps outside the door and he turned from the window, glad to be distracted from his constant and secret worry over Mark. Margaret came in ready to go home. She had put on her hat and the jacket to her new spring suit. It was a matter of course nowadays that she bought her clothes in New York, and this suit was the result of her going with him last week. She and Sandra had gone to some fancy place and picked it out, and at the same time she had bought some things for Mary. He took enormous pride in Margaret's good looks. It was an achievement when a woman kept as slim, or almost as slim, as she had been and without wrinkles. Tom's wife, Fioretta, had run to fat, in the way of Italian women.

Strange marriage that! Thomas Seaton was only cold in his grave when Tom suddenly decided to marry the pretty Italian girl who was John Carosi's youngest sister, twenty-six years younger than he, and almost as many years younger than Tom. There had been no wedding. Tom had informed the family one day that he and Fioretta would be married and sail at once for Italy, where he might stay a year. He had stayed four months, and meantime Mrs. Seaton, restless in the big empty house, had gone to live in Paris with Dorothea, her divorced sister. Tom had come back suddenly because Fioretta was pregnant and he wanted his child born an American. He had declared that he wanted no children, but that Fioretta, incurably maternal, had cheated him. She had continued to cheat him amiably, and the Seaton house was noisy with three rather spoiled but extremely beautiful little girls.

Edward was secretly fond of his Italian sister-in-law, while realizing that it was a comedown for the Seaton family. But the new times were very queer. Nothing was as it had once been. His own mother, though it had been no business of hers, had made a fuss over the marriage. "I never thought we'd be connected with South Chedbury through the Seatons," she had said acidly.

She never knew either, he supposed, how nearly Baynes and Sandra had come to a divorce five years ago. Sandra had even gone to Reno. As he had surmised, this time it was money, and no other than Harold Ames, still president of a New York bank. It had not come off, however. The directors had met and after violent argument had informed Harold that it would make people lose confidence in the bank if he divorced his old wife to marry a woman who though not young, perhaps, at least looked sinfully young, and if he persisted, another president would be chosen. Harold, confronted with loss of prestige and mindful of his bald head, at which Sandra had unwisely already poked some fun, withdrew prudently before anything was made public.

Sandra had come home at once, pretending that she had only been on a trip. She brought back, with her infallible instinct, a novel about New Mexico written by a young veteran who, dying with tuberculosis, had gone to end his days in the sun, and she had been frank to forestall scolding.

"I see now that Hal only loved me as a sort of shadow sister of yours," she had told Margaret. "I was a fool," she added honestly, "and I shan't be one again. Baynes is an archangel and too good for me."

Baynes was, in a dry way, a saint, Edward admitted. After their mother had died of double pneumonia the winter of unprecedented snows, when Chedbury was without light or fuel for nearly a week, and the whole of New England was winter-bound, Baynes had taken Louise to the New York office, where she had become a perfectionist with the adding machine and had risen to be treasurer of the company. Never again had she or Edward referred to the single dreadful night when she had revealed herself of a heart. He continued mildly affectionate toward her, as his sister, and she grew less and less affectionate toward anybody. She maintained a two-room apartment in New York, furnished with her mother's things, and developed a zeal for museums, and had become, to Edward's astonishment, something of an expert in Japanese art. She had a few friends, equally absorbed, and he supposed she was happy. At any rate, he had never been able to do anything about Louise.

Margaret was drawing on her pearl-gray gloves. The gray suit, light enough almost to match her white hair, was, as she well knew, singularly good with her pink cheeks and blue eyes. Her little vanities pleased him and made him love her the more fondly. Beside her Mary looked like a warm dark little dove—a darling dove at that, very pleasant in her swirling brown skirts. Edward liked the new long skirts, after the years of tight and narrow ones, from whose knees he had so often averted his eyes.

"Shall I tell him?" Margaret asked of her daughter.

"Tell me what?" Edward demanded. "Of course I'm to be told."

"Mary is going to have another baby," Margaret announced.

Mary smiled at her father. The marriage, contrary to all his expectations and even wishes, had been a very happy one. Enveloped in her husband's worship, Mary had grown softly dependent and willfully clinging as she left her girlhood behind.

"Lew is going to be surprised," she said sweetly.

"When's he coming back?"

"Next week."

Harrow had flown to London to quarrel with his English publishers over a cut in royalties. The internal troubles of a socialist Britain were none of his affair, he had declared loudly over the transatlantic telephone, and he did not intend to be impoverished by Englishmen. It was not as if he were a Socialist or a Communist or any of these new kinds of persons. As the son of a drunkard and a laundry woman he knew enough about people to believe that they would always sponge on others who had regular jobs, and he considered socialism a delusion, devised by the sons of the rich out of guilty conscience and idleness. Anybody else, he often said, would know better. People would take all they could get, just as he did.

"I thought you weren't going to risk this business again," Edward grumbled. "When the twins were born I certainly remember hearing Lewis say he wouldn't let you have any more children."

"He did say that," Mary replied. Her dark eyes, full of soft mischief, looked into his with deep and worldly wisdom.

"You didn't embark on this purposely, did you?" Edward inquired.

"Not really," she said, ambiguous in his presence. Her soft red lips folded with some of her old stubbornness.

Ah, well, she had grown very far away from him. The days when he had felt her very flesh was his were long gone. She had become a pretty, rather distant woman, who stirred in him only now and then the memories of a small oversensitive girl. If he had lost her there seemed nevertheless to be some sort of increasing friendship between her and her mother, though less a mother-daughter relationship, perhaps, than that of two women who were able at last to like one another. He did not pretend to understand it, especially when he remembered past antagonism and how often he had tried to console his child.

"Well, good-by," he said, sighing. "You'll have to make your own peace with your husband. At least the doctors will be better now than they were ten years ago. I suggest, however, that you don't make it twins again."

Both women laughed, which was what he had intended them to do. He stooped to kiss his daughter, his dry lips frosty and not touching the rich red of her full mouth. He had a horror of lipstick staining his clipped white mustache.

"Good-by, darling," Mary said comfortably. "If you see the Indians on the way down the mountain, please tell them to come and get ready for lunch. I wish you'd stay but Mother says you won't."

"No, no. I like my meals in peace," he declared.

From the comfortable sedan car he looked at his daughter as she stood on the stone threshold of her home. The wind was blowing her short brown curls and except for the content and the wisdom in her eyes she might have been a girl. Certainly she still looked young enough to be Harrow's daughter. He waved and then spoke to the chauffeur as the car moved away.

"Be careful how you go around the bends. My grandsons are probably hiding behind a rock somewhere."

Under the robe his hand sought Margaret's, as usual. He liked to sit beside her, hand in hand, and watch the familiar landscape of Chedbury rise nearer as they descended.

"I wondered why Mary wanted all those negligees," Margaret said, smiling.

"Is it safe to have a Caesarean after thirty-five?" he inquired anxiously. It had been apparent ten years ago when the twins were ready to make their dual appearance that Mary's frame was too delicate for normal functions—too delicate, he did not doubt, to be married at all to the grossness of a man like Lewis Harrow, but on that dark picture he would not allow himself to dwell. He had not been able to sleep the night after Mary's wedding. What was the fellow doing to his little child? It had been almost better not to know where she was, the night she ran away. But the next morning had brought them news in her own voice over the telephone. They were in some little town in Maine, having driven all night, and they were at that moment going to be married before a justice of the peace.

"Stop!" he had commanded that soft determined voice ringing in his ear. "You mustn't do this, Mary! I forbid it—absolutely!"

"I will do it," she had replied and had hung up the receiver. He heard the click which cut her off again and he had turned to Margaret, who was standing beside him, her hands clasped tightly at her throat.

"She's getting married now!" he had gasped.

"Where?" Margaret had cried.

He had stared at her blankly. "I don't know!" Only then had he realized that Mary had not even spoken the name of the town. Ah, purposely she had not told him the name of the town!

She and Lewis Harrow had not come home for nearly two years. They had gone to England and to France. When they did come home to The Eagle it was to rest and to prepare for the birth of the children. He had not been able to believe that the swollen little figure was that of his Mary, his child. For a brief while, when she lay at death's door before the doctor had decided to operate, he had reclaimed her again.

"You shouldn't have married her!" he had exclaimed in utmost agitation to Harrow. "This is your—your—excessive vitality."

In the midst of his own terror Harrow had paused to stare at him and then to burst into loud and unexplained laughter.

When Mary was saved, however, and he went in to see his grandsons, he felt no return of his brief recognition. There she lay, pale and placidly triumphant in her bed, a robust if small infant in either arm. He had been compelled to readjust himself quickly.

"Well, well," he had said with something more than his usual vigor.

"Nice, aren't they?" she had asked.

"They look healthy," he had replied with reserve.

They were healthy. He believed that his grandsons

253

were overstuffed with vitamins. It was difficult, moreover, to talk to two boys, and one could never get them separately. One boy, he sometimes thought, he could have interested in something, say in stamps, or even in some of the types at the printing shop, but two were disconcerting. They began to romp at any moment—rough-housing, they called it. And a grandparent had no chance nowadays in competition with radio programs and comic books. These preoccupations of the immature he deeply disapproved, and yet such was the softness of his heart that he could not forbear picking up a handful of the wretchedly printed books from the newsstands where he bought the morning papers on his days in New York. Two or three times, troubled by the effect of the lurid pictures on his descendants, he had tried to read some of the pages and had not the least notion of what they were about. He was appalled at the taste of his grandsons. There must be, he told himself, something in these comics that he did not see, just as he could not see what Mark had enjoyed in his endless evenings about town, aimlessly, or so he feared, pursuing pleasure. But at the thought of Mark, his heart forbade judgment.

A yell surpassing any he had ever heard before broke off his thoughts. The car came to a violent stop, and two painted heathen jabbered at the window.

"What are they saying?" he demanded of Margaret.

"Give them each a dime," she said, smiling. "They are pretending to hold us up."

"But isn't it very bad for them to think they can succeed?" he asked, anxious as always for their morals.

"It doesn't mean anything," she said comfortably and felt for her own purse.

"Oh, I'll do it," he said with some irritation, "if it has to be done, that is."

He took out his wallet and opening the window he gazed into two round and ruddy faces, so charming in smiles that his heart softened again and trying not to let Margaret see, he took out two quarters instead of dimes and pressed them into the filthiest hands he had touched for years.

"Mind you, this is all against my principles," he said earnestly in the slightly didactic voice of which he was almost entirely unconscious, except when, as now, it grated surprisingly on his own ears. "You shouldn't hold up anybody—most of all your own poor old grandfather. I need my money for my old age. What if I have to go to the poorhouse?"

Compunction appeared in the two pairs of dark eyes.

"You can come and live with us," Peter suggested.

"We'll come and bring you home," Paul added.

"You still want the quarters, I notice," he said dryly, although his heart was further softened to the point, he told himself, of folly.

"Just for the present we need them," Paul said sweetly, clutching his booty.

They let out their war whoops and seeing them dash into the underbrush, he remembered their mother's message and shouted after them, "Go home to luncheon!" He sank back panting. "I doubt they can hear anyone, they're making so much noise."

"Their stomachs will lead them homeward," Margaret replied. She felt for his hand again and leaning toward him she kissed his ear while the car started forward. He glanced involuntarily at the little mirror. The chauffeur's eyes were set coldly ahead, thank God.

"Now what's that for?" he demanded in a guarded voice.

"Because you gave them quarters, Ned," she replied. They looked at each other for a long minute, her eyes were soft and still so blue, and then he was abashed.

"Oh, well," he grumbled, "it's only once—though of course they are utterly without discipline."

He held her hand firmly and was conscious of deep inner happiness.

This welling inner happiness was something that had grown only as he approached what was commonly called old age. In years he knew that indeed he was an aging if not an old man. Mark, his youngest son, was twenty his next birthday and Mark had been a belated child. A child almost perfect, he often reflected with something like fatuousness. He had spent much time upon Mark's education. The other children had grown up in the usual round of schools and colleges, but Mark had, so to speak, been hand grown.

It had been a disappointment he did not acknowledge even to himself that this dearest son had not shown the slightest sign, as yet, of interest in the firm of Haslatt Brothers. Instead, by some astonishing twist of inheritance Tommy, after deciding not to marry Dinny and then sowing an agitating number of wild oats in that unhappy period between wars, had settled down into the family firm with a gaiety combined with a cynical prudence that forced Edward to realize that perhaps he had produced a publisher superior to himself by nature. By a process of inheritance far beyond the understanding of man, Tommy combined in himself his father's love of books and his uncle Baynes's instinct, or flair. Sandra loudly proclaimed Tommy's virtues and claimed him as the son she herself should have had, if she had only had the sense to know it earlier. After years of refusing to have any children Sandra now at a lean and chic middle age wished that she had let nature take its course with her, although she added, "Nature on the loose would probably have produced something that looked neither like Baynes or me." She remembered the grimness of the remote Uncle Henry Haslatt, now long dead, and declared finally that his visage alone made her content to be childless. Nevertheless she adored her Tommy, and was far more proud than Margaret had been when he chose as his wife the prettiest debutante of her year in New York.

After this marriage Sandra had tried to force Tom and Fioretta out of the old Seaton house, because she maintained that Fioretta made it look like something in South Chedbury whereas Diantha would have made it what it had been designed to be, a family seat.

Edward had taken the side of Tom and Fioretta, however. He was grateful to her for marrying Tom and removing him as a bad influence upon his elder son, and therefore even remotely, perhaps, from Mark. At any rate it was only after Tom's marriage that the great change had appeared in Tommy.

Thinking of Fioretta now he drew his old gold watch from his pocket.

"We have time to stop by Tom's, if you like. I don't suppose Mary would mind if we mentioned her condition. Fioretta is always so pleased at the prospect of a new child in the family."

"Very well," Margaret replied, her voice pleasant.

Some moments later Edward leaned toward the chauffeur and directed his stop at the white painted gate which Tom had set between the stone posts in order to keep his offspring within the bounds of Fioretta's hearty cries. Fioretta sensibly had not wanted the house changed and it looked as it always had, a little less spotless than of old, perhaps, as to white paint. The flowers, too, had degenerated from lilies and English tree roses to a general effect of zinnias and marigolds, and he disapproved the row of tall sunflowers against the dignified background of the house itself. Fioretta kept chickens in the back yard, and considered sunflower seeds conducive to eggs.

As usual she saw them through the window and came running out to greet them warmly. She had been plump when Tom married her, a darkly rosy creature with huge black eyes and a red mouth. Now she was frankly more than plump. She still loved the bright deep orange hues and crimsons of her girlhood and they somehow became her in spite of spread.

"Uncle Ed—Auntie Margaret!" she cried in her fresh voice. The one sign of her insecurity in this family was that she had never brought herself to call them by their first names. Only when the children grew old enough to talk had she solved the problem by calling them what she taught the children to say.

"Come in, do! I've just got lunch on the table—special ravioli Tom does love. Ah, now, sit down! For what else should you come just when I tell the girl to dish up?"

"We can't, dear," Margaret said gently. "Ned doesn't digest starches, and luncheon is waiting for us, I'm sure. And you know how it puts the cook out if we don't come home. We just wanted to see you and the children and Tom, if he's home, to tell you the latest family news."

"The children are coming home from school this minute and Tom is mending the grape arbor. I tell him every year we should have more grapes so I can make our wine at home. It is better for Tom than the boughten stuff. My poppa taught me how to make it so good, like they do at home in Italy."

"It is delicious," Margaret said.

"Now," Fioretta said in her cozy busy voice, "what's the news?"

"We've just come from The Eagle and Mary told us

257

today that she is going to have a baby." Margaret spoke simply as though to a child.

"My God, how nice!" Fioretta's great eyes rolled and she threw up her hands. "So she's goin' to get ahead of me? She's goin' to have the next baby. I'm goin' to tell Tom. He won't let me have any more little babies. What you think of that? And me with my arms empty! My children are all too big. You know what? That Viola of mine she's kissing a boy already. Can you imagine!"

Fioretta flung back her head and laughter rolled from her rich red mouth.

Edward as usual was silent. He basked in this generous presence of Fioretta. Actually they had very little to say to each other. Fioretta had never, so far as he knew, read a book. John Carosi, now, was a reader. In later years he had often quarreled with his employer over the books published by Haslatt Brothers. Last year, when Edward had chosen to publish *The Rights of Employers in a Democracy,* written by the head of a great utility firm, John had thrown his gray cap on the floor one morning when Edward came into the shop.

"Mr. Haslatt, I don't work the press on that book!"

"Very well, John," Edward had replied. "I'll give it to one of the other men."

"I don't work in this shop," John had declared next.

"I don't want you to stop with me any longer than you wish," Edward had replied with dignity. "But I do reserve the right to publish two sides of any question. Don't forget I was entirely willing to publish *The Union and the Worker* last year."

"There can't be two sides to the right," John said.

"There are two sides to everything," Edward had retorted. He had proceeded through the shop, examining, with eyes grown quick and shrewd through the years, the presses pounding out the books he had chosen to present to the world. He had steadfastly resisted both Baynes and Tommy on the matter of enlarging the works.

"I do not intend to publish more books," he said at least several times a month. "Better ones, yes, every year—but no more."

"Come next Sunday then, please," Fioretta was urging. "I will make something special for you, Uncle Ed, not starch, a beef stew like something in Italy. Please, please!"

The children had reached home and came swarming out in a dark brood, all of them more Italian than English in their looks. Their eyes were lively, their voices piercing, and their health apparent in every move and word. They surrounded their mother and hugged her ardently while she laughed. "Look, now, at my monkeys. Children, you should beg Uncle Ed to come to Sunday dinner!"

"Uncle Ed, please."

"Auntie Margaret, make him."

He was inevitably pleased at their loud desire to have his company, though why he did not know, for he found very little to say to children at any time.

"Now why do you want me to come?" he demanded, mildly jocular. "I can't run around with you and I don't play any games."

Dark eyes met dark eyes and silence fell.

"Speak, children," Fioretta commanded with the warm imperiousness born of absolute love. "Say what is in your hearts. Don't be afraid."

Viola threw back her heavy curls. "I'll tell you why, Uncle Ed—we all feel you like us."

"There!" Fioretta cried admiringly. "Isn't that the truth! Nice the way she said it!"

"Very nice!" he admitted, and putting out his hand he touched the child's warm olive cheek.

"Lovely," Margaret said tenderly, "and we will come. Now you must all go and have your luncheon."

The ardent children left their mother and pressed around them, and upon this picture in the warm spring sunshine Tom appeared, the father of this family to be sure, and yet always seeming somewhat puzzled and even astonished by what he had brought almost unwittingly into existence.

Lean and sandy hued as ever, he wore an overall of khaki color and in his hand he held a pruning knife. "They'll strangle you," he said. "I know what it's like. They try to choke me every day of their lives."

He waved the knife, pretending to stay them as they swarmed now toward him at the sound of his voice. He elbowed the older ones aside ruthlessly and opened his arms to his youngest daughter. "Come here, Baby," he said. "You're the only one that can kiss me. Here on the cheek, please!"

She planted a noisy kiss at the spot he indicated and Margaret laughed. "Tom, Tom, I wonder that our father doesn't rise from his grave!"

Fioretta turned solemn. "You think the old man wouldn't like it?"

"He'd love it, bless him," Margaret said. "He'd love you, Fioretta. Bless you, too."

She kissed Fioretta's round and rosy cheek. "We all do, darling. Don't mind me. And if I say anything you don't understand just forget it. Tom knows what I mean and he'll tell you."

"Aren't you going to stop for lunch?" Tom demanded.

"No, dear. We're coming Sunday."

Fioretta suddenly bethought herself of the news. "Tom, what you think? Mary is going to have a baby! Now, Tom, I ask you, why can she have a baby and not me?"

"Shut up, Fioretta," he answered with affection. "We've got more than we need now and there'll be an accident or two. I know you."

"Aw, Poppa, we'd like a new baby!" Viola pleaded.

"You just wait, my girl," Tom told his daughter. "You'll have your own all too soon."

He turned to his sister. "Meg, do you think Mary ought, when you consider the twins?"

"It's too late now," Margaret said with the tranquillity that was the chief sign of her years. "We'll just have to keep prodding Lew to take care of her. He means to, but he forgets when he's writing, as usual, his greatest novel."

Tom's thin and handsome lip lifted in something like a sneer. "Count upon it, Ed, there'll be a childbirth in the book, a husband, like as not, hanging over his dying wife's bed, and moaning that he'd rather have lost the child."

"Don't joke, Tom," Margaret said sharply.

Fioretta, listening, was suddenly angry. "Ain't he wicked? My God, sometimes I think I got the worst man in the world! Mary won't die—what the devil!"

When she was angry and in the bosom of the family Fioretta returned wholeheartedly to South Chedbury. Indignation burned in the hot gaze she now bestowed upon her husband.

"Shut up, Fioretta," Tom said, from habit. "Well, we'll be looking for you Sunday, Ed."

They turned away, knowing that until they left Tom's brood would delay in the sunshine, and sitting in the car again, hand in hand, they rode in silence, each aware of warmth in the other's heart.

"Do you really think your father would have approved South Chedbury in his house?" Edward asked.

"Of course it couldn't have been in his day," she replied. "Things were so defined then, somehow. Mother would have made it impossible for Fioretta. But if it had been Mother who died instead of Father, I think he could have lived there quite happily with Fioretta, growing drowsy in the grape arbor, drinking her wine and spotting his waistcoat more and more—and the little girls would have loved him extravagantly."

"They love everything extravagantly," he murmured.

He was surprised at her reply.

"Do you know, Ned, I've come to believe in extravagant love—it's the only thing that makes life in this world possible. Maybe Fioretta's children will teach us all."

He knew the deep distress in her mind these days. She had given up much that she had once done. After the war she had given up Red Cross work. "It all seems useless," she had said to him one night. "It's just patchwork. There has to be something different in the world, a new approach to the whole of life."

They talked together now more than they ever had. He looked back on his earlier years with a sort of wonder. He had been so busy when his children were young that he had very little time for talk, or indeed for anything except the anxieties of a livelihood for those whom he loved and had too little time to enjoy. It was he alone, or so he had felt, who stood between them and the overwhelming world.

One of his most successful books had been written by an explorer in the jungles of Sumatra, an adventuring sort of fellow whom he had heartily disliked when he met him at a dinner Baynes and Sandra had given for him in New York when the book was published. The jungle, however, Edward had never forgotten. It had crept up on him in the night for years until he had been able to identify it with the overwhelming world he feared. Stoutly conservative, even to the extent of present distress over the socialism now rampant in England, he would have declared himself at all times unafraid of the insecurities of extreme individualism. Yet the nightmare of the encroaching jungle had beset him until one night in his wakefulness he had confided to Margaret the recurrence of the dream.

"I seem to be walking along a narrow path, enclosed in walls of the most livid green trees and vines. They aren't ordinary greenery—nothing like what we have here in New England. They're horrible, they keep growing new branches and tentacles. The roots of the trees are not even decent. They're like great sucking mouths, clutching the earth and draining it dry. The further I go—and I must go on—I can't help myself, it seems—the tighter the green walls press around me, and I can't see ahead. You are following behind me—sometimes just you and Mark, sometimes all of you—sometimes lately only Mark. I keep fighting off the horrible green tendrils reaching out. But they get me at last and I wake, strangling."

Margaret, waked from sleep, had listened, her eyes startled. "You're worrying about something," she declared. "You haven't told me everything."

"I've told you all I know," he had protested in honesty.

For the next few months she had persuaded him toward going to a psychiatrist, which he had resisted with profound conviction that such stuff was all charlatanry. In the end he had gone, however, commanded by Wynne, his doctor these many years.

"Your blood pressure is far too high, and yet you're as lean as a hound dog," Wynne had told him. "It isn't overeating that's doing it. It's whatever is gnawing at your mind. You're a born worrier like your New England ancestors. Go and have a talk with some professional—unless you can confess to a Catholic priest."

Confession was impossible to Edward's Protestant mind, and he had in the end made a carefully noncommittal appointment with an unknown though highly recommended name in New York. There he had gone soon after the inevitability of the war had burst upon his dismayed and terrified consciousness. Dr. Hastings had proved a tall, spare, pleasantly cold-looking gentleman who had listened respectfully to Edward's halting account of his nightmare. A succession of detached though acute questions had led after two hours or so to a conclusion that had been immensely helpful.

"There is nothing wrong with you, Mr. Haslatt," Hastings had said. "You seem an exceptionally well-balanced and disciplined person. What you are suffering from is a disease called modern times. You, like all of us, have no security. Our American way of life so far does not provide it. Whether this is good or bad is beside the point. I am no moralist. But you have to recognize that though you are by nature and choice an individualist of the strongest dye, yet the fact is you are unconsciously frightened of the present hazards of extreme individualism, even while you reject anything else. You must learn to accept insecurity. As long as you live our society will not provide it for you. Say to yourself, 'I have an ample income and a satisfying wife'—you are sure you are telling me the truth there?"

"Completely," Edward replied. "I am what is called a one-woman man—that is, in my wife I have found all women. She is beautiful and intelligent."

"Very unusual," Dr. Hastings had said in a dry voice. "Such being the case, I am sure you can deal with your own fears of insecurity. Consider it part of the world state of mind, the atmosphere of our generation."

He had left the doctor's office strangely lighthearted. It was true that in the midst of the hazards of business he had always made a good and on the whole increasingly ample income, though he was sound rather than rich. He had never lost anyone he loved, his parents he supposed scarcely coming under the category of real love. Margaret had passed through her middle years without the neuroticism to which he had heard women were susceptible, and she did not find him unpleasing in their intimate relations, even as she grew older. He tried, of course, to be considerate. He had even bought a book on menopause in women, which she had snatched away from him, laughing at him as she did so.

"Don't read up on me, Ned!" she had exclaimed. "I'm as normal as possible, thank God, and I still love you."

She had been a perfect wife, or as nearly so as a mortal man could expect. Her few faults were negligible— a tendency to be careless about the house as she grew older, dust and so on seeming less important to her while it became more important to him, and his clothes were not always sent to be pressed when he wished them to be. He felt, sometimes, too, that she thought about a good many things of which she did not tell him, though when he questioned her, asking, for example, so direct a demand as, "What are you thinking about when you look like that?" she answered only vaguely. Once she had almost lost her temper.

"I do wish," she had said with some of her old girlish vigor, "that you would not ask me what I am thinking. My thoughts are ungovernable and always were. I let them lead me by the nose and I'd be ashamed sometimes to tell where I am."

"You needn't be ashamed before me," he had reminded her.

"Oh, I wouldn't be exactly ashamed," she had said carelessly. "It's just that it would be too bothersome to explain how I got to thinking whatever I'm thinking."

"Do you remember," he had reminded her, "how, when we were about to be engaged, you demanded complete and perfect truth between us?"

This she had answered inconsequentially, he thought. She had said, "I knew nothing whatever then about being married. If I had always told you the truth, you'd have divorced me by now."

"Never!" he exclaimed, much alarmed.

"Besides," she had gone on, "what I didn't know is that when two people live together long and closely they tell each other less and less in words. They know everything anyway—everything, that is, except what they don't want to know."

"Has there been something about me that you haven't wanted to know?" he had asked after some thought.

"Nothing important," she had said in the same half-careless fashion. "When you've fretted—and you do fret, Ned, though I wish you wouldn't—it doesn't always seem worth while to bother about what little thing is fretting you."

He had been a good deal hurt when she said this and had retired into silence. Then after reflecting upon it he had been compelled to acknowledge that she was right. Had she been torn by every worry that had tortured him, she would have lost her calm, that blessed atmosphere in which he found such strength and refuge. All the same, it had been his fretting, as she called it, that had made his business a success when other publishers were failing. Not even Harrow could have saved him had he been incautious.

Now on this perfect day in May all struggles were in the past. He had got rid of the jungle, by will power and by reading philosophy again. In his day at Harvard William James had been a professor of philosophy and remembering that vivid life-loving figure, he had returned to books he had not read since he left the presence of his teacher. He had been too shy to tell James what he felt about him in those college years, and had passed through his classes merely a name on a roll call.

Reading and rereading these books, Edward in his approaching old age felt a new vigor of the soul return to him. William James had been an American, he told himself, a philosopher, a thinking active man, who gloried in the pragmatism that was a part of America's very soul. He read aloud sometimes to Margaret in the evening the striding powerful words, the abhorrence of violence and war which today, in spite of the mildness of the May sunshine, overshadowed the sky of every intelligent mind.

What had happened to make Americans now think the cruelties of violence signified strength? Strength was to be found only in "the moral equivalent of war," a powerful wisdom, a discipline stronger than any military force could develop, because it was discipline of the self by the self.

He dared not voice such thoughts. Chedbury would never have understood them and he would have been smeared with red. Yet did the young men never think such thoughts, as they marched on alien roads in half the countries of the world?

He remembered a night, soon after Pearl Harbor, when Mark was a boy of thirteen. He had gone upstairs to

Mark's room to tell him good night—a discarded habit, for the growing boy did not like to be babied. But he had not been able to restrain his fears. Surely the war would be over before Mark grew up. He had bent over his son and had kissed his wind-burned cheek. Mark had been skating all day on the first thick ice of the season.

"You've had a good day," Edward had said. "I can tell it from your face."

"I've had a swell day," Mark had replied. He had gazed into his father's face for a long moment, his eyes dark with what he could not know. Then, inexplicably, he had spoken those words that were graven upon Edward's heart.

"I hope I can live," Mark had said.

Edward had restrained the first impulse of his life to weep wildly. "Of course you will live," he had said. Then unable to bear the pain in his throat he had gone into the hall and shut the door and let the silent tears flow down his cheeks. He had not been able to repeat the scene to Margaret, for shame lest he weep again, and it remained locked within him.

Neither of his sons had been interested in philosophy. Tommy had majored harmlessly in English literature and Mark had cared for nothing but science, and especially physics. Sandy had actually gone in for medicine. He did not approve of women doctors but felt it only decent not to say so while his younger daughter plowed her difficult way through to successful practice. She had put up her shingle now in Boston, and every quarter he paid such bills as she had not been able to manage and prayed that she would marry some decent man and give up the struggle. Sandy, the grimmest and the gayest of his children, was not likely to give up. She was handsome rather than pretty, her Grandfather Haslatt having left her his somewhat too long nose, but she was the favorite of her Grandmother Seaton and likely, Margaret had said one day, to come into something substantial when old Mrs. Seaton died.

"That is nothing to me," he had said stiffly.

"It's something to me, you old poker back," Margaret had retorted laughing at him. "Sandy will never get married to that nice boy who is in love with her unless she can pay her share of the expenses."

"You aren't wishing for your mother's death, I hope," he had replied.

"Of course not," Margaret had said in her most cheerful voice. "At the same time, Mother cannot live forever, and I am glad she likes Sandy and I hope she persuades Aunt Dorothea, who seems perennial, to give what she has to Sandy, too. Mary doesn't need it, and the boys can manage."

"Who's this fellow in love with Sandy?" he had then demanded.

"Don't you remember the young man she brought down last Christmas Eve?"

"Not particularly," he had been compelled to say, scraping his memory.

"The big one who broke the footstool when he sat on it?"

"That fellow! I remember thinking I wouldn't like him messing around inside me—a surgeon, wasn't he?"

"He is," Margaret said. "He has curiously delicate hands. In debt up to his neck, too, for his education—it'll be years before they can make ends meet."

This had troubled him a good deal, and he had pondered ways of making marriage possible for this daughter upon whom he had never until now spent much thought. Sandy had been so healthy, so normal, whatever that meant, that she had grown up almost without his noticing her, except to see, with an irritation which made him ashamed, that she got better grades at school than either of her brothers. Ought not parents to make it possible, he asked himself, for young people to marry at the reasonable hour of the highest biological urge? He and Margaret had been young, and the costs of living then were low. Now it was practically impossible, unless one were a war veteran, to synchronize marriage and biological needs. He had a horror of the easy sexual intercourse that seemed acceptable today even among his friends, and though he could see nothing he could do about it, he did not like the numbers of illegitimate children being born. Such polygamous children were the problems of a monogamous society. Surely there had been far fewer in his youth. Tom's daughter Viola, he feared, was not the premature infant she had been tactfully declared. Very robust, for prematurity! But nothing had been said in Chedbury, of course—not openly. Nobody had dared to say anything to him, naturally.

He preferred not to think it possible that Sandy might be sleeping with her young man, fortified by the astounding amount of protective information that she might have. Agitated, however, by this possibility, he had been casting about in his mind how he could offer her an income without offending her pride, when Mrs. Seaton died suddenly a year ago this May. He refused to think it opportune but the truth was there. He and Margaret had gone over to Paris and had brought the narrow and ancient body back with them in a metal casket. Margaret had not wept. Prepared for her tears he had been nevertheless relieved when they did not flow.

"You aren't hiding your feelings from me?" he had inquired anxiously.

Her hand on his cheek had comforted him. "No, darling. It was time."

This was all she had said. They had left an even more desiccated old woman behind them in the overdecorated French apartment, a frame so ancient, a visage so withered that it was impossible to believe that for her sake a young and ardent man had once fled both fame and fortune to live with her in happy sin for nearly twoscore years.

"Good-by children," Aunt Dorothea had said, presenting both her leathery cheeks. To her they were children, though with graying hair and grandchildren of their own.

"It is frightening to live so long," Margaret had said.

Sitting beside her as they drove into the wide gate of their comfortable home, he had wondered rather soberly if what she had said was true. It did not seem possible, this May morning, that anything could be worse than death.

The pleasant weather held through the week with increasing and unseasonable heat. In the garden after breakfast on Sunday morning Margaret exclaimed over flowers forcing themselves to premature blooming. The roses, she told Edward, were pushing out buds that could not come to maturity.

268

"I wonder if that wretched atom bomb has set up some sort of heat inside the earth," she mused.

He had been tempted by the ardent sunshine to leave his pile of manuscripts, his constant week-end task, and come out into the garden just as he was, bareheaded and without putting on his topcoat. He saw her, bareheaded too, busy with a trowel, her sleeves rolled high on her still shapely arms. Sunday was her day of gardening, the aged, vociferous, and agitating Italian, Tony Antonelli, who considered the garden his possession, being that day safely at home in South Chedbury. On Mondays Margaret did not go near the garden, allowing Tony time to get over his wrath at what she had done. By Tuesday they were able to quarrel again without rancor.

"I suppose Mark could tell you," Edward now said in answer to her question. They had discussed the atom bomb through many mealtimes together. She was positive of its entire evil, and railed at him when he could not utterly agree. It was, he said, only one evil thing in an evil business. How devastating it really was he could not find out and he had made up his mind that when Mark came back he would go into the science of this most devilish of weapons. What troubled him most was not the bomb itself so much as the lack of moral principle in the scientists who had allowed themselves to make it. Surely scientists, he had told himself, ought to be the new leaders of morality, all else having failed. When Joseph Barclay had preached a violent sermon against the use of the atomic bomb, a sermon during which Margaret had sat tense, her hands clasped tightly together, Edward had wondered at such resentment. Was not the bomb merely the logical means of an inhuman process?

This he dared not say to Margaret. Instead he remarked now with a mildness to suit the day, "I suppose we should be getting ready for church—unless the sunshine can tempt you to stay home."

"I don't want to go to church," she said, "and yet somehow these days I feel we must."

"Why?" he asked with his undying curiosity concerning all she felt and thought.

"Because we are so helpless," she answered.

He did not ask, helpless against what? He knew that in spite of all he could do she was somehow, underneath her tranquillity, allowing her personal content, even her happiness, to become involved in the incomprehensible events taking place in the world. Both of them had been vaguely cheered at the stolid way in which their own people had taken hold of the political elections six months ago. Voting Republican from long habit, he had been amazed to find that Margaret had voted against him. She had not at first wanted to vote at all, maintaining that she despised equally all the presidential candidates. She would not, she declared, even go to the polls. She would stay home and crochet a doily in her new luncheon set.

This he flouted as a gesture. She crocheted beautifully as she did all things well, and there were times when he liked to see the ivory needle in her long narrow hands flashing in and out of the daffodil yellow thread. But he had learned that when she picked up such handiwork it was in the nature of a retreat from life.

"You must go," he had exclaimed. "If you do not the whole of Chedbury will know, and after your preachments, my dear, in recent years, concerning the responsibilities of women, it would not do. You may cast a blank ballot, if you like, but you must go into the booth."

Her stupefaction the next morning had aroused his immediate question.

"I thought I was making a strong protest vote," she told him, more confounded than he had ever seen her. "Instead I'm on the winning side."

"What did you do there alone in that booth?" he demanded.

She looked at him with merry eyes. "I voted the straight Democratic ticket—that's what I did—as the strongest protest I could think of against everything I didn't like."

"Do you think you'll like what you got?" he inquired with grimness.

"How do I know what I've got?" she countered. "Maybe if I'd known I was going to get it, I wouldn't have voted for it."

He had snorted at this. "That's democracy for you!"

Afterward in his office he had thought of it again and had laughed silently and alone. All over the country, he supposed, other stupefied people were discovering that they, too, had voted on the winning side. He had written an unusually cheerful letter to Mark, describing his mother's surprise, and remarking that for his own part he was glad to see people get up a little spunk.

Now, in spite of the warmth of the sunshine on this day, he was aware .that the momentary optimism over such spunk was dying down. He did not at all like the look of certain signs on the horizon. At his age he did not care to face what he had gone through before the depression. He wished Mark would come home. He could talk to Mark. A misery of longing for his son swept over him and for a moment he saw him so vividly that he all but cried out, while Margaret bent over the hyacinth bed.

"The white hyacinths are the most beautiful," she was saying. "I believe I'll cut a few spikes and put them on the church altar."

He did not answer. Lifting his eyes he could imagine he saw Mark's face, the strong lines of jaw and high cheekbones, his eyes, dark and filled with some sort of surprise, gay or not, happy or not, he could not tell. He was leaning out of the cockpit, as he had seen him lean, when he leaped up on wings from the earth.

"What did you say, Ned?" Margaret was asking.

"I said nothing," he replied. He went on with difficulty. "Suddenly I saw Mark."

"You saw him?"

"As if he were here."

He looked at her and saw her wondering, half-frightened face.

"You've been thinking too much about him," she said. "Come, let's go to church."

Vague as he was about his religion, and in spite of basic faith being still assailed by the manifold doubt of his times, he felt comfort today in the morning service. The pew he and Margaret used had belonged to his parents, and he had sat here restlessly as a small boy, and then unwillingly in his youth. Here, too, his children had sat between their parents. Once Mark, at three, always unable to be still, had fallen backward through the seat, and he had reached after him and drawn him up and had hushed his sobs against his shoulder until he slept.

The church was sweet with the scent of early lilacs,

and Margaret had set the white hyacinths in a silver bowl between two bunches of the feathery flowers. The place was seldom filled nowadays and it fretted Joseph Barclay that his fiery messages found no response in the cool hearts of today's young. Though he loved them and yearned for their souls, they did not hear him. Mark had been the arch rebel.

"I can't and won't go to any more of old Joe's rantings," he had said.

"I see the man behind the words," Edward had replied.

"I can't see the man for the words," Mark had retorted too smartly.

"Shame," his mother had put in. "Think of all the minister used to do for you children—the tree at Christmastime, the parties, the baseball in spring in the square, coaching you at football, getting the money together for the swimming pool."

"All granted," Mark had replied instantly. "But preaching still turns my stomach, Mother."

They had not pressed him and when the minister had asked diffidently why Mark no longer came to church with them, Edward had told the truth. "They can't listen to sermons, nowadays, I'm afraid."

Of Mark's soul, Edward felt, he knew nothing at all. He had come near to a glimpse of it one night a week before Mark's enlistment when, his mother having gone to bed, he and the boy had sat together in the library, he marking a manuscript for the printer the next day, and Mark sunk in the biggest chair, and lost in a book of nuclear physics. He had shut it suddenly with so loud a bang that Edward had started and dropped his spectacles.

"Sorry, Dad," Mark had said.

"You are feeling vigorous," Edward had replied.

"No, only somehow for the first time glad I'm going across instead of staying home."

He had looked at his son and it seemed to him that the boy looked careworn, as though he had been sleepless.

"Can you tell me why?" he asked, delicate always before apparent probing.

Mark had answered after a moment with strange gravity. "It postpones what I really want to do."

"Well?"

"If I stayed at home I'd go straight on with my research work in atomic energy. It's what I want to know about, more than anything else. I've got to know. The whole future of man depends upon our knowing."

"Well?"

Mark had hesitated again. He was rubbing his dark hair slowly with both hands into something more than its usual disorder. "I know a fellow older than me—just got married. He's finished college—took exactly the course I want. He has to have a job, of course. Well, the only job he can get is in one of the new war plants. That's a fix, isn't it? You spend four years of your life learning something and then you've got to use what you know to kill people."

He had often wondered what Mark felt about war. They had never discussed it. That night he perceived that this duty was loathsome, and he longed to spare him, and did not know how. There was no escape for the young nowadays.

"It can't last," he had said, and had heard the words feeble in his own ears.

Mark had got to his feet and yawned. "It doesn't do to think. One day at a time, I guess. And maybe no tomorrow."

"Don't say that, son," Edward had remonstrated. "It sounds cynical."

"Sorry, Dad—only why are you older ones so afraid of sounding cynical?"

He had paused upon Mark's question.

"I suppose we were brought up to believe in the goodness of God," he had said at last.

Mark, kicking the coals into the fireplace, had not answered.

"I fear we have somehow failed you," Edward had continued. "I would like you to believe in the goodness of God and the value of life, but I don't know how to teach you. Things were simpler when I was young."

"Oh, I believe in the value of life, all right," Mark had replied. He had folded his arms on the big oaken mantel and leaning his head upon his arms he gazed down into the dying coals. "Life is wonderful—could be, that is."

"If what?" Edward asked, daring another step.

"If it could last," Mark said.

He shook himself like a big dog, stretched his arms their enormous length and yawned again. "Why am I getting serious at this time of night? Must be talking in my sleep! Good night, Dad."

"Good night, my dear son," he had replied.

Left alone he had sat puzzling for a while over the meaning of what Mark had said. Did he mean more or less than the words contained? Who knew? So different this world from that in which he himself had grown up that the heart even of his son was strange to him. Mark was set upon a solitary path and in spite of all the yearning of his elders, he had to tread the way alone.

The minister was proclaiming the closing hymn. What the sermon had been about Edward did not know. He had not heard a word of it. But the familiar words of the hymn fell on his ears and resounded with memory. "Lead, Kindly Light, amid th' encircling gloom." It had been his father's favorite hymn. He stood up, holding one side of the hymnbook with Margaret. He never sang, having no ear for music, but he liked to hear her clear voice singing. She had sung to the babies in the nursery, though when Mark had been born he had been compelled to remind her, so that Mark would not miss the memory of falling to sleep wrapped in the music of his mother's voice. She had been half ashamed and half laughing. "You see how much too old I am to have this baby," she had told him, pretending to pout. But she had been lovely to his eyes all over again, because he had forgotten how she looked, holding a baby in her arms, rocking and singing. Queer how they used to say a mother shouldn't rock a child! Margaret had rocked theirs because she liked to, flouting the books and doctors, and yet the other day from a manuscript that came into his office from some psychologist, he learned that after all it was the right thing to rock little babies and sing to them, to pick them up when they cried. He was glad he had always picked up Mark when he cried, and glad for the nights he had sat with him through thunderstorms until he was a big boy.

The benediction was over and he and Margaret went out of the church, greeting their friends as usual. Fioretta was a Catholic and she took Tom and the children with her to mass, early mass this morning probably, dragging them out of their sleep so that she would have plenty of time in the kitchen to prepare the huge meal that he shrank from even in contemplation. His digestion was healthy but delicate.

The sun was hotter than ever when they came out to the sloping lawn. On the horizon over Chedbury below them evil-looking clouds were looming. There would be a thunderstorm later in the afternoon, and then the night would be cool.

He paused, looking down over the green, and then feeling strangely weary he sat down for a moment on the mass of rock outside the church door. The rock had been the subject of argument and controversy in town meeting more than once. Some of the citizens of Chedbury wanted it dynamited and carried away, but he and others had opposed this stoutly. Gray and lichen covered, the huge mass had been here in the time of Chedbury's first settlers. He preferred it to grass. There was something symbolic about rock in New England. It lent character even to the church.

At the end of the war he had been inspired by an idea. He still felt it was an inspiration. Instead of the pretentious shaft of marble upon the green as a memorial to the twelve Chedbury boys who had been killed in Europe and in Asia, he had suggested a heavy bronze plate sunk into this rock. Chedbury folk had doubted so unconventional an idea, but the minister had pushed it through.

"A wonderful conception," he had declared in town meeting. "There's something eternal about rock."

The grocer had finally cast the deciding vote, won by the fact that a bronze plate cost next to nothing. Edward turned his head to read again the twelve names. John Carosi's son headed the list, "John Brown Carosi, aged nineteen." He remembered Jack as a lively small boy, squeezing his way between the presses to find his father and beg for a nickel.

"Aren't you well?" Margaret asked.

"Quite well," he replied, lying a little. He got up and they walked slowly down the sidewalk that bordered the green, circling it to the white house at the foot.

The sun poured sultry into the yard, but the old trees cast a heavy shade and they walked in silence toward the door. A croquet game was going on in the back yard and they heard the children screaming over the wickets.

"I believe the bees are out," Margaret said.

"They are thought to be fretful when a thunderstorm is coming," he replied.

So heavy was his sense of doom as he mounted the steps slowly that he wondered if he, like old Tom Seaton, was to die by a stroke. The front door was open and the house was strangely quiet. Where was Fioretta and where was Tom?

He stood for a moment looking into the shadows of the wide hall. Then he saw Tom and knew that doom had fallen. Tom stood at the wall telephone, the receiver in his hand, his face white and stiff. He hung the receiver upon the hook, and came toward them slowly.

"That was for you, Ed. A telegram. Brace yourself. It's about Mark."

They stared at him, two aging parents.

"He crashed," Tom said, "coming in from Berlin."

His first feeling, stupid with grief, was one of envy. He wished that he could wail aloud as Fioretta was wailing. She stood in the kitchen door, holding her big white apron to her face, sobbing. It would help him if Margaret could weep aloud. But she, too, could not weep.

She sat down on the carved chest beside the stair. He leaned against the wall. Tom repeated the bare words of official regret, as he could remember them.

"Hank wanted to type it out but there was nobody to send, since it's Sunday. He'll drop it in the mail."

"I'll go around and get it," Edward said quietly. He felt suddenly strong and alert.

"I'll fetch my car," Tom said.

"Let me come," Margaret begged. She turned to Fioretta. "My dear, give the children their dinner. Don't let it be spoiled for them."

"I can't eat a bite," Fioretta sobbed.

But she would eat, he knew. She would eat and cry at the same time. He never wanted to eat again. His stomach felt shriveled and dry. But he held himself straight as usual and Margaret slipped her hand into his elbow while Tom whirled the car out of the garage.

They drove in silence through the humid sunshine

toward the small railroad station where Hank Parker, the station master, received telegrams. The station was empty. Hank stood behind the window in his shirt sleeves, his eyes shaded by a piece of green paper held under his cap. He looked at them sorrowfully from behind the thin iron bars.

"I'd ha' given a million not to have got this," he said simply. He pushed the yellow slip of paper between the bars and Edward took it. He held it for Margaret to read with him and Tom waited, his face red and grave.

There was nothing told in the bare words except the monstrous fact. How it had come about he must wait to know. Mark, who had never had an accident, his genius son, was dead. He had an unutterable longing to get home, into his own house.

"Thank you, Hank," he managed to say. "We'll have to learn how to get along somehow, now."

"Folks have had to," Hank said. He scratched his ear with his pencil.

"Yes," Margaret said. "Plenty of folk have had to."

"Let's go home," Edward muttered.

"Please, Tom," Margaret said.

They climbed into the car again and Tom took them to their own gate. "I wish to God there was something I could do," he urged.

"There's nothing, of course," Edward said.

"You might tell a few people," Margaret said. "You'll know the right ones. Ask them not to call us up for a bit."

"I will," he promised.

They watched him drive away and then they walked wearily along the brick path between the two rows of flaming scarlet tulips. They mounted the steps and opened the door and shut it again. The house was empty. Even the servants were gone on a Sunday afternoon. He had never imagined such terrifying stillness. He turned to Margaret and caught her in his arms and together they began to weep.

It was Lewis Harrow, strangely, who gave him his first comfort. The amazing ineptitude of people who sought to assuage his sorrow made him ashamed for their sakes and he found himself coming to their aid with his utmost efforts. "Yes," he said, "I know—God's will is inscrutable. . . . Yet, it is good that we have our other children —and of course our grandchildren. . . . Of course," he agreed, "life is difficult today for the young. Perhaps Mark is spared a great deal."

He allowed Joseph Barclay to pray with him, first alone and then with Margaret. Margaret bowed her head, her face white and still, her hands clasped on her knees.

She had the wisdom not to try to comfort him, and he did not try to comfort her. For them there was no comfort —not yet. Together they reached the ultimate in pain, and dimly he began to perceive that of all the divisions among people, the deepest and the most universal is that abyss which lies between those who have suffered the ultimate in pain and those who have not. Those who had suffered spoke few words, but the clasp of their hands upon his was strong and warm.

He held his daughter Mary in his arms and let her sob, knowing that she, too, understood nothing yet of sorrow. "Don't cry, my dear," he said almost pleasantly. "You have a responsibility toward life, you know. You mustn't forget that."

The hardest comfort of all was from those who tried to find meaning in Mark's death. He loved Joseph Barclay because he was not one of these. When he prayed, the minister had said, "I could tell you this is God's will but I don't believe it is. I could point out to you that Mark died while he was taking food to those who had been his enemies, but we know they weren't his enemies and never had been, his or ours. He was taking food to the Germans so that they wouldn't turn Communist. Maybe that will prove worth dying for, but I can't promise you that it will."

"Joe, you are a man of God, and now I know it," Edward had replied.

It was Harrow who came flying back across the Atlantic bringing comfort. Upon receiving Mary's cable he had flown straight to Germany, slashing his way through red tape, more arrogant than any officer, inquiring of them all if they knew who he was.

"By God, I'm the most famous writer in the United States," he shouted, furrowing his thick black brows. "What I can write about you and where I can publish it would surprise you!" By such totalitarian methods he had forced his way to the scene of Mark's death.

Once home again, he rushed from the landing field to Chedbury and went straight to the house, where he found Edward and Margaret walking in the garden after the food they had tried to eat at midday.

"I've come as soon as I could," he announced. "I knew you'd want to know exactly what happened. I went to find out and I think I got it all."

"Come inside, Lew," Edward said.

"Dear Lewis," Margaret said and took his hand. "How did you know what we wanted?"

"My damned intuition, I suppose," he retorted. They were in the empty living room. Margaret had made it as pretty as usual with her flowers. Baynes and Sandra had come, of course, and most of Chedbury had streamed quietly through the door. That was over now. Edward had not allowed even Tommy and Sandy to stay. He wanted to be alone with Margaret. They were face to face with the days, one after another.

Harrow sat down. He flung off his topcoat as though it stifled him. The weather had turned cool again, after the frightful thunderstorm on the Sunday they had first heard Mark was dead.

Harrow leaned forward, his big ugly mouth working, his dark hair straight on his forehead.

"I wish to God I could tell you something wonderful," he said. "I wish Mark had died saving somebody or something. But there isn't anything wonderful. He was simply part of the machine. The planes leave every few minutes from the American zone and fly over the border into the Russian zone. It's not easy because of the hours and the Russians' potshots, and sometimes the weather. It's round-the-clock stuff. The planes keep in line—every few minutes. If they can't land at the receiving end for some reason or other they just fly back to where they started from and get in line again and start over. That's what Mark did. Something must have been wrong with his plane and he didn't dare to land and so he just went back to the starting place and tried to come down there. A ground man said he saw one of the wheels roll away, and then Mark crashed nose down into the earth and his plane began to burn."

"Was—his body—destroyed?" He put the question which he saw in Margaret's eyes.

"No—injured, of course. But it's in a coffin. I arranged for that. It'll be over—in due course. You know 'in due course'? Hah!" Lewis snorted and looked away out of the window. He said roughly. "If you have the sense I hope you have, you won't open the coffin. Just have a nice funeral."

He sighed enormously and got to his feet. "I wish I knew how to say things to you, but I don't. There's no sense to anything, I guess."

He lumbered toward the door and Margaret stopped him.

"Lew, my dear."

He turned.

Her face, wet with tears, was shining and tender. "Has Mary told you?"

"Told me what?" he demanded. "I only had the cable about Mark. I've been rushing around too much for letters."

"Then let me tell you," Margaret said. "Mary won't mind—for my comfort. She's going to have a baby. Lew, you're going to have another little child."

He stared at her for a moment and then rushed to her and fell upon his knees before her. "I worship you," he muttered. "Ed, I worship this wife of yours!"

"So do I," Edward said. "So do I."

They sat quietly looking at each other when he had gone. They smiled at each other. Once or twice he thought he might try to put into words how for him their love had passed now into something transcendental, something crystal and clear, like light enfolding them both. Life they knew and now death they knew, and nothing could separate them, not time and not eternity.

He felt unutterably weary, yet not spent. Looking into her face, he understood that she, too, felt as he did. They needed something to renew their bodies, that the spirit which dwelled in them both might live.

"Shall I fetch a little of Fioretta's wine?" he asked.

Fioretta, longing to be of use to them, had sent a jug of her homemade wine.

"That would be nice," Margaret said. She leaned back

in her chair and folded her hands on her knees. He went to her and knelt before her and kissed her hands. She leaned forward and took his head between her palms and kissed his forehead and then his lips.

"Dear love," she said, "bring a little bread with the wine."

He went away to bring that for which she had asked. He poured the wine into an old amber glass pitcher that had once been his mother's. She had poured milk from it when he was a boy. Now he filled it with the wine. He took a loaf from the breadbox of yellow painted tin and broke it upon a silver tray and putting two wine glasses too on the tray, he carried everything back to the living room. There he poured the wine and gave it to her, and he poured his own and he passed her the bread and they ate and drank.

When they had finished, Margaret took the glasses and set them on the tray.

"Now that we know everything," she said, "now that we know there is no use in trying to understand, shall we go out into the garden, Ned?"

"Yes, let us go," he said. "It looks as though the sunset would be splendid."